Magic Without Mercy

"Urban fantasy at its finest. Readers become invested in the fate of each character as they navigate the complex world Monk has created. . . . Every book is packed with action, adventure, humor, battles, romance, drama, and suspense. . . . Clear your calendar. Once you start reading, you won't want to stop."

—*Sacramento Book Review*

"Fast-paced, action-packed, and jammed full of all manner of magical mayhem, the eighth book of the Allie Beckstrom Novels puts the Hounds against the nastiest foes to date."

—*Monsters and Critics*

"One of the most impressive things about *Magic Without Mercy* was Devon Monk's ability to keep a perfect balance between action and character development. . . . From start to finish, *Magic Without Mercy* was a roller-coaster ride. I simply could not put it down!"

—*A Book Obsession*

Magic on the Line

"Monk's electric seventh Allie Beckstrom urban fantasy is the best one yet. . . . This dark and delicious novel digs deep into the characters, their relationships, and the mysterious Authority. Allie is one of urban fantasy's most entertaining heroines, and her latest adventure will leave readers desperately wanting more, especially when Monk whips out a killer cliff-hanger ending."

—*Publishers Weekly* (starred review)

"Allie Beckstrom is one of the best urban fantasy heroines out there. Monk takes risks with her writing that other authors may not feel comfortable attempting, in her quest to wring the best possible story from within the world she has created."

—*Fresh Fiction*

"Absolutely another awesome addition to this action-packed series. . . . The characters seem to grow and evolve as each book progresses the story."

—*Night Owl Reviews*

"[A] remarkable series. . . . Time and events are getting dark indeed as Monk ratchets up the threat ratio. Excellent as always!"

—*Romantic Times*

continued . . .

"The writing moves at a fast pace with plenty of exciting action. . . . This series just gets better and better with each new book."
—Night Owl Reviews

Magic in the Blood

"Tight, fast, and vividly drawn, Monk's second Allison Beckstrom novel features fresh interpretations of the paranormal, strong characters dealing with their share of faults and flaws, [and] ghoulish plot twists. Fans of Patricia Briggs or Jim Butcher will want to check out this inventive new voice."
—Monsters and Critics

"[A] highly creative series. . . . If you love action, magic, intrigue, good versus evil battles, and pure entertainment, you will not want to miss this series."
—Manic Readers

"One heck of a ride through a magical, dangerous Portland . . . imaginative, gritty, sometimes darkly humorous. . . . An un-put-downable book, *Magic in the Blood* is one fantastic read."
—Romance Reviews Today

"This series uses a system of rules for magic that is original and seems very realistic. . . . The structure of the story pulled me in right away, and kept me reading. There's action, adventure, fantasy, and even some romance."
—CA Reviews

Magic to the Bone

"Brilliantly and tightly written . . . will surprise, amuse, amaze, and absorb readers."
—*Publishers Weekly* (starred review)

"Mystery, romance, and magic cobbled together in what amounts to a solid page-turner."
—SFFWorld

"Loved it. Fiendishly original and a stay-up-all-night read. We're going to be hearing a lot more of Devon Monk."
—Patricia Briggs, #1 *New York Times* bestselling author of *Fair Game*

"Highly original and compulsively readable. Don't pick this one up before going to bed unless you want to be up all night!"
—Jenna Black, author of *Sirensong*

"Gritty setting, compelling, fully realized characters, and a frightening system of magic-with-a-price that left me awed. Devon Monk's writing is addictive, and the only cure is more, more, more."
—Rachel Vincent, *New York Times* bestselling author of *Blood Bound*

Books by Devon Monk

The Allie Beckstrom Series
Magic to the Bone
Magic in the Blood
Magic in the Shadows
Magic on the Storm
Magic at the Gate
Magic on the Hunt
Magic on the Line
Magic Without Mercy
Magic for a Price

The Age of Steam
Dead Iron
Tin Swift

Magic
for a
Price

An Allie Beckstrom Novel

Devon Monk

A ROC BOOK

ROC
Published by New American Library, a division of
Penguin Group (USA) Inc., 375 Hudson Street,
New York, New York 10014, USA
Penguin Group (Canada), 90 Eglinton Avenue East, Suite 700, Toronto,
Ontario M4P 2Y3, Canada (a division of Pearson Penguin Canada Inc.)
Penguin Books Ltd., 80 Strand, London WC2R 0RL, England
Penguin Ireland, 25 St. Stephen's Green, Dublin 2,
Ireland (a division of Penguin Books Ltd.)
Penguin Group (Australia), 250 Camberwell Road, Camberwell, Victoria 3124,
Australia (a division of Pearson Australia Group Pty. Ltd.)
Penguin Books India Pvt. Ltd., 11 Community Centre, Panchsheel Park,
New Delhi - 110 017, India
Penguin Group (NZ), 67 Apollo Drive, Rosedale, Auckland 0632,
New Zealand (a division of Pearson New Zealand Ltd.)
Penguin Books (South Africa) (Pty.) Ltd., 24 Sturdee Avenue,
Rosebank, Johannesburg 2196, South Africa

Penguin Books Ltd., Registered Offices:
80 Strand, London WC2R 0RL, England

First published by Roc, an imprint of New American Library,
a division of Penguin Group (USA) Inc.

First Printing, November 2012
10 9 8 7 6 5 4 3 2 1

ALWAYS LEARNING   PEARSON

For my family

ACKNOWLEDGMENTS

Without the many people who have contributed time and energy along the way, this book, nay, this entire series would never have seen the light of day. My deepest thanks to my agent, Miriam Kriss, for believing in Allie and her story, and also to my wonderful editor, Anne Sowards, for her keen eye and amazing knack for making each book better. A huge thank-you also to the fabulous artist Larry Rostant and to the many people within Penguin who have gone above and beyond to make this series shine.

There are two first readers who made it through every rough draft of every book, and probably deserve a medal for that. Thank you, Dean Woods and Dejsha Knight, for all the last-minute reads, for the crazy brainstorming sessions, and for your wonderful suggestions, enthusiasm, and help. I could not have done this without you. A big, squishy thanks to my family, one and all, for being there for me, offering unfailing encouragement and sharing in the joy. To my husband, Russ, and sons, Kameron and Konner—you are such strong, creative people and the very best part of my life. Thank you for putting up with me. I love you.

To you, my dear reader, go my greatest thanks. A book can only really come alive when there is someone to share it with. Thank you for giving me the chance to share these people, this world, and this journey with you.

Chapter One

I never expected cookies at the end of the world. Some other more violent dessert perhaps, like volcano cake or devil's food or heck, maybe even zucchini muffins, since everyone knows zucchini is evil. But cookies? Those are happy, life-goes-on desserts.

And that was exactly what my best friend, Nola, was cooking. By the truckload.

Two days ago I had led a small group of magic users, who were also my friends, in a magical battle for the safety of the people and magic in Portland, Oregon, against Jingo Jingo—a powerful and mad Death magic user. The only reasons they'd needed me, Allie Beckstrom, to lead them were one: we were on the run, and two: our backup for the fight—Hounds who, like me, tend to work in the shadier corners of the city tracking down illegal spells—would listen only to one of their own.

Magic had been poisoned—a problem we still haven't solved—and it was spawning the Veiled: ghosts of dead magic users who were infecting and killing the living. Not that anyone in the Authority would have believed us about any of that. We had fought Jingo Jingo, and the entire Authority—the secret group of people who decide who uses magic and how.

None of us had gotten out of that fight unscathed.

Some of us would carry those wounds, and the things magic had done to us, for the rest of our lives.

Jingo Jingo was dead but we still hadn't come up with a cure for magic.

Which was why we were all here at Kevin Cooper's estate. We had to find a way to cure magic before Leander and Isabelle, two undead and superpowerful magic users who made Jingo Jingo look like a fluffy puppy when it came to madness and magic, showed up to kick what was left of our asses.

Generally not a situation I'd expect to be celebrating with cookies.

"Nola," I said. "What's wrong?"

"Allie!" She bent in front of the oven, her honey-colored hair pulled back in a long braid, a plain white apron tied at her waist. "I didn't hear you come in."

She drew two sheets full of cookies out of the oven and turned toward me. "Nothing's wrong. Cookie?" Her freckled cheeks were pink from baking, her hair doing that cute curl-thing around her face from the heat. But she wasn't smiling.

I stared at the cookies on platters, stacked in step-mountain pyramids across the counter tops, and filling bowl after bowl in rounded domes. Chocolate chip, sugar, gingersnaps, oatmeal, and something that looked like red velvet.

"You bake when you're worried. You bake a lot when you're really worried." I pointed at the heaps of cookies. "What's wrong? Really."

She shrugged one shoulder and expertly slid the spatula under a black-and-white crinkle cookie, depositing it on the cooling rack.

"Nothing," she said. "Well, nothing new. To you, anyway."

I took a sip from my water bottle and waited for her to continue.

All this violent and secret magic stuff was new to Nola. I was afraid my friend wasn't coping with this new knowledge with her usual aplomb. Finally, I asked, "Is it Cody? Is he okay?" Nola had taken Cody in about a year ago. He had gotten mixed up with a lot of the wrong people and ended up with his memories taken away and his mind broken. We'd done what we could to heal him a couple of days ago.

Still, it was strange to see her without him by her side. Nola stopped sliding cookies onto the rack and turned to face me.

She frowned, looking worried, which I supposed was better than exhausted or injured. "He's still trying to get his footing, I think," she said. "Since Zayvion joined the two parts of his . . . soul . . . or mind . . . or memories?"

I shrugged. She jabbed the spatula at me. "That. That sums up everything."

"What 'that'?"

"The shrug. You just take all of this in stride. Like it's normal for a young man to have half of his mind and soul or whatever broken in two. One part of him nothing more than a ghost, the other part of him alive and struggling to do the simplest things. And then it's normal to shove those two pieces of him back together again so that he's someone different, even though he's the same."

"It's not normal," I said. "It's just I've been aware of this level of magic and magical cost and retributions for months. You've only just found out about it. It takes a while to get used to it all."

"You could have told me."

"About the Authority?"

She nodded.

Ah, so this was what had sparked the baking explosion.

I relied on Nola. Magic had always made me pay the price in pain like everyone else who used it, and then it had taken a chunk of my memories for good measure. I'd lost fewer memories lately, but if what Jingo Jingo had said about my father, Daniel Beckstrom, was true, it was possible people—like my dad—had also used magic to take my memories.

Nola had always been the one to give me back my memories when I lost them. For her to be able to do that, I confided in her and told her everything that was happening in my life.

Everything. Even the uncomfortable stuff . . . until I met Zayvion Jones, got framed for my father's murder, tangled with the secret organization of magic users, and realized telling Nola everything I was mixed up in might just get her killed.

"Why didn't you?" she asked.

I dragged my hand back through my hair, trying to tuck it behind my ears even though it was too short to stay put.

It was strange to think that it had been only two days ago we'd been fighting for our lives in St. Johns. Fighting against the very people who were going to be gathering now, here, to try to stop an even bigger threat.

Leander and Isabelle. We knew they possessed the Overseer, the one person who held the highest and most powerful position in the Authority.

Which meant they had every member of the Authority in the world at their beck and call.

All we had was us.

Well, and cookies.

I didn't know who was going to make the decisions about what to do next. Maybe Victor Forsythe, who had been my Faith magic teacher, or maybe Maeve Flynn, who taught Blood magic and was also my friend Shamus Flynn's mother. Hell, it could be twins Carl and La, since they'd stepped up to serve as spokespersons for the Authority right after the battle with Jingo.

Whoever it was, they'd have a plateful of hard choices in front of them. Like how to stop Leander and Isabelle. And how to convince every other magic user in the world that two dead people were possessing the highest ranking magical official in their organization.

"Must be a big reason if it's taking you that long to answer." Nola scooped dough that smelled like peanut butter onto the sheets.

"Not really," I said. "I'm just . . . not at full speed yet. On anything."

"I'm not surprised," she said. "Maybe you should get some sleep before the meeting?"

"No. Maeve wants to talk to Zay, Shame, Terric, and me to see how we might use the disks to cure magic. And I want to see how Shame and Terric handle magic now."

"Now?"

"Since the fight. When they . . . died for each other using magic." I said it as if that explained everything. Only it didn't really explain anything. Not to a woman who had spent most of her adult life living in a small town on a large farm without magic.

"Zay and I are Soul Complements," I said. "We can make magic bend the rules of what it will and won't do. All Soul Complements have that ability. I think that's why it's so rare to have two people linked together in that way. When you use magic together like that, you can do things other magic users can't do. Usually deadly things."

"How many Soul Complements are there?"

"In Portland?"

"In the world."

"I don't know. I've never asked."

For the briefest moment, a parade of faces flashed behind my eyes. Memories from my dad, who was possessing a corner of my mind. Memories of people he knew — Soul Complements. Men and women, young and old, from a variety of different ethnic backgrounds, all smiling in that over-the-moon-in-love kind of way. Several of the faces carried with them Dad's emotions, and I was surprised he thought kindly of these people. Maybe even cared for many of them.

"Maybe a dozen pairs?" I continued. "I know of Zay and myself, and probably Shame and Terric, though Shame refuses to be tested to find out if he and Terric are a match. Chase and Greyson were Soul Complements too. I haven't met anyone else, although now I kind of wish I had."

"Chase?" she asked. "Zayvion's ex-girlfriend?"

I nodded.

"Is Greyson still alive?"

"No. Leander killed him. Killed him, and used him to kill Chase."

"Allie," she breathed. Nola was no stranger to death. Behind her country girl manners, she was no shrinking flower. Still, her gaze was heavy with the knowledge that Leander, on his own, had already successfully killed two Soul Complements.

"It hasn't always been this way," I said. "Maeve and Victor told me that things aren't usually this death-y in the Authority. It's just since my dad died . . ."

"And possessed you." Again with the even gaze.

Oh, there was no way I was getting out of this now.

"I'm sorry. I didn't know how to tell you. I mean I couldn't just call and say, 'Hey, Nola, guess who's in my head? My dead dad! Yes, he's still a self-centered jerk, yes, he still wants to rule my life, but you know, no biggie.' It just sounds too crazy. You would have thought I'd really lost it. I tried to get rid of him. More than once. Thought that when I did I could tell you he was gone, and it wouldn't matter if you believed me or not. But now . . . he's been helpful lately. I guess."

"Do you trust him?"

I thought about it for a second or two. Dad had been quiet in my head since the battle. I could still feel his awareness there in my thoughts, his wintergreen presence, but he wasn't getting in my way, wasn't offering suggestions. Other than that sudden flash of his memories, it was like he was observing and meditating, resting up for a big effort of some kind.

And he might be very wise to be doing so.

"I don't know. It's weird. I want to trust him."

Nola's eyebrows went up and she smiled a little. "Really? You, the rebel child?"

"I told you it was weird. But since he's been dead, we've had to work together. He's been . . . respectful. Mostly. But he's still done things that . . . that I don't like."

"So you don't trust him?"

I sighed. "I guess I should at this point. But, no. Not with every fiber of my being."

"But you trust Zayvion." It wasn't a question. It didn't have to be. She knew.

"Down to the last drop."

"So when you use magic together, as Soul Complements, you can make magic bend the rules," she said. "Can Shame and Terric do that too?"

"If what they did out on the battlefield against Jingo Jingo is any indication, yes."

"Is it more dangerous to use magic that way?"

"I guess so. But magic is always dangerous. Zay and I try not to cast together like that because when we do, we sort of get lost in each other's minds."

"That doesn't sound so bad."

"It's not. At all. But it's hard to let go of him and want to stay breathing in my own body when I'm wrapped up in the man I love."

"Oh," she exhaled.

She was such a romantic.

I took a drink of water to cover my smile. "We're okay. Zay and I are pretty good at not using magic together in ways that make us do something . . . disastrous."

"How disastrous?"

"Well, Leander and Isabelle were Soul Complements. They were the first pair ever discovered. A few hundred years ago they used magic to torture, kill, and destroy anyone who disagreed with them throughout the world. The only way the Authority stopped them was by breaking magic into two forms—light and dark—which drastically changed how it can be used."

"Wait," she said. "A few hundred years ago?"

I nodded.

"After breaking magic, the Authority killed Leander, and broke Isabelle's mind. But apparently that wasn't enough. They found their way back from death and possessed people, starting with Sedra, who used to be the head of Portland's Authority, and was Cody Miller's mom. And now they want all the magic, which we won't let them have, and all the world, which we won't let them take. They'll be headed this way to go all apocalypse on anyone standing in their way." I gave her a smile to try to take the sting out of all of that.

"Is that what this is, then? An apocalypse?"

"Naw. Not with all these happy cookies to eat." But my smile faded, and I ran my fingers through my hair again, nervous. I may talk a big game, but the truth was, I was scared out of my pants to have to face Leander and Isabelle again.

"Maybe," I said quietly. "If we can stop them and send them both back to death, maybe it won't be the end of the world. We'll still need to find a way to counteract the poison in magic, and find a cure for people who have been infected by it, and make sure the Veiled aren't going around trying to hurt people. I guess someone will have to rebuild the Authority since we've lost a lot of people in the last few months."

I swallowed hard against the flashing images—my memories—of Bartholomew with the bullet hole I had put in his head, gasping his last breath; of Jingo Jingo sucking the life out of dozens of people; of Shame, more dead than alive, crushing Jingo Jingo's heart until it stopped beating.

"We'll figure it out," I said, even though my voice quavered a little.

"You mean you'll figure it out," she said firmly.

"I doubt it." I reached over and dug up a finger full of cookie dough. "I bet I'll be ground troops in this fight. There are much wiser minds than mine who can deal with all of this."

She shrugged and went back to scooping drops of dough onto the sheet. "I think you're underestimating yourself. And you still didn't tell me why."

"Why I've been keeping secrets? Sure you don't want to discuss it some day over a case or two of wine?"

"I don't think we're going to get a 'some day' anytime soon, do you?"

"No."

"Then right now, over a mountain of apocalyptic cookies, will have to do. Spill."

"Fine." I popped the raw dough into my mouth. "Mmm. So good. You really must be worried."

"I'm not worried," she said archly. "I'm trying to feed an army. And putting this industrial dream kitchen through its paces. I don't think it's been used in years."

Kevin Cooper's kitchen was just as grand as the rest of his house. When he'd first suggested we all gather at his place—and stay if we wanted—I hadn't thought it was a good idea.

But then, Zayvion hadn't bothered to tell me Kevin was rich. Like old-school, going-back-generations rich.

Kevin certainly had the house—well, manor—to show for it. Kevin said he didn't live here, preferring a modest house in a quiet neighborhood. I didn't blame him. This place was big enough to be a hotel.

"Have you looked at these ovens?" Nola continued with a wave of the spatula. "Gorgeous. And you are getting off topic."

"All right. When I first joined the Authority to learn how to use magic, they told me I'd be Closed—have my memories taken away—if I ever told anyone about them."

"Who told you that?"

"Everyone. Victor, Maeve, Jingo Jingo, Zay, Shame. All my teachers. Don't get angry. It's the rule—the same rule for everyone who is a part of the Authority. I was worried that if I told you anything, they'd Close you too. I couldn't do that to you, couldn't know that I was responsible for your memories being taken away."

"They wouldn't really take your memories away."

"They very much really would. Without a moment's hesitation."

"Even Zayvion?"

I held my breath on that. "Not now," I finally said. "Definitely not now. But a while ago? Probably."

She raised one eyebrow.

"It's his job, Nola, or it was. He's practically grown up in the Authority. He's very . . . loyal."

"And you didn't think I should know any of this? That I shouldn't be there to help you out if you were Closed? You should have told me. I'd rather be at your side—even if things are bad—than not in your life at all."

"You were always in my life. I didn't push you away."

"No, you just didn't tell me the truth. I hate being lied to." She scowled and hooked her thumb in the bowl, scooping out dough.

"Okay," I said, "it wasn't the most honest thing I could have done. But I was trying to keep you safe. And"—I held up my hand to cut off whatever she'd been about to say—"I wanted you safe for purely selfish reasons. You're my best friend. If it came down to it, if I had to do this last year over again, I might try to do it differently."

Memories of Grounding a wild magic storm, walking through death, fighting and failing to stop Leander and Isabelle as they dragged me out of my body and tried to kill me and all of my friends stuttered through my mind.

I winced.

"I'd definitely do things differently. For one thing, I'd try to tell you about all of this—the people, the secret magic, the risks—sooner. But, Nola, if it all goes to hell again, I'm still going to try to protect you from the worst of it."

She shook her head. "Have you ever thought about just leaving?"

Huh. Strangely, I hadn't. "No. This is my home. Well, not right here at Kevin's, but this city. No one can make me leave it. Even my dad couldn't make me leave it, and he drove me nuts."

She smiled and finally popped the dough in her mouth. "Now that so many people know about the Authority, what's going to happen to us and our memories?"

"Honestly? I have no idea."

The kitchen door opened and in walked Kevin Cooper. Sandy-haired, sad-eyed, he was one of Zay's long-standing friends. He was also a hell of a magic user. He'd somehow gotten himself assigned, by my dad of all people, as a bodyguard to Violet, my dad's wife. Somewhere along the way, Kevin had fallen in love with Violet, and he was still her stalwart guard.

"Allie," he said, "we have a problem."

"We have a lot of problems."

"Seattle's been scrambled."

"What does that mean?" I asked.

I'd never seen Kevin shaken. I'd never even seen the man sweat, and I'd seen him in the middle of a magical battle against overwhelming odds. He was sweating now.

"The Authority members in Seattle have been ordered by the Overseer to secure Portland."

"Secure?" I asked. "How?"

"They are going to lock us down so that no one can enter or exit, and Close or kill any member of Portland's Authority who stands in their way."

"My God," Nola said.

"It's okay." I gave her an encouraging nod, which was a big fat lie. "We can handle this. Right, Kevin?"

He didn't say a word. Just stood there looking grim.

Note to self: Kevin sucks at the big fat lie.

"What can I do to help?" she asked.

"Right now? Don't burn the cookies."

"Allie," she admonished.

"As soon as I figure out how bad it is, I will tell you what we need to do. Give me a second or two to talk to a few people, okay?"

She nodded. "Paul said he'd be here in a half hour or so."

"Good." Paul—Detective Paul Stotts—was her boyfriend, and was now just as deep in Authority business and end-of-the-world magic users targeting Portland as any of us who had been a part of the Authority for years. It would be good to have him on our side. I had the feeling we were going to need the cooperation of the police to get through this.

I jogged out of the kitchen, Kevin right on my heels.

Kevin's place had the feel of a grander sort of living, of balls and ceremonies and social events from a century prior. Not a speck of dust though. Kevin may not be living here, but he still had someone come in once a week to clean and air out the place.

"How bad is it?" I asked.

"They're coming to kill us."

"Right. Heard that. Can they do it?"

"With magic poisoned and most of us still not recovered from fighting Jingo Jingo? Yes."

Not the answer I was looking for. My heart was beating too fast. All I wanted to do was run, hide. Get the hell out of town. But too many people were relying on me being here, and hadn't I just told Nola I'd never run?

"How much time do we have before they get here?" We crossed the long, carpeted hall accented with woods and paintings that were probably priceless. I took a left, heading to one of the smaller meeting rooms.

"Three hours at the least. Four at the most."

"Then it's time to make some plans." I pulled open the double door to the room and strode into the sparsely furnished space.

"About time you got here," Shame said as soon as I crossed the threshold. "I was getting tired waiting for the world to end."

Chapter Two

There were three people in the room: Zayvion, Maeve, and Shame. Shame sat in a bright red cushioned arm chair with gold tassels across the bottom of it. It did not fit in with the rest of the room's decor of silk white wallpaper, dark wooden central table, matching chairs, and gigantic lead crystal chandelier.

Okay, maybe it fit with the chandelier, but it was obvious someone had dragged it in here from one of the other more elegant sitting rooms.

He wore a heavy, black cabled sweater with a black turtleneck under it, black fingerless gloves, black beanie, and blue jeans.

Out of all that blackness, his eyes shone through, startlingly green against his sallow skin. I could still see magic with my bare eyes, which was, as far as any of us could tell, a side effect of magic being poisoned and me hitting my head on concrete a few days ago.

Sometimes, when I had a spare minute to give in to my fears and suspicion, I wondered if it was being possessed by my dad for nearly a year that had changed me.

Looking at Shame made me wonder how much I was seeing him, and how much I was seeing what magic had done to him.

He wasn't just wearing dark clothing; he was surrounded by shadows.

Shame looked like death.

He'd been on the thin side lately, but the fight with Jingo Jingo had made it only worse. Every angle of his face stood at hard relief to the shadows surrounding him. Both physical and magical blackness covered him and roiled like inky smoke, licking outward with questing tendrils, as if looking for something to taste.

Shame sat in the center of that sliding darkness, burning like a hard white flame.

I didn't want to admit it, but the shadows reminded me of the souls and Veiled I used to see hovering around Jingo Jingo. Except the darkness and magic around Shame wasn't made of dead people, it just seemed to be made of magic and death.

He gave me a slight smile. Suddenly it was the very much alive Shame staring back at me.

He might have been changed by magic, but he was still Shame.

"Done getting your beauty sleep?" he asked.

"I wasn't sleeping. I was talking to Nola," I said. "And if I remember right, we were waiting for you to wake up."

"Behold my awakeness," he said, spreading his long, thin fingers. "Let's party."

Zay, in jeans and a T-shirt, had been leaning against the wall with his arms crossed over his chest. He strode toward me, his left hip bothering him enough that he didn't try to hide the catch in his stride with his usual swagger. The doctors had done a lot of good for us over the last two days, but anyone who had been a part of that fight in St. Johns was still nursing pain.

Zay's dark, thick hair was cut short against his skull, giving his high cheekbones a prominent angle beneath golden-brown eyes that seemed to see right through my soul. He wasn't scowling, but his eyebrows were creased in question and concern.

Beyond the physical Zayvion, I could see the magic that marked him—that had always marked him since I'd first met him. Glyphs of spells branded into his dark skin burned with silver fire tipped in red and blue. He'd told me once they were the mark and power of his position as Guardian of the gate. The glyphs were part of why he could work both light and dark magic for short amounts of time, which was in turn why he was such a strong magic user.

Some of those glyphs no longer burned. They traced dusty gray lines of ash across his bare arms and hands, used, exhausted, burned out.

Ever since he'd fallen into a coma, fought Leander and Isabelle, then Jingo Jingo, the glyphs had changed. The magic he carried, magic spells he wore as part of his job of Guardian of the gate, were burning out. I didn't know what it meant. He didn't want to talk about it.

"Allie?" Zay took my hands. His pain and fatigue rolled through me, just as I was sure mine carried to him.

My heart literally skipped a beat. Not because we were both hurting and tired. It seemed like we were always hurting and tired.

But because I loved him, and I hated knowing that we were both headed into a fight underpowered and outmatched. I couldn't bear the thought of losing him. There was no guarantee either of us would get out of this alive.

What he needed, what we all needed, was about a month of sleep. What we didn't have was one damn second to spare.

Terric walked into the room. "Are we ready?"

"I'm okay," I said to Zay, then, "I have some news."

I turned toward Terric.

Shame was darkness and death, but Terric seemed to glow as if moonlight pooled beneath his skin. His white hair, now streaked with black, gave him an edgier look, and his face, which I'd always thought was handsome, carried that underlying light. It was hard to look away from him, especially when he lifted his gaze to me, catching me with his clear blue eyes.

"Oh," I said. "Wow."

Terric's chin lifted just a fraction more and I found myself fascinated by the hard line of his jaw, the soft curve of his lips, the set of his wide shoulders tapering down to a narrow waist.

"What wow?" he asked.

His voice buzzed under my skin, soft as a lover's finger.

Influence? Some kind of Illusion, or mesmerizing spell? One thing was for sure, I'd never felt like this looking at Terric before. He wasn't my type. I certainly wasn't his either.

It had to be magic.

"You've kind of got your charisma set on high beam," I said, breaking eye contact and looking instead at my shoe.

As soon as I did so, my head cleared. It had to be magic.

"It better be magic," Zayvion rumbled, catching both my thoughts, and probably all my emotions too.

Fabulous.

"Did you cast a spell?" he asked Terric.

"No."

"What do you see, Allie?" Zay asked.

I blinked a couple of times, then looked back up at Terric.

Magic shifted around him in a golden white light that illuminated every lovely feature that boy had. He looked like an angel. I wanted to touch him. Wanted to stand nearer to him and be touched by him.

"It's magic," I said, managing not to add "of course" to it. "Terric looks like he's made out of sunlight and sex, and Shame looks like the dead."

"The sexy dead?" Shame asked.

Zayvion shot him a look, then glanced over at Terric.

"I'm not seeing what you see," he said.

"Maybe cast Sight?"

"I have. But I can again."

He let go of my hand and I tucked it into my pocket, laying my palm against the warmth of my hip so it wasn't empty, hollow.

Every inch of my body wanted to be closer to Zayvion, held by him, holding him far from the danger I knew was coming.

"Make it quick," I said. "I do have news."

"Just tell us," Shame said. "Z has ears."

I shook my head. "After he casts."

Zay took several steps away from me, putting himself between Terric and Shame, and I strolled over to the other side of the room, closer to Maeve. Magic made me sick. Getting too close to someone using magic made me sick too.

Zay drew a Disbursement, which he Proxied.

Huh. I didn't know the Authority was using Proxies again. I wasn't sure that I approved of other people bearing the price for the magic we were using. Especially when that magic was poisoned.

Zayvion set magic into the glyph and the Disbursement formed in front of him, then sifted away, as if tugged apart by a breeze. A pink string of magic circled his wrist.

The Disbursement glyph should find the person who was holding Proxy and attach to them in some manner.

In just a moment, a pink string slipped back in through the wall and drifted across the room, tying to the magic band on Zay's wrist. His Proxy was set.

Zay cast a nice tight Sight. He held it over his fingertips as if balancing a globe, and looked through it at Terric.

"The light around him?" Zay asked.

"Yes," I said.

"Light?" Terric asked. "Seriously?"

"Look at Shame," I said.

Zay pivoted so he could see Shame through the spell.

Shame made a kissy face.

"Shadow," Zay said. "I see darkness around him." Zay dropped the Sight spell, which was good because it was starting to stink up the place.

I liked it better when I couldn't see magic with my bare eyes and smell it like it was hot garbage.

"All you saw was light and darkness?" I asked.

Zay nodded. "None of it particularly sexy."

"But then we all know you have no discerning taste, mate," Shame said. "And why does it matter? Let's hear the news."

"Seattle has been scrambled," I said.

Everyone in the room went silent.

Shame finally whistled quietly. "You ever heard of an entire city being sent to lock down another city, Mum?"

Maeve, who had been quiet all this time, shifted in the chair at the table. She had braided her hair back in a single band, and it somehow made her look younger even though she still had to use a cane to get around since Jingo Jingo had tried to kill her. Dark circles stood out like bruises against her pale skin. "No, I haven't. Do you know when they'll be here, Allie?"

"Kevin has the details."

"Three or four hours at the most," he said. "They have orders from the Overseer to lock us down, refuse any magic user entrance or exit and to Close or kill if we don't like it."

"To what ends?" she asked.

"Buying time," Zayvion said. "Keeping us under their thumb until Leander and Isabelle can get here."

"Swell," Shame said. "Other than a fight for our lives in a few hours, is there anything else I have to know about? Tired, hungry, and in a foul mood over here."

"Which is different than when?" Terric said.

"Fuck you is when," Shame said.

"We need to make a plan," I said.

"You need to make a plan," Shame said. "You're good at that."

"Fine. My plan is this: Kevin, call every member of the Authority you can reach and tell them to get out here in the next half hour. We need to explain this once, to as many people as possible."

Kevin pulled out his phone and was already talking to someone by the time he left the room.

"Shame, Terric," I said. "I want you to use magic together so we know what you can and can't do with it."

"Like hell," Shame said.

"Now?" Terric asked.

"Yes, now."

"So, you want us to waste time messing with magic when there's an entire city of people coming our way to fight?" Shame asked. "Forget what I said about plans. You suck at them."

"We do this now because I don't want to be on the front line with you and have something unexpected happen."

"You've fought alongside us before," Terric said.

"Magic changed you. Changed both of you when you died for each other on the battlefield."

"No," Shame corrected. "No, we did not die for each other. We died to kill Jingo Jingo. Isn't that right, Ter?"

Terric didn't say anything.

"Don't care how you want to remember it, Shame," I said. "I want to know what you can do with magic before we are in another life-or-death situation."

"Did I mention I hate this idea?" he grumbled.

"Don't care."

"Let's be done with it then, Son," Maeve said. "It should only take a minute or two."

She obviously wasn't in the mood to deal with delays either. Shame had killed Jingo Jingo, and changed greatly to come back from that. Her boyfriend, Hayden, was recovering in one of Kevin's bedrooms, heavily medicated and missing a hand.

It had not been a good last few days.

"We need someone to Ground," Maeve said.

Zayvion held up his fingers.

"Good." She walked around the edge of the table to stand at the foot of it. "Zayvion will Ground and I will Block the room."

Shame clapped his gloved hands together and pushed up out of his chair. "Fine. I'm starving anyway."

Maeve looked surprised. "Didn't you just eat?"

"Dying makes me hungry."

"Shamus. Don't," she said quietly.

"Die? Not planning on it. Once was enough." He didn't say it like he was angry or worried. Just maybe . . . resigned to the way things had turned out. "The sooner we find out that Terric and I cast magic *exactly the same as we always have*, the sooner I can eat something, or hell, get a damn smoke."

Zayvion positioned himself near the door.

Terric, who still had a case of the glowing gorgeous, moved to stand in front of Shame.

I wasn't sure where, exactly, I should be. Didn't even know what good I was since I couldn't use magic.

"Shamus and Terric," Maeve said, "I will tell you each what spell to cast. You will do so, in the order I tell you and at the smallest level possible. If it becomes too difficult, tell me immediately. We're going to see what you can and can't do alone, then together."

"Bullcrap," Shame said, shaking out his hands as if getting ready to arm wrestle. "You're going to test to see if we're Soul Complements."

"Ah, Son, no," Maeve said. "You already took that test."

"When?"

"When we died for each other," Terric said softly.

Shame glared at him. "I didn't die for . . ."

Terric held him with a patient gaze.

Shame shut his mouth. Must have finally figured out there was no use denying it when we all knew the truth.

"Terric," Maeve said, "let's begin with you. Please cast a small Light spell."

I decided it was time to find a wall, and walked to the far end of the room, at the head of the table.

Zayvion drew a glyph in the air, but didn't pull magic up into it yet, holding it ready for when or if Terric or Shame slipped.

Terric traced a Disbursement, waited for the Proxy to connect, and drew a small, beautiful spell of Light that looked like a lacy globe. He called magic into it, and the globe became visible, glowing in front of him with a butter-soft light.

"Can you control it?" Maeve asked.

Terric nodded, then made the light grow to the size of a basketball, then shrink to a pinpoint.

"Let it go," Maeve said.

The light winked out.

"Shame, please cast a small Light spell."

Light was one of the easiest spells to cast, and usually one of the first anyone learned. It really couldn't do much harm.

Shame drew a Disbursement, set it free to Proxy, and as soon as the returning ribbon slipped around his wrist, he traced a basic no-frills Light spell. It popped into existence with a snap of red, then rolled into a hot orange flicker.

"Control it," Maeve said.

Shame whispered and the light became a single candle flame; then he said another word and the light roared out into a heatless fireball.

He extinguished it with a flick of his fingers.

"Very good." Maeve sounded relieved. Was she that worried that they wouldn't be able to handle the simplest of magic?

"Now," she said, "cast Light together."

Terric looked at Shame. "How do you want to do it?"

"Quickly, so I can get a drink."

"Cast, then combine?"

"And hope we don't blow up the place."

"Let's hope for a little more than that," Terric said.

The faint pink Disbursement spell was still wrapped

around Terric's wrist from his last cast. Shame was holding a thin tether of Disbursement for Proxy on his wrist too. The price of this spell would be paid by someone else.

When Shame and Terric stood this close together, the glow around Terric seemed to dim to a more normal level. He was still radiating charisma, but it wasn't so strong, so alluring. Shame looked more normal too. The darkness around him thinned to flickering tendrils of smoke that drifted gently around him.

Terric drew Light.

And so did Shame.

Then they pulled magic up into the glyphs. Just as before, Terric's Light spell was a soft lacy orb, and Shame's was a ball of flame.

They each sent the spells closer together, their movements in perfect synch. The two spells joined and the orb flickered with orange flame. A beautiful combined spell of Light.

"Very nice," Maeve said. "Now make it smaller and larger."

Terric pulled magic up from the ground. It leaped to his hands like lightning, and burned there, a crackling stream of pure white light snapping with gold.

That was a lot of magic. Too much magic for such a small spell.

Shame drew on magic. It burned upward into his hands like black fire, a ragged river of black heat. Hard, strong.

Magic is invisible to the bare eye. Shame and Terric could not see what the magic looked like as it poured into their hands. But I could.

White and black magic arced between them, light and darkness biting, clashing, and finally, blending. Shame and Terric didn't say anything. They didn't have to. Soul Complements knew what the other was thinking. Or at least Zayvion and I did. Even if Shame and Terric couldn't read each other's minds, they were certainly working magic as if they had an intimate knowledge of what the other was going to do.

It was more than a little hypnotizing to watch them work magic together.

I licked my lips, and wished I were standing next to Zay. Wished he and I were joined together, lost in the magic between us.

Hot white magic jumped from Terric's hand to Shame's, becoming ebony flame that dripped from Shame's fingertips back into the ground.

With his other hand, Shame pulled magic out of the ground. It leaped to Terric's palm and melted into gold and white drops that slipped through his fingers, falling back to the ground.

Within that loop, that infinite band of drawing on the magic given and releasing the magic taken, the Light spell changed and changed until it crackled with unmatched brilliance.

Then two sets of hands adjusted the spell and the light grew smaller and smaller until it was only the tiniest speck, like the glitter of a single star resting in the space between them.

That kind of work, that kind of finesse in joint-spell manipulation, took a hell of a lot of concentration.

Without any outward signal I could see, the light began to grow. Shame glanced at Terric with a satisfied smirk. Terric chuckled as he exhaled slowly, sharing some silent, private connection that made me ache again for Zayvion.

Terric and Shame threw their hands wide.

The loop of magic between them spun into a spiral around them, the symbol for infinity. The Light spell grew larger until it was big enough to engulf them. Then it pushed outward, lacy orange fire reaching up to the huge crystal chandelier and setting it to glow, with diamonds and firelight covering every inch of its surface.

"Beautiful," I said. And beautiful didn't even cover it. The magic danced through every crystal, as if winged creatures out of some kind of fairy tale fluttered there.

Zay lifted his hands, waiting, ready to Ground if the magic slipped their grip.

The cinnamon sweetness of the Block spell Maeve was supporting around the room grew strong enough to make my eyes water. The Block strained to keep the magic Terric and Shame gleefully pulled upon contained in this room. The sheer weight of magic in the air pressed like hands on my shoulders.

The Light spell grew brighter, rays touching the corners of the room, falling like warm honey as it caressed faces, hands.

When the spell touched me, the magic caught fire to the patterns of magic down my arms, bringing the metallic markings alive like incandescent flame that wound down to wrap each of my fingertips.

I glanced around the room. It wasn't just me. We were all glowing.

Shame and Terric shifted their stance, drawing new spells in the air between them, and pulling even more magic into the room.

Shame no longer looked sick, tired, dead.

He burned with light, just as mesmerizing as Terric had been, just as alluring. Except Terric had shone with pure angelic light. Shame, on the other hand, radiated darkness and sin, blackness and a hard edge that drew my eye and made my pulse beat faster. He was beautiful. Forbidden. And promising every dark desire with those emerald eyes.

What did you know? Sexy dead.

Terric, in contrast, no longer looked as angelic. The magic around him carved him into something so powerful as to feel alien. He was gold and white light, his blue eyes heartless, cold, judging.

And they were pulling on more magic. So much more.

"Zay?" I said, taking a step backward and bumping into the wall behind me.

Whatever Shame and Terric were doing, whatever it was they were *becoming* from using magic together as Soul Complements, I wasn't sure it was a good thing, a safe thing.

I wanted my friends to use magic.

I didn't want them to become it.

The floor trembled as darkness fed light and light bloomed from darkness. Magic burned to ash only to catch fire again. Shame and Terric called magic as easily as breathing, commanding it to rise, fall, extinguish, and live to the beat of their hearts.

The walls shook, the chandelier rattled and chimed. The Block spell seared the satin wallpaper to a black crisp.

So much magic, so much power. I couldn't breathe.

"Enough!" Zayvion cast the Ground spell.

Magic exploded in a flash of light. Darkness poured into its wake.

And for several heartbeats all I did was try to breathe.

I blinked hard, trying to adjust to the darkness and lack of magic in the room. Only it wasn't dark—the room was lit. Normal electricity seemed feeble compared to the light Shame and Terric had just called upon.

Shame and Terric were on the floor. Maeve was already hurrying over to them. So was Zayvion.

I just stood there, stunned, unable to figure out what had happened. It had been only a minute, maybe two, since they drew on magic. But that had been a staggering amount of magic for two people to use together.

Maeve knelt next to Shame, her hand trembling as she pressed fingertips against his neck.

"They're alive," she said, checking Terric's pulse next.

The door burst opened and Kevin strode into the room. "What the hell just happened?"

"They used magic," I said. "Together."

He lifted his phone. "That was Thomas over at the Proxy pool. Every Proxy working the day shift for the Authority just passed out."

"All of them?" Maeve said.

"All of them."

"Is that why Shame and Terric passed out?" I asked.

"No," Zayvion said quietly. "Shame and Terric passed out because they blew the Proxies."

Everyone was silent for a second. I wasn't grasping the scope of the situation.

"How many Proxies were working?"

"Three hundred," Kevin said.

Okay. Now I got it. They had pulled on so much magic that the price to pay for it had knocked three hundred people unconscious. Well, three hundred and two, counting Shame and Terric.

Holy shit.

I looked down at Shame and Terric—two men who had lived and died for each other, two men who could use magic like I'd never seen before—and wondered who or what they really were now.

Soul Complements, Dad said quietly in my head. Even he sounded afraid.

Chapter Three

"It was just a Light spell," Maeve supplied over our silence.

"They blew all the Proxies?" I repeated slowly. "All of them?"

"Thomas doesn't exaggerate," Kevin said. "Do they need Dr. Fischer? A hospital?"

"I don't think so," Maeve said. "Let's give them a few minutes and see if they come to. Kevin, do you have any medical equipment here?"

"The staff isn't here today, but I can pull up the list of what we have in inventory and get that for you." He started toward the door, then put his hand on the doorknob. "Everyone's coming," he said to me. "We'll be ready in less than twenty minutes."

"Good," I said. "We'll be there."

Zay was already trying to get Shame and Terric into more comfortable positions, rolled onto their backs, legs straightened instead of where they'd fallen in a heap.

I bent down to help with Shame.

"Maybe we can move them to beds?" Maeve asked.

She was looking at me expectantly. Right. Other than Shame and Terric, Zay and I were the only Soul Complements around.

"I think distance from each other might make it

harder on them," I said, standing back up again. "Especially since they were working so closely together to use magic."

Maeve nodded and checked their pulses again.

"We need to have a plan," I said. "Less than twenty minutes until everyone in the Authority will be here."

Zayvion straightened and slipped his arm down my back, mine sliding around his waist. "Have you talked to Violet about the disks?"

"Using them to cleanse the wells? Briefly, yesterday. She said she'll bring the remaining disks here so we can use them if we need too. She should be here any minute."

I glanced back down at Shame and Terric. I didn't want to leave to see if Violet was here until I knew if they were going to be okay. "They weren't anywhere close to controlling that spell."

"Obviously." Zay smiled. "No one's ever knocked out every Proxy in Portland."

"Was that every Proxy?"

"Only the day crew. Still, impressive."

"And frightening," I said.

His hand tightened on my hip. If that's the way Terric and Shame were going to pull on magic, they'd kill themselves before they finished drawing the first line of a spell. We could not afford to lose three hundred people to pay the price for their spells every time they cast simple magic. They would be useless in a fight.

"They can't work magic together," I said.

"They're not dead," Zay pointed out.

"They should be. Three hundred Proxies? For a Light spell?"

"It was their first time," Zay said. "I think they got a little . . . drunk on the power. It's a heady thing to find yourself soul-to-soul with someone who perfectly matches you. It's very hard to stay in control."

A thrill of need stroked a low, slow heat beneath my skin, burning down my stomach to my thighs. Just thinking about casting magic with Zayvion, held by him, holding him, made me want to take a quick break from all this serious business and opt for some sexy-private time.

Shame moaned, then swore. "Hell. What. Ter?"

Then a little louder, a little panicked, "Terric?"

"He's right here, Son," Maeve said. "Still unconscious. You knocked yourselves out."

Shame slipped his hand from his eyes and looked up at his mother.

The blackness around him seemed to have faded some. I wondered if the physical distance between him and Terric made some sort of difference in how magic manifested around them. When Shame was near Terric the blackness wasn't so encompassing. He seemed less skeletal, less death-y. When Terric was near Shame, that fall-to-your-knees charisma and light damped down.

Yin-yang.

Maeve shook her head, but she was smiling. "You never do anything in a small way, do you?"

"What? And be boring?" Shame exhaled a shaky breath. "Can't have that."

She and Zay helped Shame sit. He stared at Terric, who was still out. An expression of respect crossed Shame's face. He swallowed, and shook his head just slightly. Then, with what looked like some effort, he looked away from Terric, to us.

"Tell me we blew something up in a most spectacular way." His hand trembled as he dug in his pocket for cigarettes.

"No, not really," Zay said, without a trace of a smile. "Well, you did blow through a few Proxies."

Shame tapped the pack in his hand and slipped a cigarette free. "Few?"

"Three hundred," Zay said, obviously enjoying this.

"Fucking ballsicles. Are you shitting me?"

"Every damn Proxy on duty in the city."

Shame smiled. No, Shame grinned. It was a wicked, wicked thing. "Top that, Jones."

"Don't have to," Zay said, pulling me in a little tighter. "We took on Leander and Isabelle."

"Sure, but they got free, didn't they?" He nodded toward Terric as he slipped the cigarette in his mouth. "We killed Jingo Jingo."

"As I remember it, there were a few other people on that battlefield doing their part so you could kill him. And Allie and I didn't have to die to take down Leander and Isabelle," Zay said.

"Dying, schmying. How many Proxies have you blown through today?"

"This is not a contest, boys," Maeve said.

"C'mon, Mum." Shame patted his pocket for a lighter. "Z here has been trying to get me to admit Ter and I can use magic together for years. And now that we've done it—better than he and his girl there—"

"Girl has a name," I reminded him.

"You can't expect me not to rub it in a little."

"Jesus," Terric said softly. "Shame?"

"Over here," Shame said.

Terric blinked up at the ceiling. "What the hell?"

"Mostly magic," I said. "And mostly impressive magic."

"Yay?" he said.

"Do you feel like sitting?" Maeve asked.

"I don't know. I can try."

Zay and I helped Terric sit. He looked at Shame, waiting, I thought, for Shame's normal rebuke.

"We blew three hundred Proxies," Shame said smugly. "Smoke?" He offered the pack of cigarettes.

"Three hundred?" Terric took the pack, tapped out a cigarette. I'd never seen him smoke. He handed Shame back the pack and just sort of held the cigarette in his hand, as if he didn't remember it was there. He looked up at Maeve, then Zay and me.

Concern, and maybe a little panic, clouded his eyes. "Are they all right? Is everyone all right?"

"We had all the safeties in place," Maeve said. "The Proxy spells blew, but the people paying the price for your magic aren't harmed. They probably won't be able to Proxy for a few weeks though."

"Thomas is getting a second line in place," Zay said.

"Jesus," Terric said again. "Jesus, Shame."

Shame slanted him a look. "You're the one who wanted this."

"I wanted us to use magic together, yes," Terric said, groaning as he pushed up onto his feet. He made it, even though he held his hands out to the side for a second before getting his balance. "I didn't want us to lay out half of the Proxy pool."

Shame shrugged. "It is what it is."

"No." Terric rubbed his fingers over his eyes. "It is a mess. Next time we do that, *if* we do it, we Proxy our own price. And we make damn sure magic doesn't become . . ."

Shame just watched him, waiting for the rest of the sentence. Maybe daring him to say that what they had done—cast magic together—was wrong.

". . . dangerous," Terric finally said. "We need better control."

Shame huffed out a laugh. "Speak for yourself. I liked it. Control is overrated."

"You're wrong," Terric said.

"Getting tired of you telling me that."

"Why, because I'm always right?"

Shame shook his head and shoved up to his feet like it didn't hurt, even though I was sure it did.

"You're fucking amazing," he said, getting in Terric's face and jabbing a finger in his chest. "You hassle me for months to cast magic with you, and now that I have, you want nothing to do with me? Fine. You got what you wanted. It's not my problem you can't deal with it."

"I didn't say—" Terric started.

Davy Silvers, one of my Hounds who still couldn't get it through his head that I didn't need him to look after me, appeared in the doorway of the room.

"Hey, boss. Noticed half of Portland is headed this way. Something going down I should know about?"

Davy had been so close to death in the last week it was startling to see him on his feet. If Eli Collins, a man who had once worked on developing magical technology with my dad, hadn't literally cut spells into Davy's skin to give the poisoned magic he was infected with a way out of his body, Davy would be dead.

But like all things with magic, that "cure" had come with a price. Davy had to work hard to stay solid. Those spells made him insubstantial. If he didn't keep his mind on being a solid physical person, he'd fall through the floor he was standing on.

"Seattle's on the way to kick our ass," I said.

His eyebrows jerked up into the ragged edge of his bangs. "The entire city, Space Needle and everything?"

I grinned. "I hope not. Can you call the Hounds? I want them in on this."

"They're already in the kitchen eating cookies."

God, I loved Hounds. Never late to a disaster. Or a free meal.

"Tell them to be in the main ballroom in five."

"On it." He headed down the hall at a jog.

"So what's the plan?" Zayvion asked. I glanced at Shame and Terric, who were scowling at each other, and Maeve, who looked at me with a mix of sadness and determination.

"We tell Seattle to stay the hell out of our city."

Chapter Four

The ballroom looked like something out of an old movie. Two staircases spiraled down from three stories up, joined at a grand landing, then split one last time to create a perfect arch over a huge fountain in the center of the marble-floored room. The upper two floors came with open balconies looking over the ballroom that I'm sure could be romantically lit for waltzers back in the day.

Nobody was waltzing today.

One wall of the main floor was set with a stage. That is where I and Maeve, Zayvion, Kevin, and Victor stood, waiting for the crowd to settle down.

Victor had been the Voice of Faith magic, and my teacher. A tall, gray-haired man, he was old enough to be my father. He had traded in his slacks and jacket for jeans and a dark brown sweater. His eyes were still bandaged from the flash of magic he'd taken in the face out on the battlefield. We weren't sure if he was going to regain his sight or not.

He didn't seem to be in pain, talking quietly to the woman, Grace, who was at his elbow.

Grace was maybe ten years younger than Victor, and had been away in Canada for the last year or so, doing some Authority work there. I'd just met her today and already liked her. Her dark hair swung at her shoulders and was pulled back with combs to show off her deep-set brown eyes and soft, rounded features. She spoke quietly to Victor, explaining the size and shape of the room, and the people it contained.

Shame wasn't on the stage. Neither was Terric. I scanned the crowd for them, and finally saw them standing on opposite sides of the room, doing their best to fade into the shadows and completely ignore each other.

The room wasn't quite shoulder-to-shoulder packed with people, but that was only because it was such a large space. Quick count told me we had at least five hundred people here.

All those bodies, all those faces, all those people between me and any exit I could see—not to mention more people streaming onto the balconies—kicked my claustrophobia into high gear.

My chest tightened; my breathing hitched. Sweat peppered my upper lip. My little panic mantra of "I'm gonna die, I'm gonna die" sang through my head.

I hated that mantra.

Zayvion, standing beside me, took my hand.

At just that touch, the fear pushed away, the panic quieted. I was still freaking out, but Zayvion's calm did me a world of good. I squeezed his hand. I just needed to get through this, lay out a plan, and then I'd go find some fresh air and wide-open spaces.

Antarctica might be nice this time of year.

Victor and Grace walked up to the microphone. Then Grace stepped away so that all eyes would be on Victor alone. We'd agreed to let him tell the news since he had been a respected figure in the Authority for years.

Victor waited patiently. If it weren't for the gauze

around his eyes, you'd think that he was fine, that everything was good, normal.

But everything was not normal. Not at all. Seattle was on its way. Leander and Isabelle were on their way. Magic was poisoned. We were about to enter a battle, then probably a war with an army of magic users, and two of the most powerful Soul Complements who had ever used magic.

We were nowhere near ready for this fight.

But we had no choice, and no time left.

"We have information," Victor said, "that Seattle has been scrambled by the Overseer. They are coming to shut Portland down and kill or Close us."

It was so quiet in the room, you could hear feet shift over marble, fabric shush, and distantly, the clatter from the kitchen.

Zayvion pressed his shoulder against mine and I took a deep breath, trying to get my oxygen evenly and calmly through the claustrophobia.

"We need the entire Authority in Portland working together against this threat," Victor said. "We have the ear of the police department via the MERCs and Detective Stotts. We have all the Hounds in the city willing to assist us. The mayor, other governing officials, and emergency departments are in the loop, and ready to lend whatever help and resources we need. In short, the entire city of Portland is joined in this fight.

"We do not make as strong a front as we might like. Magic is poisoned. We are not certain what caused magic to go bad, but we are certain that it is magic itself that has been tampered with, not the cisterns, networked lines, or other storage facilities.

"The more we use magic, the more we will fall ill from

it. We've sent out public warnings telling people to stop using magic while the networks are being upgraded, allowing us time to try to purify the wells, but we are not seeing any decrease in magic use. The number of ill and infected is growing."

"What about other cities?" a man in the crowd asked. "Do they know about magic being poisoned?"

Victor paused. Then, "We sent out word to the Authority in Washington, California, Idaho, and Nevada warning them that magic has been poisoned and that it might spread. We also shared our information that the Overseer has been compromised by Leander and Isabelle. We have not received word back. From anyone."

A low murmur rolled through the room.

"Is that unusual?" I asked Zay quietly.

He nodded. "We usually receive communication instantly from other cities. Especially in times of crisis."

Okay. So that meant either our communication didn't get out, it fell into the wrong hands, or the Authority members outside the city had decided not to talk to us.

Or had been told by someone not to talk to us.

Someone like the Overseer.

A chill washed over me as I took that idea a step further. *Dad,* I thought, *if you had possessed me fully— killed me and taken over my body as I'm guessing Leander and Isabelle did with the Overseer—would you have access to my memories?*

Just because I am possessing you, Allison, doesn't make me an expert on the phenomenon, he said dryly.

Throw me an educated guess, I said.

He was quiet for a bit.

Victor stepped away from the microphone, and moved toward the side of the stage, where Grace helped him sit on one of the chairs there. That was my cue, I guess. To stand up and lay out a plan. To figure out who was going to lead this fight.

If I wanted to preserve your memories, Dad finally said, *I would have found a way to do so while in your body. Even if you died.*

I suddenly realized what a strange question that had been. And I didn't much like his answer: If he had wanted me dead, he could have killed me, taken my memories *and* my body.

Hells.

I shivered.

Zayvion rubbed his hand down my arm. "Your father?" he asked.

"Yes. I just asked him if he could have killed me but kept my memories intact when he possessed me."

Anger rolled through Zay, through me, a hot, bitter wave. "God, Allie. Why would you ask him that?"

"I wanted to know if it was possible. If I were Leander and Isabelle and had just possessed the head of all of the Authority worldwide, I'd want more than her address book as a resource."

"Son of a bitch," he breathed.

I nodded.

"What did he say?"

"That if he wanted my memories, he'd have found a way to keep them even if he killed me."

"Leander and Isabelle have the Overseer's memories," he said. "They know everything we know. You should take the mic."

"No. You can do it. I hate spotlights, remember?"

He slipped his arm from around me and paused just a moment, turning toward me, his long fingers resting on my hips as he looked me straight in the eye.

Too much gold in his gaze, where only warm brown should be.

"Your voice is stronger in this crowd than you think."

"It's not my voice I'm worried about. I hate public speaking. Or public standing."

"They need to know, Allie."

"Then tell them."

"You underestimate your position."

"What position? Just a couple days ago, I was on the run for my life from the Authority."

"Things have changed."

"Sure, I agree. But not enough for people to care what I have to say about it."

"You'd be surprised." He let go of my hip and stalked over to the microphone. Even in boots on the hard wood, with what I knew was an aching hip and back, he made only the slightest sound as he smoothly crossed the stage.

He stood in front of the microphone. Man had a presence, even when he wasn't speaking. Maybe especially then.

Voices quieted and went silent.

"I'd like to bring up a few things Victor didn't address," Zay said. "The Authority in Portland is largely without officially appointed Voices. Since there are four wells of magic beneath our city, it has always been tradition for a Voice to not only stand guard over the well that corresponded with his or her discipline, but to also speak for the users of that discipline.

"Bartholomew Wray changed that when he reassigned the position of Voices. Jingo Jingo did even more damage, killing our coworkers, family, and friends.

"Other cities would buckle under the strain of these

setbacks. But not Portland. Other people would turn from this fight. Not the people of Portland.

"Leander and Isabelle retained the Overseer's memories when they possessed her body. They know everything we know. Every procedure, every rule, every regulation and resource. They know what we have, they know how we'll use it, and they know how to use it against us.

"We need a leader in this battle. Someone the Overseer doesn't have much information on, and therefore neither do Leander and Isabelle. Someone who knows how to fight and how to survive. Someone who is willing to use unconventional tactics against them.

"We need Allison Beckstrom."

The entire room seemed to fade away, replaced by fuzzy gray fog that came rolling in from the edges of my vision. A high ringing started up. Me, sliding into shock. Really didn't have time for that.

I so didn't want to be the one calling the shots in this fight. I'd already taken the responsibility for one fight. People had died, people had been crippled. I didn't think I could handle all these lives in my hands again.

You are strong, Allison. Dad's voice was as comforting and confident as I'd ever heard.

I have no battle experience . . .

. . . You have done nothing but fight since I died, he said.

I don't know how to coordinate a city full of people. Thousands, Dad. Thousands of people could die, are dying right now. I don't know enough to make everything turn out right.

They're not looking to you to make everything right, Allison. They are looking to you to stand and be their strength. To make the hard decisions they know must be made. To lead them when they are lost. Each person will make their own choices, will live and die by their own actions. Your place, a leader's place, is to make them believe they can win this war. And if not win, then survive.

Even if they can't? I asked.

Is that what you believe?

I thought about it. I didn't know what to believe. Things had been changing so quickly. Magic had changed. My friends had changed. Hell, even I had changed.

I'd killed a man.

I swallowed hard, trying to push away the memory of Bartholomew's death that always hovered just below my conscious thought.

I'd managed to handle whatever had been thrown my way, but could I handle this?

It's a war, I said. *We're talking about waging a magical battle against Seattle, Leander and Isabelle, and all the people they are going to send against us. We fought Jingo Jingo—one man—and almost died. He wasn't nearly as strong as Leander and Isabelle—he wasn't even a Soul Complement. They are. I don't know how we can take on someone more powerful than him.*

You are a Soul Complement, Allison. Do not think that is without advantage.

I can't even cast magic without puking.

Dad sighed, which is sort of weird since he couldn't breathe. *You simply refuse to admit your power. It has always been a vexing and disappointing flaw in your character.*

"Disappointing? From a dead guy? You have no right to judge me."

It is not a judgment if it is the truth. Why must you turn every conversation into an argument?

"I'm not arguing. I'm being logical and you're talking crazy!"

Someone coughed.

That's when I realized I wasn't just thinking to my dad. I was talking. Out loud. On stage. While everyone across that floor stared at me, silent.

Oh, just so classy.

You have their attention now, Dad said. *Be their strength, even if you are uncertain. Give them a reason to refute their fears even if you can not refute yours. They need hope. They need you.*

I tipped my chin up a little and swallowed. "Well, I heard about half of what Zayvion said."

"Mic!" someone from the back yelled. It was Jack Quinn, one of my Hounds. I knew he could hear me. Hounds had good ears. But he was probably right that other people might need me to speak up.

I brushed my fingers above my ears again, trying to tuck too-short hair. Yes, it was a nervous habit. I had a lot to be nervous about.

Spotlight, for one thing.

End of the world, for another.

I strolled over to Zayvion, fixing him with a glare. He held one hand out for me, and I took it, very aware of all the eyes on us.

I wondered, for a moment, how they saw us. A man and a woman? An ex-guardian of the gate and a Hound? A poor boy and rich girl? Black and white?

Or maybe, did they see more? See us as we really were: lovers, companions, friends. Magic users. Survivors. Warriors. Soul Complements.

From the slight snap of saltiness in the air, I knew at least a few people were casting Sight to see what, exactly, we looked like through magic.

I don't want to do this, I thought, not to Dad, but to Zayvion.

You won't do it alone. Zay rubbed his thumb over the side of my hand.

I'd rather have him at my side than anyone else in the world.

I pulled my shoulders back, let go of his hand, and faced the microphone. "Hi," I said a little too close, causing the feedback to buzz.

"For those of you who haven't met me, I'm Allie Beckstrom. I don't think I'm the best person to lead this fight. I only joined the Authority this year, have never been a Voice or held any other position of leadership, and I tend to think like a Hound more than a commander. Please reconsider Zayvion's suggestion. I am sure there are other people more experienced than I who should lead."

"I will follow Allie," a voice called out from the back of the room. It wasn't Jack. No, that voice was Davy Silvers, who was pretty much my right-hand Hound.

Davy sat on the edge of the fountain, his girlfriend, Sunny, who was both punk-rock chic and a hell of a Blood magic user, right next to him. They were both eating cookies. He grinned and raised his hand in a wave.

Great.

"I will follow Allie," another voice called out. This, to my surprise, was Detective Paul Stotts, who stood near one of the exit doors with his team: officers Roberts, Garnett, and Julian. They all seemed very interested in the entire assemblage, probably because this sort of stuff had never been seen by the police before.

I guess Stotts had decided that since we'd been through so much together, he might as well stick it out with me. Also, I expected his feelings for Nola had something to do with his loyalty.

The next voice was Maeve's, behind me. "I will follow

Allie." Then Victor. That started off a chorus of people, a rising river of voices, carrying my name.

Not everyone said they'd follow me. As I scanned the faces and the body language, I could tell not everyone was happy about the decision. But no one was angry enough to leave, or to stand up and throw their hat into the ring.

Which meant it was time to come up with a plan. Fast. I shook my head, not believing I was about to do this. But who else would? No one had come forward when Victor had left the microphone open. Only Zayvion. Only me.

We had probably just sealed our deaths. Might have sealed the deaths of hundreds.

I couldn't think about that now. All that mattered was curing magic, stopping Seattle, and killing Leander and Isabelle.

It was certainly what I was aiming for.

Right now we'd be lucky to pull off two out of the three things.

No, we'd be lucky if we managed to do even one of those things.

The crowd quieted.

"Seattle is coming to Close us and lock down Portland," I said. "We're not going to let them do that."

That got their attention.

"We know they're going to use magic to shut the city down. We know they're going to use magic to Close us, hold us, and whatever else their orders might be. We know using magic will make us ill—and it will make them ill too.

"So we are going to take magic off the playing field. We are going to shut down the networks so that no one can use magic."

Silence filled the room.

"The hell," Shame's gleeful voice called out. "We can do that?"

Can we, Dad? I asked.

There is a way.

"Yes," I said, "we can. And we are going to. What I need from everyone are two things. One—do not draw upon the magic from the wells. Magic is too damn dangerous for anyone to be using right now, and that includes the people who are going to defend the city—us.

"The Seattle crew knows about the wells, so the sooner we can cleanse the wells and close them, the less we'll have to worry about them pulling on the tainted magic and us needing to do the same to fight them."

"Then how are we going to fight them?" a voice in the crowd asked.

"Once we shut down the wells and there is no magic to draw from, it shouldn't be that difficult. Detective Stotts? Is there some way we can legally keep them contained until we deal with the Overseer?"

All eyes turned to Detective Paul Stotts.

"There is," he said. "I will expect that the people in this room, and all other members of the Authority, will leave their detention to the police. We will, of course, also expect that everyone here will work closely with us if problems or concerns arise."

"Thank you," I said. "Any questions about apprehending the Seattle members *after* magic has been closed, when, hopefully, they and we will not be using magic, check in with Detective Stotts. Any questions about apprehending the Seattle members *before* magic has been closed, when I am sure they will be trying to use magic against us, contact me, Victor, Maeve, or Zayvion and Kevin. We will keep everyone up to date on any and all information we receive.

"Second thing," I continued. "I want all the hospitals, emergency services, communications, ports, and plants to be contacted to make sure they are ready for the switchover to straight electricity, natural gas, and oil."

A roll of conversation swelled and silenced. It had been years since Portland had gone traditional power only for any length of time. Years since a spell hadn't been used to bolster a piece of equipment, or a person's medical recovery.

But humankind had lived without easy access to magic for centuries. I figured we could handle a few days—maybe weeks at the most without it.

From the sound of the crowd, they were not as sure about that.

The Hounds were still in the crowd. No surprise. Life as a Hound meant you didn't turn down a job if one was offered. Actually, it was more than that. The Hounds had thrown in their lot with me. They'd stood beside me when there was no reason for them to believe any of us would walk out of the fight alive.

They were loyal friends. And furious, dirty fighters.

My people.

They didn't appear to be at all concerned about shutting magic down.

"You expect us to convince everyone in the entire city to run on electricity alone?" a sallow-faced man somewhere in the middle of the crowd called out. "We haven't been nonmagic for nearly thirty years. No one will do it. There will be riots in the street."

I didn't know who he was. Didn't much care, really.

"You have a good point," I said. "Unfortunately, it

doesn't matter. The city has all the backup systems to go magic-free. We've done it for short stints during wild magic storms. It's in all the emergency plans. It can be done. And it's going to be done. Get ready, and spread the word. Because whether or not anyone likes it, I am shutting this city down in exactly one hour."

I picked up the mic, switched it off, then strode across the stage.

Chapter Five

"**N**icely done," Zay murmured as we stepped off the stage.

"Do *not* talk to me, Jones." I tromped down the stairs.

The only problem with my plan of storming off was the hundreds of people standing in my way. Well, that, and a feet-freezing rush of claustrophobia. I got three steps down the side of the stage before I could go no farther.

Zay was on my heels. He didn't have to be touching me for me to know what he was thinking. I was confusing the hell out of him.

"What's wrong?" His hand landed on my shoulder, and he hissed as the full force of my phobia stomped through our bond.

He pulled his hand away and exhaled, then was down the stairs, next to me. His arm looped around my back, propelling me through the crowd that parted like magic in front of us, with nothing more than his glare clearing the path.

We crossed the room and were out the double doors to the wide-open hallway, and through that so fast, I couldn't keep track of which doors we had passed. Then we were walking up the steps to the main doors—beveled glass and lead caught with rainbows from a century ago—and on the wide columned front porch of the estate.

Air. Real air.

Zay let go of me and walked across the porch as if shaking off a pain, then paced back toward me, but keeping his distance.

I just stood there, alone, with an armload of space, a world full of air and roominess. The wind was warm, even though evening was setting in, but it left me shaking and cold. Barging our way through that many people had made me break out in a sweat.

Zay leaned one shoulder against a column and watched me.

"Why?" I finally said, when my heart was slow enough not to make my words stutter. "Why did you tell them I would lead?"

"Because there isn't anyone else I would follow."

"Bull. You've followed the Authority all your life. Followed Victor. Followed Maeve."

He gave me a smoldering look, his arms crossed over his wide chest. "I don't follow them anymore, Allie. I follow you. Better than that—I stand with you. You are the only one who kept us alive on that battlefield. You are the only one the Hounds trust and follow, Stotts trusts and follows. You are the only one I trust."

"You trust Victor."

"As a teacher, yes."

"You'd follow him into battle."

He shrugged. "This isn't just about a fight. It's about magic. How we fix it. *Who* fixes it. What it will be when that is done. It would be too easy, too tempting for any other person in that room to make choices for magic I refuse to live by."

"Like what?"

He paused, frowning as he realized I didn't understand what he was getting at.

"The Authority is an ancient organization. It is not a democracy. We are given our positions, appointed to them by our superiors. But there is always room to move up. And every person in that room has a reason to want to be the one person with the power and ability to decide what should be done with magic."

"Done with it?" I asked. "Heal it. Cleanse it. Fix it," I said. "What the hell else would anyone want to do with it?"

"Control it," he said. "Use it. Rule it. Own it. Just like Bartholomew Wray. Just like Jingo Jingo."

I was going to tell him he was wrong. Magic was poisoned and killing people. Anyone in their right mind would want to fix it and let it go back to being what it has always been.

But not all magic users cared about the greater good. Certainly Leander and Isabelle didn't care. There were others. My dead father still placed his desires above all others. He had once told me he suspected even Victor had done things to tip the balance of what was done with magic to what he thought was right.

Which Victor had as much as admitted to when he'd told us he'd taken away more of Eli Collins' memories than was required by the Authority.

"I don't want to control it," I said, all the breath out of me.

Zay waited a moment more. Then he unfolded his arms and started toward me. "I know."

"Other people don't want to control it," I said, though it came out more like a question. "They want it fixed."

"Those other people can't lead like you can."

"Why didn't you volunteer to do it? They would follow you."

"No. Too many people don't like things I've done in the past as the Guardian of the gate. They won't follow me."

I looked up at him. He had stopped about six inches away, his thumbs tucked into his front pockets. I could smell his familiar pine cologne and wished I were home, in bed with him, in some kind of world where magic didn't make everything and everyone it touched hurt.

"Tell me," I said, "that you weren't setting me up all along."

The corner of his mouth quirked up, then pressed back down into a serious line. "Hmm. Like this entire mess was some kind of master plan I put in place a year ago just so I could see if you'd try to purify magic and save the world from two psychotic dead people?"

"Not that," I said. "Expecting me to jump in and lead just because you said I should. Did you have that planned?"

He shook his head. "It just seemed right at the time. I overstepped a bit, didn't I?"

I nodded. "More than a bit. Tell me first."

"I will. If there's a next time."

"Good." I placed my hands on either side of his hips, and felt his muscles contract. I rubbed my palms up his back, gently since I knew how damn much he was still hurting despite painkillers and a good doctor.

Then I kissed him.

His faint surprise was quickly washed away in a rush of passion as his arms surrounded me, one hand dragging warm fingers across the bare back of my neck, then stroking up through my hair.

If I surrendered myself to this, to my want of him, the thrumming electricity pricking to life beneath my skin, the amazing awareness of who I was, and how alive I was in Zayvion's arms, I might not let go.

I'd told Nola it wasn't hard for us to remain in our own bodies. That he and I handled the draw of being Soul Complements just fine.

But that was not the full truth. It wasn't just when we were using magic that I wanted to be part of him, breathing his breath, feeling his heartbeat as if it were my own.

It would be easy to let go of everything, to just slip into his mind, his soul, and never feel alone again.

I love you, I thought, and felt it ripple through him.

Then I pulled away, making sure I was soundly in my own mind, my own body. That I was just me, Allie, and he was just him, Zayvion.

He inhaled, placing his forehead against mine. "Tell me that wasn't good-bye."

"That was I love you. Weren't you paying attention? You'd know if I said good-bye."

I stepped back, and he caught my fingertips with his own.

"I'd better," he said. "Because I'm pretty sure I'd have something to say about that."

"Allie?" Kevin strode out onto the porch. "Violet's upstairs with the disks."

I gave Zay's hand a squeeze. "I'll be right there. Do we know how many people from Seattle are on the way yet?"

Kevin shook his head.

Zay let go of my hand. "I'll see if I can find out."

We walked into the house, Zay right behind me. He jogged down the hall to the left while Kevin and I picked up the pace and made for a staircase at the right. We took the stairs two at a time, then walked a short distance down the hall.

"She's in this room." He stopped outside a door that looked like the other dozen doors down the hall. This place really could be a hotel.

Kevin was a man of economical movements and words. He wasn't the sort of person to waste time. Still, he stopped a moment, adjusted his shirt, and brushed the sweat from his face. When his hand came down, he looked very placid: sad eyes calm, body language just carrying a hint of worry, but not the tension I had seen in him moments ago.

I wondered if he even knew he was doing this. If he understood how much he cared about the way Violet saw him.

"Have you told Violet you love her?"

He paused, hand halfway to the doorknob. "She knows."

I didn't say anything.

He gave me a sideways look. "She must know," he insisted. "All this time. I mean, I haven't come out and said it . . ."

"You should."

"She's a very intelligent woman. I'm sure she's aware of how much I care, and of . . . my other feelings."

He sounded uncomfortable and worried.

It was kind of adorable.

"I wouldn't count on it," I said. "She's smart. But sometimes the smartest people are blind to what's right in front of them."

"I don't see how this is any of your concern," he said.

"She's my friend, Kevin. And you know, the mother to my only sibling. I'd like to see her happy. I think you can make her happy. But she's not a mind reader. Tell her. Tell her you have feelings for her, or that she's important to you or . . . something, before it's too late."

He blinked and waited to see if I was going to continue. Then, slowly, "We're not going to lose this fight, Allie. After things settle down, really settle down, I'll talk to her. I'll have time to tell her and show her how I feel."

"Two undead magic users who are Soul Complements have the firepower of the entire Authority outside this city behind them and they're coming our way. There's no guarantee which of us will survive this, Cooper. No guarantee any of us will survive. Please. Tell her before the night is over. Or I might have to tell her myself."

"I'd appreciate it if you stayed out of my personal business. And my love life."

"I'd appreciate it if you wouldn't leave her in the dark. If it helps any, Dad doesn't seem to hate you as much—"

"I don't give a damn what your father thinks about me."

Sore spot. Well, who could blame him? Even I wasn't sure why Violet loved my dad. Although, from the wisps of memories I'd gotten from Dad, he very much loved her in his own emotionally stunted way.

"Neither do I," I said. "This isn't about Dad. This is about Violet, and I'm guessing the baby. If you want to stay in her life and stay in his life, you're going to have to let her know about it. Soon." Then I added, "Please."

His expression didn't change. I couldn't tell if anything I'd said made a bit of difference to him. He just turned, shoulders stiff, and opened the door for me.

I walked past him. I'd meant what I said. Violet was my friend, Daniel was my little brother, and Kevin was a decent man. Decent men didn't hide their feelings from the people they loved.

The room was a bedroom, not a meeting room, fine linens across the bed, a tasteful, almost feminine touch to the decor. Sheer curtains spilled at the corners of the window, letting in the evening light.

A little happy-baby squeal and the sound of water

splashing came from behind a second door. The bathroom. Violet's voice carried out into the main room. "Be right there."

Kevin walked over to the window and gazed out it. Maybe thinking about what I had said. Maybe just looking for trouble like a good bodyguard should.

Violet strolled out of the bathroom with little Daniel wrapped up in a white towel. The corner of the towel was tucked over Daniel's head like a hat. It had little black eyes and a pink nose stitched onto it and bunny ears that flopped at the top.

He looked ridiculously cute.

"Aw," I said.

Violet smiled. She wore a T-shirt and jeans, her auburn hair a little messy and damp as if someone had gotten his soggy little hands all over it. She didn't have her glasses on.

I felt a strange melancholy drift through my mind. For a moment, I didn't know if it was my feelings or my dad's. That baby brother of mine made me think about what it might be like to have kids of my own, to hold Zayvion's child in my arms.

Made me think about how wonderful that would be.

I pushed that knot of unexpected desire away. No time for that now. Maybe . . . maybe if we survived.

But the melancholy remained. Sadness. It wasn't my emotion. It was Dad's. He missed Violet. Deeply regretted that he'd died before she had given birth to their only child.

His only son he would never know.

"Hey," I said, trying to distance myself from Dad's feelings and not doing a very good job of it. "Any luck with the disks?"

"Some. We have them set and ready for anyone to access." She made a silly face at Daniel and he squirmed and made another happy noise, waving her glasses at her before stuffing them awkwardly in his mouth.

"I don't, however, have any clue about how to get the magic samples from each well out of Stone," she said.

"I think I know how."

"Good." She was all business now, putting Daniel on the bed with a pillow on either side of him, though I had no idea why.

Kevin moved away from the window to one of the chairs. He picked up a tote bag with little bears decorating the edges of it and gave it to Violet.

"Thank you." She proceeded to pull out the tiniest little shirt and pants and socks I'd ever seen. "Keep going, Allie. I'm listening."

Right. Stop being distracted by the cute.

"I need to know how many disks you still have."

She gently pried her glasses out of Daniel's hands and he set off crying. Kevin produced a little giraffe toy out of the bag and jingled it sweetly. Then he pressed it on Daniel's chest and made duckie noises until the baby noticed it and started chewing on the thing's nose.

Kevin and Violet looked good together. Very natural. Like a father and mother should look. I had never once doubted Violet loved her son. And now I had no doubt that Kevin did too.

Another ache rolled through me, hard enough I held my breath against it. It was strange—Dad wasn't usually this haphazard with letting his feelings leak. He usually kept them tightly controlled and sealed away from me.

But then, Violet was the only person—well, maybe besides baby Daniel—that I thought he actually loved.

I have always loved you, Allison, he said with the same kind of bittersweet note. *Perhaps, someday, you will believe that.*

His sorrow was so palpable, I had no idea what to say to him. I had never been in the position to comfort my father. I'd never thought he'd needed or wanted comforting. Certainly not from me.

Violet quickly dressed the baby, then sat on the edge of the bed, her hand on his belly, while he contentedly slobbered on the toy.

"Nineteen," she said.

"Disks?" I asked, trying to remember what we were talking about.

"Yes. They are each charged with enough untainted magic to power one spell. What exactly is your plan, Allie?"

"We're going to shut down all the magic in Portland."

"Do you even know how to do that?" she asked. "There are agencies, paperwork involved. A review process."

"Not today. Today I'm making the decisions. And if we're going to stop the hit squad from Seattle and keep more people from getting sick and dying from using magic, we are going dark."

She shook her head, but a small smile played across her lips. "It isn't a bad idea. Reckless. Untested, but not without merit. I'm not sure there is a way to safely shut down all access to magic. Your father might have known. He was always planning for any emergency. But if he knew, he never told me."

And that's when I knew I'd have to do something I'd been avoiding for almost a year.

"I need to tell you something else," I said, steeling myself for this. "It's going to be hard for you to hear. I'd hoped I would never have to say it. Not like this, but I think you need to know. About Dad."

Kevin's body language suddenly stiffened. He very much looked like a man who could take me down with one well-placed hit. I looked over at him, met his gaze.

"I have to tell her. They'll need to work together on the disks."

Kevin swallowed, then, "Hell. I object. Just so you know."

"I know."

"Allie?" Violet said. "What?"

"Violet, Dad died. I know you know that. You were there for his burial. Both of them. But there was a man, a doctor, who was a part of the Authority. He worked in Death and Blood magic and dabbled in dark magic. He was trying to raise my father from the dead."

Violet was holding very still, listening, absorbing. She had known about the Authority before I did. But Dad had been very careful to keep her sheltered from the worst aspects of it.

"And?" she asked calmly, as if I were a student who hadn't fully expressed my thesis.

Allison, Dad breathed, *no. Oh, please, daughter, no.*

His plea made my breath catch in my throat.

"That man contacted Dad's spirit and chained it down. I tried to free him. Things got confusing—there was a lot of magic being thrown around. By the end of it, Dad was possessing me. A corner of my mind. And he still is."

Violet had gone a ghastly shade of gray. Little Daniel lost hold of the giraffe and was fussing beneath her hand. She didn't seem to notice.

"I'm . . . I'm sorry I didn't tell you," I said. "I'm sorry it happened."

"Daniel?" she exhaled, her eyes searching my face. Looking for a lie, looking for him.

She pulled herself together with visible will and turned to Kevin.

"Is it true?"

"Yes."

"And you didn't tell me?"

He opened and closed his hands. Uncomfortable. Guilty. "None of us thought it would be an ongoing concern. We all thought — We all hoped it would pass. Quickly."

Those accusing eyes turned to me. "I don't understand," she said. "Why did you keep this from me? All this time?"

"I — no — *we* didn't want you to be hurt. Again," I said honestly. "Dad — I think he thought it was enough for you to go through two burials. He . . . he still cares for you. And he wants you to live a good life. A happy life."

"He can speak to you?" she asked.

I opened my mouth, but she stood.

"Let me speak to him. Now."

Allie, please, Dad begged. *I cannot . . .*

You need to. She needs you to.

I stepped aside to allow Dad to come forward in my mind.

He didn't. So, I reached over to him and dragged him forward, forcing him to stand, mentally, beside me.

Talk to her, I thought.

"Hello, Vi," he said softly through me.

Her eyes fluttered closed and tears caught in her lashes.

Shame had once told me that everything about me changed when Dad talked through me. My body language, the cadence of my voice, my tone. Zay had told me it was like looking at a different soul behind my eyes.

With just that one sentence, Violet could tell it was Dad.

His emotions flooded through me. He wanted to reach out and comfort her, wanted to pull her into his arms and tell her all of his regrets, wanted to apologize, wanted to tell her he loved her. He had always loved her. But he held still. Uncertain.

After a long moment, she swallowed several times, then tipped her head up just a little to meet my gaze.

"Oh, Daniel," she said. "I've missed you terribly. Every moment."

"I've missed you too, my love," he said. "This"—he held up my hands in a most helpless gesture—"is not what I wanted for us."

She bit her lip, holding back tears. "Have you seen our son? Your beautiful baby boy?"

My head nodded. Dad was at a loss for words, struggling with his sorrow.

"I named him Daniel," she said. "He has your smile. And your temper." She tried to smile.

The baby had moved from fuss mode to intermittent hollering. Kevin finally picked him up and bounced him in his arms until he settled.

Kevin cast wary glances my way.

"We . . . I . . ." Dad's voice caught and he cleared my throat. "There are times when I can see through Allison's eyes. She visited you at the hospital the day he was born."

"You were there?" she asked.

He nodded. "He is beautiful. Just like you. There are so many things I want to apologize for. Things I regret—"

"Don't," she said. "I don't regret a single moment. The time we had was brilliant. You were brilliant."

I felt myself smile sadly. "Brilliant?" He shook my head. "Oh, Violet, I had such plans for us. For our life together. I wanted long years with you. With our children. I am sorry for my failures."

"You didn't fail me," she said gently. "You have never failed me. Even this"—she pressed her hand gently against my cheek and laughed a little—"it's amazing. You are an amazing man."

"You make me so," he said.

"Sorry to interrupt," I said.

Violet's eyebrows slipped up in surprise. She pulled her hand away.

"It's me," I said. "Allie. I'm sorry I can't give you more time together. Maybe later, after this fight, you can both talk again."

"I'd like that," Violet said, searching my eyes.

"As would I," Dad said.

Violet wiped her fingers across her eyes and stepped back. She took a moment to stare over my shoulder. Then, "We need to access the magic samples in Stone. Can he do that with the disks?" she asked.

Dad's love and pride slipped through my mind and I knew that this was something he respected and admired in her. Her ability to set her emotions aside and tackle a problem with scientific objectivity when necessary.

I can, he thought.

"He said he can."

"Good," Violet said. "And do you have a way to shut down magic?"

Dad was thoughtful. *There is a master switch we can throw. It will cause a backwash into the wells, but should flush the networks of quiescent magic.*

Will there be explosions? I asked.

In theory? It is unlikely. But possible.

And will it hurt people?

Allison, he said, *magic always hurts people.*

"Dad says there is a master switch we can throw to shut down magic. Where is it?"

"I'm not sure," she said.

"Sorry. That was for Dad."

At our condominium. Behind the mantelpiece. Mr. Cooper should be able to find it behind a hollow stone in the stonework.

"Okay," I said. "It's at the condo on the mantel behind a hollow stone. He thinks you can find it, Kevin."

"How do I activate it?" Kevin asked.

Dad stepped forward, and I let him. "Cast Cradle."

"Cradle? That's a very gentle spell for an entire city's network to respond to."

"It is only as gentle as the user. Cradle will trigger the magic back to its source—the wells. Then an automatic backwash will seal the glyphs and close the networks and cisterns, rendering them inactive until we need the system to be accessible again."

"You built an off switch into the networks?" Kevin asked. "Did you even tell anyone about it? About having a switch—in your living room—that could override spells you worked into the lifeblood of this city's magic to shut down magic for good?"

"The network was my project, Mr. Cooper," Dad said, sounding annoyed. "My technology, my money, my risk. The decisions I made were of my own counsel. Of course I built an override for the system at my disposal."

Okay, that was enough of that. I shut my mouth. Firmly.

Dad wasn't very happy with Kevin, but I was pretty sure it had more to do with the fact that Kevin was holding his only son in his arms than that he was questioning his morals with magic technology.

Or hell, maybe it was both.

Dad didn't like losing. And when it came to being alive, Kevin had him beat.

"The details don't matter," I said, glad to have my voice, mouth, and words again. "Right now, the fact that no one knows about this override means the Overseer probably doesn't know about it and Seattle probably doesn't know about it. Kevin, can you cast Cradle?"

"It's not a difficult spell," he groused. "I was just surprised that he chose it."

Which is why I chose it, Dad said, exasperated.

I didn't let him forward again because I was so not going to get in a yelling match with Kevin.

"Kevin, please take however many people you'll need with you and shut the networks immediately."

"I can do it alone."

"No, take someone," I said, heading toward the door. "If something goes wrong, you want backup. No argument. None of us travels alone."

Violet took Daniel from Kevin's arms. There was a moment, fleeting, when their eyes met and they both smiled.

Dad, inside my head, closed himself away, leaving the sharp bite of his sorrow and regret behind.

Chapter Six

We'd lost almost an hour getting everyone on the same page. Frankly, I was more than a little surprised that all these high-level officials in the city were just falling into place and taking my word for what was going on and what needed to be done.

This was probably not the first time in Authority history that unforeseeable changes had called for quick thinking and across-all-lines cooperation. Magic, after all, had never been an easy force to deal with.

"What we need right now," I said to Shame, Terric, and Zayvion as I strode with them toward the library where Violet said she'd have the disks ready for us, "is to decide what combination of spells we will cast on the wells. We need something that will bite if anyone tries to tap into the magic."

"I don't recall anyone ever asking me to booby-trap magic before," Shame said. "May I just say it is about time. What do you think, Z? Know some counterspells with a bite?"

"That Seattle won't know?" Zay pressed his lips together, thinking about it.

"Reflect?" Terric suggested.

"It casts a shadow in the stream. They'd see it in time to break it," Zay said.

"Tangle," Shame said. "You know, old school." He pointed one finger and started drawing the spell.

"Don't!" Zay and I said at the same time.

He paused, his finger still stuck out in front of him. "What? I was just illustrating my point."

"We know what Tangle looks like," Zay said. "And we've seen the way you handled Light."

Shame's eyes twinkled. "That little scuffle back there with the Proxies? Aw, that was just for kicks. I know how to control magic."

Zay and I didn't say anything.

"What?" Shame asked.

"Maybe," I said. The one test they'd taken had laid low three hundred people.

They were a huge unknown right now.

"You don't trust me."

"I understand you," I said. "I know what it's like to be changed by magic. To have it take over and make everything about using magic different. I've been there, Shame."

He was still smiling, but there was a hardness to him, an anger, a darkness. My very good friend was also a dangerous man.

"I trust *you*, Shame. I just don't trust you with magic right now."

He gave me this look—I didn't know if it was anger, or hate, or something else. Something dark and hungry. I didn't know what was going through his mind.

Terric must have. He just said one word, quietly, "Shame." Not a warning. More like a reminder.

Shame inhaled and exhaled, the darkness lashing around him like whips, then settling again.

"Really annoyed I have to prove this to you," he said.

"You don't. You don't have to prove anything to me."

"Leave it, Flynn," Zayvion said. "We're all tired. None of us should be trusted with magic right now. But it is what it is."

We had stopped outside the door to the library and Zayvion took half a step toward Shame, sort of positioning himself between us, and wrapped his arm around me.

"And," Zay said, "if you ever look at Allie like that again, I'm going to put you flat on your back to give you a little time to reconsider your manners."

Shame actually laughed and leaned back on one foot, giving Zay a long look. "Really? You're going there? It has been forever since you've threatened me, Jones. Are you feeling a little uncertain about your abilities? Want to test them out on me, mate?"

"You and I are not getting in a fight," Zayvion said. "Not unless you want to spend the next week unconscious."

Shame narrowed his eyes, considering Zayvion.

Since Zay's arm was around me, I knew that even though he looked calm and magnanimous while he was threatening Shame, he was in no mood for bullshit. If Shame decided to push this, he was going to put him down.

And beneath that decision, I felt another thread of emotion from Zay. Not fear, but a wariness, a concern. For his friend. His brother, who had changed so much in such a short time and who had had no chance to recover or regain his footing.

Zayvion knew he might have to be the one to stop Shame if he lost control.

Any magic user who lost control was dangerous. But when a Death magic user lost control, people were going to die.

Like Jingo? I thought, surprised at what had crossed Zay's mind.

Shame could never be like Jingo, Zayvion thought. And he meant it.

But I watched the darkness and death roil around Shame, just as Death magic had cloaked Jingo, and had my doubts.

Shame could be like Jingo Jingo. Just as powerful, just as deadly. Maybe more deadly since he'd been the one who killed Jingo Jingo.

Holy shit.

"Set a combination of Rebound and Tangle on it," Terric said, changing the subject to my great relief. "On the wells, beneath Tangle. One disk can also power a combined spell. They won't see that unless they're on the edge of the wells looking in. Rebound isn't used any-more, so even if Seattle suspects we booby-trapped the wells—which they shouldn't because, who does that?— they won't be looking for Rebound. I assume we aren't going to let them get close enough to the wells to actu-ally look into them?"

"That's right," I said, while Shame and Zayvion glared at each other. "I have the Hounds out to trip them up and slow them down. Can we make the spells on the well refresh so that anyone who pulls magic will get their wrists slapped?"

"If we set Refresh over Tangle and Rebound, it won't be their wrists that are slapped," Terric said, "it will be their heads. And they will be unconscious."

"Even though we're only using one disk to power all three spells?" I asked.

"The spells will be drawn and cast as one spell," Ter-ric said. "Each component of that combined spell will only take a third of the magic in the disk to work. To-gether the parts will be much more powerful than the sum."

"Good," I said.

"Good?" Terric asked. "You do know if we set those spells, everyone who draws magic from the wells will also get slapped. Including us."

"I know," I said. "Are you two done?" I asked Shame and Zayvion.

"Are we?" Zay asked Shame.

"Not hardly," Shame said.

Fine. They could glare and threaten. I had things to take care of. I noticed Eli Collins standing in the shadows at the end of the hallway and ducked out from under Zay's arm. I strolled over to him.

Collins the Cutter had been Closed and kicked out of the Authority years ago. But he had also saved Davy's life and stood with us against Jingo Jingo. He possessed a sharp, if immoral, intellect and was currently one of the people I planned to use to help us win the fight with Seattle and the battle with Leander and Isabelle.

"Allie," Terric called after me, "you're shutting down the networks, you're booby-trapping the wells. How are we supposed to defend ourselves without magic?"

Zayvion followed me, but Shame stayed behind, hopefully cooling down.

"We are going to fight the old-fashioned way," I said. "Dirty. Dr. Collins, I need to talk to you."

The bruising on his face had faded some, though a ragged edge of brownish red licked along his hairline and jaw. He was still a little puffy from the price he'd paid using magic to save Davy, and then to fight Jingo Jingo. He didn't seem to be in pain, standing cool and crisp in a button-down shirt, vest, and slacks. His round wire-rimmed glasses gave him that stiff, educated air that made him seem older than the thirty or thirty-two I guessed his age to be.

"Allison," he said. "Zayvion."

I didn't have to look over my shoulder to know Zay was scowling at him.

Eli shifted away from the wall, and nodded toward Terric and Shame.

"What about them?" he asked.

"What about them?" I asked.

"Do you think they're stable?" he asked.

"*You* asking if they're stable?" Zayvion said. "Ironic."

Eli just gave Zay a droll look.

"If you have a point," I said, "tell me now. I'm a little busy."

"Terric and Shame aren't stable, is my point. If I were in a position to have a say in such things, I'd get them out of Portland to some place with little to zero naturally occurring magic for a month at least. Then I'd slowly re-introduce them to magic."

"Do you think they're that much of a danger?"

He shrugged one shoulder. "I can only assume. I may be wrong. There is very little . . . research on Soul Complements. That's what they are, isn't it? That's why they were able to do what they did on the battlefield together?"

"Yes." I figured there was no point hiding it.

"Two men," Collins mused. "Since I am certain Victor hasn't fully restored my memories, would you, Zayvion, tell me if in the history of the Authority there have ever been Soul Complements of the same gender?"

"None that were tested," Zay said. "It doesn't mean they didn't exist. It just means either they didn't find each other, or they did, but were never tested."

"Still . . . I am curious. What is Shame and Terric's sexual orientation?"

"None of your business," Zay said, short. Final.

"So I can assume there's tension in that aspect of the relationship," he mused. "Interesting."

Zayvion cracked his knuckles, giving Eli the kind of look that I'd seen him use only right before he was going to punch someone in the face.

"You," I said, touching Zayvion's arm, but talking to Collins, "should not assume anything. Not with Shame. Not with Terric. All I need from you is an informed opinion on one of my father's technologies."

"I would have thought you, of all people, would have access to that information," Collins murmured.

I knew he was talking about Dad being in my head. Maybe I could trust Dad to tell me everything I needed to know. But habit, caution, and lack of time made me want to bring all hands on deck before we destroyed Portland with guesswork.

"The more opinions I have, the better." I strode down to the library and through the open door. Violet was there, and little Daniel was in a playpen. Kevin leaned over the soft netted walls of the playpen and placed several toys next to him.

I took in the rest of the room. A few chairs stood along the walls of books, and a table centered the room, as if waiting for a banquet.

"Hello, everyone," I said. "We're short on time, so let's get to this."

I thought about sitting down but couldn't stop pacing. Time was ticking. We needed answers on how to cleanse the wells, and quickly.

"Where are the disks?" I asked.

"I've sent for them," Violet said. "They should be here any moment. I see several approaches to this problem."

Dad, in my mind, stirred. He wanted to listen to Violet,

hear her voice, even if he couldn't talk to her. Even if he could never be with her again.

"I believe we can use nonmagical resources to find a solution to this problem," she said, "but I'm not sure they would do enough fast enough. I suggest we use magic to cleanse magic."

"Fire with fire?" Eli Collins walked across the room and gave Violet a fetching smile. "I do like the way you think, Mrs. Beckstrom."

I had forgotten he was following us.

Distracted much?

"And you are?" she asked.

"Collins. Dr. Eli Collins." He extended his hand. "I did some . . . work with your husband several years ago, when the concept for the disks was still in its infancy."

"He never mentioned you."

Collins smiled. "I don't suppose he would have. Mr. Beckstrom was a very private man."

Violet shot a glance my way, then pressed her lips together. "Yes," she said evenly, "he was. I believe we can use the stored magic in the disks to inject the cure we've been working on. Magic appears to respond quickly and positively to the mix of magic in the Animate—Stone—when combined with the stronger restorative spells."

"So you think if we add the magic from Stone into a disk, we can then pour that into a well to purify it?" I asked.

"I believe so." She looked up at me. "Do you think the disks can be calibrated to respond to casting through each magical discipline?"

Wow. I had no fricking idea. I didn't even know why she was asking me that.

She wasn't asking you, Dad said. *Tell her yes. Each user can first cast a Prime on the disk. The disk should allow for the subtleties of discipline to transfer that specific expression of the spell to its host well.*

I took a breath, hoping I was going to repeat this correctly. "Yes. Each user should cast Prime first. Then the disk will allow the details—"

Subtleties of discipline, Dad corrected.

"—I mean subtleties of discipline to transfer that spell to its host well." *Did that cover it?* I asked him.

Close enough, yes.

"Good," she said with a small smile. "We have a theory. We'll need to do testing."

"No time for testing," I said. "We're going to take the disks out to one of the wells, cast the spells you think are best, and hope it works."

Everyone in the room stared at me like I'd just announced there was no such thing as gravity.

"No," Violet said. "That's a very bad idea, Allie. If cast incorrectly, it could kill the user and possibly damage the well."

"We don't have time to be careful," I said. "A handful of us will take this risk and then we can make a better decision after we see the results."

"I don't think you understand how dangerous this is," she said.

"Each disk holds enough magic to power one strong spell, right?" I asked.

She nodded.

"So we use one disk to open the well, one disk to purify it, one to close it, and one to cast a triple spell to keep people out of it. Four disks per well, four magic users per well. I do understand how dangerous this is."

Zay, standing behind me at the head of the room, didn't shift, but I could feel his presence as if he were pressed against me. There was no chance he'd leave me to do this alone.

"Since I can't use magic, I'll need at least two more people other than Zayvion to volunteer to go with us. If someone has a good knowledge of the disks, that would be welcome."

"I believe I'm your man," Collins said.

Good. I was hoping he'd step up.

Violet frowned. I could tell she was torn between going with us to deal with magic and science, and staying here with little Daniel.

Finally, she nodded. "I want you to have a cell phone. Also, Kevin, I'm going with you to shut down the networks."

"Mrs. Beckstrom," he said, "I don't think that's wise."

After all this time together, he still called her Mrs. Beckstrom? How old-fashioned could he get?

"It is wise," she said. "It is in my home, after all."

Jamar, one of my Hounds, came strolling into the room. "Your disks, Mrs. Beckstrom." He looked cool and composed, but his dark eyes took in every inch of strained body language in the room, finally resting on me. "You stirring things up again, Allie?"

"Not again. Still."

He grinned, his teeth a flash of white against his dark complexion. "Where would you like these?" He pointed at the messenger bag slung across his chest.

"On the table please, Mr. Legare," Violet said. "And thank you for retrieving them."

He nodded and placed the messenger bag, gently, on the table. "Anything else I can help with?"

"Davy is coordinating the Hounds who are running interference with Seattle hitting Portland. You can talk to him if you want in on that," I said. "It's going to be

street work, holding up taxis, slowing luggage check-
outs, killing cell phone signals. No magic."

"I heard," he nodded toward Zayvion. "You'll let me
know if you need any other assistance."

"I will," Zay said.

I had to smile. A lot of the Hounds seemed to have
found a new respect for Zayvion. Zay had moved about
the streets of Portland like a drifter for years and none
of the Hounds had suspected how powerful a magic user
he was.

That impressed them.

Then the magic fight on the field with Jingo Jingo had
left more than one Hound talking about Zayvion Jones.
There had been bets placed and a lot of speculation
about what the man could really do with magic and with
weapons.

Not that Zayvion would tell them what he was capable of.

That only made them all the more curious.

If I wasn't careful, the Hounds might vote me out and
make Zayvion the next den mother. Which would probably drive him crazy and entertain me to no end.

Note to self: Suggest to the Hounds that they elect
Zay as leader once all this was over.

Jamar gave me half a salute, then was out of the room.

Violet opened the bag and set all nineteen disks out
on the table.

I moved closer to get a look. Dad was just as interested as I was, and I could feel his subtle request to see
clearer through my eyes, which I let him do.

I ignored how frightening it was that he and I were
starting to operate seamlessly in my mind and my body,
like roommates who had finally figured out how to live
with each other's dirty laundry all over the place. He

had been in my head for almost a year now. It was becoming, not exactly normal, but sort of comfortable to have him with me.

If I thought about it too much, it would probably freak me out. So I stared at the disks instead.

The disks were all the same size and shape, made of lead and silver, with flecks of black and glints of glass worked into them. I'd gotten a little better at reading obscure glyphs since I'd last seen one of these babies, but the symbols carved into the palm-sized pieces of metal still escaped me.

One thing that didn't escape me was the electric tingle of magic that hovered around the disks.

The magic in the disks smelled a little like flowers.

I had forgotten how nice magic smelled when it wasn't tainted. It almost made me want to touch the things.

Almost.

Then I stepped aside while Violet and Collins got busy adjusting the glyphs on the disks so that they would do what we needed them to do: Save the world.

Chapter Seven

It felt like my life was being measured out against the ticking of the second hand. Violet and Collins had worked on sixteen of the disks in record time, leaving three disks we might not have to use.

A group of us—Zay, Collins, me, Stone, and to my surprise, both Shame and Terric—were headed out to the Blood magic well to see if the cure would work. We'd decided to let Shame and Terric come because Soul Complements, even those with little or no control, still had a better chance of making magic do what they wanted it to do.

Plus, it kept them in our line of sight so Zay could shut them down if needed.

Zay drove Terric's van, with Terric in the passenger's seat and Shame and me in the middle seat. Collins rested with his eyes closed in the backseat, while Stone, next to him, watched the city rush past.

Stone was a gargoyle and Animate, which meant he was built to carry magic and to seem lifelike. He glowed a soft blue-white and threw shadows and light around the inside of the van as he hopped on and off the seat.

Ever since Cody had unlocked him, Stone had gone glowbug on us. It was cute, really. Not so bright that it hurt my eyes, nor was he any warmer to the touch than he usually was. He seemed to take all the recent chaos in stride, as if becoming a lightbulb was simply the newest fashion for the modern gargoyle on the town.

I didn't know how long his glow was going to last, but if the electricity ever went out, he was going to be a handy four-footed flashlight to have around.

Despite Detective Stotts reminding people not to do anything illegal, all of us were carrying our weapons.

The Hounds were already on the road, having decided who was going to throw roadblocks in the Seattle crew's path when and where. Davy had done a good job coordinating it with the police, and it looked like they weren't going to have any trouble slowing down the people from Seattle. The reports we'd gotten indicated that at least a dozen people—far less than I'd expected and an even mix of men and women—were coming our way. Some were driving, a few were flying.

I didn't know how they thought twelve people could shut down an entire city, but I wasn't going to underestimate their ability either.

We had a half hour lead on them, tops, even with the Hounds running interference.

"So we go in," Shame said, crunching his way through a bag of potato chips, "open the well, make Stone spit in it, then close it up?"

"No," I said. "We open the well with one disk. We use another disk to extract some of the magic Stone is carrying and pour it into the well. Then we close the well with another disk and set the blended spells of Rebound, Refresh, and Tangle with a last disk."

"Isn't that what I said?" He dug out another handful of crisps.

Maeve had practically forced Shame to eat something before we left, and he'd finally chowed down on a sandwich. His mood had improved like a thousand percent, something that did not escape Zayvion's, Terric's, or my notice.

But the thing that was really telling to me was that the darkness around him seemed more settled and quiet, with fewer tentacles reaching out.

Death magic was a discipline of energy transference and exchange. A very real one-to-one cost for giving and receiving, using and accepting. A fuel-and-burn kind of approach to magic. I wondered if food would help to sate the hunger of dark magic that hovered around Shame.

He dipped his fingers into the bag again, then paused with the chips halfway to his mouth. "When are Kevin and Violet throwing the switch?"

"Should be any time now," I said. "Why?"

"Because I think—" He glanced at Terric, then looked away quickly.

I looked at Terric too. He nodded. "It's coming."

The light across the city around us snuffed out—a wave of darkness washing over the hills and streets. We were just hitting the bridge to Vancouver. Streetlamps blacked, lights from boats on the river, from houses along the river flickered and were gone. The headlights, luckily, stayed on as it was a requirement that all moving vehicles operate under nonmagical force.

Terric whistled. "That's something to see."

The darkness rolled across the river, snuffed out the lights and towers on the other side, reaching like a hand, fingers stretching north.

Then, like intermittent strikes of flint, sparks of light flickered to life in the wave of darkness.

The city came back to life, glowing white and yellow with electricity alone, without any of the enhanced hues of pink, lavender, blue, or green. It was strangely beautiful, almost like a city out of an old-fashioned, nonmagical past, like someone had thrown gold and diamonds against the velvet hills and set them to shine with watery, earthly light.

And then the bridge caught fire, bright hard white snapping alive and carving cones of silver down around the road and all the cars, red emergency lights at the top of the metalwork pulsing like a silent, defiant heartbeat.

Alive, the city seemed to be saying. Even without magic, Portland still lived.

"Almost pretty," Shame said, wiping his fingers before rolling up the empty bag. "Although I'm sure that's not what most people are thinking right now."

He was right. It had been years, for some people their entire lifetime, since the city had been run without magic. Even though all of the services were bolstered by magic, the regulations and laws early on had made it a requirement that all businesses and residences could function on alternate power sources.

Most homes ran on nonmagic power anyway. It cost too much in pain to run your house on magic.

The people who would probably be the most inconvenienced with the lack of magic were businesses that catered to the luxuries magic could provide, and the hospitals that would be without medical spells.

Which was why we'd take care of this as quickly as we could. Cure magic. Stop the Seattle crew from shutting down Portland and Closing magic users. Then we'd find a way to stop Leander and Isabelle, or convince someone outside Portland that the Overseer had been possessed, and needed to be unpossessed.

"Seattle is following orders from the Overseer, right?" I said.

"Uh, Allie?" Shame said. "That news flashed about an hour ago."

"What I'm asking is, do we have anyone else on our side? Someone outside of Portland who would listen to us instead of the Overseer?"

"There might be a few individuals," Zay said. "But no one speaks against the Overseer's direct orders. Not without heavy evidence."

"We have evidence," I said. "I'd say it's even heavy."

"What, Roman Grimshaw telling us they were possessed?" Shame asked. "That's testimony from a dead ex-con ex-Guardian of the gate who was jailed for life because he accused leaders in the Authority of being possessed. And yes, sure, he was right, but no one will care."

"We can prove it," I said.

"No one will listen," Terric said. "Portland hasn't been in good standing with other cities for the last year or so. We've broken too many rules, had too much strife between magic users. Most members of the Authority don't get into magical battles, or try to raise people from the dead. We are without leverage in this argument."

"There has to be someone we can contact," I said. "Some way we can make sure we don't have the entire country west of the Mississippi down our throats. And if we do, if we fall, I want a backup, a plan C. I want someone, somewhere to know what's going on."

Silence. They'd been thinking it too. If the Overseer wanted to turn all the guns in the world on us, she could. Leander and Isabelle had chosen well when they'd taken her body to possess. They had every contact, every resource in the world at their disposal.

Hell, we'd be lucky if the military from three states around us didn't roll up to our doorstep.

And I was a little worried that it hadn't happened yet. If I were the Overseer, my first order would have been to take us down immediately. Not in some sneaky scramble-Seattle kind of way either. I'd bring the big guns to bear against the city.

Maybe they hadn't done that because they didn't know Roman Grimshaw had made it back to us and told us they'd possessed the Overseer.

He'd bought us more than time; he'd bought us an upper hand.

And then it hit me.

"They don't know," I said. "They don't know we know. That's why they only sent twelve people. They don't know."

"Guess who else doesn't know?" Shame said. "Us. What the hell are you talking about, Beckstrom?"

"Allie?" Zayvion glanced in the rearview mirror.

"Leander and Isabelle," I said. "Twelve people. That's not enough. They don't know."

"It sounds like English," Shame said. "But it makes no sense. Zay, do you speak the babble?"

"Shut up, Shame," I said. "Listen, Leander and Isabelle would have scrambled more than twelve people from Seattle if they thought we knew they had possessed the Overseer. They would have sent the entire military force against us expecting us to fight, right?"

"Maybe," Zayvion said cautiously.

"I don't think they're getting information from anyone here in Portland, which means no one's turned on us yet."

"You're expecting a betrayal in the ranks?" Terric asked.

"In a fight like this, of course," I said absently. "People will always look after their personal good over the good of others. But that doesn't matter. I think Leander and Isabelle don't know Roman made it through the gate to us. That's the point I'm trying to make. Roman said it exhausted them to take over the Overseer. He said they couldn't use magic yet, and they might not be able to use the gates to get here from England."

"Still not seeing the shiny side of it," Shame said. "Try short, clear sentences."

"We're not a step behind them—we're a step ahead of them, maybe more than that. They probably think they can take their time getting to us. That we'll be surprised by Seattle's people coming down, infiltrating the city, and quietly taking out key players among our Authority. They think they can shut us down, easily. And then Leander and Isabelle can take their time to deal with us and the rest of the Authority any way they want."

"We still don't know what, exactly, they want to do," Shame pointed out.

"Probably imprison the people they think will cause the most trouble," Zayvion said, "and kill the others who object."

"Look at you with the morbid, mate," Shame said with a grin. "Sure, yah. They're going to kill, torture, lock away. But then what? What is their real goal? What do they want? Because that's where they'll show their throat."

"Magic," I said.

"They have that," Shame said. "Power of rulership over the world of magic users too. What's left?"

"They'll tip their hand," Terric said. "As soon as they recover, we'll know what they want."

"It's not Portland, is it?" I asked. "Is there something unusual about Portland?"

Shame chuckled, and shoved the bag of chips in the

pocket of the side door. "How about I give you a list of things that aren't unusual about Portland. It'd be shorter."

I shoved his shoulder.

"Hey, now," he said, "fragile Death magic user here."

"Fragile? Three hundred Proxies," I reminded him. "Is there something specific about Portland that Leander and Isabelle want?" I asked Zayvion.

My dad shifted uneasily in my mind.

And there was the one advantage to sharing emotions with the dead guy. I knew he knew something. Something Leander and Isabelle wanted.

What? I asked.

He seemed to fade away, retreating to those far corners of my mind where it would take me a lot of concentration, time, and effort to dig him out.

"Dad knows something," I said. "How close to the Blood well are we?" The Blood well was in the basement of Maeve's inn, on the other side of the river in Vancouver.

"Less than five minutes," Zay said.

Shit. Not enough time to stage a war in my head. Didn't mean I wouldn't do it anyway.

"Shake me when we get there." I closed my eyes and took a few deep breaths, shutting away the sound of the car, the rocking hum of tires over pavement, the shifting and creaking of the seat as Stone moved around.

I pushed away my awareness of Stone and Collins, of the light and darkness of Terric and Shame, pushed away the tactile knowledge of Zayvion just inches away from me.

Inward. Quiet. Centered.

Breathe.

I'd never tried this exact way to communicate with

my dad before. But then, I'd mostly tried not to communicate with him at all.

Dad, I said, letting my voice reach out into all of the edges of what made me me. *I know you have secrets you don't want me to find out. I can respect that, even if I don't agree with it. There are a lot of things you've done that I don't agree with. But Leander knew you. He came back from death specifically looking to kill you. And I think you know why. Maybe you've been holding the information about Leander and Isabelle away from me for some good reason.*

But we don't have time for that now. Leander and Isabelle care enough about Portland, or the Authority members here, or you, or something, that they want the city closed down and people killed.

What do they want from us?

He was silent for so long, I didn't think I was going to get an answer.

But then he drew forward, stepping out of the nooks and crannies he had retreated into—places in my mind I wasn't aware of, and didn't know if I could access. I'd be lying if I said it wasn't kind of creepy.

I tried not to hear Jingo Jingo's words: "He owns your mind. He stole away anything he didn't want you to know and fed you full of the things he wanted you to believe. Made-up memories. And when you had nothing of your own left, he moved into you, into those places he'd made for himself."

Dad finally spoke, shaking me from my dark thoughts.

Leander and Isabelle want to rule magic. All magic. Light and dark, all disciplines, he said. *They want to live the life they were cheated out of, here in the living world, together. If they have control of all the magic in the world, they will change it, bend it to their desires, their vision of what magic should be. And then they will find a way to become immortal. Even if that means killing and repossessing over and over again.*

This, I knew. *Why Portland? Why send Seattle after us? There are . . . four wells under Portland.*

I noticed the hesitation, but before I could ask, he went on.

That many wells in such a small area is unheard of and gives the location an unmatched advantage. If one wanted to change magic, poison it, or . . . or perhaps join dark and light magic together in the world again, Portland is the place for that.

I knew that couldn't be everything he knew. *Is that all you're going to tell me?*

Again the hesitation. *It is all I can tell you that I know is absolutely true. When . . . if I know more, or have additional data, I will tell you . . . I will tell you everything, Allison.*

You'd better, I thought.

"Allie," Terric said. "We're there."

I opened my eyes. Zay had stopped the van around the back of Maeve's inn, so it wouldn't be seen from the road or parking lot. No one had gotten out yet, but Collins was awake, and stretching. At least one of us was rested.

"Okay," I said. "Why are we waiting?"

Shame nodded toward Zayvion.

Zay's eyes were half-lidded, his breathing deep and steady. It took me a second; then I realized what he was doing because I'd felt him do this before. Zay had a sense of the city. It was like he could feel it, feel the magic flowing through it and the people using that magic as if it were juxtaposed over his skin. I'd thought it had something to do with him being the Guardian of the gate but had never asked if that were the case.

"Zayvion?"

He rubbed his palms down his face, then opened his eyes as if coming back from a distance. His eyes glowed gold in the low light.

"They haven't tapped the wells yet," he said. "No one from Seattle has made it to the wells. Let's make this fast."

He opened the door and everyone piled out of the van.

Collins took a few steps in the gravel, and stared at the inn, smiling. "Never thought I'd see the old place again. Well, and remember what it really is."

"That makes two of us, Cutter." Shame walked to the back door and produced a set of keys from his pocket. He stepped through the door and flipped on the hall's interior light.

Terric hesitated for a moment, then stepped in behind him without a word or glance to any of us. Stone sat next to me, one foot resting on my boot, giving off a little cloud of light. I put my hand on his head and rubbed behind his ears. He cooed, but instead of the vacuum cleaner growl I was used to, he made a musical croon that was more like a cello and French horn harmonizing.

"Well, that's new," I said quietly.

He tipped his head up, one ear flopping to one side making him look like a dork. *That* was not new.

Collins had already walked into the inn, so I started after him.

Zayvion caught my left hand, and tugged me so quick, I didn't have time to do anything but a sort of awkward turn toward him.

"Hey," I said softly.

He kept his fingers threaded through mine, our hands raised just above shoulder height, his arm pulled possessively across my back, hand resting on my butt.

As if we were paused, waiting for the first step in the dance.

"Zay?"

He pulled me closer, leaned down, just a fraction of an inch.

"I love you," he breathed over my lips.

And before I could reply, he kissed me, his thoughts, his mind, reaching into me, my mind, my soul, claiming me. I didn't want to let him go even though he was so close it would be easy to surrender, and lose myself in him.

I knew he felt my fear of being lost as if it were his own.

But he didn't give into it, didn't pull away. He gently evaded my concern and stepped through my fears. And found me. There, in my mind, alone, maybe not lost, but not exactly sure of where I belonged either.

"With me," he said.

I wanted that. I wanted to hold him. Forever.

"Don't leave me," I whispered.

"Never. I will love you until my last breath. Don't forget that." His words had a weight to them that sank into me and anchored. It was comforting. Strong. "Don't ever forget us." Those words caught and held too, digging deep into my psyche and setting roots there.

It wasn't magic. Or not exactly.

Soul Complements, Dad said softly from what seemed a far distance.

And I knew he was right. Zayvion had just done something I'd never managed to do. He'd found a way to plant a knowledge in me, a memory I knew I'd never forget. No matter what magic did to me. No matter who tried to Close me.

This was tied to my soul. His words. His love. Him.

I would never forget him. Never forget us. And never forget our love.

Zayvion gently pulled away and the awareness of my body, his body, of the air and world around me, came rushing back.

"How?" I asked, when I could find words again.

"We can make magic break its own rules for good things too," he whispered to me. "I don't want to lose you."

"You never will." I rested my head against his chest and he pressed his cheek against the side of my face.

For that moment, we were safe, secure. And everything was right.

But only for that moment. We had work to do, a city to save, a war to fight.

We both let go, and stepped apart. Zayvion had the messenger bag over his shoulder, the disks wrapped carefully within it. He started toward the door, crossing the rest of the way to the inn, and so did I.

Stone wove his way in front of me and tromped into the inn ahead of us. I followed him, and then Zayvion shut the door behind us.

The inn was quiet, no diners, no movement, no light. It was dark beyond the hall and the triangle of light coming from the door that led to the staircase going down.

Stone stopped at that door, looked over his shoulder at me, his hand on the jamb.

"Yes, we're going down to the well," I said.

I wasn't sure if Stone liked coming to this well, but he made a funny little chirring sound that kind of sounded like a flock of little birds.

I grinned. "You've gotten pretty musical all of a sudden," I said. "Think it's from all that magic mixed up inside you?"

Yes. From Dad.

"Probably," Zay said.

"Dad agrees with you." I gave Zay an isn't-that-interesting look, then clomped down the stairs.

Chapter Eight

It didn't take us long to get to the huge arched-ceiling room that looked more like a chapel than a basement below the inn.

"So, how do you want to approach this, Beckstrom?" Collins asked. He was standing at the foot of the stairs. So were Shame and Terric, though they were as far apart from each other as they could be without stepping out into the room.

The well was closed, which meant the floor looked like beautiful old marble with a gradation of white to black happening so subtly it was difficult to say where, exactly, white left off to become gray, and gray poured into ever-deepening darkness.

I could feel the well just beneath that marble surface. Feel magic lashing, pressing, digging at the stone above it. Magic trying to break free.

"If we open it, do you think it'll explode?" I asked.

"Only one way to find out, now isn't there?" Shame bent and pulled off his shoes. Then he tugged off his socks and stuffed them back in the toes of the shoes. "Give me a disk."

He held his hand out to Zay.

"You'll have to use Blood magic," Zay said, not moving.

"I know, Jones. I've opened the well before. Live here, remember? Give over."

Zay still wasn't moving. "Terric?"

"Fuckssake," Shame groaned.

"Shame can open it," Terric said.

"Do *not* need your permission," Shame grumbled.

Terric continued as if he hadn't heard him. "You or Collins can purify the well with a disk and the magic in Stone."

Stone warbled at the sound of his name.

"I'll close the well," Terric said. "I don't know which of us will still be standing to cast the Tangle, Rebound, and Refresh combination, but whoever is, will handle that."

Zay weighed those options for a split second. I had the sudden feeling that he and Terric had worked through a lot of situations with pretty much this same approach. Making fast, hard decisions, and largely ignoring Shame's impulses. He trusted Terric. Trusted his opinion.

Zay slid his hand into the bag and pulled out one disk that shone hard flat silver against his dark palm. "Don't screw this up, Flynn."

Shame smiled. "Don't you know me better than that, Z? Or do you think I've changed that much too?"

"Just do the job," Zay said with no heat in his words.

Shame tossed the disk as if getting the weight of it. The dark magic that surrounded him reached out to touch the disk, to taste it, lick it.

I didn't see the darkness actually pull on the disk, didn't see any magic transfer between the disk and Shame. But after the darkness around Shame pulled away from the disk, he nodded once, as if knowing more clearly just what it was he had in his hands.

That was different. I didn't even know if he was aware of what he had just done with darkness. I didn't know if it was a good thing or not.

"I'll make this fast," he said. "And I mean fast. Someone better be ready with the other disk and rock boy over there in case this all does explode."

Shame paced across the room. Even though he'd said he'd take it fast, he moved a lot more slowly than I would have, and took a circuitous route toward the center of the room, pausing for the briefest of moments, and tipping his head down as if he could hear the magic, feel the magic pulsing beneath his bare feet.

He finally made his way to the center of the room, and then knelt there. He placed the disk, carefully, on the ground directly between his bare feet, wiggling his toes just a bit before standing very still.

Then he drew a glyph in the air in front of him with both hands. It was an Unlocking spell of some kind, though the order of it didn't make any sense to me until he drew a switchblade out of his pocket, snicked the blade free, and cut the side of his hand.

Blood fell in crimson droplets, pattering against the disk between his feet.

The spell exploded to life, carving out a pattern of power in black and red ribbons. Shame was whispering, coaxing, guiding the spell in a singsong that I had a hard time trying to follow.

The magic spooled a line from the glyph in the air, combined with Shame's blood and breath, and joined the glyph in the disk on the floor.

The floor spun open, marble moving as smoothly as a watchmaker's spring, stones sliding soundlessly outward like a flower opening.

Shame bent and plucked up the disk before it fell into

the ever-widening maw in the center of the floor. But he continued chanting, whispering, controlling the spell as he paced slowly backward at the growing edge of the well.

The bulk of the floor opened to the twisting, glowing mass of magic that pooled beneath the ground. Shame was on the other side of the room, the well between him and us.

A situation Terric did not seem entirely comfortable with. He was pacing, just four short steps to the side and four short steps back, his hands opening and closing, as if wishing for something, or someone, to hold on to.

I was happy about two things. One, the well was open.

Two, I could still breathe even though the well stank of tainted magic. I didn't know if that meant I'd become more immune to the foul smell, or if by turning off the networks, we'd already done some good for magic.

Shame lifted his hands over his head, then out to each side, as if bracing against a doorway. One last word tumbled from his lips, and the floor stopped moving. The Unlock spell faded from sight. The well was open.

"Allie?" Zay asked.

"The magic in the well looks like black sludge to me, almost solid, with just a center of light."

"That's not how Maeve and Hayden described seeing it just a day or so ago," Terric said.

"The poison has spread," I said. "That's why we're here. Collins, I think it would be best if you access the magic in Stone and fix the well."

"Of course," Collins said.

"Like hell he will," Terric said.

"Collins," I amended, "will hold the disk and Dad will access the magic in the disks and in Stone." I glanced at Zay, who didn't look like he approved of that idea either.

"Let us do this part," I said. "Dad knows what he's doing with Stone and Collins understands how the disks work if something goes wrong. I think Terric should close the well and you should set the spells to keep people out of it."

I looked between the three men. Grim, but silent. "Glad we all agree," I said. Besides, if I had to work with my dad—let him take over my body—they had better not complain about letting Collins pull his weight too.

"Come on, Stone," I said. "Let's get closer to the well."

We do need to be closer, right? I asked Dad.

I would assume so. You'll need a disk.

Right. I turned to ask Zayvion for one. But he was already handing one to Collins and giving him his patented glare of death.

Collins took the disk without a flicker of emotion, but when he turned my way, I could see the fire of curiosity in his eyes as he studied the glyphs carved into it.

"Beautiful," he said, walking my way. "Just. Stunning. To hold a working product after all those years of trial and error." He glanced up at me. "Your father is possibly one of the greatest minds ever to modify magical techniques and technology. Think of what he could have done if the accident could have been avoided."

His smile faded as he saw my scowl.

"Murder isn't an accident," I said.

"Not that," he said. "Not his death. The accident. When you were younger?" He pushed his glasses back on his face, then tipped his chin just a bit as if suddenly realizing I had no idea what he was talking about. "Well, perhaps you were too young to remember. Shall we?"

Shall we, hell. I wanted to know about that accident.

Allison, Dad said, *the well.*

"Allie?" Shame said from the other side of the room. "Really be great if you'd get in the game here, love."

Magic—well, black tar sticky, smelly stuff—was lapping up the walls of the well, splashing just over the edge of the marble floor. Where it touched marble, it burned, sending up steam that stank to high heaven.

"Anyone else see that?" I asked.

"Magic burning through stone?" Terric said. "Yes. Even without Sight. Need help?"

"We got it." I looked at Collins. "I'm going to let Dad forward, but I'll be here too."

He nodded, not looking at all concerned. "He and I will figure this out. If I know your father he already has a plan in place."

We stepped as close to the well as we could get, about three feet away from the edge so the sludge couldn't reach us.

Stone hesitantly padded up next to me, his wings unfurled and quivering. His ears were back, and he was no longer crooning. He didn't look like he wanted to be here at all.

"It's okay, Stone," I said, putting my hand on his head to comfort him and keep him beside me. I knew he didn't like working with my dad. "I'll be right here."

"Ah," Collins said, eyeing the magic that was steaming and burning its way closer to us. "We should get to this immediately."

I stepped aside in my mind, allowing Dad equal access to my eyes, body, hands. *Please, Dad,* I thought. *Do this right.*

He paused, and I could feel his sigh. *I have never endeavored to do anything less.* Then, with my mouth, he said, "Eli, I'll need you to simply hold the disk. I want to alleviate Allison's sensitivity to the poison in magic as much as I can."

Eli's smile spread into a grin. He held the disk across his right palm. "Good to be working with you again, sir."

"And you," Dad said. "I'll tap into the Animate. Do not activate the disk yet."

I felt my head turn to look down at Stone, which was, as always, a weird sensation. "As I understand the desired outcome, we'll be performing this on all four wells. Is that correct, gentlemen?"

"Yes," Zayvion said, his voice tight.

Oh. I hadn't put a lot of thought into it before, but suddenly realized it must be really weird for him to watch me become not me, when Dad took over.

That anchor, the promise of me remembering us, and remembering what we were together that Zayvion had given me was still strong and comforting in my mind. I wanted to tell him not to worry, but we didn't have time for that.

"I'll need a small portion of the purified magic in this . . . in Stone," Dad added awkwardly.

Stone narrowed his big round eyes and showed some teeth.

He did not like Dad. At all.

"It's okay, Stoney," I said, taking over my mouth without even having to negotiate with Dad. Once again the ease in which we were living in the same space freaked me out.

Stone's ears flipped up and he wrapped one wing around my leg. He knew I was here, but still didn't seem convinced he should do what Dad said.

"Better make it quick," I said to Dad. "I don't know how long he'll let you work with him."

Collins shook his head, his mouth open. "It's fascinating. You truly are two different beings in one body. Just, well, impossible would have been my first thought, but obviously this is more than possible. You must be very pleased," he said.

"Pleased?" I asked.

Dad took over my mouth again, a little more quickly than I'd expected. "I am pleased only in that I can lend my assistance to purify magic and see that Portland is safe once again."

Okay, I believed about half of that. I knew Dad really did care about keeping Portland safe, even if it was only for little Daniel and Violet. But the rest of what he'd just said didn't ring true.

Collins knew something about my dad I didn't know. Some reason why he'd be pleased about all this happening. About him possessing me. Maybe he knew what my dad's plans had been before he died.

Maybe he could guess at what his plans were now.

After we cleansed the wells, if we did so and survived, I was going to pin Collins down and bribe or beat information out of him.

"Allison," Dad said with my voice. "It is easier if I have your attention."

Could have done without the condescending tone, but I paid attention.

Collins was tracing a very delicate spell with the fingers of his left hand, something that reminded me of Illusion, but not quite.

"It is an Enhancement," Dad said in answer to my thought. "We will use it to carry the small portion of purified magic contained within the Animate."

Stone growled.

He has a name, I thought. *You might want to use it before he bites your hand off. Well, my hand off.*

"Stone," Dad said. "Stone will not be harmed in this work."

Stone just growled again. He didn't trust Dad. Smart rock.

"Easy, Stone," Zayvion said, walking up to stand on the other side of him. Stone looked between Zayvion and Dad behind my eyes and whimpered a little.

Apparently Dad in me was confusing the heck out of him.

Still, having Zayvion there helped him settle down a bit.

"I am going to draw out some of the magic in the Animate—in Stone," Dad said. "Mr. Jones, please stand ready to Ground if I have miscalculated the force of this endeavor."

"Have you ever miscalculated before?" Zay asked quietly.

I, well, we held his gaze. Heavy with gold, with un-spent power. Dad saw Zayvion differently than I did. He saw him more of an immovable force, an uncertain accomplice who could just as easily become his most formidable enemy.

"Yes, Mr. Jones," Dad said mildly. "I have often been wrong."

A memory, of blood on his hands, his blood, someone else's blood. The rising fear and panic choking him, his voice, begging. For the briefest moment, I saw a woman's bloody face in profile. She seemed familiar. He snapped that image away and into darkness so quickly, I couldn't even remember what she looked like.

"But I will not be in error today," he said calmly. He

didn't use Influence, which made sense. Zayvion had told me he was immune to Influence. But there was something about my dad, a kind of charisma that gave his words weight, strength. Most people found themselves nodding along with anything he said.

He'd used that to his advantage for his entire life. Strange that he didn't do so now.

"Continue," Zayvion said.

Dad's irritation swept across the edges of my thoughts. He didn't like anyone telling him what to do.

"Stone," Dad said. "Hold still. Do not fear." Dad actually put just the slightest Influence on that last command, maybe to comfort Stone, but more likely to try to keep Stone subdued.

It had not escaped our attention that our single hope to cleanse the wells was locked inside a stone creature who was powered by magic, and oh, yes, had wings. Stone could fly away if he wanted to and we'd be so far up shit creek, not even a boatload of paddles would float our boat.

We very much did not want Stone to get stubborn about this.

Zayvion reached over and rubbed behind Stone's ears. Stone huffed and mumbled, sounding pretty put out over the entire thing. But he wasn't moving away, and wasn't looking as worried as before.

"Very good," Dad said. "Let us begin." He pulled the blood knife I had in my belt—the same knife Zayvion had given me months ago, and pricked my left ring finger.

Distantly, I felt the hot sting of the blade, and then the oily slick of blood flowing from my finger across the knife.

Dad shifted how I was standing and I had to take a

deep mental breath not to reach out and steady myself. He took a wide-legged stance I never used, and then began chanting. I didn't know the words. If someone asked me to repeat even one of them, I wouldn't be able to.

But Dad not only knew them, he seemed to understand them. I caught a string of his thoughts, the calculations put into play to create the correct tonal quality of the words, along with the correct spacing between them, the flow, the rhythm. All painstakingly thought through so that this one spell, on this one Animate, would respond in the way he predicted.

This wasn't a language—these were words my father had created.

Stone tipped his big head up, and opened his mouth as if panting. He was still glowing that soft blue-white, but as Dad raised my hand and knife and carved a spell, or maybe two, into the air, glyphs began to burn across Stone's skin.

I heard Shame inhale with a kind of caught wonder, or hunger. And Terric whispered something that sounded a lot like a small prayer.

Stone was beautiful, transformed. Magic played over him and through him with an easy, flowing gracefulness. It was like seeing the dance of the northern lights for the first time, a sunset painting the sky with fire, an ocean churning with deep jewel tones and shadow.

Magic, this magic of each discipline combined, joined with both light and dark magic, was a force, a beauty I'd never seen before.

Dad finished the spell, having hooked part of the spell Collins was still drawing up out of the disk with the tip of the blood blade.

And then he pressed my finger on Stone's head, just below his right ear. Blood bloomed there, spreading out to trace the form of a rose blossom that reached from the base of his ear, out over his eye where an eyebrow would be, if he had an eyebrow.

Dad pulled my finger away, and liquid red fire followed my hand, arcing through the air to catch the invisible spell he'd drawn with light and flame.

The spell was intricate, complex, a three-dimensional ball of flame that seemed to burn through a series of smaller glyphs, smaller magics. And when it had burned just enough, Dad sent it spinning, wrapped in the threads of magic Collins had unraveled from the disk, before plunging into the well.

The spell zeroed straight for the center of the well, where magic was still untouched by the poison, and sank.

The world shook. A sound louder than thunder rolled with physical force, crushing through the room, as if a bomb had gone off. A shriek of voices like metal twisting and snapping scorched through the room.

I reached out for Zayvion, only Dad was holding my body very, very still so I couldn't even wiggle a finger.

The world shivered under my feet. Reality, the room, the walls, the arched ceiling, the marble floor, and all of us seemed to shift back into place as if our colors blurred for an instant before coming back into focus even sharper than before.

The soft sound of chimes, distant and high, stirred on an unfelt breeze.

"It is done," Dad said with a kind of reverence I'd never heard in his voice. And then he stumbled back in my mind, no longer in control of my body.

Chapter Nine

I rushed up into my body in a wave of heat, my ears ringing, flashes of light swimming at the edge of my vision. My mouth was dry and tasted of blood. I swallowed, which hurt, licked my lips, which stung, and tried to get a grip on what had just happened.

Everyone in the room looked like they'd survived. Stone was sitting clear across the room on the bottom stair, his wings tucked tightly around him, big round eyes narrowed as he glared at the well.

Zayvion, next to me, was talking. I caught only every third word or so. Something about Close and Terric and spells.

"Are you well?" Collins touched my elbow, his fingers shaking, just like his voice.

"Fine," I said, even though it came out more air than word.

He pulled his hand away, as if surprised by my voice. What had he been expecting? Dad? Then I realized, yes, that's exactly what he'd expected.

He still had the disk in his hand. It was dark, the dusty gray-black of dry cast iron.

"Good," he said a little stiffly. "Very good."

I glanced at the well. The black sludge was much, much less, just a thin lining at the very edges of the well.

Magic, pure, clear magic shifted in crystal glints and shattered rainbows.

"Did we do it?" I asked.

Collins took off his glasses and wiped them on the edge of his shirt. "Purify the well? I believe we have. At least for now. That remnant of sludge"—he pointed his glasses toward the tar sticking at the edges of the floor—"may be inert."

"Or it may not?" I asked. "How about a guess?"

"We have bought ourselves some time and rid the well of the bulk of the taint so that pure magic is flowing. But it won't stay that way forever. We will have to do more testing as time goes on. Purifying the other wells might be enough to clarify all the magic."

"What about the Veiled? What about all the people hospitalized from using poison magic?"

"I am not sure." He gave me a smile that seemed sincere. "I am not an expert. Your father would be the one to ask. I have a few questions for him myself, if you wouldn't mind."

I felt through my head. Dad was there, but sort of half-conscious. Dull pain radiated from his general direction. Casting that magic in Stone, the mix of dark and light magic, had taken a lot out of him.

I was surprised it hadn't completely knocked me out.

"He needs some time," I said.

"Interesting." Collins slipped his glasses back on.

Zayvion was walking back toward me, and I realized I'd sort of checked out of paying attention to everything else that was happening in the room.

I took a quick look around. Stone was still on the stairs, looking sullen. Shame strolled across the floor, which was now seamless marble, no well to be found.

Terric had positioned himself in the center of the room, a disk in his hand, apparently getting ready to cast the booby trap spells. Zayvion, just a few feet away, was shaking his right hand and sending sparks of black and gold magic crackling down to the floor.

"Closed?" I asked him.

"Locked. Are you all right?"

The flash of gold in his eyes and the taste of blood in my throat told me he already knew the answer to that question.

"Still standing. Terric setting the traps?"

He nodded. "Thought I'd Ground in case anything . . . slipped."

I glanced over at Shame and Terric. Shame was still walking our way, slowly. Terric had his eyes closed and was tracing a spell—two different spells—with each hand. The light around Terric was growing stronger, white going yellow and green. He was ramping up into gorgeousness again, magic shifting around him and making me want to be closer to him.

Then he set both spells free, and I had to bite the inside of my cheek to keep from making any small, embarrassing noise.

Terric was beautiful, just amazingly alluring when he used magic like that.

Shame exhaled, though I couldn't tell if it was a curse or wonder. I slid my gaze away from Terric to him.

Shame looked ice pale, pasty, as if working that magic to open the well, or having that magic worked around him had made him ill. He was thin, too damn thin. If he weren't moving, if those emerald eyes weren't glittering with caught light from the magic Terric was tossing around, I'd think he was death itself coming my way.

"Probably a good idea," I said, answering Zayvion. Only Zayvion was already halfway to Terric. I hadn't even seen him move away.

"Holy hells," I whispered.

"He is hard to resist," Collins said mildly, though I noticed he was staring at the ceiling, acting suddenly interested in the architecture instead of Terric. "I tried to explain that to Zayvion, but he did not seem pleased."

I lifted my hand and dragged fingers through my hair, trying to sort my head, trying to gather my thoughts and put some space between my ache—because being around this much magic was no picnic—and Dad's pain. My left finger hurt from the cut Dad had given me, and all my muscles were sore as if I'd been running too hard and too long.

Casting that spell hadn't just worn Dad out. It had exhausted me too.

"That was fun," Shame said as he came up beside me. "Next time we rattle reality, piss off your gargoyle, and make Zayvion so angry he almost botches a Close spell, can we bring popcorn?"

"Zay almost botched the spell?" I looked over at Zay, who stood facing Terric, steady as a rock, hands at his sides, ready to cast Ground for Terric if anything went wrong.

"Oh, he pulled it off," Shame said. "This is Z we're talking about. But it was a sloppy showing. Think he's losing his touch?"

He glanced at Zayvion; then his gaze slid to Terric. Shame narrowed his eyes. He didn't seem as affected by the light and allure that surrounded Terric, but a faint smile played on his lips.

"Always so anal about closing off the connections,"

he muttered as he pawed at his pocket and pulled out a pack of cigarettes. "Give it a rest, Ter. We know you're good. Ain't no gold stars for perfection."

Shame dug out a cigarette and stuck it in his mouth, then lit it with the lighter he had palmed. He sucked until the cigarette was a bright cherry red, then flicked the lighter closed and exhaled smoke in a thin stream away from Collins and me.

The cigarette burned hot between his fingers. Too hot. In a matter of just a few seconds, the cigarette was half ashes. Shame didn't seem to notice that the Death magic around him was consuming the cigarette, burning it down to a line of gray ash. He just tapped the ashes onto the floor, then put the cigarette to his mouth again and breathed the last of the life out of it.

He flicked it to the floor and went to rub his foot over it, then paused, one bare foot poised over the smoldering coal.

"Jesus." He pulled his foot away and looked around for his shoes. Found them on the stairs by Stone and headed that way. "I'm going up for coffee. Call me if something explodes."

He bent with a groan, grabbed his shoes, and started up the stairs, one hand holding the railing as if he were worried he'd fall. Stone took that as an invitation and clattered up the stairs after him, though trailing at a distance so the Death magic snapping around Shame wouldn't touch him.

It was strange to see Shame forget he was barefoot, strange to see him wandering away to find coffee before finishing a job. But then, he looked exhausted from unlocking the well. I didn't know how he was still standing, much less climbing stairs.

Terric was still casting the last part of the spell, the Refresh that would keep Tangle and Rebound working even if they were triggered more than once.

It wasn't that difficult of a spell to cast, although it took a steady hand to thread it through the other two spells that pulsed in deep blue and red weaves hovering above the floor.

The Refresh spell poured out from his fingers like thin ribbons of green that planted deep into the flooring, then stretched up to catch hold of the red and blue Tangle and Rebound before sinking back into the floor again.

It was literally like watching someone hand stitch a patchwork quilt together. And Terric was indeed taking his time to make sure that every connection held and was tied off.

At this rate, he'd be done in a few seconds. Almost every red and blue line had a green ribbon connected to it.

I rubbed my sore finger with my thumb, wishing Terric would hurry up. We had three more wells to hit and the Seattle people were getting closer with every minute.

It made me itchy. I knew closing down the wells and making sure that no one, not the crew from Seattle, and hopefully, not anyone else Leander and Isabelle sent this way—including Leander and Isabelle—would be able to access magic.

Still, I wondered how the Hounds were doing, if anyone had been hurt, if they were staying one step ahead of the smart and powerful magic users from Seattle coming to Close us, kill us.

And I wondered if everything else was going according to the very hasty plan we'd thrown together. Had the hospitals been warned in time to switch to electricity only? Was the lack of magic causing fewer people to get sick, or was it making people angry, or vulnerable?

It didn't take much of a stretch of the imagination to think that the city that had been bathed in magic for the last thirty years might be a little restless without it.

There could be riots, looting.

A phone rang. It took me until the second ring to realize it was coming from my pocket. I dug it out, didn't recognize the number, answered anyway. "This is Allie."

"Two cars headed your way," Davy said, breathless. "Lost them about half hour ago."

"How many people?" I asked.

"Sid said nine."

"In all?"

"Just headed to Vancouver. We've stalled the rest—closing down the networks was brilliant. Plenty of chaos. But they're just about to head out of the airport now. Six cars. Thirty people."

So much for only twelve being sent to shut us down.

"Stall but do not engage, Silvers," I said. "I don't want dead bodies. On either side."

"Got it. Any luck?"

"One well is secure."

"Only one? Pick up the pace, boss."

"Working as fast as I can. Gotta go."

Terric and Zayvion were walking my way. Terric seemed a little dazed, although the bright beauty of him was nearly blinding. Zay had ahold of his arm and was guiding him through the tangled threads of the spells, which passed right through them.

"Seattle's headed this way." I shoved the phone in my pocket. "Fight or run?"

"Run," Zay said. "We need to get the cure to the wells."

Collins made a little "hm" sound. "I always thought you'd choose to fight no matter the situation."

"Let's you and I get one thing straight, Collins," Zay said, walking past us, Terric still caught in his grip. "You don't know me. I know you better than you do. You don't have to understand what I do, but you damn well better not get in my way."

He was at the stairs and climbing. Terric seemed to be coming to his senses the farther away from the well they got.

I hurried up after them. Collins took one last look at the room, then followed.

The smell of coffee reached me about a dozen steps from the main floor. Terric was walking on his own now, and Zayvion had let go of his arm though remained close enough to catch him.

I didn't think Terric looked that unsteady on his feet, but if Zayvion thought so, I trusted him.

"We done with this bag of tricks?" Shame stood in the hall, a cup of coffee in his hand.

"Seattle's on the way," Zayvion said once we were all in the hall. "Here."

Shame swigged down the last of the steaming coffee, wincing a little. "Rather not have to deal with them here at Mum's inn. She's barely got it back together from the last fight." He followed behind, falling into step with Terric, though I didn't think he noticed it.

Zay was in the lead, and flicked off the light in the hall. He glanced out through the leaded glass window of the door.

"We have company. Two cars."

"Davy said it's nine people," I said. "Plan?"

"Isn't that what you're here for?" Shame said.

Terric slipped up beside Zayvion and looked out. "I know three, no, five of them. Decent people. Excellent magic users. Fast. I'd rather not see them dead."

"Nobody dies," I said. "Understand? These people could be us. They're just following orders and don't know their boss's head has been possessed."

"Hey, they really *could* be us," Shame said giving me a grin. "Our boss's head is possessed too."

"Don't kill them," I repeated.

"Why do you keep looking at me?" he asked. "Collins is the guy with the bloody past."

"Don't kill them," I said over my shoulder to Collins.

"Not my plan nor desire. But, well . . . accidents happen."

"Not today they don't," I said. "We have the advantage. They're going to pull on the magic from the well. That should knock a few of them out. Can anyone tap the magic from the other wells from this distance?"

"We all can," Zayvion said. "And so can they."

"Yes, but we're going to do it first. Now would be good."

Zayvion inhaled, and I felt him call magic to his hands. Shame and Terric both chanted something like a low, slow lullaby, and Collins rolled his shoulders back and carved a spell into the air, setting his mind and his concentration on the task at hand.

As for me, well, so far magic hadn't knocked me out. And even though it still stank, I wasn't sure if I could draw on magic and use it without giving myself a concussion. Dad had said it was the poison in the magic that was making me sick to use it. That seemed right to me. Ever since magic had been poisoned, I'd been having a hard time using it. I guess I was just more sensitive to it.

Dad had kept me safe from it when he used it, but he was still in some corner of my mind licking his wounds.

Stone would fight, and I suppose I could use him as protection. But I hated walking into this with nothing but a knife in my hand and a sword on my back.

There was a chance I could use magic, pull it in from the nearest unclosed well, and maybe cast one spell before I was barfing in the bushes.

Okay, maybe not. Didn't mean I wouldn't try it though.

Zay opened the door and strolled outside, his boots crunching the gravel.

He wasn't holding up a Cloak, or Camouflage, or Illusion. Still, it seemed to take the Seattle people an extended moment to realize the door was open, and all of us were walking out of it. They probably hadn't expected us to be expecting them.

"The Overseer has been possessed by Leander and Isabelle," I said. Might as well tell them the truth. Even though there was no way they'd believe me.

The short, stocky guy in flannel with a dark beard and mustache stepped in front of the group.

Nine people. Just like Davy had said. Five men, four woman. All facing us. All ready to fight. Kill. Close.

"The magic in Portland has been compromised," the man said. "We're here to make sure everyone gets the help and treatment they need. We don't want a fight."

Sounded great. Except he was lying.

Two of the women and a man snapped their fingers, reaching out for the magic in the Blood well. Terric threw a Shield around us, grunting as he pulled the tainted magic from the unclosed Faith well, miles to the south near the Japanese Gardens.

The finger snappers all jerked backward as if an invisible force had slammed into their chests.

That would be the Tangle. They were working Cancel spells to try to unravel the magic tying up their hands and fingers.

The man tried a different spell, pulling on more magic. He grunted and passed out, unconscious on the gravel.

And that would be Rebound.

"Magic has been compromised, Rodney," Terric said, "and so has the Overseer."

"So I've heard," he said, taking a step backward.

They were all walking backward. No, they were spreading out, creating a circle that literally formed the basic glyph for Enhance. A glyph that when cast with another spell did just as its name suggested.

It wasn't often I saw a group use their positions to each other as a way to boost magic.

Okay, it was never.

"You were involved in overthrowing the Voices here, Terric," the man said. "In killing Bartholomew Wray. You've lost your way."

Not another word. Not a signal I could see. But they simultaneously pulled on magic and cast.

Two of the men went down, pulling on the well's magic. They quickly disengaged from the spells and were on their feet recasting, drawing on magic from a more distant well.

Silver and black lightning bolts skittered across the Shield Terric held around us.

They'd caught on quick and were no longer trying to draw magic out of the Blood well.

But then, neither were we.

Zayvion and Shame strode through the Shield at the

same time, Zay throwing Sleep and Shame chanting, one hand held out, not throwing magic, but instead catching it in a spell that pulsed like a black heart in his hand.

Collins threw Illusion. In the eyes of people who couldn't actually see the spells tearing through the air, it would look like he had disappeared. But I could easily see him as he jogged to the van and opened the side door, ducking inside.

He emerged with a baseball bat and a nasty grin on his face.

He refreshed the Illusion, then circled around behind them. I hoped he remembered our deal. No killing.

"Allie," Terric said, "run!"

Suddenly, there was a hell of a lot of magic raining down in flaming blades.

Terric pivoted back, his left hand gathering a fistful of magic and twisting it into a spell—Impact—that he heaved at the Seattle crew just as the Shield broke and burned down like hot glass.

Shit.

I ducked my head and ran. There wasn't a lot of cover by the inn, but Collins had gotten around behind the group. He took one woman out at the back of the knees. She screamed and fell. I didn't have time to see if he stopped there or not. More screams filled the darkness, and I ducked behind the Dumpster.

Use magic, I said to Dad, frantic.

I can't. He sounded exhausted.

If you can't, then I have to. Can you fix me, do something to my brain or body so I can tolerate using magic again?

I am not sure it would work, Allison.

I glanced out at the fight. The people from Seattle

knew what they were doing, and had no qualms about using deadly force. We were not winning this fight.

Do something, I thought. *Anything.*

I didn't know if Dad could do anything to help, but he knew my head probably better than I did.

Dad stirred. He reached into places and parts of me that were tender and vulnerable. I didn't like him touching me there. Oh, this was going to hurt.

There is one way I can open you to using the tainted magic, he said. *But every time you use magic it will harm you. Permanently.*

Do it.

This will hurt, he said.

It felt like he stabbed a knife into the middle of my brain. Whatever it was he did, I felt the hot liquid rush through my head, like blood pouring free.

No, not blood. Magic.

I yelled as pain tracked through me, scraping down the paths of magic Cody had stitched into me months ago, catching my face, my neck, my arm all the way down to my fingertips on fire. My left arm went heavy and cold as magic ravaged me again.

As magic awoke in me again.

The pain didn't seem to have an ending. I lost myself to agony for a second, for more than that. For ever.

Then I inhaled, tasting sharp heat on my tongue as if someone had just struck a hundred matches at once, as if I had been on fire and suddenly extinguished.

Something in me was gone. Snuffed. A sliding fear, a knowledge, whether mine or my father's, of what that thing might be shifted through me and was gone.

Then the rest of the world came back.

I was still behind the Dumpster.

Stone had both wings wrapped around me, protecting me from the magic raging through the night. They were still fighting. What had felt like an eternity had happened in an instant.

I had been burning, and now I was freezing. Shaking. Not quite shock, but not exactly on my feet either.

Stone growled and the glyphs on his body flowed through waves of gold, deep blue-black.

I put my hand on his back and looked over his shoulder.

I could still see magic without casting Sight, so whatever Dad had just done to me hadn't taken that away. But magic no longer stank like rot.

Terric was slumped against the inn behind me. His eyes were squeezed closed, his hands in fists as hot white magic rolled around him. Bright enough to hurt my eyes and destroy my night vision.

I looked away as quickly as I could. He was breathing heavily but controlled, as if he were enduring pain.

"Shame," he said.

I looked back at the fight. Shame was pulling on a hell of a lot of magic. And it looked like it was everything he could do not to lose control of it.

Which is probably why he didn't see the two guys throw spells that hit Zayvion so hard, he was knocked off his feet.

"Zay!" I stepped out from behind the Dumpster and drew Impact without hesitation. Magic sank hot claws under my skin, around my bones. I yelled, unable to hold back the agony of that spell. But I did not lose focus. The spell took shape at my command.

And lashed out at the remaining people from Seattle, knocking them out before they even had a chance to block.

I felt like I'd just been wrapped in fire, every inch of

me stinging in the suddenly cold air. But it had been worth it. The fight was over. Unconscious people littered the ground. The only people standing were Collins, who as far as I could tell didn't have blood on him, and Zayvion, who had regained his feet and was striding toward me. Zay looked angry, a little singed, but whole.

Over his shoulder, I finally saw Shame. He stood behind a young woman, one arm wrapped around her waist, the other clamped over her mouth. He leaned down just enough so he could whisper in her ear, his eyes burning green beneath the black of his bangs, his face the cold white of the moon. He was a figure carved in alabaster and ink.

It took me a second to register what seemed strange about him.

Something was wrong with the woman. Like a fly held by a spider, she was stiff, wide-eyed, and terrified. And yet she didn't raise her hands to cast magic, didn't made a single sound.

Shame was doing something to her—no, the magic around Shame was doing something to her. I didn't think Shame was in control of it anymore.

"Shame?" I said quietly.

Zay stopped. Spun on his heel. Collins was backing away from Shame, fast.

"Shame!" Zayvion yelled.

"No!" I pushed Stone out of the way and ran. Not to Shame. To Zay. I caught Zayvion's arm and pulled him back out of Shame's reach.

Just as the darkness around Shame lashed out, whipping through the unconscious people lying in the gravel. Shame stopped whispering. He tipped his head up to the starry sky. And laughed.

As he drank their lives down.

"Stop," I said. "Shamus, don't do this. Don't kill them!"

But Shame could not hear me.

Ghostly shapes lifted up from each body, faint and misty. Whips of Death magic snapped out and pierced the ghosts. That darkness drank them down until there was nothing left, not a ghost, not a shadow. And then, not even the bodies in the gravel.

"Fuck," Zay whispered. "Eleanor." I felt his fear roll through me, as mine washed through him. And in that second, neither he nor I wanted to do what we knew must be done.

Take Shame down. No matter the cost.

Chapter Ten

The woman, Eleanor, was still in Shame's arms, cradled almost lovingly against him. I didn't know why he hadn't killed her yet.

Shame was no longer gaunt and skeletal, no longer as pale. He no longer looked like standing and breathing hurt. He tipped his face down and smiled at Zayvion and me. The man looked amazing. Healthy. Strong.

But that was not our friend looking out from those eyes.

That was a man lost to the madness of power. The power of Death magic.

The last person I'd seen drink lives down like that was Jingo Jingo.

"Jesus," I breathed. "Please, Shame, let her go. We don't want to kill anyone. That's not who we are. That's not who you are."

Zay very quietly pulled a knife from his belt. I could tell he was ready to cast a spell, to throw the knife, to shut Shame down.

But if insane Shame put his hands on Zay, I didn't think Zay would survive.

"Let her go, Shame," I tried again.

Shame blinked. Slow, languid. Caught in the thrall, the sensual embrace of Death magic.

"So. Sweet," Shame said.

Darkness around him stroked slowly, sensually over Eleanor, surrounding her. Consuming her. Her eyes closed and she slumped in his arms.

"No!"

Zay ran, knife and magic cutting a wicked spell. I ran, casting Shield to hold Zayvion, to keep Zayvion out of Shame's reach, away from his touch. I couldn't lose Zay. Refused to watch him die, even if he was trying to save Shame.

I threw Shield around Zay, around me. It spun out like a pure blue glass, wrapping us in a bubble.

I moaned from the pain of it, the grinding weight of magic. It felt like that single spell weighed a ton, as if magic were bleeding out of me, pulling from my skin, my bones, to feed that spell.

Zay flicked his wrist and the spell that was caught on the edge of his blade sliced through my Shield and razored toward Shame.

The Death magic and darkness around Shame licked out, tentacles drinking Zay's spell down. He turned those un-Shame eyes on us again. And began chanting.

The woman's ghost stepped out of her body, looking confused and afraid. She tried to take a step away from Shame, tried to run, but the blackness around him snaked out and wrapped a thread around her insubstantial wrist and pulled her in close.

"Shame?" Terric's voice was soft, but somehow carried across the air. Even filtered through my Shield I heard it as if he were standing at my shoulder, even though he was just now pushing himself away from the inn and walking our way.

Shame heard him too. He looked away from us to Terric.

Terric radiated pure light, achingly beautiful. As he walked, grass sprung up around his footsteps, vines pushed through soil and rock to brush his boots, to unfurl and catch at the edge of his coat, the cuff of his sleeve.

He was surrounded by magic, Life magic. And the world came to life around him. Life magic poured just as strong from him as Death magic poured from Shame.

I could not tell if Terric was in control of the magic. I didn't know if letting Terric and Shame get near each other would stop Shame or if it would spark off something else. Create something even more dangerous.

Soul Complements can make magic break its rules. Was this how Leander and Isabelle used magic when they were alive? Was this how their madness began?

"Don't," Shame said. He still hadn't let go of Eleanor's body. But her body hadn't dissolved like the others. Yet.

Terric shrugged. "I know what you want, Shamus," he said in a voice that promised all the pleasures of mind and body. He strode over to Shame, graceful, intense.

Shame blinked, as if trying to parse what Terric had just said. As if trying to decipher the meaning behind the words. A hint of the man I knew shadowed his eyes. "No," he said. "You don't."

Terric smiled and my breath caught at the unworldly beauty. My concentration faltered. The Shield around Zayvion and me broke and fell soundlessly to our feet.

Zayvion's arm was around me, holding me tight. It was the only reason I wasn't walking toward Terric.

That, and my fear. Of what he was. Of what he and Shame might become together.

"Yes," Terric said, stepping so close to Shame he could touch him if he lifted his hand. "I do."

He paused, held Shame's gaze.

And Shame could not look away.

Terric raised his hand. Shame flinched. But Terric didn't touch Shame. Instead, light and Life magic washed outward from his palms.

Trees shivered from the touch of that magic, the wind stirred and the world sighed. All around Terric life sprang forth, rising in great green twisting fronds and branches at his feet, rolling outward as if stirred by a gentle breeze, brush and vines reaching to engulf them. All of that green, all of that life, created by magic, answering a call only magic could utter.

Shame closed his eyes again, only this time, his face was tipped to a new light, to Terric. Serenity played across his features as the darkness around him drank down the light that poured free from Terric's hands.

As quickly as the living green vines and grasses grew, they were just as quickly drained to dust by the hunger of Death magic surrounding Shame.

Neither Zay nor I moved. I didn't know where Stone was, where Collins was. Maybe inside the inn, maybe back in the car. A fleeting thought crossed my mind: This was our chance. To stop Shame and Terric, or maybe to do something more. Knock them out. End them.

I knew we should. Zay knew we should. But neither of us wanted to destroy them.

There are no happily ever afters for Soul Complements. I'd been told that over and over again. I'd seen Chase and Greyson die. I'd faced the horror of what Leander and Isabelle had become.

And even though I knew watching Shame and Terric lose themselves to the give and take, the light and dark, life and death of magic might mean I was standing by and watching them lose hold on their own minds, their own humanity, I could not bring myself to stop them.

They were beautiful. Powerful. Primal. This was what magic was supposed to be. Dark and Light, balanced.

Well, without the dead girl between them.

The greenery dancing around them rose shoulder high now, bending toward Shame, reaching to him with soft green fingers.

Death magic lashed at the green, tearing through it, burning, destroying, consuming. The plants dissolved into silver rain that pattered against gravel, and which Terric drew up again so that greenery and life bounded back, growing, thriving with riotous joy.

Shame could not destroy faster than Terric could create. They were equal, matched. Soul Complements.

And then, finally, Shame shuddered as if waking from a deep, hard sleep.

The plants stopped growing. Darkness around Shame thinned to the faintest of shadows in the hollows of his skin. The light around Terric dimmed to a slight nimbus.

And they both took that last step toward each other. Terric wrapped one arm around Shame's shoulder, supporting him as Shame nearly fell forward with the dead woman between them.

"Ter?" he said, realizing there was a woman in his arms. "Shit. Oh, shit. No. Eleanor."

Terric seemed to come to his senses, and shifted his grip so he could help Shame lower the woman to the ground.

Her ghost stood nearby, watching, sadly.

"No," Shame said again, on his knees now next to her. "I didn't. God in heaven, tell me I didn't. Terric. Tell me I didn't kill her."

Terric sat on the ground next to him. He put his hand firmly on Shame's shoulder, as if that contact alone could hold back the panic, the horror of what Shame had done.

"She wasn't the only one," Terric said softly. "They're all dead."

Loss and horror hollowed Shame's face. He swallowed, shaking his head, then stumbled up to his feet. Got about ten feet away before he was on his knees again, retching.

Eleanor's ghost stayed where she was, staring down at her body, and then at Terric. She seemed to make a decision and drifted over to Shame, standing several feet off to one side of him.

Even at this distance, I could see the faint silver line that tied her to him.

Terric didn't get up to help Shame. I wasn't sure if Terric could get up. He was still on his knees next to the body, his eyes closed, hands loose on his thighs. In the dark of the night, he looked bruised and beaten.

With an unspoken agreement, Zayvion started toward Shame and I walked over to Terric.

It was strange to push my way through ankle-high grass where just a moment ago there had been gravel. Stone was suddenly at my side and paced along with me, burbling and sniffing at the grass, before sitting on his haunches and ripping out handfuls of it that he tossed over his shoulder.

It smelled like grass. It felt like grass and sounded like grass.

What had they done? Magic. And using magic meant it used you back. I could not imagine what the price for this would be.

"Terric?" I didn't touch him.

He opened his eyes, looked up at me. "Allie. I think . . ." He paused as Shame retched again. "I'm sorry. We're sorry. It was . . ." His words drifted off and he just stared at me, his eyes too glassy, as if a fever raged beneath his skin.

Zayvion was talking quietly to Shame. I heard Collins walking their way.

"It's done," I said, touching Terric's shoulder gently. I didn't know what I expected. Heat, I guess. Or some kind of magical backlash. But he just felt like Terric, his coat a little cool in the evening air, and the soft warmth of a fever radiating from his bare skin.

"We'll figure it out," I said. "Can you stand?"

"I think so." He moved to push up on his feet, and groaned. "God, my head." He pressed his hand gingerly over his forehead and eyes. "Hurts."

I was surprised he wasn't unconscious. That was a hell of a lot of magic to call on, and Soul Complements or not, magic always found a way to make you pay.

"Let's get you in the van," I said. "Can you take a step?" I guided him away from the body, and we moved toward the van. Zayvion had already gotten Shame on his feet, and was walking with him, his hand supporting his arm.

Shame walked like he was in a daze.

Shock, I figured. It wasn't that Shame hadn't killed before. But this time he'd let magic take control of him to drink down lives and consume bodies.

Just like the one man he most hated, Jingo Jingo, had done.

Is this what a master of Death magic really was? A monster?

Collins opened the van door for Zay and Shame, and they both helped Shame step inside. Eleanor sort of floated into the van to sit behind him. Then Zayvion came back and helped me with Terric, who still had one hand over his eyes.

We got him in the van too, in the middle seat next to Shame, who was sitting upright and stiff, staring straight ahead.

The three of us—Collins, Zay, and I—stood outside the van for a second.

"They didn't mean for this to happen," I said.

Collins just shrugged. "There is no nice way to wage a war," he said. "We went into this knowing there would be victims. Innocent or not, those people came here with one goal—to kill us. I prefer this outcome, if you must know. Let's get to the next well."

He climbed in the van and slid around to the backseat. Stone whuffled under my hand, bumped his head on Zay's thigh, then eased his way into the back of the vehicle.

Zay pulled the door closed. "I don't know," he said, answering my unspoken question of what we should do. "Shame's in shock. How's Terric?"

"Speaking some. In pain. We need to take them to a doctor, or someplace where their magic can be monitored. Kevin's?"

"We don't have time. Let's call someone. Have them meet us at the Faith well."

"Good," I said. "That should work. Help me with . . . Eleanor, okay?"

War or not, I wasn't going to leave her body out there in the cold where animals could get to her. Not that I had a great idea of what we should do with her body, but the least we could do was get her inside the inn.

Zay thankfully didn't argue with me. We walked back

to where the body was lying, picked her up, and carried her to the back door.

It occurred to me that this wasn't the first dead body Zay and I had moved in the last couple of days.

"Are you okay?" Zay asked.

"I hate this," I said.

"I know. But you cast magic. Impact and Shield. Are you all right? You . . . something hurt you and you feel different to me, Allie."

Oh. That. I sighed. "Dad did something in my head. It hurt. A lot. And then I could access magic again. That hurts too. Of course."

"Did you ask him what he did?"

"He's unconscious." We paused and Zayvion opened the door to the inn. The wind stirred in the trees, louder now with all that grass and shrubbery to riffle through.

"Why can't Shame and Terric control magic?" I asked as we brought her body down the hall we had used to get to the well. But instead of going down the stairs to the left, we opened one of the unlocked side rooms on the right.

"Soul Complements. They came about it on the battlefield—killed people as they were drawing on each other, drawing on magic," Zay said. "They died for each other, lived for each other. It . . . changed them."

"We died for each other," I said. "Hell, I walked straight into death for you, Zayvion Jones."

We placed Eleanor gently on the floor and I looked around for a blanket or cover of some sort. This was one of the spare office areas Maeve used when running the inn as an inn. There was a nice leather couch with a throw blanket on the back of it.

"I've been thinking about that," Zayvion said.

I gathered up the blanket and paused before spreading it out over her. Eleanor had straight blond hair and a soft heart-shaped face with a long thin nose. I thought she might be in her early twenties but still looked like a teenager. "She was so young," I said. "Too young for this."

Zay didn't say anything.

"Did you know her?" I asked.

He nodded. "Her name was Eleanor Roth. She trained with Maeve several years ago. Had a huge crush on Shame. Not that he noticed."

"Why didn't he notice her?"

"Said she was too young and too sweet for him. That he'd ruin her."

I didn't know what to say. He'd been right. He did ruin her. Although I didn't know how young and sweet she was anymore, since she'd come here to kill us.

I placed the blanket over Eleanor, covering her still face.

"It's your dad," he said.

"What's my dad?"

"I think he's the reason we have control over magic. Or at least the reason why we haven't done what Shame and Terric just did."

"Dad is the reason we haven't lost control?" I didn't like that idea.

"When we last fought Leander and Isabelle, at the Life well, you left your body and came to me." He waited until I nodded.

"How did you let go of me, of us, and return to your body?" he asked.

I didn't want to say it, but I did. "Dad pulled me back."

Zay's jaw tightened. He didn't like it any more than I did. But he wasn't the kind of man who looked away when the truth was staring right at him.

"He was possessing you when we first tested to see if we were Soul Complements," he said, "he's been . . . in you for almost as long as he's been dead. For almost as long as we've been together. Nearly a year now."

"So you and I haven't really had the chance to work magic as Soul Complements, like Shame and Terric, without someone else's interference," I said.

He rolled one shoulder, not quite a shrug, more like trying to dislodge an uncomfortable weight. "I think so."

"Great," I said. "Just fab. And what if what Jingo Jingo said is true—if Dad's been carving out holes in my head, preparing me all my damn life for him to possess me—what does that mean? I can't live with him in my head my entire life. But if the only reason we don't self-destruct is because Dad's in me, what are we supposed to do? Stop using magic forever? Stop being with each other? I will not give up on you because of magic, Zay."

He was in front of me so fast, I swear I didn't see him move. He put his hands gently on both of my arms.

"Then don't. We'll find a way to remove your dad from your head. As soon as we deal with Leander and Isabelle and make magic safe to use again, then we can figure out how you and I can be together without him. If that means giving up magic, then, yes, I will give up magic for you."

I nodded, knowing he had just told me he'd give up the life he had built for himself to be with me.

"I don't want you to give up magic for me, Zay. Not out of fear of what might happen. I'm just tired. I don't want to fight Leander and Isabelle to the death. I don't want to have to . . . kill Shame and Terric. I still can't deal with what . . . what I did to Bartholomew Wray. And Collins said this is war and a lot of people are going to die. I'm not a leader . . . not really, not with this much at stake. The entire city. The world. I'm just . . ." I shook my head. "Nothing."

Zay gently tipped my chin up, the fingers of his hand warm against my jaw, his other hand on my hip. Magic, caught in whorls through my skin, heated at his touch, straining to be nearer him.

"You are not nothing."

"How would you know?"

"Because I know what you have done. You saved Cody when he was just a stranger to you. You killed Lon Tragger and stood up to a Death magic user who was killing girls to use magic. You fought a Necromorph, and walked through a gate into death to bargain with my captor to bring me back to life. No matter what has been thrown at you, you have found a way forward, found a way to fight for innocent people to stay alive, for the Hounds to find pride in their work and each other, and for Portland to remain safe."

I was shaking my head. I knew all those things he said were true, but were they enough?

"And," he said, "because you are mine. As long as you want to be. We will walk this to the end. We will find our way, and a way to get rid of your father. This fight? That's right now. Just right now."

"Promise?" I searched his gaze, soft brown, heated by gold.

He brushed his thumb down my cheek. "With my dying breath."

I swallowed back something that felt a lot like tears. "Thank you."

I wanted to say more, to tell him how much I loved him. But if I kissed him right now, there was no way I was going to be able to let go and face everything else we needed to do. Things we should have done hours ago.

I stepped away.

Zayvion stepped with me, his hand never leaving my hip. "Allie."

I knew he saw the fear in my eyes, saw my very uncertain need to be with him and my certainty that I should not be. Not now.

Then he kissed me, gently, his lips pressing softly against just the corner of my mouth. Before I could return the kiss, he whispered, "There are a whole lot of tomorrows ahead of us. And I plan on spending every damn one of them with you."

That certainty, his firm belief that we were going to have our happily ever after no matter what, did me a lot of good.

I nodded, and we both pulled away, the distance between us much easier to bear. Which was good. We had a lot to take care of. "I'll call for someone to see to her body," I said, walking toward the door.

Zay didn't follow me. I glanced back. He was staring at the wall. I followed his gaze to the shelves inset there.

And on those shelves were Void stones.

I knew exactly what he was thinking.

"Will they help?" I asked, stepping over to the other wall where more Void stones were displayed as art, jewelry, and just plain stones. I gathered up as many as I could carry. A strange numbing relief flowed out from those stones, like a balm on a burn. It was kind of wonderful.

"They might," he said. "One way to find out."

We hurried out of the inn, our hands loaded with Void stones of every size and style, from the plain gray pet rock–looking thing, to the polished and really quite beautiful stones set into necklaces, bracelets, and rings.

The Void stones had helped me when I was having

trouble controlling magic. It made sense that they could help Shame and Terric too.

We left the building and Zay locked it before slamming the door shut. We marched through the grass to the van. Zay got in the driver's seat and I stepped up into the passenger's side.

"What took you so long?" Collins asked. It didn't sound like he cared what I answered.

"Void stones," I said, turning and crawling back toward Shame and Terric while Zay got the van moving. "Help me with them."

"You stole them?" Suddenly Collins was alert and more than willing to help me place Void stone necklaces on Shame and Terric, latch bracelets on their wrists, and set stones on their laps, at their feet, and beside them on the seat.

Eleanor hovered just behind where Shame was sitting, and placed her fingers on the Void stone necklace against the back of his neck. Shame shivered, but his blank stare didn't falter. I didn't know if he was aware of the stones around him, but he could at least in some manner sense Eleanor's ghost.

"Borrowed." I braced as Zay made a hard left.

Zay was trying to make up for some lost time by breaking the speed limit. "Faith well, right?" I asked.

"That's the plan," he said.

My phone rang, and I shook my hands to clear the soft numbness from handling the Void stones, then planted myself back in the front seat and pulled the phone out of my pocket. "Beckstrom."

"Seattle's on the road and furious," Davy said. It sounded like he was running. "Go, go!" A car door slammed behind him and all I could hear was clattering, squealing wheels, and something that sounded like the cell phone hitting the ground.

"Still there?" Davy asked.

"What's going on?"

"They're headed into Portland. Should make the city limits in a half hour. We'll do what we can."

"Stay low," I said. "Stay out of sight."

"They'll never see us coming."

"No. Davy, no. That's not what I mean. Stay out of their range. Do not fight them."

He hung up.

"Davy says more from Seattle are headed to the city. Half an hour out," I said.

Zay took a hard turn and crossed three lanes to hit an exit.

"What are you doing?" I asked as soon as we were on four wheels again.

"Heading to the Life well."

"All the way out to Multnomah Falls?" I asked. "Faith well. We're supposed to be headed to the Faith well. Southwest. Under the Japanese Gardens. Not headed east."

"Seattle's coming into the city," he said. "Life well is the farthest out. We need to purify it and close it, lock it, to take it out of play. Faith and Death wells are close enough we can get to each of them fast after the Life well is closed."

"So, change of plans," I said.

I could call Kevin and tell him to get a car out to the falls to take Shame and Terric back, and tell him to send me two more people who could help us with the wells, but we didn't have the time to wait for them.

Maybe I'd tell Terric and Shame to stay in the car.

They should be fine with the Void stones if they didn't try to cast magic. I had cast magic twice. It hurt, but maybe I could take up some of the slack. Between Collins, Zayvion, and me, we still might be able to do this.

I glanced over my shoulder. Shame was staring straight ahead, like he'd just had a front-row-seat view of the end of the world. Terric's eyes were closed, though I thought I saw a glimmer of a tear slipping down his jaw.

Okay, maybe they wouldn't be fine. But they probably wouldn't cause themselves, or anyone else, damage if we left them in the car. I guess I could leave Collins in the car to keep an eye on them.

No. We'd need at least three of us to purify the well. Zay, Collins, and me, and of course, my dad.

Dad, I thought, *we're going to need you to be ready for this.*

Nothing.

Dad?

Okay. So it might just be me, Zayvion, and Collins. Yes, I could use magic again. I hoped. But I hadn't paid close enough attention to the spells Dad used to get the magic out of Stone. I didn't know if I could do this without him.

I glanced at the speedometer. Zayvion was at a hundred miles an hour and climbing. It felt like the miles crawled by. Finally, finally, he turned into the parking area. We'd have to cross under the train trestle to get to the well.

Zay parked and turned off the engine. He got out of the van and so did I, pulling open the van side door.

"You're staying—" I said to Terric.

"We are not." Terric pushed his way past me. His shoulder brushed against mine and sent a weird numbing tingle down my spine. Not magic. Rather, the lack of it. He was covered in Void stones. So many that even a brush felt like a cool breeze sucking magic away from me.

Terric turned so he was facing the inside of the van, blocking Collins' and Stone's exit.

"Shame," Terric said, "we have work to do."

Shame didn't budge, didn't move an inch. He was still sitting stiff and straight, staring without blinking. Eleanor had moved to sit between him and the window. She seemed a little less sad, and a little more curious as she considered him in profile. She put her hand hesitantly on his shoulder and he twitched at the contact.

One of the traits all good Hounds learn quickly is how to read lips. I couldn't hear Eleanor, but I knew she said, "Shame. You have to go."

Shame shivered just slightly. I knew he could hear her.

"Terric," I said. "Maybe you should give Shame some time."

"Maybe you should let me handle this." Terric flared, gold white, and the Void stones heated red before expelling that cool breeze sensation again. He wasn't glowing anymore.

Didn't mean he wasn't angry.

Terric was a nice guy. Someone I counted as one of my closest friends. Magic had changed him. Yeah, well, welcome to the club.

This angry-killer look wasn't anything magic had done to him. I was pretty sure that was just Terric, pissed off and ready to fight anything unlucky enough to get in his way.

I hoped that included the magic he tried to use.

Stone pushed his big head against Terric's arm and Terric moved aside enough for him to tromp out of the van. Collins slid out behind him, carefully avoiding touching Terric.

"Nice place for an ambush," Collins noted, staring up at Multnomah Falls caught by moonlight as it tumbled down against the cliff side on the other side of the railroad trestle and parking lot.

I took a couple of steps away from the van. Zay came around from the front and walked up to Terric. "You're both staying here."

Terric ignored him. "Shame." He reached into the van and touched Shame's wrist. A Void stone rattled and rolled toward the back of the seat.

Shame turned his head. Looked at Terric. His eyes were more black than green, but there was no anger in them. Actually, there was no emotion on his face at all. He just looked broken. Blank.

Sweet hells.

"This isn't over for us," Terric said. "We can't change what we've done. But we don't have time to deal with the fallout. Not now. You've been here before, Shame. Been to this darkness. You lost control of magic like this, when you broke me, broke my ability to use magic when we were younger. You almost killed me. Would have if Zay hadn't stopped you.

"You found your way out of that darkness. You found your way to a place of sanity. Without my help. I'm here to help you this time.

"So pull yourself the fuck together, Flynn. You can cry over the horror later. Flynns don't give up. Flynns come up swinging. You told me that. You told me Flynn blood isn't smart enough to know when to stop fighting. And right now, we need that. Need you. Because we have a war to fight. More than just a handful of lives are on the line. I'm not going to sit this fight out. You damn well better not either."

Shame tipped his head down; his shoulders slumped.

"I'm going in there without you," Terric said. "So are Zay and Allie. Are you going to sit in the car and cry?"

Shame lifted his head. "Hate you," he rasped.

"I know." Terric held out his hand.

Shame took it and pulled himself out of the van. He stood next to Terric for a minute and seemed to suddenly notice all the rocks hanging from his neck and wrists.

He nodded, absently, not taking any of them off. "You think this will do any good?" There was no tone in his voice, no emotion. He was on his feet, but he sure as hell wasn't all together yet.

"It won't hurt," Terric said. "Plus, if you try that shit you did back there again, I will knock you on your ass."

Shame didn't say anything, didn't glare, didn't flip Terric off. He just stood there, as if waiting to be told what to do next. As if all the fire in him had been snuffed out.

It was strange. Frightening to see him like this. Just as frightening as seeing him mindlessly drinking down the dead.

"Enough talking," Zay said. "Let's close this well."

Chapter Eleven

Zay and I jogged across the parking lot. Stone seemed to think we'd come out to play some kind of running game and was zipping around all of us like a race car doing laps. Each time he passed by me he made a little happy croon, which just made him sound like a tiny train zooming by with its whistle stuck.

I didn't look back to check on Shame and Terric or Collins, but from the sound of footfalls, they were all right behind us.

There were only a few people leaving the parking lot since it was completely dark now. They looked our way, probably surprised to see a gargoyle running around like a dog off a leash. Not that I cared. No time for stealth. No time for secrets.

We'd gotten the word out not to use magic. We'd gotten the word out that magic was getting shut down. But that hadn't stopped people from coming to see the falls.

We jogged past the parking area, past the espresso stand, up the concrete pathway that wound between green ferns and moss to our right and trees and scrub to our left with nothing but moonlight to guide us. Hit the bridge at the midpoint of the falls.

I slowed, because, damn, I was hurt, tired, and out of

shape. I did manage to keep it to a fast walk as we took the next rise in the hill.

Zay slowed too, probably more for my burning lungs than for his own limitations.

No matter how fast we ran up this hill, then down those damn stairs to the well, there was no chance we'd get back to town before the rest of the people from Seattle got there first.

Unless the Hounds managed to trip them up, slow them down.

Maybe. Davy sounded like he was on the chase behind them, not in front of them. And Hounds weren't the sort of people who gave up easily.

Zay stopped, and I nearly ran into his wide back.

We must have reached the doorway to the Life well. I never could recognize the exact spot where it was hidden in the hillside.

I stepped to the side of the trail while Zay drew magic from the well to cast an Illusion in case someone came upon us, although it was unlikely so late at night. Then he cast the spell that would reveal the doorway in the side of the hill that would lead down to the well.

"Very nice," Collins said, a little out of breath. "This is well hidden."

Great. This must be part of the memories he'd had Closed and taken away from him by the Authority.

Shame and Terric didn't look tired. Standing there, blank darkness and brooding light, they weren't even breathing hard.

Even better, the darkness and light around them was very subtle. The Void stones were doing a good job of keeping the magic that was available to them dampened.

Of course, neither of them was actually trying to draw

on magic. I had a feeling if they did, not even the half-dozen Void stones they each wore would be enough to slow them down.

The door opened and we all stepped through it onto the platform at the top of the stairs.

Terric flipped on the light switch and electric lights flickered to life all the way down the staircase, shining wet and yellow against the stone walls.

Stone burbled, still standing outside on the trail.

"Come on, Stone," I said. "This isn't going to hurt."

His ears flapped back, and then up, his wings stretched.

"Come on, boy," I said again as I started down the stairs. "Let's do magic."

He finally clambered in, then pushed past me, so that I had to hug the wooden rail. Stone galloped down the stairs, with his very humanlike hands wrapping around each step as he went, his wings out for balance.

I took the stairs as fast as I could, trying not to think about having to run back up the damn things in a few minutes.

At the bottom of the stairs, I stopped to get my breathing in order while Zay unlocked the big double doors with that ribbonlike spell that spooled out from his fingertips.

Then he slammed the doors open and strode into the room. "Terric, you think you can open this one?"

If Terric was surprised by Zay asking for his help, the only indication of it was a slight pause in his step. "Should be able to."

"Then you do that," Zayvion said. "Shame, I'll want you to close it. Allie, you and your dad will purify the well with Stone. Collins, you and I handle Shield and Ground and anything else you might need. Let's make it fast."

Terric pulled off the stones on his wrist, and then the three he wore around his neck. He handed all of those to Shame. "If I turn this place into a rain forest, stop me."

Shame just nodded.

As soon as the last Void stone was off of him, the glow around Terric flared and that otherworldly beauty infused him.

Zayvion dug a disk out of the messenger bag and handed it to Terric, then handed another one to me. I was worried about touching it at first, but it wasn't a problem. It held magic locked and ready for my dad to release just like Collins had released it. The disk itself was just metal.

I noted he didn't give a disk to Shame yet.

Terric walked out into the middle of the room. He took a deep breath, then began whispering while he very carefully traced one finger over the disk in the palm of his hand.

Shame, beside me, shifted slightly, maybe getting ready to use magic.

I glanced at him. The laughter that had always seemed to be leashed just beneath his surface was gone.

He wasn't standing like he was getting ready to use magic. He was standing like he was trying hard not to turn and walk away. Eleanor was pacing, well, floating, at a distance behind him, glancing over at Shame and Terric with a worried look on her face.

"You okay?" I asked Shame quietly.

"On a scale from one to ten?" he said. "No."

I couldn't help but smile a little. That sounded more like the Shame I knew.

"Going to get through this?"

"You mean am I going to try not to kill anyone?"

"No," I said, pressing my fingers gently against his sleeve. He jerked at the contact, looked over at me.

"Are you ready to use magic?"

He was breathing a little hard and sweat slicked his forehead, sticking his bangs into points. He pulled his arm away. "Don't. Just . . ." He shook his head, then looked back out at Terric. "You don't want to be holding on to me if I fall, Beckstrom."

"So don't fall," I said.

Terric said one last word and flicked his fingers. An Open spell spread out at his feet, glowing in soft orchid light. The wooden floor shifted and slid, pulling away from the well.

Terric paced away from the ever-growing hole in the floor, the disk in his hand dark and empty of magic. He strode over to where Shame and I were standing and nodded.

"It wasn't impossible to control," he said to Shame. "But it took . . . effort."

Shame handed Terric the Void stones and Terric put them on with a look of relief.

"Allie?" Zay said.

Right. I was up. *Dad?*

He seemed to draw himself forward from a far corner of my mind. He was tired.

Can you do this? I asked him.

Don't be ridiculous, Allison. Of course I can. Step aside.

Think you can do it with a little less pain this time? I asked.

I didn't expect the . . . amount of effort required to tap into the magic in the Animate. If I'd been in my own body, it wouldn't have been as difficult. But in yours? He paused, and I knew what he was thinking. That my body, my skills, and my mind were inferior for the task he could have carried out just fine on his own.

Say it, you egotistical jerk, I thought.

In your body, with the damage to your mind, he said with something that hinted at fatigue, or, I don't know, kindness, *there are variables I hadn't taken into account.*

Had he just called me brain-damaged?

"Allie?" Zayvion said again. "Can he do it?"

"He can do it," I snarled. "Come on, Stone." I marched over to the edge of the well. The white and crystal light of magic was muddied with black tar that lapped at the edges like cooling lava. And just like at the last well, there was only a center of pure magic left.

Stone paced up next to me, keeping a wise distance from the edge of the well even though the tar didn't seem to be lapping over onto the floor this time.

I patted his head. "Good, Stoney. We'll make this quick."

Collins stepped up beside me. "Shall I draw from the disk?"

"I don't know. Ask my dad."

"I was," he said.

Oh.

I mentally moved aside so that Dad could see through my eyes, use my hands and mouth. I wanted to be as far away from him using magic as possible. He'd told me the thing he'd done so I could use magic would hurt me. No, he'd said every time I used magic it would do me permanent harm.

Maybe staying out of his way while he accessed the magic in Stone would keep the damage down to a minimum.

"You will need to tap into the disk via Life magic, Eli," Dad said through me. "Can you do that?"

"Certainly," Eli said.

"Let us begin."

Collins pulled the magic from the disk, holding it steady over his palm.

Dad once again chanted, strange tonal shifts in a non-language as he drew a glyph in the style of Life magic over Stone. Magic flowed through the glyphs carved in Stone, rippling with green light like a stroke of wind crossing a grassy field.

It hurt. The longer Dad used magic, the harder magic stretched my veins and burned my bones, like a beast trying to claw its way out of my body.

I didn't moan, but only because Dad had my mouth clamped tight as he concentrated on bringing the spell to completion.

It was not quite an Open spell, not quite a Clarify. It resembled Confluence, which didn't make a lot of sense. Confluence was usually used to connect two spells, like putting a Refresh on a Relax spell at a dentist's office. Confluence made the spells join into a seamless harmony. Not exactly what I would have expected him to use, and I'm pretty sure not what he used on the Blood well.

Stone opened his mouth again, standing very still except for the twitch of his wings.

My arms shook with fatigue, but Dad kept my hands steady enough to guide the magic pouring out of Stone to wrap with the disk magic Collins set free. The spells wove together, then arced in a lazy whirlwind down into the pure liquid crystal center of the well.

The world shuddered beneath my feet. A thousand drums and gongs all struck at once, crashing with physical force through the air. I couldn't breathe, couldn't scream.

Then everything stilled. The faintest scent of roses hung in the room.

I drew in a harsh breath, heard the others doing the same.

Blood, hot and thick, ran from my nose. I wiped it away with the back of my hand, and blinked until the white stars stopped swimming around in the fuzzy gray mess of my vision. I wanted to puke, but even that would take more energy than I had to spare. At least I was still on my feet.

Is that it? I asked Dad. *Dad?*

There was no response. No sense of him at all.

For the first time in a long, long time, I suddenly wondered if he could die. I mean, I knew he was dead already, but could working magic at this level, through me, kill him?

Dad? I cast out my awareness, searching for the feel of him, the sense of him in my mind.

Finally, a flicker, a slight stirring. He was there, still with me. But not conscious.

". . . out of the way, now." Someone had a hard grip on my arm and was dragging me backward.

That someone was Eli Collins, and we were headed to the base of the stairs where Stone was already rubbing his head against the railing post and grumbling.

"What?" I managed. My throat felt like I'd just gargled with gravel.

"We're getting out of the way. In case."

"In case of what?"

He nodded toward the well.

In case of Shame.

Shame stood at the edge of the well. His back was toward me, but turned just enough that I could see his profile. Terric stood next to him, wearing the Void stones, several more hanging from leather cords in his left hand. His right hand was on Shame's shoulder.

Shame didn't have any Void stones on him. The darkness of magic roiled around him like a storm cloud.

Zayvion stood at Shame's other side, both hands gripping the edges of a Ground spell. He hadn't drawn any magic into the glyph yet, but the interconnecting glyphs of Ground hung quiescent in the air like a woven blanket he could throw on Shame if needed.

Shame visibly took a deep breath, then lifted his chin and held the disk in his left hand as if he were looking into a mirror.

His fingers sliced through a clean, strong Lock spell. The magic from the disk crawled out across the fingers of his left hand, then skipped into his right and filled the glyph he had drawn there.

The well responded, shuttering like a camera lens, the wood floor once again just a wooden floor. The well was closed. Now someone needed to cast the combined spells of Tangle, Rebound, and Refresh.

Terric reached across Shame and took the disk out of his hand, and pressed another disk into it.

Shame hesitated.

Eleanor, who stood right behind both Shame and Terric, put her hand on Shame's other shoulder. I couldn't see what she said, but I saw her nod.

Shame drew the blended glyphs for Rebound, Tangle, and Refresh in quick, sure strokes that fell across the entire room like deep blue tendrils of fog covering the floor with tiny spots of candle flames flickering.

It was beautiful, really, and very well done.

Shame handed Zayvion the spent disk. Zay took it and shook the Grounding spell free, letting it unravel and fade away.

Terric held out the Void stones and Shame put them

all back on with the rhythm of a man sliding prayer beads through his fingers.

They all turned toward me.

Shame was sweating, his color a little high as if he'd just come off a hard workout. Still, he gave me just the slightest quirk of a smile, his eyes burning green.

That boy had not fallen.

Terric looked calm, and incredibly pleased. Maybe even a little relieved.

Shame had always been a hell of a magic user. My dad had once said he was a master of Death magic. Without control, he was also very dangerous. But he'd proven to us, to himself maybe most of all, that he could still make magic his bitch.

And not kill everyone within a three-block radius.

Go, team.

Zayvion met my gaze. Accusing. Angry. A wall of grim and pissed off.

Whoa. Wait. What had I done to make him so angry?

"Let's go," he said.

Collins took one last look around the room as if trying to fix it in his memory, which was probably exactly what he was doing, and then headed up the stairs. Stone was already out of sight.

The thought of hauling up all those damn stairs made me nauseous. No choice. I got moving.

After a dozen steps, Zay jogged up next to me. "You're bleeding."

"Backlash. The spell Dad used wasn't exactly a walk in the park."

"Is your dad making you pay the brunt of the price?"

"I don't think so. He's unconscious, I'm not. I wasn't even sure if he'd survived that last spell."

We walked and I counted stairs by ten, then ten again, then ten again. My thighs were burning. And not in a sexy way.

"I watched you cast the spell," he said.

"Dad . . . cast it."

"Doesn't matter. Magic tore through you."

"Tear seems a little—"

"It's killing you."

And that faint knowledge, that awareness the moment my dad had so very painfully "fixed" me whispered: *yes.*

A chill washed over my skin. *Permanent harm.* I knew he was right.

"When you cast magic, it's killing you." Zay's voice was so very, very calm. "It's draining you. Draining your life."

"I know. Now. Maybe if I don't do much . . ."

"Two more wells," he said.

"We can do it. Dad can." That was all the breath I had. If air were plentiful I might add that I'd watched Dad pulling the magic out of Stone. It was the blend of light and dark magic inside Stone that was kicking our respective mental and physical asses. Back when Dad had first combined the samples from the wells into Stone, he'd also added a little dark magic. I'd never been very tolerant of dark magic. Hell, no one was.

"Maybe Dad can find a way . . . to use magic through me without it having to . . . to harm me."

"No. You're done."

I stopped right there in the middle of the climb. "That's not your call, Zayvion."

He walked back down two stairs toward me and stood so close I could feel the brush of his coat against mine as he leaned down over me. "It is now."

"Really? And who are you going to get to pull the magic out of Stone? You've heard that weird language Dad's using. It isn't even real words. It's something he's made up to trigger magic in a certain way. I've never heard it before. I don't think anyone else has either. There isn't anyone except him who can do this."

"I do not give a single damn," he said. "You are done."

"I'm done when the wells are closed. I'm done when this city is safe. I'm done when I say I'm done."

"That's not how this is going down," he said. "Not this time."

My phone rang. I pulled the phone from my pocket and glared at it. Victor.

"What?"

"Are you safe?" He sounded concerned.

"Yes. The Blood and Life wells are closed." Then to Zayvion, "Walk."

We started up the stairs again.

"Where are you now?" Victor asked.

"Done with Life well. Going to . . ."

"Faith," Zay said.

". . . Faith well next. Ran into Seattle crew outside the Blood well. They didn't survive."

I glanced over my shoulder.

Eleanor's ghost was floating just ahead of Shame, who kept his gaze doggedly on his feet.

"There's one body, um . . . Eleanor Roth's body is in one of the rooms at the inn and needs to be taken care of."

"Oh," Victor said, a little of the air taken out of him. "That is so unfortunate."

That's right. Zay had told me she trained with Maeve. Victor might have known her too. "I'm sorry," I said.

"We will take care of it. I want you all to return to

Kevin's place immediately. Do you understand me, Allison?"

Wow. It had been a while since Victor had ordered me around. Since Zayvion had also decided it was suddenly time to tell me what to do, I found myself not liking it much.

"Why?"

"We just received a report from London. Leander and Isabelle are on the move."

"Where are they?"

"They've left England. They've killed George and Lorraine in Wales, John and Cherie in France, and Alessandro and Anna in Italy."

"Who are those people?"

"Soul Complements. Allie, they're all Soul Complements. Leander and Isabelle are taking out every known Soul Complement pair in the world."

Holy shit. "Are you sure?"

"Yes. Get back here, now. All of you."

"I'll call you . . . when we are on the road."

I turned off the phone.

"What?" Zay asked. He wasn't even out of breath.

Unfair.

"Victor," I said. "Hold on." I kept my air to myself until we got to the platform at the top of the stairs. I leaned on the railing for a good thirty seconds, trying to reacquaint myself with oxygen.

Sure, I'd been running pretty hard lately and paying more than one price for magic, but Zayvion was right. Whatever spells Dad was working through Stone were murder on me. Literally.

"He said Leander and Isabelle are on the move. Said they're killing Soul Complements. Just like they killed Chase and Greyson."

Shame and Terric stepped up on the platform.

"Who else is dead?" Zay asked. "Where?"

I repeated the names Victor had told me. Zay swore softly and tipped his head down, shaking it. He knew those people, the happy faces I'd seen in my dad's memories.

"God," I said, realizing I hadn't handled that announcement with much compassion. "I'm sorry, Zay. Were you friends of theirs?"

He nodded. "I've met them all. They . . . they made me think there was a chance, a life together for Soul Complements. A good life, you know?" He looked up at me, sorrow and pain tugging at his mouth and eyes.

There was no happily ever after for Soul Complements. I'd been told that many times. And these deaths just proved, once again, our future. Shame and Terric's future too.

"Victor wants us to return to Kevin's. Do we go?"

"No," Terric said. "We finish this. We get to the other two wells before anyone can access them. We cleanse magic and close the wells. We make these sacrifices . . . all of them . . . worth it."

"If Victor knows Soul Complements are being killed by the Overseer, so does everyone else in the Authority," Shame said. "Zay, you and Allie are walking targets."

"So are you and Terric," I said.

Shame just shrugged, his gaze on Zayvion alone. "Best way to survive this is to step down, mate," he said. "Keep Allie off the battlefield, keep her safe."

"There is no way I'm staying out of this fight," I said. "I can't, remember? Dad is the only one who can access the magic in Stone."

The Zen mask slipped and Zay looked like he wanted

to pull someone's spine out of their skin. He took a deep breath and composed himself. Calm on the outside, raging in the inside.

"We know all the Soul Complements too," he said. "We have the same list the Overseer has—the same list Leander and Isabelle have. We could get to the Soul Complements before the Overseer. I can open a gate. They wouldn't expect that. We could save them."

"No," Shame and Terric said at the same time.

"When Roman Grimshaw died," Terric said, "Allie said his spirit stepped into a gate to lock down that system of travel, so the Overseer couldn't just open a gate and appear on our doorstep. Even if you can undo what Grimshaw did and open a gate, all it will do is tip our hand. You might be able to save one pair of Soul Complements, but as soon as you opened the next gate, there would be an army of magic users under orders to kill, waiting for you to walk through."

"I agree," I said. "Leaving Portland right now only plays into their hands."

Zay glared at me. "So you think we should hide while Soul Complements, good people, are killed?"

"No," I said. "We need to do something for them. Try to get someone out to help them, or guard them. But not you."

Not us, I thought but didn't say. "Plus, it's not really news that we're targets."

"I'm not," Collins said.

We all ignored him.

"Did Victor say where the Overseer is?" Zay asked.

"No. Just that they, well, she, was out of England and on the move. Which is what we should be. On the move," I clarified. "Is someone opening this door, or am I?"

Zay pushed off the wall he'd been leaning on and

walked past me. I didn't have to touch him to feel his anger. At me. Maybe at this entire situation. At his friends dying. At not being able to attack the problem the way he wanted to.

"So are we going back to Kevin's?" I asked.

"You think someone else can run the gargoyle?" Shame asked.

"No."

"Then we go to the wells," Terric said.

"Fuck." Zay blew the spell he'd been drawing. He took a deep breath, then started another spell to open the door.

"That's new," Shame noted.

Terric frowned at Zay. But Collins, who had been closest to Zay and me on the stairs and had the best chance to hear our recent conversation, just gave me a placid stare.

Asking me without words if I was going to tell Shame and Terric what Zay had confronted me with before Victor called.

"Magic's hurting me," I said, holding Collins' gaze.

He blinked. The low light cast crescent moons on the lenses of his glasses but otherwise didn't show any reaction to my half truth.

"That's not new," Shame said.

"How bad?" Terric asked.

Zay triggered the spell to open the door. He grunted, but held steady so that the glyphs in the air could rotate into position. He was pulling magic in from one of the other wells miles away, since we'd just made sure no one could tap into this well.

It was not easy. Especially if you were distracted. Or angry.

Magic finally responded, rising a little sluggishly into

the spell he'd cast. The door opened and we stepped out onto the concrete path. It was still dark out. We hadn't lost much time.

"Pretty bad," I said to Terric. "I agree that we should hit the next well before heading back to Kevin's. Try to reach both the Faith and Death wells. Then see what we can do for the Soul Complements."

"Victor may have sent someone to help them already," Collins said.

"There isn't anyone else who can help them," Zayvion said.

"Truly? Are you so deluded to think you are the only one who can help a person under attack?" Collins asked.

"From Leander and Isabelle?" Zayvion said. "I am one of the few left who can fight them. They have no qualms breaking the rules of magic. If we're to have a chance against them, we're going to have to break magic to fight them. I can break magic. With Allie. Terric and Shame can too. Because we're Soul Complements."

"So are the people they're killing," Collins noted.

"But I can use dark magic. Other Soul Complements can't."

Collins' eyebrows rose up into his sandy hair. He, apparently, hadn't thought that all through.

We stopped talking and negotiated the pathway down. I needed all the breath I could get anyway. Things were getting suspiciously dark at the edges of my vision, as if I were low on oxygen, or exhausted.

Or dying from magic.

I pushed that thought away because it just made me want to scream in terror. All the screaming in the world wouldn't change anything. I just needed to make it through two more wells and two more spells. Then someone else would have to handle magic.

We reached the base of the falls where the path spread out wide enough to handle the crowds that usually gathered here. Zayvion stormed past me and just kept right on walking toward the car.

"Tantrum much?" Shame asked, coming up beside me, but watching Zayvion. "What did you do to make him so angry?"

"Like I'm the only one screwing up today?"

Shame stiffened just slightly, but didn't go away.

Damn it.

"Blunt," he said, as if sampling wine. "Sharp. Also true. I know my sins, love. What I want to know is why you're suddenly afraid of yours."

I stuffed my hands in my pockets. Even after that hike, I was cold. "He's angry that magic is hurting me."

"The bloody nose back there?" he asked.

"Yes."

"Is that all?"

"Yes."

We walked for a little while, through the train trestle tunnel and to the parking lot.

"When this is all over," he said, "and if we survive, I will teach you how to lie."

"Promise?"

We were at the van now.

"Cross what's left of my heart." Shame pulled the side door open and climbed in, saying no more. Eleanor drifted in beside him, then faded through him to hover near the window. Shame shivered at her passing, but otherwise didn't acknowledge her.

I thought about crawling into the back next to Stone. I didn't want to be so close to Zayvion that I could feel his anger against my skin.

We didn't have time for his anger. We didn't have

time for my fear. What we had time for was trying to get the cure to the wells so the people in the hospitals infected with the poison—and all the people in Portland—might be safe when they used magic again.

If we could keep magic shut down, we could keep Leander and Isabelle from tapping into the wells to fight us.

Not that I had a plan for how to actually fight Leander and Isabelle without magic. At this point I think a few dozen snipers with high-powered rifles might not be out of the question.

Terric pressed his fingers gently on the center of my back. "Go ahead and get in, Allie," he said softly. "We got you."

Then he was past me, climbing into the van next to Shame. Collins had already wedged himself in the backseat next to Stone.

Not liking the idea of getting so lost in my thoughts I wasn't paying attention to what was going on around me. I took a deep breath and wiped at my eyes, then opened the door and got into the front seat.

Chapter Twelve

Zay took the road at speed. The Faith well was clear across town on the west side. We had a half-hour drive time at least, if we were obeying the speed limits. I thought Zay was going to do it in fifteen minutes.

My phone rang.

I dug it out of my pocket past my seat belt, trying not to watch the cars that Zay wove in and out of, leaving millimeters between paint jobs.

"Beckstrom," I said.

"Where the hell are you?" Davy asked.

"Headed to the Japanese Gardens. Where are you?"

"There now. Allie, I know you told us not to get involved, not to engage, but they are killing anyone who gets in their way."

"Don't get in their way."

"We aren't, but other people are. We won't stand aside and watch people die. Sorry, boss. All bets are off. We're going to stop them. Any way we can."

He hung up.

"Damn it."

"Who was it?" Terric asked.

"Davy. He said the Seattle crew is at the Japanese Gardens killing anyone who gets in their way."

If they were at the Gardens, they were just steps away

from the Faith well, which was somewhere in the house built underneath the gardens—a house that used to be, and maybe still was, Victor's home.

Zayvion floored it and rocketed through traffic, weaving through lanes.

My heart was beating too fast and the sword on my back dug against my spine and ribs as Zay narrowly missed every damn thing on the road ahead of us.

I stopped counting near misses. Stopped counting how much time we had left before Davy and the Hounds would be dead.

Instead, I took several deep breaths and let them out. What I needed was focus. We were hurtling toward a fight. I'd either have to use magic to defend myself or I'd have to use magic to purify the well.

Either way, I wanted to do what I could to make sure magic didn't knock the crap out of me again. Being calm and centered before using spells was Magic 101.

Dad, I thought, *are you there?*

Nothing. Not even that stir of his awareness.

I took a deep breath again, two. Tried again.

Dad. I need you to wake up. We need you to use magic. To help us purify the wells. You're the only one who knows which spells to use on Stone.

At the mention of Stone's name, I felt the slightest movement, as if he were trying to drag himself up out of a deep sleep.

Or a coma.

Dad, we need you. Stone needs you. I need you. Hey, I figured flattery couldn't hurt. Plus, we did need him.

"We're here," Zayvion said, turning a hard corner into the parking lot. "Shame, Terric, keep the Void stones on," he said. "I don't care if you use magic to fight, but if you suck the life out of anyone here—especially us—I will find a way to fuck you up from the other side of the grave."

Wow. Guess who had woken up on the wrong side of the battlefield today?

"Wait here," he ordered.

Zay swung out of the van, slamming the door behind him. I never had been very good at taking orders. I got out of the van too, but instead of storming off, which frankly, I was not up to, I leaned against the front bumper, assessing the mess we'd gotten ourselves into.

The Faith well was deep beneath the Japanese Gardens through underground tunnels that were locked down as tight as Fort Knox. This parking area, however, was open to the public. If Seattle had been stopped, this would be the logical place.

I didn't see the Hounds anywhere. I didn't see anyone from Seattle either.

Zayvion hadn't stormed off far. He scanned the hillside.

"No one," he said, heading back to the van. "They must be down at the well."

We got back in the van and raced down the hard-to-see road that led to what looked like a garage, but was actually the access point for the tunnels that would open to Victor's underground home, and somewhere beyond that, the Faith well.

Zay parked in the garage area and we all piled out and jogged to the first door, which was blown open and sagging on its hinges. The air stank of stale magic.

No one said anything. We ran down the next well-lit tunnel that seemed to stretch on forever.

My side hurt. My head hurt. In through the nose, out through the mouth. When was this tunnel going to end?

We heard the fighting before the open door was in

sight. Zay tossed one of the disks to Shame, another to Terric. I expected him to give me one. Waited.

"Zay?" I panted. "Disk?"

Nothing.

Oh, do not make me tackle you, Jones.

He stopped next to the door, up against the wall so he could look around it and through the second set of doors, which led to Victor's home.

He glanced through the door.

"Shame, Terric, I want you to use Shield and Block. No attack spells. Collins, you and I hit them from two sides. I'll take the right, you take the left."

What? Wasn't I good enough to be a part of this little plan? It occurred to me that Zayvion and I might be experiencing some difficulty in communicating.

I stopped beside him, but couldn't see past him to the other room. I could hear the fight going on in there. "Do you want this well purified?" I said with the breath I had left. "Give me a disk."

"No." Zay pushed off of the wall and pivoted toward the room.

That was so not how this was going down.

I pushed in front of him, blocking his route into the room, and yes, putting myself in direct line of fire.

"You don't make that decision." I held out my hand.

Zay wrapped his hand around my wrist and yanked me toward him.

I lost what air I had left slamming against his chest, back in the hall and out of line of fire as he spun to put me against the wall, his body between me and the fight in the other room.

"Can't you hear me?" He was as close to desperate as I'd seen him. "Magic is killing you. *Killing* you, Allie."

I could feel the pain and fear behind those words as if

they were my own. I knew he wanted to protect me. I knew he didn't want me hurt.

"This is a war," I said. "In my city, hurting my people. I can't stand on the sidelines while other people fight it."

For a moment, for longer than that, he held me, searching my eyes for mercy. Only I had none. Not for myself. Not for him. Not for us.

I held out my other hand. "Give me the disk, Zay. Just one spell."

The shattered look in his eyes nearly broke me, but I tipped my chin up a little, bearing the weight of our pain.

"One spell." He drew the disk out of the bag. "God. Just one. Please, Allie."

I nodded. "That's probably all I'm good for. I can do this. I promise. Go."

I didn't want to think about the Death well that still had to be closed. Couldn't worry about how I would survive that until I survived this.

I stuffed the disk in my coat pocket and stepped out of the way to draw my knife.

Zay looked at the others.

Terric and Shame had taken off all of the Void stones except for a single necklace they each wore against their chests. Collins had that open-mouth grin he always got when he sensed a chance for violence and pain.

"Keep it tight," Zay said. "Let's shut this down."

Terric and Shame strode into the room, shoulder to shoulder, magic crackling like caught lightning against Terric's fingers and burning black flames from Shame's. The Faith well wasn't closed yet, so it was easy to draw on the magic here.

Shield burst into the room in front of them, arcing to the ceiling and slamming down behind me.

Victor's once elegantly decorated home was in

shambles. I took a quick head count. Davy, Jack, Maeve, Sunny, and other members of the Authority were on the left side of the room, casting magic, while twenty or so people I did not recognize—the Seattle crew—were on the right side, casting magic.

Outnumbered two to one.

We had to get across the room to the short hallway and door beyond to reach the well.

Zay and Collins were on Shame and Terric's heels. They threw Impact, slicing through the Shield to strike at Seattle's crew. Collins' spells seemed to come with greater effort, while Zayvion handled magic with calm and deadly ease.

Strobe flashes of magic ricocheted around the room, blinding and confusing my vision.

A flash: brief images of people fighting. Darkness: nothing but chanting and yelling and screams filling the air.

Stone, beside me, grumbled and glowed.

The room burned with red light. The Seattle people all used magic, and were wrapped in the strongest Shield spells I'd ever seen.

Thick darkness burned my throat and collapsed my sight again.

Shame and Terric chanted just ahead of us. Magic, gold white, stained green and violet-black, rolled out at our feet, lighting the room, and taking the hard edges off both the darkness and light.

Shame and Terric were walking right down the middle of the room and had made it about a quarter of the way across it. Zay and Collins threw Hold, Freeze, Stun. Things to knock people out, knock them off their feet. Hopefully things that could get through those Shields Seattle held. Hopefully things that would end this fight.

There was no way we'd be able to purify the well in the middle of a war zone.

I didn't even know where the well was in this structure. I'd been only in the main room, and then in that little closet where Victor and Shame and Zay had done their best to wrap Dad up in my head so he couldn't use me anymore.

Which hadn't worked for long. Obviously.

Although, right now, I wished Dad were a little more involved in what was going on.

Dad, I thought. *You have to wake up. Now.* I mentally reached out for him, aiming for those parts of my head that felt "Dad" and dragging them closer to the parts that felt "me."

I must have hit something right. He jolted awake in my head, and was suddenly standing next to me like I'd just dragged him out of sleep by his heels.

Allison?

Do you know where the Faith well is?

Even so obviously fatigued, Dad still had the sense to check his surroundings. Well, my surroundings.

There is a room. A small room with four doors.

I remember.

It is through that room.

Everyone around me seemed to be moving in slow motion. I didn't know if one of the spells Zay and Collins had cast was doing that, or if my perception of reality was that far off.

My heart beat too loudly in my ears. I could taste the magic in the air. It stung my nose and bit at my skin, as if a thousand tiny needles were being thrown at me.

Magic skittered off the Shield around us. We'd made it halfway across the room. Three quarters of the way.

Zay and Collins finally, finally, blew through Seattle's Shields.

The Hounds, Authority, and my friends hit the people from Seattle with everything they had.

Even wrapped in the Shield Terric and Shame were supporting, I hissed at the sudden pain of magic colliding with magic. Too many people. Too much magic. In too small a space.

I wanted to run, wanted to get out under an open sky where I could think, where I could breathe, where I could inhale without so many people and so much magic pressing in on me. Claustrophobia slowed my feet, threatened to freeze me in place.

Zayvion spun on his heel and wrapped his arm around me even while still walking, like a dancer moving to an unheard song, his steps locked with mine, guiding me forward, as he walked backward, his gaze on me, and only me, across the room.

Telling me we could do this. Telling me I could do this.

The sky opened above me, blue and clear and endless. Air surrounded me, like his arms, and sunlight warmed me, like the heat of his body.

I didn't know if it was a spell or just his presence giving me that comfort, that illusion, that memory of a soft summer day with endless horizons.

But I held on to it. I wanted that sky, that air, that space.

I think it was him, just him, holding between me and the magic around us, giving me space, giving me what I needed so I could get through this. So I could stand strong when all the world was falling around me.

"The well," he said, or maybe thought. It was hard to tell over the strangely muted sounds of the fight, of the curses and litany of spells all around us.

"Only one spell," he said.

And then he was gone. His heat, his strength, his steady hand. And all the blue of my sky.

But that respite he had given me had been enough. I no longer felt like I was trapped, boxed in, suffocating. I felt like I was going to get this done so we could get out of here.

We jogged the last few paces across the living room and down the slightly curving hallway to the little room.

I didn't like that little room. Painful things had happened to me there.

Right now, I didn't have time to care about that either.

Shame kicked the door, then stumbled back, hopping on one foot. "Son of a bitch!"

Terric tried the handle, then rammed his shoulder into the door, which burst open. We rushed in, then through the opposite door to another space. Zay took point and Collins lingered behind, walking backward and talking to himself—no, reciting a poem . . . "The Raven" by Poe; I realized he'd been reciting it during the entire fight—watching our backs.

The room with the Faith well was fairly small. It didn't have a high arcing ceiling like the other well rooms. It was a solidly built space, with wooden walls carved in a scattering of symbols, beautiful in their simplicity. It was serene here, a place suited for meditation. There were even lit candles burning in a row on the low shelves built across each wall.

In the center of the room was the well. It didn't appear to be closed . . . which was good news as far as I was concerned.

But then I looked at it again and realized there was a finely etched glass floor worked over much of the center of the room and directly over the well. Magic shifted, flickering in tones of blue and gold and setting opalescent fire to the glyphs in the glass above it.

"It's . . ." Beautiful didn't seem like enough. "Amazing," I finally said.

No one was paying any attention to me.

"Drop the Shield." Zay's voice was a crack of command.

Shame and Terric stopped chanting and took a step away from each other, then another step, in synch, fingers stretching to the floor, releasing the magic they had used back into the well.

The Shield fell around us like gossamer threads, collecting in a wispy pile at our feet and ankles, before melting into the floor.

"Shame, open the damn thing," Zay said. "Terric, close it. Allie, one spell. One." He held up his finger just in case I'd forgotten how much one was.

"Collins," Zayvion said, "watch them. Ground them. Hell, knock them all out if you have to. Keep them safe."

"You have my word," Collins said.

Then Zay started toward the door we'd just come through.

"Wait," I said. "Where are you going?"

"We're in the middle of a war," he said. "I'm not going to stand by and watch my people die either."

He jogged out of the room.

Past me.

Gone.

No.

I couldn't do this without him.

Yes, Dad said, sounding a whole lot stronger and clearer than just moments before. *You can. And so can I. We play our part, or his sacrifice will be for naught.*

Sacrifice? The hell he's going to sacrifice anything.

I tramped toward the door. Then my feet weren't working. I was standing very, very still. I was no longer in control of my body. Dad was.

We all play our part, Allison. From the moment we take our first breath, and until the day of our last exhalation. Our part, your part, is to stay here. With me. With Stone. To purify the well. To use that single spell to the best of our ability. Then we'll let fate fall where it may.

Shame was finishing the Open spell. The glass floor cracked like ice, each of the glyphs smoking and heating and burning outward until the glass appeared to have melted back out of the way so that the well was there, open, accessible. It wasn't nearly as dark as the other wells.

Maybe setting the purification spells in the other wells was making a difference. Or maybe this well hadn't been as tainted as the others.

I still wanted to go to Zay. I could hear the cries and his commands over the voices of the other people out there.

But I didn't go to him. Instead, I did what my father said. I turned my back on my lover and set myself to the job at hand.

Chapter Thirteen

"Done," Shame panted. Tendrils of smoke rose from the disk in his hand. The dark magic around him reached toward the well with hungry fingers, snapping back before actually touching it.

Shame turned his back on the well with what looked like effort and walked the very narrow glass path that spun out like a crystal brick road over the well to where the rest of us stood against one wall on a wide band of solid wood.

He fixed me with a look. Not a lot of green in that gaze. Just hungry, dangerous blackness. He licked his lips and smiled. "Your turn, Beckstrom."

I glanced around for Stone. He was pacing behind us nearest the wall, wings up, head down. Snarling at the sounds of the fight in the other room.

"Stone," I called.

He came to me.

Collins took a step forward too.

"I don't think there's room for all of us on that path," I said.

Collins' eyes narrowed behind his glasses. He nodded once. "I can cast from here."

Stone walked behind me as I took the glass path.

I'm not afraid of heights. However, the path was only

about a foot wide, made of glass, and the well swirling beneath me was something that Shame had once told me would kill me fast if I ever fell in.

Who designed this thing?

It's an older approach, Dad said. *Originally capped by interlocking wooden boards that could be moved by pulley. That was destroyed in a fire. An artist in the industrial age replaced it with glass and lead. He was experimenting with art, magic, and the possibility of creating a public feed from the well, much like the networks we now have.*

Wow, ask a question and get a history lesson.

The path seemed to be getting narrower the closer I came to the center of the room.

It doesn't, Dad said. *But you are close enough.*

Good, because I was starting to remember that I completely sucked at the balance beam back in grade school.

Be careful, I said to Dad, *but make it fast.*

I will make it right, Allison. No matter how long that takes.

He stood beside me at the front of my mind. Even though neither of us were physical in any real manner in my head, I got the sense that if he'd been physical, he'd look like he'd just been hit by a bus. I sensed pain, breaks, and bruises from him.

One of the things about sharing a mind with someone was that they pretty much knew what you knew. He felt my awareness of his pain. Then that pain was gone, replaced by a convincing illusion of him standing strong, perhaps bored, but plenty able to handle magic.

You don't have to put on a show for me, I said. *I know what magic is doing to us.*

Did I raise you to give up so easily?

I'm not giving up. I'm stating the facts.

You don't have the facts, Allison. Not all of them. Not enough of them. And I would appreciate it if you were quiet so I could concentrate on this spell.

Had he just told me to shut up? In my own head?

I hated being possessed.

But I kept my opinion to myself.

"Begin, Eli," Dad said. "Faith magic, of course."

Collins got busy with drawing on the disk in his hand.

Dad called the magic out of Stone.

Me? I kept myself distracted by trying not to scream in agony.

A new spell and new glyphs burned to life across Stone's body.

Maybe it was pretty. I couldn't tell. Couldn't even hear Dad anymore. I was surrounded by pain.

I wanted out of my body. Out of my head. Dad could have it. Have my brain and body if he would make the pain end.

I couldn't see, couldn't hear, couldn't feel anything but the pain. I didn't know if Dad had finished the spell and combined it with the magic from the disk or if he had just begun casting. I didn't know if I was standing anymore.

It felt like I was falling.

Everything went black.

Allison! Dad yelled, his voice a slap across my mind.

I opened my eyes.

Holy shit. I was falling, backward, tipping off the path. I reached out to catch myself but was too slow.

I felt that sickening slip of solid ground pulling away from my boots.

And then two rock-hard hands grabbed under my arms and yanked on me. Hard.

It took me a second or three, longer than I'd like to

admit, to figure out what the hell was happening. The room seemed to be swaying as it fell away from me. The ceiling was getting awfully close.

A grumble over my shoulder, and I finally put two and two together.

Stone had caught me. Stone's hands were under my arms, lifting me up, flying me back away from the well.

"Good boy," I said, or tried to say. I think all that came out was a croak.

I felt scorched. Burned from the inside out. Sick. Exhausted.

I closed my eyes. Just for a minute . . .

"Oxygen," Collins yelled.

. . . of sweet . . .

"Breathe," Zayvion said.

. . . sweet . . .

Allison? Dad said.

. . . sleep.

"Allie." Zayvion again. "Wake up."

I opened my eyes, suddenly awake. Very awake. I was lying on my back, somewhere dark. Zay's face was so near mine I could make out the lines at the corners of his eyes when he smiled.

"God," he exhaled. He closed his eyes and swallowed hard, as if he'd just been screaming, or crying.

"She's okay," Collins said.

I hated to break it to the good doctor, but I didn't think he knew what he was talking about. I wasn't even in the same zip code as okay. Everything hurt, like whoa.

"Let's see if she can sit," he continued. "Then we can go."

"I can," I started. Okay, wow. Just those two words took a lot of effort.

This was ridiculous. I hadn't done anything out of

the ordinary. One little spell couldn't knock me out. Could it?

Permanent Damage.

"Ready?" Zay asked me. His voice was calm; so was his expression. I couldn't tell if he was angry, pleased, or, well . . . anything. Even though his hand was on my arm, I didn't sense anything from him.

I nodded. With Zay's help, I sat. The world did one circle on the merry-go-round, and then everything was solid, set. Normal.

"I'm good," I said, even though I was shaking and weak. "Help me up."

Zayvion did me one better than that. He scooped me up like I didn't weigh a pound and started walking.

I didn't know where we were going. Hell, I didn't know where we were, though from the smell of all the magic, I'd say we were still at the Faith well.

I suppose I could get all tough and tell him I could walk, to put me down, and all that. But I didn't think I could walk. And even though I felt sort of stupid having him cart me around like an armful of kindling, I decided to take this chance to get my head together.

Using magic hadn't just been painful. It had been incapacitating.

So, that was bad.

"Did Terric close the well?" I asked.

"Yes." Man was not in a talking mood.

"Seattle?"

"Closing the well broke their hold. They had no magic to pull upon. Then we . . . restrained them in a more conventional manner."

"How many are dead?"

"None."

That didn't seem likely. There had been a hell of a lot of magic thrown around in that room.

"I wouldn't lie to you."

So that whole he-could-tell-what-I-was-thinking, I-could-tell-what-he-was-thinking thing was working again. Nifty.

"I want to walk," I said.

He took six more strides before finally stopping, then very gently lowered me so that my feet touched the ground.

Surprisingly, my knees held. "I got it," I said.

Zay shifted and kept hold of my elbow. I took a look around. Garage. Van not far off. Good. "Any news on Leander and Isabelle?"

"Some," Victor said.

I jerked. Suddenly, the rest of the world seemed to come into focus. It wasn't just Zay and me walking toward the van. And there wasn't just the van parked here.

Six other vehicles, including Detective Stott's big white box van, were parked, doors open, people standing beside them, police lights spreading blue and red across the ceiling and walls.

People were getting into those cars. Some with police escorts who had guns strapped at their hips — when had we called the police? Others, people I knew — my Hounds Jack, Bea, Jamar — and members of the Authority — Carl, La, Sunny, Kevin. More people and faces I didn't have names for, helping to make sure the people from Seattle were handcuffed and seated in the vehicles.

A lot of those people I'd seen at the meeting at Kevin's place.

"How long was I out?"

"About a half an hour," Victor said. "Dr. Collins

recommended we let you come up out of the faint without magical assistance."

"Faint? I did not faint."

Victor was walking just slightly ahead of me. "Unconsciousness," he corrected with a nod. "He tells me you are having difficulty with your father using magic through you."

I glanced back at Collins. So he hadn't told him that magic was killing me. And from the slight tightening of Zay's fingers on my arm, I guessed he hadn't said anything either.

Why didn't they want him to know? Did they think Victor would be able to stop me, or rather, stop Dad from using the magic to purify the last well?

"It's more painful than before. But we only have one well left to cleanse. We can do that. Have you heard anything more about Leander and Isabelle?"

We were at the van now, and Grace appeared from across the garage. That's when I realized Victor had been walking without her help.

"Can you see?" I asked.

He shook his head. "No more than before. Just variations of light and darkness. But I have lived here for years. I could walk it blindfolded. As for my news, we have received reports that the Overseer landed in New York. Unfortunately, we also received news that Hector and Chloe were found dead."

"Were they Soul Complements?" I asked, already knowing the answer.

"Yes."

"Where do the other Soul Complements live?"

"Chicago, Atlanta, and San Diego."

"Have you alerted people there? Have you contacted

the Soul Complements and told them to get out of
there?"

"Yes," he said, his voice soft. "We have called. They
don't believe us. The last person I spoke with accused us
of setting up these rumors of poisoned magic and possession to frame the Overseer. It's . . . horrifying how
little we can do."

"Who can open gates?" I asked. I was still tired as
hell, but wanted to do something for these people. There
had to be a happy ending for Soul Complements in this
world. If it wasn't going to be Zay and me—and considering how much hell magic was putting me through, our
luck was running thin—then it damn well better be someone out there.

Terric and Shame strode off, putting distance between themselves and everyone else. They looked
strained. Uncomfortable. They hadn't started growing
anything or killing anything or fighting each other. But I
didn't have the highest hopes of them getting through
this in one piece either.

Eleanor paced between them, her arms crossed over
her chest, occasionally pausing to say something to
Shame I couldn't make out.

"Any Guardian of the gate can open a gate," Zay said.

"Is there one Guardian in each city?" I asked.

"If there's a well in a city, there's a Guardian."

"So, yes?"

"Yes," Victor said.

"Do you know the Guardians?" I asked Zay. "Is there
some kind of club or yearly get-together where Guardians get drunk, wear funny hats, and compare war stories?"

Stone sat next to me and leaned against my leg and

hip, which helped me stay on my feet. I put one hand on his shoulder for stability.

"We don't gather," Zay said, "but over the years I've crossed paths with several Guardians. Why?"

"Because we need someone who can open gates to where the remaining Soul Complements are, and somehow remove them from the playing field. Knock them out, tie them up, drug them if necessary. And then hide the hell out of them so Leander and Isabelle will come here while we have people left to fight them."

Zay was silent, thinking.

Victor just shook his head. "There isn't anyone who believes us, Allie. Not even the Guardians."

"I'll do it," Collins said.

Zay's head jerked up and he leveled a piercing gaze at Collins, who was leaning on the front bumper of the van.

Collins lifted his hands and gave Zayvion a disarming smile that did nothing to disarm him.

"I'm not a Guardian of the gate," Collins said, "never have been. But I've opened gates and have done some . . . experimenting with technology that should allow me to nail my arrival point."

"Let me guess," I said. "It's something you were working on with my dad."

"No, although my time with him was part of what led me to begin the research. It was something even you weren't able to Close from me, Victor."

Victor and Zayvion had mirrored expressions—very carefully Zen. Which was really their go-to cover for when they were pissed as hell.

They didn't like this idea. Didn't like putting the safety of Soul Complements in the hands of Collins the

Cutter. But it was the best plan we had. No, it was the only plan we had.

"Yes," I said.

"Excellent." Collins said. "Am I to assume I am free to use any method necessary to see to their concealment and safety?"

"You are to keep them safe," I said, "from Leander and Isabelle and anyone else who wants them dead. But you are not to do them any permanent physical, mental, emotional, or magical harm. Understand?"

"Perfectly," he said. "I will need the list of names and addresses if you have them, Victor."

"Allie," Victor finally said. "You can't trust him with this."

"When my choices are to do nothing and know that people will be slaughtered, or send Collins to try to hide them, I'm going to send Collins. Even though I don't exactly trust him—no offense—"

"None taken," he accepted.

"—I trust he knows that if he fails in this mission, I will personally tear this planet apart and boil him alive in his own skin."

That got a smile out of Collins, his eyes alight with way too much interest. "I would relish the day that you, Allison Beckstrom, could actually be pushed to such extremes."

"If she won't," Zay rumbled, "I will. No push necessary."

Collins pursed his lips and nodded. I didn't care who he thought would kick his ass to the ends of the earth, just as long as he believed we were serious about him working with, not against, us.

"Anyway, you aren't going alone," I said.

He tipped his chin to the side. "I think that's a bad idea."

"Good," I said. Then I yelled, "Davy?"

Collins lost his smile and the twinkle in his eye became a hard light.

"I think that's a *very* bad idea," he said.

Davy strolled over to us. Davy was infected with the poisoned magic. To keep it from killing him, Collins had carved several spells into his skin and forced magic to follow those paths out of Davy's body.

It had saved Davy's life. But in doing so, those spells had pulled him away from living and so close to death that Davy was not quite alive or dead. When he didn't concentrate, he went insubstantial. He ghosted out. That was the bad side effect of Dr. Collins the Cutter's not-so-gentle administrations.

The good side effect was that when Davy used magic, he was a frickin' demon. He could absorb magic thrown at him, and then use it on the caster with vicious, whip-like accuracy. I figured he could give even the good doctor a run for his money when it came to magic.

On the outside, Davy didn't look any the worse for wear: still a twenty-ish guy I mostly thought of as a little brother. I'd just seen him in the middle of that fight, half ghost and using enough magic to knock out an elephant.

Sunny was at his side, a hair band in her teeth as she combed her fingers through her jet black hair and gathered it up in a ponytail.

"Boss," Davy said, reading the situation with the speed and accuracy of a Hound. "Where do you need me?"

"I want you and Sunny to go with Collins. He says he has tech that will open gates and take him, and the both of you, across the country."

"And what are we doing there?"

"You're gathering up Soul Complements, people who use magic like Zay and I, and you are taking them to some place safe."

"Is it dangerous?"

"Very."

"Does Collins want me along for the ride?"

"Not at all."

Davy grinned. "Well, then. This sounds like fun."

"Victor, please give Davy and Sunny the Soul Complement list, and then send someone . . . capable to collect Collins' technology."

"We'll go with him to get it," Sunny said. "C'mon, Dr. Collins. I'll drive."

"You'll put them at risk?" Collins asked me. "Put them in the path of Leander and Isabelle?"

"I will send them to make sure you and the Soul Complements stay alive. They can handle the risks."

Collins shook his head. He didn't look angry, just frustrated. "We may not come back from this," he said.

"*You* might not," Davy said with a chuckle, "but I sure as hell am. That all, boss?"

I nodded. "Please—"

"Yes, I'll be careful. And we'll make sure the job gets done."

"I know you will." I gave him a smile, and he and Sunny started off toward Sunny's car.

Collins pushed away from the van, but before walking off, he said, "I'll need to use the Death well to power the first gate. Don't close it until I get free of Portland, okay?"

"Meet us out there," Zay said. "At the Death well. That way we'll be sure all of you get off safely."

Collins took off his glasses and polished them on the

edge of his shirt. "Of course. I'll be there in just under an hour."

"Do you remember where the Death well is?" Victor asked.

"As a matter of fact, Victor, I do." Collins put his glasses back on, and walked off to Sunny's car.

Victor carefully rubbed at the bridge of his nose. "I didn't give him those memories back."

"Do you think he does know where the Death well is?" I asked.

"If he worked with your father and has some kind of access to his research, yes."

"Well, that's working in our favor for a change," I said.

"Allie." Detective Stotts, in his usual trench coat and scarf, strode across the garage, stopping in front of me. I caught the orange spice of his cologne. "Are you all right?"

"Sure," I said, trying out a smile. "I'm good. Do I need to handle anything else with the people from Seattle being arrested? You are arresting them, aren't you?"

"I most certainly am. Breaking and entering to begin with, using magic with intent to harm, then every other charge I can think of. They will stay securely behind bars for a few days. Have you had any luck with cleansing the wells?"

"There's only one left to go," I said with a confidence I did not feel. "Shouldn't be a problem. Do you have everyone in place in case more people are coming down from Seattle?"

"We do. Seattle, LA, or anywhere else. They'll never get past the airports or across the borders without us detaining them. We've made the city as safe, prepared, and as aware as we can be."

His eyes narrowed a little in concern. "Nola's worried about you. She gave me this, in case I saw you."

He reached in his coat pocket and pulled out a chocolate chip cookie covered in plastic wrap. He handed me the cookie.

I glanced down at it. She had arranged the chocolate chips in the shape of a smiley face.

I couldn't help but laugh a little. "Is she okay?" I asked.

He nodded. "Worried."

"If you see her before I do, tell her I'm fine."

"I'll do that," he said.

He hesitated, then looked down at the pavement before deciding something and looking back up at me.

"In case I haven't said it, I'm sorry, Allie. For not believing you when you first came to me and told me about the things going on with magic, and the people working behind it all. For a man who has spent most of his career trying to track down illegal magic, and trusting Hounds to help him do so, it took me far too long to believe in you."

"It's okay," I said faintly. "It is a little hard to believe."

"I should have listened. I trust you, Allie. And when this is done, I hope we can be friends."

"I think that's a good idea. Especially if you're marrying my best friend."

That caught him by such surprise, he took a step backward. Then a huge grin spread across his face. "Well. Then we're definitely going to become friends."

"Good," I said.

"Detective!" someone called from across the garage.

"If you need me," he said, already walking away, "call. Anytime."

I would have responded, but my second wind was so

depleted, my vision was starting to go a little foggy at the edges.

"So," I said to Victor and Zay. "All that's left is purifying and locking the Death well. Hurray."

"And to deal with Leander and Isabelle if they arrive," Victor added.

"Oh, I'm sure they will," I said. "We'll have to take them down without magic. I'm thinking SWAT team, fire hoses and Tasers. Can I please sit down now?"

Zayvion moved past me to the van and opened the side door so I could get in. I crawled in, and lay across the middle seat. Stone hopped in after me and rubbed his head on my thigh. I scratched between his ears. "You're a good boy, Stone. You saved me from falling. Good job."

He flicked his ears up and burbled happily, then trotted around to the backseat.

"Shall I look into the assault forces at our command?" Victor asked.

"Yes. I know it's two powerful magic users possessing one body, but without magic, it's only one human, mortal body. If we can restrain her, or hell, shoot her with a tranquilizer dart, we might have a chance to make them unpossess her body."

"Even incorporeal, they are powerful," he said.

"I know. That's why Zay and I and Shame and Terric are going to throw them back into death."

"With magic?"

I nodded, then rubbed at my eyes, unable to keep them open any longer. Sweet hells, I was tired. "After we cleanse the wells, we'll have three disks left. They don't know that, don't know about the disks. We should be able to tap that magic, and use it to open a gate to death, bind them, and kick them over the threshold and into death where they belong."

I yawned and unwrapped my cookie. "How's that sound?"

"Brilliant," Victor said from a soft distance.

I took a bite of the cookie and closed my eyes. Sugar, butter, vanilla, with just a hint of toasty brown sugar, and pockets of deep, rich chocolate. Heaven. Nola should worry more often.

"I had my doubts on closing down magic," Victor was saying, "but I think it might be just enough to throw them off, limit their abilities, and give us the upper hand. You're doing very well with this leadership role, Allison."

"Yay, me," I mumbled. "Someone wake me up when we get to the Death well, okay?" I didn't even hear an answer, or get another bite of cookie, before I fell into a deep sleep.

Chapter Fourteen

"How many do you see?" Zayvion asked.

"What's more than a swarm?" Shame said.

"A mob?" Terric suggested.

"No, like if a girl mob met a boy mob and then they decided to repopulate the earth with billions of baby mobs, how many is that?"

"Too many," Zay said. "Are we talking thousands?"

There was a pause, then from Shame, "Yes." And that was his serious voice.

"We go in anyway," Zay said.

"Not without a plan we don't."

"Damn," Terric said.

"What?"

"You, Flynn? Planning? Now I believe it's the end of the world."

"We could always tell Collins to stroll out there and crank up his gate-making gizmo. See what happens," Shame said. "I bet they would find it very interesting."

"He is not expendable," Zay said. "Yet. And Davy and Sunny would be injured."

"Well, we could warn *them*," Shame said.

"I just don't see how, Zayvion," Terric said.

"Maybe a Grounding spell?" Zay suggested.

"For that many?" Terric paused a second. "No. At best you'd knock yourself out."

Okay, that was enough of that. I had no idea what they were talking about. And since they were also talking too loudly for me to ignore, I opened my eyes.

I was in the van, in the same position I'd fallen asleep in, the cookie clutched tightly in my hand.

The engine was not running. Hadn't we left yet?

"What are you talking about?" I muttered.

"Veiled," Shame supplied. "A fuckload of them."

"Fuckload is good," Terric said.

"Shame says the grounds are covered in Veiled," Zay said.

"What grounds? Tell me someone has coffee."

"We did not take the time to stop for your latte, your highness," Shame said. "And we're at the cemetery."

I sat up, glanced out the window. It was still night. We were outside the cemetery and inside the van for good reason. There was a fuckload of Veiled beyond that iron-fenced gate.

"It's kind of pretty," I said, wolfing down the rest of my cookie.

Shame was sitting behind me. He leaned forward. "Dead people are pretty? Well, that explains your attraction to the emotionless, stoic types."

Zay, in the front seat, just shook his head.

"Maybe you don't see them the way I do," I said. Then, "Wait. You see them, Shame? Without a Sight spell?"

He inhaled. Thought better of whatever he was going to say, and just said, "Yes."

It must be a side effect of what Death magic had done to him. Of whatever it was he had become.

"Do you see them, Terric?"

"No. Only Shame and you see them. We've agreed it's not worth drawing their attention by casting a Sight spell."

"Good choice," I said. The Veiled were always hungry for magic. We'd closed down every network, every cistern, and almost every well. It only made sense that they'd be here, swarming around the crypt, drinking from the last resource in Portland.

"Do you see thousands?" Terric asked.

"At least a thousand," I said. "It's hard to tell. They're . . . well, I see them as sort of water-colored people shapes. Kind of ghostly, but with holes where their eyes should be and serrated teeth in their mouths."

"Pretty much dead on," Shame said. "And now that we agree on what they look like, we need an idea for getting into that crypt and taking care of the well."

"They'll be drawn to the disks," I said.

Zay shook his head. "Maybe not. They're right here and the Veiled haven't come close to the van."

"So maybe they don't sense the magic in them because the well has more and easier magic to access?" I said.

"A sound theory," Terric said. "Which means they might not even bother us. Until we close the well."

"Will they disappear when we do that?" I asked. "I mean, like ghosts?"

"I don't think it's just magic that keeps them here," Shame said, his voice low, as if dragging old memories out of a long, dark drawer. "They would be here even if there was no magic. But they are hungry. For magic. Or life. Either will sate them."

"Okay," I said, "so here's an idea. We are not going to use magic until we get to the well. Hopefully, they won't be interested in us. We get to the well and open it. I'm sure that will catch their attention, but I don't care if they all dive into it. I'll cast the purification spell. That's when things might get tricky. We'll need to keep them off Stone, and off the magic inside of him. Zay, I want you to open the well. Shame and Terric, you'll deal with the Veiled. Kill them, distract them, hell, make them waltz, just keep them off Stone. Once the well is purified, Zay, I want you to close it."

"What about the Veiled?" Zay asked. "If Shame's right"—he shifted in the seat so he could look back at both of us—"then once the well is closed, the Veiled will turn toward the living and begin draining them."

"Right." I dragged my fingers through my hair, thinking. My hands were shaking a little. "I don't know. Ideas?"

No one said anything.

"Have you asked your father?" Zay asked quietly.

I shook my head. "He's not . . . I don't know. That last spell really took a lot out of him. I don't think he's conscious."

"I think you'd better ask," Shame said. "That's Davy's car over there, isn't it?"

I squinted past the headlights slowly rolling our way. "Yes," I said. "Give me a minute. Don't let them do anything stupid, okay?"

Zay opened the door. "I'll go talk to them."

The cool air gave me chills. I was sweating, not hot, just tired, hurting, and all around uncomfortable. My dad wasn't the only person that last spell had taken a lot out of.

The weaving and shifting colors of the Veiled not far beyond the window was distracting, so I closed my eyes.

Dad, are you awake?

Silence. Then the distinct feeling of pain, but distant, and not my own, rolled through my thoughts. I could almost hear his thoughts as he steeled himself to be conscious, aware, and focused enough to cast magic. He knew he had to pull himself up for this last effort.

It frightened me how difficult that was for him.

Dad? Okay, now I was concerned. I'd never felt him so ragged, so weak in all my life. *Do you need help? Can I help you?*

I . . . Give me a moment, Allison, he said softly. *Just a moment more.*

I'll try, I said. *We don't have a lot of time.*

I opened my eyes.

"Any luck with the old man?" Shame was sitting next to me now, his legs stretched out between the two front seats of the van.

"He's . . . he needs a minute."

Shame's eyebrows lifted. "Really. Your da needs a minute? For what? A shower and a shave?"

"We've all been working hard, Shame," I said. "He's been doing everything we've been doing, only dead and in someone else's brain. If he needs a minute, I'll give him one."

"Maybe you're right, Ter," Shame said. "It is the end of the world. Beckstrom's gone soft on her dear ol' da."

"I'm not soft on him," I said evenly. "But I don't want him to decide to let go and slip into death right when we most need his knowledge."

Terric, in the front seat, nodded. "Were you able to ask him if the Veiled are going to go after people if there's no magic available to them?"

"Not yet."

Zay climbed back into the car and sat sideways—

well, as much as those shoulders of his allowed him to—and looked back at me.

"Davy, Sunny, and Collins will wait for our signal. Collins said the device he's rigged up runs on electricity, and is only triggered by magic. So once it starts, they won't need more magic to fuel it."

"What about Davy?" Shame asked. "Are the Veiled staying away from him?"

Oh, I hadn't thought about that. Davy had magic worked into him. He might look like a very tasty treat to the Veiled.

"None of them approached," Zay said. "Davy can see them too. Very clearly. Allie, what about your dad?"

"I'll check again."

I closed my eyes, blocking out Shame, Zay, and Terric's quiet conversation.

We're out of time, Dad, I said. *We need your help.*

Dad formed next to me, as if he and I were standing together in a dark room. He looked haggard, the lines in his face more pronounced, his bottle-green eyes faded to a thin silver sheen.

However, even here, in the middle of my head, he appeared to be wearing a three-piece suit, his gray hair combed back and neat, his shoulders set square as if he were ready to end the negotiations of a very long business meeting.

Open your eyes, Allison, he said. *I'll be no good to you blind.*

Before we purify the last well, I have a question, I said.

He waited.

We need some way to make sure the Veiled don't attack the living once we close the well. Do you know of any way to get rid of them all at once?

I've never experimented with removing Veiled from the living world. It seems to me, Zayvion would be able to open a gate to death and perhaps force them through, Close them.

Wouldn't that risk letting more Veiled through into life? I asked.

Yes. He was quiet for a moment. *I don't know, Allie. It is not a tested method.*

I had to admit that surprised me. It didn't seem like there was any magical problem we'd faced that Dad didn't have some kind of answer to or plan for.

He could Ground them, he said.

But I'd seen Zay Ground a mob of Veiled before. It had almost knocked him unconscious and that had only been maybe a couple hundred Veiled. There were a thousand out there.

I don't think that's going to work, I said. *Don't you have any other ideas?*

I am not a Death magic user, Allison.

He sounded irritated. So: normal. I couldn't believe I was actually glad to hear that tone of voice, well, *thought* from him.

Why don't you ask Mr. Flynn if he can't do something with them, he said. End of conversation.

I opened my eyes.

"Well?" Shame said.

"Dad said you should do something with them."

"Me?" Shame said. "No. And you may stick a hell no up that no."

"Shame," Zayvion said. "We don't have the luxury of you saying no."

"Fuck you, Jones. I have sworn off interaction with the dead. Permanently."

Eleanor, who was sort of hovering in the seat behind

him, slapped him across the back of the head. Shame twitched.

She started talking again, though I couldn't hear her. I didn't know if Shame could hear her either, though one shoulder hitched up as if he were trying very hard not to turn around and look at her.

"Shame," Terric said. "I think Allie's right. You and I . . . we can take care of the Veiled."

"We? You're no Death magic user," Shame said.

"No, I'm not. But if they want life, I can give them all they want."

"Jesus, have you all gone mental? You're going to feed them?"

"I'm going to keep them away from Stone and the well."

"Good," Zay said opening the door. "It's settled. Let's go."

I didn't think anything had been settled. But Zay was right. The longer we sat in the van arguing, the more chance there was Leander and Isabelle had tracked down another Soul Complement pair.

Terric got out of the car.

Shame reached over for the side door. Eleanor's hand was already there. He hesitated, then gripped the handle and pulled anyway.

"You can see her, can't you?" I asked.

"Who?"

"Eleanor."

Eleanor stopped midrant and slid through the seat and Shame so that she was hovering in front of him.

He shivered at her passing, but didn't look at her. "I don't know what you're talking about."

Eleanor threw up her hands in exasperation.

"Lying won't change anything, Shame."

He took in a deep breath. "I don't want to talk about it. Not . . . I'm not going to talk about it now. I can't," he added in a whisper.

Then he started off toward the cemetery gate. Eleanor gave me a considering look, then nodded and mouthed "thank you." She drifted off after Shame. We might not be able to hear her, but she could hear us and it was clear she was going to remember Shame wasn't the only one who could see her.

Stone cooed.

"You ready for this, Stoney?" He squeezed around from the back of the van and rested his chin on the seat so I could rub his head. I did so. Yes, I was procrastinating. As soon as I got out of this van, I would be only minutes away from having Dad use magic through me again.

The idea of going through that much pain so soon made me want to slip into the driver's seat and drive this van until I ran out of land.

But that wasn't going to happen. We were going to lock magic down. We were going to fight Leander and Isabelle. We were going to save the world.

And if it meant I'd have to go through a little pain for that to happen, so be it.

I shoved at Stone's nose and he rubbed his forehead on my arm. "Come on, you big lug. Let's go be heroes."

Stone clomped out of the van and toward the graveyard.

I walked over to Zayvion, who was still on this side of the open cemetery gate.

"We have a plan?" he asked.

"We go in there, open the well. That will keep the Veiled interested enough that I don't think they'll notice Collins opening the gate."

I glanced over at Collins, who was only a few yards away. He wore a jacket and leather gloves, and was setting up something that looked, at the moment, like a pair of tripods.

Davy was watching. Intently. Probably so he could set the thing up himself if he needed to. Boy was smart that way.

Sunny was keeping an eye on both of them. They had all changed into dark coats and gloves, and were carrying backpacks. Probably supplies they'd need if they had to go into hiding or were on the run.

Not for the first time, my stomach clenched at the thought of throwing Davy and Sunny into the path of Leander and Isabelle with Collins at their side.

"That's it," Collins said.

Davy nodded and shoved his hands in his pockets. He walked over to me. He was frowning, and his shoulders were hitched up against the cold.

"Don't power that thing until Shame and Terric give you the all clear, okay?" I said.

Davy nodded. "Boss? You're not looking too good. There are a hell of a lot of dead people in there. Someone got your back?"

I gave him half a smile. "Zay's got my back. Shame and Terric too. If you get in too deep, if things get too tight, I want you to haul ass for home, you understand me, Silvers?"

"If there's one thing I've found that I colossally suck at, it's dying." He glanced at Sunny, who was keeping close tabs on Collins, then at Collins, who was adjusting a netting of thin silver wires in a circle around the tripods.

"I'll make sure we find our way back. Breathing," he added. "Do not do some damn stupid heroic thing while

I'm gone, okay? Pike would kill me if he found out I left you alone."

"I promise not to do anything heroic—stupid or smart."

Collins dusted his hands together. "We should be going, Mr. Silvers."

"See you soon, Davy," I said.

"See you soon," he said.

There were no good-byes between Hounds, unless it was spoken to a gravestone.

"Shame, Terric," I said. "When Zay opens the well, and when you think we're making enough magical noise to keep the Veiled off Collins and his machine, tell him to fire it up."

"Been thinking." Shame exhaled smoke from his cigarette. "This could be suicide."

"Don't like the odds?" Terric asked.

"Dead people, untested magic, untested technology all stirred up together?" Shame paused and brushed his trembling fingers through his bangs, his bravado broken. A shadow crossed his eyes. Sorrow, or maybe fear. "I'm sure it's all going to work out perfectly," he said softly.

Chapter Fifteen

Zay stepped through the gate and headed down the road that cut the graveyard east and west. I was at his right, and Shame and Terric were at his left. The graveyard was only about the size of a city block, and tucked right in the middle of what were busy streets and bustling businesses during the day.

During the night, with all the spells stripped from the buildings and city, the cemetery glinted like cut obsidian, slices of electric light sliding off the polished edges of tombstones and statuary, shining white on marble carvings, catching deep indigo ink under the branches of tall pines, firs, hollies, and maple trees.

Sliding among the shadow and light were the Veiled. Flashes of watercolors, pastel shades that had once been people and were now shabby opalescent reflections of their lives. Hungry, lost, and restless.

They stirred as we passed, looking our way with empty pits where their eyes should be, mouths open. They were silent. They were always silent. But they did not move toward us, did not follow us.

Almost, I felt as if I were the ghost in their world. Felt that as I walked that long ribbon of gray concrete toward the shadows, this might be a dream. I might wake up and find myself curled in bed next to Zayvion in a world where dead magic users didn't possess their daughter's mind, where friends weren't crippled and mutated by magic, where immortal monsters didn't walk in flesh hunting down Soul Complements and killing them.

But I knew this was not a dream. It was a living nightmare. And it was up to us to make sure the good guys won.

Even if we weren't standing by the end of the fight.

The crypt was off the path, tucked up against several old cedar trees. We'd been here before, well, Shame and Terric and I had been here before. Zay had been in a coma then. We'd closed the Death well, thinking it would stop the spread of Veiled.

Boy, had we been wrong.

"How do we get in?" I asked, eyeing the iron-worked fence that surrounded the crypt. There were so damn many Veiled, I was having a hard time seeing through them to the actual building.

"Let Shame and me handle that." Terric paced back to the middle of the roads that met from east, west, north, and south.

He chanted the words to an old blues song and a flood of gold white light poured out around him.

Along with the light he'd gone super-beautiful. As the magic around him grew, he shifted from beautiful to cold, then alien, burning with power.

The Veiled were suddenly still, caught by his voice, caught by the light and magic. Then they rushed toward him and lapped up the magic that poured from his fingertips and the ground around him like droplets of fiery rain.

Shame threw his cigarette to the dirt, his words carried by smoke. "Get on with it," he said, not looking at me or Zay. "We'll try not to destroy the world while you're gone."

He walked through the Veiled toward Terric. Where Shame passed, the Veiled bowed down on one knee, reaching out hands to catch at the blackness that lashed around him like fire, as if trying to touch the coattails of a god.

Eleanor was there too, but stayed as far away from the Veiled as she could, mouthing, "Careful, careful," over and over.

Shame stopped in front of Terric. "And you say I have suicidal tendencies."

He turned his back on Terric, and Terric turned his back on Shame. Magic rolled to them, leaping to their call, filling Shame's hands with darkness, and Terric's with light. That mesmerizing loop of inhale, and exhale, magic turning from one man's hand to the other, changing from light to darkness, like a pulse of blood between them, caught me so I could not look away.

My eyes closed. *Allison. There is no time.*

Dad. He had closed my eyes. And when I opened them, I was facing the crypt, Shame and Terric behind me.

Shame whistled once, a hard piercing blast. "Fire it!" he yelled.

Magic poured in a ribbon of muted red and black, snaking across the graves, between the trees, to answer Collins' gate device.

We needed to get in that crypt to that well to lock it down.

Zay called on magic and casually blew open the locked fence.

"Allie," he called, holding his hand out for me.

I was walking toward him. I really was. But it was like quicksand up to my ankles. Every step was slower and slower, harder and harder. I was sweating, hurting. This much magic, this close to me, even though the Veiled were no longer covering the crypt quite so thickly, made me feel like I was trying to breathe through a sandstorm.

There wasn't enough air in the air, and there was way too much magic everywhere else.

Zay grabbed my hands and pressed a disk into my palm.

"You got this," he said. His words, his strength, cleared my head a little.

Just enough that I could feel how damn much pain I was in. My skin was on fire. A part of my mind was already screaming. I hurt. Yeah, well, I was going to hurt a lot more by the end of this.

But the well would be purified. The well would be closed. The spread of the poison magic would be stopped. Portland's magic would be shut down. And without magic, Leander and Isabelle would be vulnerable. Killable.

I wanted them killable. More than I wanted to get away from the pain.

"I got this," I said to Zay. "Go. Open it." My words sounded like I was underwater.

Zay pushed the door to the crypt and stepped inside.

I pulled the disk up to my chest, holding it with both hands to make sure I wouldn't drop it. I was having a hard time feeling my fingers.

By the time I walked into the crypt, Zay had already opened the well. I swallowed back a moan as the weight of that magic dug hooks into my flesh.

Dad? I thought. *Ready?*

Yes.

Dad stood beside me in my mind, a steady, powerful

presence that bolstered me. My vision cleared, and so did my mind.

We Beckstroms were determined people when we needed to be. Stubborn as hell too.

Dad said a word or two, and the pain slipped away. It was still there. In one corner of my mind, I was still screaming, but that part of me was so far away, I could no longer feel it.

What I felt was Zayvion on the other side of the crypt, which was ten times as large as it looked from the outside, drawing magic up from the well and throwing it out to the perimeter of the room. He'd set some kind of spell to circle the room and was filling it with so much magic, the Veiled who weren't outside gorging on Shame and Terric were here, gorging on that spell like pigs at a trough.

Which meant that here, inside that circle of protection, the magic was at least a little less concentrated, though it radiated out of the well like a roaring fire.

Dad, or maybe I, walked to the edge of the well. Stone, who had been awfully quiet this whole time, was right there beside me.

I tried to convince myself I could handle this. Too bad most of me knew I was lying.

Stone and I stopped several feet away from the well. Magic was making me a little dizzy—well, a lot dizzy— and I didn't want to accidentally fall in when Dad took over.

Be careful, I told Dad. *I'm not . . . I'm not as steady as I'd like to be.*

I'll be done as quickly as I can.

Don't do it quickly. Do it right.

Always, he promised.

I set my mental feet and let Dad take over. He started

the spell, drawing it with my fingertips and whispering it with my mouth.

Pain rushed at me, crashing down and swallowing me whole. I tried to hold on, to see if Stone responded to Dad's spell, to see if Dad could also trigger the magic out of the disk and get everything all blended up and tossed into the well together.

But I was having a hard time seeing anything, thinking anything. The pain grew stronger and bigger with every syllable Dad spoke, with every line of the glyphs he drew.

Until it was an agony, and there was no escape.

I remembered falling to my knees and wondering why that didn't hurt. I remembered wondering how Dad kept his concentration when the world was tearing apart and magic was ripping holes in me.

He was nothing if not a very determined man.

Darkness folded in around me. Even the hard shush of blood in my ears and stuttering beat of my heart were replaced by a distant cool grayness.

And then I wasn't wondering about anything anymore.

I was walking. There was no pain. There was no worry, no sorrow. Only peace. I was content. Complete.

Dad was walking next to me, silent.

Ahead of me the world seemed to be filled with light. The softest, most beautiful light I had ever seen.

It welcomed me, beckoned me. I knew I belonged there. In that light. I knew I would never feel pain again. I knew I would be loved.

Was that wrong? To want that? To want peace? To want comfort and ease?

And then, even that faint worry was whisked away. There was no wrong here. Everything was as it should be.

I was almost to that soft light. Just a few steps more and I would be there. Could stay there forever.

Someone stood in the light. Waiting for me.

My father. The younger him, his hair dark instead of gray, his smile kind.

"Allison Angel," he said. "What are you doing here, sweetheart? So soon?"

"I don't know," I said. "It's nice to be here."

"Was there no other choice?" he asked older Dad, who stood next to me.

"I still have some hope," older Dad said. "There are factors still working in our favor."

Younger Dad shook his head, but he was smiling. "I had hoped there would be years for you yet, Allison. We both wished things could have been much different."

"There is still some time," older Dad said. "Still a chance—"

"No," younger Dad said. "It was a grand gamble, Daniel. But it is over now. Our part has been played."

"You are wrong," older Dad said softly.

It was a little strange seeing the two of them, or the one of him, arguing with himself. You'd think the same person would hold the same opinion. Obviously not.

Also, I wasn't quite sure what they were talking about.

"What are you talking about?" I asked.

"You, Angel," younger Dad said. "We tried to give you as much as we could. So you could live a long life. But even our careful plans are subject to things beyond our control."

"There is still a chance . . ." older Dad said.

"I disagree," younger Dad said. "It is done. And you are welcome here now, my daughter. Welcome and loved." He held his hand out for me.

Dad, beside me, did not move.

I reached for younger Dad in the light. Just a step or two, maybe three, and I would be with him. In that light. In that love. Where I belonged.

A dark figure appeared in front of the younger Dad. Wrapped in black from head to foot, darkness clung to him. He tipped his pale, pale face up, revealing eyes that burned green. Shadows slid away and I knew who he was.

Shamus Flynn.

"There," Older Dad said smugly. "Our second chance."

"Sorry, love," Shame said. "But I can't let you leave."

He punched both hands out in front of him.

Even though his hands didn't touch me, darkness slammed into my chest.

I screamed as pain broke over me. Too much pain.

I tried to get away from the pain, from anything that wasn't the soft light. I took a swing at Shame, but my fist passed through him as if he were not solid.

Or as if I weren't.

"Time to go home," Shame said gently. He opened his arms and wrapped them around me, holding me tight.

It was cold in his arms, bitingly so. And then that cold sank in so deep, I was numb and didn't feel anything at all.

"Allie?" he said. "I need you to open your eyes."

I couldn't seem to resist. I did as he said.

Something was glowing, but the glow wasn't coming from Shame. We were standing in complete darkness. I glanced down, still in Shame's arms, trying to find where the soft glowing light was coming from.

The beautiful, fragile light glowed where my heart should be.

Zayvion.

It was the promise he had planted inside of me, the

memory of us together that I could never lose. I didn't want to walk into any other light. I just wanted that. Wanted Zayvion. Wanted to be anywhere he was.

Shame placed his cold, cold fingertips under my chin and tipped my face up so he could gaze directly into my eyes.

We were so close, we could kiss. Not that I'd ever thought of him that way before. But right here, in this . . . wherever I was . . . I wondered if a kiss would make this all go away. Make everything peaceful again. Let me rest. Forever.

The moment that thought crossed my mind, Shame's concerned expression was broken by a smile. "We won't tell Jones you were just thinking about that, will we?"

Instead of kissing me, he turned me around so that my back was against him. His hands gripped both my arms, and he whispered in my ear.

"Do you see where that light inside you is shining out to?"

I nodded. The light was reaching toward another light. This one was harder edged and held a different promise of peace. It held love. It held Zayvion. I wanted to go to that light. I wanted to run there.

"All you have to do is take one step," Shame said. "He's there to catch you."

Shame let go of my arms. And shoved me.

I stumbled forward.

But I did not fall.

"Allie?" Terric stood in front of me, his hands gripping the exact same place on my arms that were still cold from Shame's palms. Terric's palms were warm. So very warm.

"Terric?" I had expected Zayvion. Why was Terric catching me?

"It's time to wake up. He's waiting for you."

Terric leaned forward and planted a very brotherly kiss in the middle of my forehead.

And then there was life. And there was noise.

". . . give a rat's ass," Zayvion said.

". . . fucking trust me," Shame said.

"Got her." That was Terric, panting. "She's back. She's breathing, Zay. Come here and give me the knife."

Wait. What? Knife? I tried to open my eyes. Didn't do it on the first go. Or the second or third. But when fingers gently brushed my hair back from my face, warm fingers, Zayvion's fingers, I gave it all I had.

Finally did it.

And then there was Zayvion.

His face took up my world and his smile gave it light and blue skies. "Allie? You're okay. Everything's fine. Just stay awake. Just stay with me, love."

"Not . . ." Wow, my tongue felt like it weighed a million pounds. "Going."

"It's okay," he said again. "I've got you. Try to rest."

And then there was movement. A lot of it. The whole—I don't know . . . room?—rushing away, and darkness and light making shadows and bright spots. I thought maybe closing my eyes would help with the vertigo, so I tried it.

I was wrong. Open eyes was better. Much better.

We were still in the crypt. Walking toward the door. There were a lot of bright colors beyond it.

Wait. Wasn't it night still? Where were the colors coming from?

"Shamus," Zayvion commanded. "Take care of that. Now."

"No."

Zay was silent for a moment. Not a good sign. Then he turned enough, he was facing Shame.

"You are a Death magic user. Fucking act like one. If Allie is harmed by the Veiled out there because of something you're too afraid to deal with, I will beat you until Terric begs me for mercy, and then I'll start in on him."

"Whoa," I said, only it came out all soft and whispery. Since I wasn't getting words out, I tried for that emotional connection, basically trying to tell Zay to calm down and not threaten his best friends, who, I thought, might have just brought me back to life somehow.

Shame considered Zayvion as if weighing just what exactly he was going to do to him. He nodded and walked up to Zay, so close I could feel the crackling Death magic that licked around him.

"I will do this. For Allie," Shame said. "But if you ever threaten to drag Terric into something between you and me again? You can kiss our friendship good-bye."

Shame shoved past Zay. A flash of deathly cold lashed through Zay, strong enough even I could feel it. Then Shame took that storm and cold with him outside.

We did not need to be fighting among ourselves. They knew better than that. They knew we had real problems to deal with. Hell, I didn't even know if we'd closed the well.

"Don't let him," I started. "Zay, don't let him get hurt."

Zay was not listening.

Fab.

I took a couple of breaths, gauging my strength. A lot of me was sore—my chest particularly so, as if someone had been pounding on it. Still, I might be able to stand. I didn't think I'd be walking yet. God, I wanted coffee.

"Terric?" I asked.

Terric put his hand on Zayvion's arm where Shame had hit him when he shoved past. Warmth replaced the icy pain Shame had planted there. "Be patient with him, Zay. No matter what happens, I don't want to live in a world where you and he are at odds." Terric gave Zayvion one more pat, and then stepped outside.

"I'm fine," I finally managed. "Zay. I'm really fine." To prove my point, I lifted my hand and brushed my fingers across the back of his neck, then down his back. "I think I can walk."

"Let me get you to the van," he said. "To a doctor."

Okay. Hero-man was not listening. I could fight him, but frankly, it wasn't worth it. Besides, if his arms and hands were full of carrying me around, then he wouldn't be able to cast spells, or get in a fistfight with Shame. So that was a win.

"The well?" I asked.

"Closed. Tangle, Refresh, and Rebound."

More good news.

"Stone?"

A rocky rumble-hum answered me from somewhere ahead of us—maybe just outside the door.

"Davy and Collins?"

Zay took in a deep breath and let it out in what sounded suspiciously like a sigh. "Allie, you don't need to worry about that right now."

"I worry. It's what I do. Did they?"

"They did. As far as we know they opened the gate and are fine. They haven't checked in."

He walked out of the crypt and into the night. The colors and light I'd seen wasn't an early sunrise. It was the Veiled. In watercolor reds, oranges, greens, and gold.

Still angry, still hungry though they were not moving. Someone had cast a Hold spell on them that was still strong, though fading at the edges.

Casting a spell that big, to stop that many people — well, creatures — must have taken a hell of a lot of magic and skill.

And from the look of the spell, it was something Shame had cast. Shame and Terric together.

"What happened?" I asked.

Zay stopped walking. Waiting for Shame to do something, I supposed.

Shame was doing something. He was smoking a cigarette as he walked out into the middle of the mob of frozen Veiled. It was strange. The fir trees, bushes, and grass outside the crypt were brown. Dead. I didn't remember there being so many dead trees when we'd arrived.

Terric followed Shame, talking to him quietly. They weren't quite arguing. They were discussing spells, discussing probable outcomes. It sounded like they had decided Shame would pull the magic out of the Hold spell and use that magic to cast a second spell.

I'd never seen anyone reuse magic like that before.

But then, Shame and Terric were Soul Complements. They could make magic break its own rules.

Eleanor hovered next to Shame, the silver tie around her wrist holding her to him. She was offering suggestions too. Shame nodded, listening to her.

"I opened the well while Shame and Terric kept the Veiled busy," Zay said. "You and your father unlocked the magic in Stone and purified the well. Then . . . then you died."

I heard him. Really, I did. But it still took several seconds for those words to actually make sense. "What?"

"You died. Stopped breathing. I did CPR. Shame . . . I don't know what Shame did. Something with Blood magic and Death magic."

"He found me," I said, remembering the soft light and love that had welcomed me. Remembering my dad in that light and Shame pushing me away from it.

"And then you called me back," I said. "The promise you gave me made me remember. Remember you. Remember us. Shame wouldn't let me go to the light. Terric caught me, you pulled me back."

Zay frowned. Looked down at me. Knew I was not lying. Then looked out at the two of them standing hip-deep in the dead. "Jesus. They did that with magic?"

"I think so. I don't know. I was walking to the light. Dad was there waiting for me. Then Shame was there. And he pushed me toward Terric. It's a little fuzzy."

"Can you see what spell they're casting now?" Zay asked.

Oh, right. He couldn't see magic with his bare eyes like I could. I studied what they were doing.

Shame was taking off the Void stone cuffs, amulets, and rings, with the same kind of brisk let's-get-this-done motions of a man about to get in a fist fight. Terric was doing the same.

Without those stones on, they'd be using magic without a safety net. But with those stones on, I wasn't sure they'd be able to access the magic in the Hold spell at all.

"They talked about using the magic in the Hold spell to cast another spell. I don't know which one they decided on. The Hold spell on the Veiled is crumbling. I think Terric's going to pull on the magic, and Shame's going to cast it into a second spell."

Shame dropped the last Void stone off his wrist and

onto the pile of other stones. He tossed his cigarette to the dewy ground, then he walked several yards away.

Terric toed the stones a little closer together, then strolled over to Shame and stood, shoulder to shoulder with him, facing the opposite way so their backs were toward the other. That's how they'd been standing when we first came into the graveyard and they'd taken on the Veiled.

Yin-yang. Darkness and light. Terric began the spell. Shame rocked up on the balls of his feet and shook out his hands. Then he waited, a stillness, a calm in that darkness he carried as he turned his hands out to the side, palms up.

Terric didn't just cast a spell. He yanked the magic out of the Hold spell like pulling a rip cord on a parachute.

Magic sped to his fingers, then arced to Shame's waiting hands, like lightning seeking the earth.

In Shame's hands, the bright flash of magic turned painfully dark, a blackness that hurt the eyes.

I looked away from the spell to the Veiled. They didn't seem to be having any problem looking at the magic. As a matter of fact, they were drawn toward it.

"The Veiled are closing in on them," I said. "They broke the Hold spell and Terric is feeding the magic in a thin stream to Shame."

"What's Shame doing with it?"

"Nothing. Nothing I can see."

And then Shame turned his palms over, letting all that black crackling far-too-bright magic pour into the ground at his feet. The Veiled moaned as if he'd just poured away the last drop of water in a desert.

Which was, in a way, exactly what he had done. We

closed the wells. All of them. The Veiled were always hungry for magic. And now, the only magic left was in Terric's hands, in Shame's hands, fading and unusable into the ground.

Still, the Veiled were fascinated by Shame, crowding closer and closer to him but not touching him. Not yet.

Shame looked up. Looked back at Zay and me. He was angry, but beneath that thin veneer, I saw terror in his eyes.

Terric took a step to the side, so that his back was braced against Shame's. He still held a tangle of magic in his fingers, though I couldn't tell what glyph he had twisted it into.

Shame licked his lips, dug his feet in, and then he said one word: "Come."

The Veiled hit him like a freight train.

Shame shuddered under the barrage of impact after impact, his arms spread wide as Veiled after Veiled poured into him. They hit him again and again.

Shame drank them down, growing stronger, more and more healthy and darkly beautiful as the Veiled fed him.

I didn't want to watch. This is what Jingo Jingo had done. Drinking down the souls of people, the lives of people, so that he could live.

"Shame," I said softly. "No."

But he couldn't hear me. And I knew, from the hunger in his eyes, from the rapture on his face, that he wouldn't stop even if he could.

And then Shame reached one trembling hand back for Terric. At the same time, Terric reached for Shame. They gripped hands, back to back.

Terric said one word.

"Leave."

A Veiled that was hovering in the darkness around Shame shot through Terric. And when that spirit, that reflection of a dead magic user, passed through Shame and through Terric, it . . . no, he . . . walked away a few steps, then turned to look at them.

Now he seemed to be a middle-aged man with a wide, pleasant face, eyes where the black holes had been, a very normal mouth where before had been a hungry maw. He frowned, as if trying to get his bearings.

Eleanor said something, waving the man toward her. He drifted over to her, spoke for a moment, then glanced around, chose a direction, and walked off through the trees until he faded from sight. He wasn't the only one. For every Veiled that Shame drank down, a person, a ghost, exited through the magic in Terric's hands.

And were guided on their way by Eleanor.

"Allie?" Zay said. "What do you see?"

"It's . . . I guess it's Death magic. Transference, right? Somehow Shame's drinking down the Veiled, and they're passing through him to Terric and turning out to be ghosts. Regular ghosts. Like Eleanor."

"Eleanor?"

"Eleanor Roth. She's a ghost now. Haunting Shame."

"Now?"

"Ever since he killed her."

"Are you sure?"

"Totally."

"My God. Only her?"

I nodded. Zay was walking down the slight hill from the crypt and up the road away from Shame and Terric. Toward the van.

"The others he killed and um . . . consumed . . . didn't do the ghost thing," I said.

Zay didn't answer, saving his breath for the walk. We

were about halfway across the graveyard, heading slightly uphill.

"I think I can walk."

"No."

"Zayvion?" That was Maeve's voice.

"Over here," he called.

An ambulance rolled down the street toward us. Zay moved out of the middle of the road as the vehicle came to a stop.

Two EMTs rushed out of the ambulance and Zayvion carried me around to the back, where they opened the doors.

"I can stand," I said. "I can sit."

"Let's see if she can," one of the EMTs, a woman, said.

Zay eased me down so my feet were on the ground.

I stood for a couple of seconds, then decided that was as macho as I could manage. With the help of Zay and the woman, I sat in the back of the ambulance.

Maeve, and a man and a woman I hadn't met, got out of the SUV that was idling behind the ambulance and headed toward Zay. There was another person, a woman, still sitting behind the wheel.

"We're all fine," Zay said as Maeve came up to us. "Shame and Terric are back at the crypt, dealing with the Veiled. Using a lot of magic. Bending it. They might need to be Grounded."

"Brant," she said. "Come with me. Irene, please stay here." Then to Zayvion. "Are you sure you're okay? Both of you?"

"I'm good," I said. It came out a little quiet, but not too bad. She gave me second look, the kind of expression moms get when they're deciding if their kid is lying about being too sick for school or not.

I must have passed the test because she headed back to the car with the man, Brant.

"We should take her to the hospital," Zay said.

"No," I said a little stronger. "We should not."

"Allie. You need a doctor."

I glanced at the man who had taken my pulse and checked my eyes. "How am I doing?" I asked.

"Your vitals are normal. I think you should see a physician. Just to check things out."

"I can see Dr. Fischer. Is she still at Kevin's?" I glanced up at Zay. He just frowned at me.

So I tried the woman Maeve had asked to stay with us. "Irene, do you know where Dr. Fischer is?"

She shook her head. "I could call."

"Please."

The EMTs were done checking me over and were typing the results into their handhelds.

"If you're going to scowl at me," I said, "could you sit here next to me so I don't have to squint against that streetlight to see you?"

Zay didn't move for a moment. Then he sat down next to me on the bumper of the ambulance.

"I'm tired," I said, taking his hand. "But breathing. That's good, right?"

He let go of my hand and put his arm around me. He didn't say anything. He didn't have to. I could feel every confusing emotion rolling through him.

I'd died.

I couldn't blame him for being a little overprotective.

"She's at Mr. Cooper's place," Irene said. "She said she'd be happy to see you there, or meet you at a hospital."

"I'll see her there," I said. "After we find out if Shame and Terric are okay. Maybe we should send the ambulance down for them?"

Just as I said that, the SUV drove up.

Zay stood, and I stood with him. He kept his arm around me, and I was grateful for it.

Maeve stepped out of the car. "They're fine. The Veiled are gone and the well is locked. You're done. All of you. Is she all right?" Maeve asked.

The woman nodded. "Wouldn't hurt her to be seen by a doctor. But she checks out."

"Come back with us," Maeve said. "Dr. Fischer is there, Zayvion. She has all the equipment needed to make sure Allison is well."

"Let's go," I said when Zay didn't move.

That's when I realized it wasn't just me who was hurting. He was in a fair share of pain too.

"You okay?" I asked.

"Yes."

I thought about making the EMTs check him out, but we were at the car door by the time that whole idea came together. And all I really wanted was a place to sit and close my eyes for a few minutes. I didn't think Zayvion was in a deadly amount of pain. We'd be at Kevin's soon. So I let it slide and got into the car, hauling myself across the middle seat.

Terric and Shame were already sleeping or passed out in the backseat. They were both leaning against opposite windows, each of them pillowing their heads with one hand. Their other hands were still clasped.

I didn't see magic around them. At all. Hell, I didn't see any magic, not even around Stone, who finally decided to crawl up into the SUV and plant himself in the space between the driver's and passenger's seats.

Eleanor was sitting behind Shame, her back against the seatback, facing out the rear window.

Zay stretched one leg out beside Stone, and then draped his arm over the back of the seat. I didn't even bother with the seat belt. I leaned into Zay, inhaled the familiar, comforting scent of pine, and gratefully closed my eyes.

Chapter Sixteen

The short nap in the car turned into a longer nap, curled up beside Zayvion in one of the luxurious beds at Kevin's place. I heard Dr. Fischer come in and check on us. I suppose she ran some tests, though I didn't feel a thing, nor did I care to.

I really woke up to the sound of Zay snoring. I pushed at his shoulder to tell him to roll over. He didn't move. So I opened my eyes and stared at the ceiling for a couple of minutes, listening to him breathe.

From the light coming in through the window I could tell it was morning. Still pretty early though; the light washing the room fell in tepid blues.

I knew I should push myself out of bed, get an update on Leander and Isabelle, check to see if Davy, Sunny, or Collins had checked in. Maybe find out if the people sick from tainted magic were doing any better.

You know, be a leader.

Instead, I rolled over and put my forehead into the side of Zay's arm, holding on to him.

I'd died.

I'd walked toward that light willingly, not caring what I was leaving behind. Not caring who I was leaving behind. I would have lost him, left him alone in the middle of a fight that we hadn't even finished preparing for, if it hadn't been for the promise he had anchored inside me.

"You didn't leave me," he said softly.

I must have been thinking too loudly.

"If Shame hadn't stopped me, I would have," I mumbled into his arm. "I'm so sorry."

He wiped his face with his other hand and checked the bedside clock.

"I would have come for you," he said. "I would have brought you home."

"Is that what you and Shame were arguing about when I woke up?"

"At the crypt? Yes. I knew I could open a gate, pull your spirit out of death."

"Why didn't you?"

"Because Roman has all the gates locked down. No one opens a gate—a real one, not technologically created with whatever sort of thing Collins used—until Roman's spirit crosses, finally, into death. It's one of the final things a Guardian of the gate can do. Lock all gates in their city so that no one can get in, or out."

"Sounds like Collins made a gate."

"He created a hole in space."

"That's different?"

"Yes."

"What if we wanted to open a gate? Or needed to?"

Zay rolled over, propped his head on one hand, and brushed my bangs away from my face. "I'd take care of it."

"What? Just you?"

"Yes. Guardian of the gate. I'm the only one who can open the lock that Roman's soul set on the gates when he died."

"Oh. Well, that's good."

"It is. And I'm not going to open the gates, so Leander and Isabelle will have to get here the old-fashioned way. Car or plane. We'll know when they're coming. We'll have warning."

"That's even better." I shifted closer to him, wrapping one leg over his and scooting so I was pressed against him.

"God, you feel good," he said.

"So do you."

He slipped his hand away from my face, and slid it up under my shirt instead, his palm warm and calloused, stroking across my stomach and ribs, and then resting beneath my breast. "How good?"

"Mm." I tipped my face up and kissed him. It felt like it had been forever since I'd kissed him, since we'd touched. I got lost in that, lost in the sensation of being here with him, of being alive, warm, and needful.

A lazy stroke of heat pushed down my chest, my stomach, and slid between my legs.

I wanted more than a kiss. Much, much more.

Zay shifted onto his back so I could straddle him and get my hands up under his shirt. Why was he even wearing a shirt in bed? Wasn't that against some kind of guy rule?

He chuckled, catching my thought, then half sat so I could pull his shirt off over his head.

"Hey, lover," I said, softly, resting my hands on his bare chest.

"Hey." He gently massaged his thumbs over my hip bones. I was still wearing my jeans. Not for long.

The door burst open. "Allie, Zayvion," Kevin said. "Sorry to wake you but we have news. Oh. I should have knocked."

I took a deep breath and let it out, not looking away from Zayvion.

He was still looking at me too. But we both knew that was all the time we were going to get for a while.

"Would have been nice," Zayvion said to Kevin, or maybe to me.

I smiled softly, agreeing. "What news?" I asked as I eased off of Zayvion's lap, trying not to get tangled in the blankets.

Zay fished around for his shirt, found it, unwadded it, and pulled it back on.

I swung my legs over the edge of the bed and tried out my first standing maneuver. Landed it. Go, me.

"It's Eli Collins." Kevin held out a cell phone. "He wants to talk to you, Allie."

I stayed where I was, holding on to the bedpost, and stuck out one hand. Kevin crossed the room and handed the phone to me.

"Really," he said to Zayvion, "sorry."

"Forgiven," Zay said. "Did he tell you anything?"

"Just that he had to speak to Allie. Immediately. Sounds like he's on the run."

"This is Allie," I said, thumbing it on speaker so Zay and Kevin could hear too.

"We have Michael and Lark. It took some . . . convincing." He paused to breathe for a second. "They're willing to come with us. I have a place I'm taking them. Safe. I'm dumping the phone after this call. I have one more stop to make."

"Understood." The stop was probably another set of Soul Complements. "Is everyone alive?"

"No casualties. The Overseer is in total control. Everyone in the Authority, in the world, believes she is still

Margaret Stafford. She told them the Authority has been infiltrated and compromised by a man who is controlling Soul Complements to bring the organization and magic into his control."

"Who?"

"Daniel Beckstrom."

"What the hell? They know he's dead. Everyone knows he's dead."

"Listen to me, Allie. They believe her. They believe anything Leander and Isabelle say while they are wearing her skin. If she says Daniel Beckstrom, one of the strongest and most brilliant magic users of our generation, found a way to cheat death, they'll believe her. She sent teams to lock up Soul Complements until she can be there personally to kill them."

"Holy shit," I said. "Where is she now?"

"She's been through New York and Chicago. As I understand it, she's on her way to Nebraska. We'll try to get there first."

"Good. Be careful."

"Wait," he said. The phone crinkled with static, as if he had to drop it, or hide it, and then pull it up to his mouth again. "She has an army. Poised in every city. Magic users waiting for her signal."

"Signal for what?"

"To blow Portland, Oregon, off the map."

Chapter Seventeen

"They want to destroy us with magic?" I asked Collins, who was still on speakerphone.

"Yes."

If they really wanted to blow up the entire city, magic was the worst way to do it. For one thing, all those deaths carried a huge price to pay. For another, a well-placed bomb would do just as much or more damage.

"Do you know any more on that?"

"No."

"Stay safe and stay out of the way," I said. "Keep the people with you safe, got that?"

"Allison," he started. "I thought I'd have time. To talk to you. To explain some things."

"You will. After this is all over. Don't do anything stupid. Just do the job, okay?"

"In case we don't have time . . . this isn't how I hoped the world would be. I wanted a chance to tell you, I'm sorry. For our past. I was an idiot. I never should have doubted you. I never should have turned away."

"Later," I said, not knowing what the hell he was talking about. "If you can get us word that you've secured Nebraska, do so."

"Good-bye, Allison," he said.

It sounded strangely permanent. What a drama queen.

"Good-bye, Eli."

I hung up. During the phone call, several people had walked into the room. Maeve, Victor, and Detective Stotts. I was really glad I was wearing clothes.

"Did you get most of that?" I asked.

Everyone nodded.

"We have magic locked down, right?" I asked.

"Yes," Victor said. "All the wells are closed."

"Then we need to know what resources we'll have against their attack," I said. "If they're traveling by conventional means and they're in Nebraska, we only have a few hours at best before they're on our doorstep. Let's take this somewhere else other than the bedroom. Someplace where enough of us can talk this out."

Nola showed up at the door with a bed tray of coffee and two covered plates. "Oh," she said. "I didn't realize there was a meeting going on."

"Just started," I said. "We're moving to a different room. Kevin, want to lead the way?"

"Sure." Kevin took his phone back and started out the door.

I was the last out of the room, having taken the time to shove my feet into my boots and grab up my coat from the back of the door. Zayvion took the time to do the same.

Before I stepped out into the hallway, he caught my hand.

"Is there any way I can talk you out of being in the middle of this?" he asked.

"Weren't you the one who voted me into the middle of this in the first place?"

"Yes, I was. That was before I knew magic was killing you. That was before I knew they were going to name your father—in you—their target. That was before I . . . lost you."

I studied his face. Zay was always so careful not to let too many emotions show, always so careful to be the dutiful and upstanding Guardian of the gate, protector of the city. But the man before me was more than just a soldier in the fight. He was my lover, my soul. And he looked so very worried about me.

I stepped in closer to him and brushed my fingers over the lines across his forehead. "I'm going to be okay. But I can't just walk away from this now. At least now we know they want Dad dead. That's something, right? Maybe it will help us anticipate their actions, give us an advantage."

Zay drew his arms around me. "I could take us away. Open the gates. We could run."

"For the rest of our lives?" I searched his eyes. "That's what we'd be doing. Running forever. Even if we found a way to exorcize Dad from my brain, Leander and Isabelle aren't going to let any Soul Complements live. And who's going to stop them if we're gone?"

"I didn't expect you to say yes," he said quietly.

"I know," I said.

He kissed me and I lost myself to that—to the awareness of him, alive, holding me, loving me, his heart beating so strong I could feel it against my chest. I refused to believe this would be the last time he and I would be together. We weren't going to lose this fight. We couldn't.

When he finally drew away, I wanted to tell him I'd changed my mind. That maybe we could just run for the rest of our lives. Instead, I pulled my shoulders back and walked down the hall toward whichever meeting room Kevin was headed to.

Zayvion hesitated. Long enough, I almost slowed to see if he was following me. Finally, I heard his footsteps on the carpet behind me. And then he was beside me.

At his touch, my heartbeat settled into a more normal rhythm. I did not want to do this alone. Didn't want to even think of doing it without Zayvion beside me.

It was time to make plans. And I needed every resource we had.

Including my father.

Dad? I thought as we walked down the curved staircase to the main floor.

I'm here, he said.

He may still be in my head, but he sounded very, very weak. I could usually feel his presence, sense his thoughts. But he was nothing but a disembodied voice.

Are you okay?

Allison, he said, irritated, *I'm dead. Of course I'm not okay.*

He didn't sound any stronger, but at least I knew he was in his normal humor.

Kevin walked toward us across the ballroom floor. "I've put us up in the first meeting room."

"Is there coffee?" I asked, falling into step behind him.

"And breakfast. Nola's made sure there's plenty for everyone."

I smiled. That sounded like her. "Good. I'm starving."

The meeting room was probably half the size of the ballroom. There was a small stage at one side of the room, but the rest of it was set up with tables. Nola and a crew had brought in restaurant-style warmers filled with food and were serving up plates. Cody Miller was beside her, chatting with people and dishing up eggs.

I got in line, Zay right behind me.

Stone, Dad said.

What about him?

Where is he?

It was my turn in line and I held my plate for Nola. "You've been busy," I said.

She nodded. "So have you. Are you okay?"

"Now that there isn't a speck of magic left accessible in Portland? Yeah, I'm feeling pretty good."

Which was true. Nonmagic and me were getting along splendidly right now.

"Plus, I got your cookie."

She placed a pile of silver-dollar pancakes on my plate, then added several strips of bacon.

"They called the ambulance for you," she said as I moved down to Cody and eggs, and Zay stepped up for pancakes and bacon.

"They overreacted. I was knocked out. That's all."

Nola looked a question at Zay.

"We did not overreact. She wasn't breathing."

"You shouldn't even be out of bed," Nola said.

"Dr. Fischer cleared me, right?" I nodded to Cody, who spooned spiced scrambled eggs next to the bacon.

"Yes," Nola said hesitantly.

"Then I'm okay. For now. Trust me, when this is all over, I'm going to sleep for a month."

"Is that enough?" Cody asked. Then, "Eggs. Is that enough eggs?"

It was still a little strange to talk to Cody now that both parts of his mind had been rejoined. Sometimes, he still seemed young and uncertain. Other times much older. And then there were times, like this moment, when he seemed his age—somewhere comfortably in his twenties.

"I'll come back for seconds if it isn't," I said. I scooted

to one side so Zay could get his share. He went for a double helping.

Stone, Dad said again.

"Cody," I said, "have you seen Stone?"

He pushed the eggs in the warmer over to one corner. "Who's asking? You or your father?"

"Both."

"He's here. Sleeping back in one of the storage rooms. Why?"

"I don't know why Dad wants him, but I wanted to make sure he'd made it through all this unscathed. Does he seem okay?"

Cody smiled and nodded, a little of his younger self shining through. "He's fine. Still just Stone."

"Good." I picked up a piece of bacon and crunched through it as I walked over to one of the long tables.

I paused, looking for a couple of open seats. Then noticed Hayden. He was a bear of a man, so really, pretty hard to miss, but I had not expected him here. He pointed his fork at the chairs next to him and Maeve, and I smiled and walked that way.

"You finally out of bed?" I asked as I took the chair next to him.

"No infection, everything's healing fine," he said around a mouthful of pancake. "And damn good pain-killers."

Hayden's arm was wrapped in thick gauze, especially the stump where his hand had been severed. He wore a sling, braced tight to his wide chest. Even though his eyes were a little bloodshot, he looked a hell of a lot better than when I'd last checked in on him.

For someone who had been so severely wounded just a couple of days ago, he looked amazing.

"Also, I'm a part of this," he said. "Don't have to be front line, but not going to be in bed when the battle hits. Understand?"

"I'll keep it in mind."

Zay came up beside me. Paused before sitting. I glanced over to where he was looking. Shame and Terric walked into the room, both of them with their respective dark and light on full throttle. More than one head turned to look at them.

But they didn't seem to notice that.

There was a long moment while Zay stood there, and they stood there, looking at each other across the room.

I touched Zay's hip. "Sit down. We'll figure it out after food."

Zay broke eye contact and sat next to me. He didn't say anything, just started in on his food.

I didn't say anything either. I had a new rule. I would not deal with the apocalypse, or arguments between men, before breakfast.

Zay, however, was keeping an eye on where Terric and Shame were in the room. He surreptitiously watched them make their way through the breakfast line, then tensed as they walked between tables, coming closer and closer to where we sat.

Since there were several open chairs next to us and Maeve was sitting here too, I assumed they'd sit with us.

Shame took a couple of steps past our table, but Terric stopped. "Mind if we sit with you, Maeve?" he said.

"Of course not," she said, her sharp eyes weighing the situation over her cup of tea. "Shamus. Come sit with your mother."

Shame paused midstep. Then turned and sat next to Terric, who was sitting directly across from Zay. That meant Shame was sitting directly across from me. He set his coffee down, and forked an entire pancake into his mouth.

Hayden slurped down some coffee, looking at Terric, who was quietly eating his eggs; to Zayvion, who was doggedly working his way through a piece of toast; to Shame, who was glaring at Zay.

"You boys fighting?" Hayden asked.

"Not yet," Shame said.

Terric shook his head. "How are you feeling, Allie?"

"I'm good. Are you two okay?"

"We're fine. Well, I'm fine. Shame is angry at Zay."

"Really, Ter?" Shame said. "You'll stoop to honesty so quickly?"

"Shame," Zay said. "Can we talk?" He stood.

Shame glanced up at him. Maybe weighing his mood. Maybe weighing his own mood. We all looked at the both of them.

"If it's going to be a fight," Hayden said, "there better not be weapons involved."

"No fights," Maeve said.

Shame pushed up to his feet. "I'll be right back, Mum."

Zay turned and walked off, and Shame followed.

"What are they fighting over?" Maeve asked.

"Zay threatened to beat Shame if he didn't do something about the Veiled," Terric said.

"Zay's been threatening to beat Shame for one thing or another for most of their lives," Hayden said. "What got him riled up this time?"

"He threatened to hurt me." Terric sat back and took a drink of his coffee. He stared out the door, an unreadable expression in his eyes.

"Ah," Maeve said as if that explained all.

"You can handle yourself in a fight," Hayden said.

"I know," Terric said. "That wasn't what made Shame angry."

"I do not understand that boy of yours, Maeve," Hayden said.

She just nodded. "He's a curiosity at the best of times."

I knew what had made Shame angry. She probably knew it too. Zay had pointed out that Shame was vulnerable in a new way. He had pointed out that he knew if Terric suffered for Shame's choices and actions, it would make Shame angry.

Shame had once told me it wasn't the fact that Terric was gay that kept him from wanting to know if they were Soul Complements. It was that if they *were* Soul Complements, that meant Shame belonged, in some way, to someone. And someone belonged, in some way, to him. Which put him in the very vulnerable position of having someone tied to his life, and tied to his actions.

Shame didn't want to be the kind of person someone else relied on. I thought he might have spent years making sure that people didn't expect too much of him.

And Zay had thrown that very new, very fresh vulnerability in Shame's face.

I finished my food and got up to get a refill on my coffee.

Most of the people in the room were nearly done with breakfast; only a few stragglers were helping themselves to seconds.

I looked around for Nola, but didn't see her or Cody. Maybe dealing with the kitchen. I thought it would be better to wait for Zay and Shame to come back before I opened up the discussion of how we were going to stop Leander and Isabelle.

Violet was sitting in the corner of the room, in a comfortable chair I figured Kevin had dragged in here for her. She had little Daniel on her lap, and was holding him up so he could stand on her thighs.

Kevin stood beside her, alternately looking like he would mess up anyone who came too near and making goo-goo baby faces at Daniel.

Since I had a little time to kill for once, I walked over to them. "Hey," I said. "How's my little bro?"

Violet looked up, smiled. "Slobbery. Want to hold him?" She turned him so that he was facing me. He had his entire fist shoved in his mouth, his eyes blue and bright. Drool coated his cheeks, chin, and fist, and made the cuff of his shirt soggy.

"Um . . . sure." I put my coffee down on the closest table and picked up little Daniel. "You are such a goofy little thing."

He smiled, forgetting his fist for a minute, then started sucking on it again.

Violet took a deep breath and let it out, sitting back more comfortably in the chair. "He has developed a superpower in the last week," she said. "He is immune to naps. Mind if I get a cup of coffee?"

"No, that's fine," I said.

Kevin touched her shoulder. "I'll get it." He walked off and Violet just looked after him with curiosity knitting her brows.

"He's been different the last day or so," she said. "I think there's something on his mind."

"Has he talked to you?" I awkwardly shifted Daniel so that he was lying in my arms, with a minimum of baby slobber coating me in the process.

"We've spoken. About the situation with Leander and Isabelle."

"Has he brought up anything personal?"

She frowned. "No."

"Well, you're right. There's something on his mind. Something personal he wants to tell you. You should ask him about it."

"Do you know what it is?"

"Yes. And it's not my place to say." I looked away from the slobber monster and met her worried gaze. "It's nothing bad. Nothing dangerous. A more mundane sort of thing." I smiled.

"I'll talk to him," she said. "How is . . . how are things with you?"

"I'm good," I said, avoiding the rest of her question. She wanted to know if Dad was all right. Maybe even wanted to talk with him. I'd told her I'd give them a chance. Later. When the fight was over.

It wasn't later yet. "He's fine. Dad," I said. "Resting from the magic work. He's been . . . amazing."

She smiled.

Kevin chose that perfect moment to walk up with the coffee and hand it to Violet.

"I think everyone's here," he said. "Are you going to call the meeting to order?"

"Just waiting for Zay and Shame."

Kevin pointed across the room. Zay and Shame were walking in. Didn't look like either of them were bleeding or sporting any new bruises that I could see. So apparently they did know how to talk things out like adults. Who knew?

"Sure," I said. "Here, have a baby." I handed Daniel over to Kevin, who handled the transition with a lot more grace than I did.

I retrieved my coffee and took a drink trying to think this out. All of these people were members of the

Authority. Well, except for a few people like Detective Stotts, Nola, and Cody.

Really, we all knew what was going on. I just needed to make sure we were covering our bases, and had a plan in place for when the Overseer showed up.

Or at least that's all I hoped I needed to do.

Stone, Dad said softly again as if working hard to drag himself out of a fevered sleep. *There is one more thing we need him for.*

I stepped up on the small stage at the end of the room. *Tell me later.*

You need to know this now.

It can wait a few minutes.

There is another source of magic in Portland.

All the people in the room turned to look at me, quieting their conversations.

Except now I had no idea what I should say.

What?

There is another source of magic in Portland. A secret source. We will need to make sure it hasn't been poisoned and make sure no one is using it.

Secret? How secret?

There is only one other person in Portland besides myself who knows about it.

Apparently I had been quiet long enough that it was looking unusual. Zay got up and walked over to me. Dr. Fischer was on her way too.

I held up my hand. "I'm fine. Hold on a minute." I walked over to the side of the room so I could get my head around what Dad was saying.

Who? I asked.

Mama Rossitto.

"What's wrong?" Zay asked. "Are you hurting?"

I shook my head.

"There is no magic in St. Johns," I said. Yes, out loud.

"There's no magic in any of Portland," Zay said.

"Dad," I said.

Dr. Fischer raised her eyebrows. "Are you talking to him?"

"Yes. Give me a minute."

I grabbed Zay's wrist and dragged him with me out of the room and into the hall. Then back a little farther so I could talk to him and Dad uninterrupted.

"He said there's another source of magic in Portland."

"Other than the networks and wells?"

"He said it's in St. Johns."

Zayvion shook his head. "We would know."

Mama knows, Dad said. *She is its protector.*

"Why tell me now?" I asked. "All this time you couldn't have told us?"

I am only telling you now because I feel that I must. I gave my word to her, years ago, that I would never reveal it to anyone. But we must be sure all magic is guarded. If Leander and Isabelle know of it they will use it against us.

"Do they?" I asked. "Do Leander and Isabelle know about it? Or the Overseer? Did she know about it?"

I don't know. I don't think so, but I can't be certain.

"Allie?" Zay said. "Tell me."

"Okay. He says there's another source of magic in St. Johns and that Mama Rossitto knows about it. He doesn't know if Leander and Isabelle or if the Overseer also know about it. We would have known, right?" I said. "All those times we ended up in St. Johns? We would have known if there was a source of magic there, wouldn't we?"

"Let's talk to Victor and Maeve. Maybe they have some idea."

We walked back into the meeting room, and everyone stopped talking. Right. Still needed to make a plan. Well, no time like the present.

"Here's where we're at," I said, heading to the front of the room so Zayvion could go talk to Victor and Maeve.

"We know the Overseer is possessed by Leander and Isabelle. The gates have been sealed by Roman Grimshaw's death. They can't get here by magical means. But they're moving. We just got word that they're possibly headed to Nebraska. That puts them a few hours away by conventional transportation."

I was pacing, trying to think this through. "We've closed down the wells and the cisterns, and put out a restriction so that no one in the city is using magic. The cisterns are inaccessible. The wells, which only members of the Authority know about, will kick back if anyone tries to use them, so that's inaccessible too.

"There is one last report of a magic source we are going to investigate and shut down.

"If we can stop Leander and Isabelle by nonmagic means, and not engage in a magical fight, that would be best. Do we have forces on the ground to carry that out?"

Detective Stotts took a couple of steps away from the wall. He looked well rested and sharp, his light jacket unzipped to reveal a nice button-down shirt.

"We have police, fire, and National Guard at our disposal," he said. "All the roads are covered; all flights in and out are being monitored. We'll know as soon as they are in the area. Since this is a matter of national security, we will take them into custody immediately, unless lethal force is necessary."

"Good," I said. "With magic in Portland blocked and locked, they will not be able to use magic to defend or attack. That gives us an edge. They should be considered armed and dangerous. Treat them as such. Detective Stotts, is there anything else?"

"We have fail-safes in place on all the hospitals and emergency services," he said. "Businesses have been encouraged to stay closed; the majority of the city is at home; the streets are relatively clear."

"Excellent," I said. "Detective Stotts, please continue to coordinate our resources along with Hayden Grimshaw and Dr. Fischer. I volunteered to help us figure out what to do with the magical side of this attack, but you are far better suited to deal with guns and bullets and the people who use them."

"Maeve and I will also stay to assist and coordinate," Victor said.

Bless him. Just the sound of his voice calmed a lot of concerned mumbling. These people were used to seeing him as a figure of authority, not me. Which was great. Right now I needed to get myself and Dad to St. Johns to see if there really was some source of magic we hadn't accounted for.

Maeve and Victor were already surrounded by people asking them questions. So I nodded to Zay.

"Coming?"

"Of course. St. Johns?"

"If there's magic there, we need to close it." I headed out of the room.

Shame and Terric were waiting just a short way down the hall, and so were Cody and Nola.

"Hi," I said to Nola. "I need to go check on that magic source. We'll catch up when I get back."

"We're coming," Cody said.

I thought about it, made a decision. A part of Cody had been connected to Mama out in St. Johns. Maybe he'd be able to get her to listen to us if things got dicey. And since Mama always had guns on her premises, it might be best to have any bargaining power available.

"I'd rather you stayed here, Nola," I said.

"You said it yourself: This isn't a magic fight right now." She pulled her shotgun and a box of shells out of a hall closet. "I know how to use a gun, and I'm not afraid to."

"I like her," Shame said as he and Terric continued down the hall.

"Sweet hells. If you get hurt—"

"I won't. Let's go."

Stone, Dad said. *We'll need him. Don't let him stay behind, Allison.*

Crap. "Anyone know where Stone is?"

We crossed the main room and stepped out onto the porch. Stone was sitting on top of the van, his ears perked up, sniffing the wind.

At least it wasn't raining. The sky was a patchwork of blue and clouds, but promised to be warm and dry.

Cody laughed. "Get down," he said. "You'll break the roof."

Stone burbled and took a step. The thunk of metal denting under his feet popped through the quiet morning air.

"Wings," Cody said. "You should use them."

Stone did so, pushing up into the air, and landing down the driveway just a bit. He folded his wings and trotted over to us.

"Why is he still working?" I asked.

"What do you mean?" Cody rubbed Stone's head;

then Stone came over to me and walked a tight circle around my legs.

"When magic was shut down back when the wild magic storm hit, he sort of . . . wound down."

"He probably wasn't fully activated."

"Is he now? Fully activated?"

Cody had made Stone. I figured he knew a lot about him I didn't. Cody paused, and held my gaze, his eyes bluer than the sky. "Have you talked to your father about Stone?"

"I think so."

"Well, then you know Stone is a very complicated construct. We've only seen some of what he can do." Cody stepped up into the van.

That was kind of . . . mysterious.

"You don't mean stacking blocks, do you?" I asked.

Shame stopped beside me to toss a cigarette on the ground. "Weren't you in a hurry just a minute ago?"

"I'm still in a hurry," I said. "Are you and Zay all right?"

Shame tipped his head so he was considering me through his bangs. "We have an understanding that will do for now."

"If I can help—"

"Bloody hell, Beckstrom," he said with a smile. "Who told you it was your job to fix every damn thing in the world?"

"Pretty much everyone," I said.

"Stop listening to them, okay? We're fine. And, as I understand it, we have a wild goose to chase."

"You don't think there's magic in St. Johns?" I asked.

He hitched one shoulder. "I don't think your da would tell us about it now, after all this time, unless there was a reason for him to. A big reason."

That's exactly what I'd been thinking.

Shame climbed into the van behind Terric and slid the side door closed. I was the last person to get in the van. I stepped up into the passenger's seat, got in and held on as Zay headed toward St. Johns.

Chapter Eighteen

*W*hy do we need Stone with us? I asked Dad as we careened down the noticeably empty streets.

To make sure the magic there is purified. I am . . . tired, Allison. Let me rest until I am needed.

He pulled away to some corner of my mind and essentially closed the door behind him.

Something about his answer didn't feel right even though it made perfect sense. Sure, we had used Stone to purify the wells, but the only thing we'd done with the cisterns was shut them down. Dad had been deliberately vague about what the source of magic in St. Johns was, exactly. If we needed Stone, then it must be a well.

Shame leaned forward and tapped my shoulder. "Mum said to give you this." He handed me a phone.

"Thanks." It was the one I'd been using before. I must have left it by the bed. I still wasn't all that used to carrying one around.

"Shame." I turned in my seat so I could more or less face him. "Thank you. For before. When I . . ." I swallowed. I was having a hard time saying it. I had died. Didn't mean I wasn't in deep, deep denial about the reality of that.

"You know I wasn't going to let you go that easy," he

said. "Last time you walked into death, Jones was miserable to be around."

"I was in a coma," Zay said.

"Like I said. No fun at all. I have pictures to prove it." Shame smiled and leaned back in the seat.

I opened my mouth, trying to get him to understand how grateful I was that he had pushed me away from death. That he hadn't let me take the easy way out.

"You're welcome, Beckstrom," he said. "Anytime."

I nodded. I guess that would have to be enough for now. Maybe later I could make him understand what it meant to me, to know he had my back like that.

We didn't talk for the rest of the drive, everyone lost in their own thoughts.

"This is it." Zay slowed the van and parked it across the street from Mama's place.

It was weird. I almost always felt some kind of immediate relief coming to St. Johns. Today was no different. My shoulders relaxed and the headache I'd been ignoring removed its teeth from my forehead.

We piled out of the van and I strode up the steps to Mama's diner door.

It was early, but the diner had probably been open for hours now.

One of the Boys, since Mama called all the strays and orphans she took in Boy, stood behind the counter. He didn't have his hand on the gun I knew was under the shelf. I was flattered.

"Is Mama here?"

He tipped his chin toward the dining room.

I started off that way. The tables were empty except for one elderly couple, who got a look at me and Zay and settled back with their coffee to see what was about to go down.

"Mama?" I called.

She was in the back of the room, wiping off a table. Mama stood barely five feet tall, and had the disposition of a wet cat. She and I were almost friends back when I was barely making rent taking Hounding jobs. That was before I knew about the Authority and all this secret magic stuff. She'd hired me to investigate a hit on one of the kids she'd taken in. A hit that had led to my father's murder.

I'd helped out her boy, but in doing so, had gotten her son, James, thrown in jail for killing my dad. To say our relationship suffered from that turn of events was an understatement.

She turned toward me and her face darkened. "Why are you here, Allie girl? You want breakfast?"

"No. I want to talk to you. In private."

She glanced up at Zayvion, who just shrugged, then over at the patrons.

Mama shook her head. "Okay, okay. Come this way, we talk."

She stomped off and opened a door I hadn't paid much attention to with an EMPLOYEES ONLY sign on it.

I had expected a storage room but it was a large, modern office with a desk, shelves, and a computer. There was an old map of St. Johns on the wall, displaying roads that I didn't recognize.

Mama turned and put her hands on her hips. "What do you both want with me? Is the Boy you took all right?"

"Cody's fine," I said, guessing his spirit, who had pretty much haunted this place for a while before he was rejoined with the living Cody, was the "Boy" she was talking about.

"So?"

"First, you need to know something. Two undead spirits are coming to Portland to tear the city apart. They want to rule all magic. And they will kill anyone who gets in their way."

She opened her mouth, but I held up my hand.

"We don't have a lot of time. They've been moving across the world killing powerful magic users. That's why we locked down the wells, and turned off the cisterns. We don't want them to have access to Portland's magic."

I rubbed my fingers back through my bangs, wishing they'd stay out of my eyes. "They will make our fight with Jingo Jingo out in Cathedral Park look like child's play. They're going to kill people, Mama. A lot of people. If there's magic here, in St. Johns, they will use it to destroy St. Johns, and then the rest of Portland."

"Why are you telling me these things?"

"Because my father told me there is another source of magic in the city. He said it's here in St. Johns. And he told me you and he were the only two people who knew about it."

"He lied. Your father was a liar." She started forward as if to leave the room, but Zayvion simply stood in front of the door, his bulk blocking her escape.

"Mama," I said, "please. Everything is at risk. All of Portland. St. Johns too. If there is some kind of magic here, something that might be tapped into, or could have been tainted—"

She scoffed.

"—we have to know. My dad believed it was important enough for us to know about it that he risked breaking his word to you."

"Who knows what was in your father's head? He was

a desperate man, Allie girl. Did such things . . ." She shook her head. "Terrible things. I want nothing of him."

"You don't have to have anything of him. I just need to know if there is magic in St. Johns."

She looked down for a moment. "You tell me, Allie. Is there magic here?"

"I don't know." I ran my fingers through my hair again. My chest ached. Not from where I was still sore from the CPR. Someplace deeper inside me ached.

"You don't know, I don't know."

Allison, Dad said. *Just tell her yes. Trust me.*

I rolled my shoulders. "Give me a sec." I closed my eyes, ignored Dad, and tried to clear my mind. I refused to lie to her.

Did I feel magic here? Was that possibly why I always felt welcome, more comfortable here? No, that didn't make sense. Magic made me sick. In one way or another, magic always did some kind of harm to me. There wasn't any magic that could make you feel good.

Somewhere inside me though, I knew the truth. Not because Dad had said it. Not because it was what I wanted to believe.

There was something magic about St. Johns. There always had been.

My dad moved aside, lifting his hand away from some small point in the center of my chest.

That was where my small magic used to be. Since I had traded that bit of magic to get Zayvion's soul out of death, I'd had nothing but a hollow coldness there.

But I remembered what it was like to carry that small flame of magic. It felt like being here in St. Johns—warm, safe, home.

Why? I asked Dad.

None of this made sense to me.

You were hurt, he said. *I . . . she, Mama, healed you.*

How?

With the magic of St. Johns.

And the truth of his words was undeniable. I knew he was right. I knew there was magic here.

"Yes," I said. "There's magic here. I can't exactly feel it. Not like other magic, but I know it is here."

She considered me for a moment or two. "Who are the undead who come this way?"

"Leander and Isabelle. They were alive hundreds of years ago. Do you know about them?"

She shook her head. "Why here?"

I could lie. But I didn't want to ruin what trust might be building between us.

"They want to control magic, and Portland has four wells of magic, plus whatever St. Johns has. And I think they want to destroy my dad."

"Your dead father?"

"He isn't dead now. He's more like a ghost who possessed a corner of my mind."

Her scowl grew deeper with every word.

"The possession thing was an accident," I said.

"Nothing that man does is an accident." She sliced her hands through the air. "There is no magic here. Never has been. You tell your dead father to go to hell. And stay there."

She stormed past me and glared at Zayvion.

"This is my house. Get out of my way."

Zay moved aside, and Mama strode out the door.

"That went well," Zay said.

"Shit," I said. "I wasn't lying. There's magic here. Some kind. I just don't know where, or what."

"Maybe it doesn't matter," he said. "If we haven't

been able to find it for the last thirty years, then maybe
it's hidden enough that Leander and Isabelle won't find
it either."

"Do you want to take that chance?"

"Not really."

We headed out of the office, out through the dining
area where two Boys were now positioned, making no
effort to hide the guns on their hips. We took the hint
and walked out the front doors.

Shame, Terric, Cody, and Nola were standing by the
van, waiting.

"Any luck?" Shame asked.

"Just the bad kind," I said. "I think there's magic here.
Dad is positive there's magic here. Mama won't admit to
it. Suggestions?"

"Can you sort of feel for it, Jones?" Shame asked.
"That thing you do?"

"I don't feel any magic here," Zay said. "Never have."

"Cody?" I asked. "Do you remember any draw of
magic in the area? When you were . . . um . . ."

"Dead?" he asked. He frowned, thinking. "I don't
think so. That . . . it's hard to really remember anything
clearly. A lot of that time is sort of fuzzy and dreamlike.
I get images, maybe memories, but it's hard to tell.
Sorry."

"How about Stone?" Shame lit a cigarette, exhaled.
"Think he could sniff it out?"

No, Dad said.

"No," Cody said at the same time.

Interesting.

"So what?" I asked. "We just hope Leander and Isabelle don't find it?"

Terric shook his head. "I hate that idea."

"How about a Truth spell?" Nola said.

We all turned to her. I, for one, was shocked.

"Just because I don't use magic doesn't mean I don't know how it's used," she said. "And I know Truth is usually only effective between blood relatives . . ."

"Not at all," Shame said. "That's just what we tell people."

"So . . . ?" she asked.

"We'll need to use magic," I said. "In the disks. You have them, right?"

Zay nodded. "Three left."

"Who's the best at Blood magic?" I asked.

"Shame or I," Zay said.

"I'll do it," Shame said. "But someone's going to have to make sure I'm not shot to hell by her gun-toting Boys."

"Easier done with magic," Terric said.

"Then we use magic on them too," I said. "We use one disk to cast a Hold, or knock them out, and one to work a Truth spell on Mama."

"Which leaves us only one disk left to deal with, Close, or hide the source of magic here in St. Johns," Zay said.

"And no magic up our sleeve if we get into a wrestling match with the Overseer." Shame was staring down the street, thinking.

"Is there another option we're overlooking?" I asked.

Zay shook his head.

"Say, I have a question," Shame said.

"What?" I asked.

"Anyone else see that?" He pointed.

I followed the angle of his finger.

Roman Grimshaw, the ex-guardian of the gate, was striding our way. Or rather, the ghost of him was sort of floating our way. His spirit that should be locking the gates and keeping them closed was no longer in those gates.

Holy shit.

"Roman?" I said.

Our phones started ringing. All of them.

"Zay?" I said. "The gates?"

"They are coming," Roman whispered.

And then an explosion rocked the world.

Chapter Nineteen

Not one explosion. Ten, in quick succession. I ducked and covered my ears as the roaring blasts filled my skull. The blue morning sky burned yellow then bled down to a deep umber red.

"What the hell?" I yelled.

"Gates," Zay said, hauling me up onto my feet. "Roman's soul must have been released so now the gates can be used."

"How?" I asked.

"I don't know," he said. "Maybe a Guardian of the gates from some other city. Get in the van!"

We hauled into the van. Shame and Terric were on their phones, and when my hearing came back I realized someone was talking on my phone too. I pulled it up to my ear.

"This is Allie," I said.

"We have confirmation that gates have opened around the outer edges of Portland," Victor said.

"How many?" I asked.

"Twenty-four at last report."

"Shit. What's coming through?"

"Magic users. Groups of ten. They're staying near the gates, keeping them open."

"What are they keeping them open for?"

"Magic. They're pulling on magic from the other sides of the gates."

"Can they do that?"

"Not for long. We're going to close the gates."

"We're in St. Johns. Didn't find the source of magic. Where do you need us?"

"Is Zayvion still with you?"

"Yes."

"Let me talk to him."

I handed him the phone. "Victor," I said.

"Zay."

I can usually hear both sides of a conversation over a phone. It's one of the good things about being a Hound. But whatever Victor was saying was covered by the muffled ringing in my ears from the blast and other voices in the van as Terric and Shame and Nola talked on their phones.

The sky was still bloodred. Somewhere not too far off sirens started up. A lot of sirens.

Mama stepped out of her diner, a shotgun resting casually in her hands. Four Boys stood behind her.

Don't leave St. Johns, Dad said. *This will be the only hope to stand against them.*

Mama hadn't raised her weapon yet. She glanced up at the sky, then turned and disappeared into the diner. A hand in the window turned the sign from OPEN to CLOSED.

But Dad's plea got me thinking.

Why did Leander and Isabelle name you as the person behind this all?

What?

Leander and Isabelle. Why would ancient, dead Soul Complements want you dead? What did you do?

I suspected early that Sedra was possessed by Isabelle and tried to remove her as the head of the Authority. I suspected that she killed Mikhale. It made them notice me, and tipped my hand as a person to be reckoned with. But what matters now, Allison, is your decision. Victor will tell Zayvion he wants to Close the gates. It will take an immense amount of magic to do that. Will you unlock the wells so that magic is available for everyone, including the armies at the gates, or trust me that there is magic here that can be accessed and can be used against them all?

You seem to have a lot riding on whether or not we access the magic in St. Johns. Why?

Allison . . .

Why? I repeated.

It is a crystal well, he said. *The magic in St. Johns is old, untapped, crystallized. Kept untouched and pure, a relic of light and dark magic still joined. Mama and generations before her for hundreds of years have kept it secret and safe. It is a magic even Leander and Isabelle don't know about. It can do things other magic cannot.*

Because it's light and dark magic joined? Would have been terrific to have known that a long time ago. What else aren't you telling me?

So many things.

"We're heading back to the Death well." Zay started the van and was halfway out of St. Johns in seconds.

"Why? What did Victor tell you?"

"I need to Close the gates. I need a well opened to do it. Death well is the closest."

"They know where our wells are, mate," Shame said. "They're just waiting for you to pick one so they can take you out."

"If I Close the gates, they won't have magic. Then you can take them out."

"No," I said.

"I don't see another option."

"You will not die to save this city. Not like that."

"Allie," Terric started.

"Stop the van." When Zay didn't do anything, I touched his arm, hoping our connection would carry more than my words could.

"I mean it, Zay. Stop the van." St. Johns was already miles behind us. "We can't do what they expect. Listen to me."

"Leander and Isabelle are going to step through one of those gates," he said. "But not if I Close them first."

In the back of the van Stone snarled.

"Stone?" Cody said.

And then Stone literally tore the back door off the van and jumped out into the street.

"Zay!" I yelled.

Not because of Stone.

The road in front of us exploded in a blast, chunks of concrete and dirt hurled our way.

Zay yanked on the wheel and slammed on the brakes. I don't know how he did it but somehow, the van did not roll over. We skidded sideways for several yards, then finally stopped.

"Fuck," Shame said. "Anyone hurt?"

"Fine," Nola said. "We're fine."

I glanced at Zay. He was stock still, hands clenched on the steering wheel. Staring out the window.

I looked out the window too.

At the woman standing in the middle of the broken street.

She wore a pair of dark slacks, sensible shoes, and a long, expensive wool jacket. Older than me . . . maybe even Maeve's age. Short gray hair cut straight at the forehead and into spiky edges everywhere else. A thin, firm mouth and a hard jawline.

Her eyes were wide—maybe they had been blue, maybe brown. Right now they were black. No color, no whites, just pure black. She was possessed by the oldest Soul Complements, two people who had been so powerful when they were alive, only breaking magic into light and dark had stopped their killing spree. They had been strong enough to escape death, to tear souls apart, to possess powerful magic users. And now, joined together in one body, they became the strongest form of magic user.

I'd never seen her before.

She, apparently, knew me.

"Daniel Beckstrom," she said. Her voice was that of a woman, but I heard her in double, a second voice echoing in my head. And that other voice was straight out of my nightmares. It was a blending of male and female. Leander and Isabelle.

"Now you will die."

She pointed both hands at the ground. Like a hard wind rising, a storm of magic pounded through the air. I didn't know how she was accessing magic, although the only thing that made sense was she had her own source, like the disks.

No, she was using the people at the gates to feed magic from surrounding cities to her.

That had to come with a hell of a price. I was sure they wouldn't be able to bear it for long.

Horizontal lightning strikes hissed across the sky like no wild magic storm I had ever seen before. Fire balls seared down and burned up from the ground.

"Fuck it all." Shame and Terric got out of the van at the same time Zay did. They all strode out onto the street.

No. They did not just do that.

Hell. So much for planning, for taking some kind of guerilla tactic against her.

Hound instincts told me this was suicide. Never meet the enemy on the grounds they choose. Never fight an enemy straight on, on the terms they set.

Unless you wanted to die quickly.

And I refused to die. Not here in the middle of the street. Not at Leander and Isabelle's beck and call.

They weren't the only pissed-off Soul Complements in this town.

As a matter of fact, when it came to angry Soul Complements around here, they were outnumbered.

"Stay here," I said to Nola and Cody. I didn't wait for their answer as I took off after Zay, Terric, and Shame.

Zay stood several paces in front of the van, facing the Overseer, Shame and Terric on either side of him.

I didn't see Stone anywhere.

"Stay back, Allie," Zay said.

Oh, like hell I would.

"Beckstrom." Their voices dug painfully into my head. "This game of yours is done. We have the final hand now. All magic is ours, light and dark, as it has always been meant to be. You have lost."

The Overseer hooked a finger, and the magic in the sky bent to her command.

I didn't know if I could use it. Didn't know if even drawing a Block spell out of that mess of magic would kill me.

The fear of death, so close, so recent, made me hesitate.

Stupid, stupid, stupid.

Everything seemed to slow.

Allison! Dad yelled.

I felt his fear, tasted the sour copper of it against the back of my throat.

He had good reasons to be worried. The sky was breaking. The ground was breaking. A building fell, the dust rolling out in strangely liquid slow motion.

Magic licked like fire. From the sky. From the ground.

Headed toward me.

Toward me and Dad.

To kill us.

I drew on that same magic. Just like Shame had drawn on the Hold spell around the Veiled.

Too late, much, much too late. Magic answered me, but scraped ice through the black mark in my left palm, pulled fire through the opalescent metal marks on my right.

Shield.

It wouldn't save me.

But I refused to die this easily. From one strike.

Because I was angry. More than angry. Furious. They had no right. No right to tear my world apart. To kill so many. They had no right to try to kill my already dead father.

The Shield carved a wall around me, flames of magic weaving a tight netting that could not be breeched.

My skin was on fire. My bones were freezing. I couldn't do this, couldn't survive drawing on their magic to use magic against them.

Their attack pounded down.

It was like standing on a rock while the entire ocean rose up . . .

. . . and crashed on top of me.

Only it wasn't water. It was magic. Too damn much magic.

Drowning, crushing.

Enough to kill me.

And then Zay was there, his hand on my right wrist,

his hand on my left. Warm, solid, real. He pulled me against him. Taking my pain, paying my price without even casting a Proxy spell.

He had walked right through my Shield like it wasn't even solid, though it reformed around him, and became stronger as he drew upon the stream of attack to bolster my Shield.

Breaking the rules of magic. Making it bend to his command. Pushing magic away so that I wasn't drowning anymore. Wasn't hurting anymore.

Leander and Isabelle weren't the only people who could break magic.

"We can't win," I tried to yell. I couldn't hear my own voice over the roar of magic.

"Not here," he said. "Can you reach St. Johns?"

The magic there. He wanted me to reach for St. Johns' magic. "I'll try."

Zay shifted to hold the Shield around us. That was unpleasant.

I reached out, seeking the promise of magic miles from us. If it was there, I couldn't reach it.

I bit down on a moan, though he wouldn't have heard me if I screamed. The pain I felt for using magic, he felt too. And on top of that, he was paying the price for using this magic.

Pain didn't stop him. He drew on even more magic being thrown at us and twisted it into a spear, cursing more than chanting. Then he heaved it straight at the Overseer's heart.

She raised one palm and the spear of magic slipped sideways to burn a hole into the concrete at her feet.

"Guardian," they said with her mouth. "You hold what we want. Give us the dead man."

She carved a glyph into the air.

Magic stalled. It refused to fill that glyph, falling away from her like fog tattered by a strong wind.

Shame drank down the magic she tried to pull on, and poured that magic into Terric's hands. Terric shaped magic, and wielded spells that he threw at her again and again.

They were amazing, fast, fluid.

Blood ran down one side of Shame's face. Terric wasn't using his left hand very well. They didn't pause, didn't stop.

They threw a spell that sucked all the magic out of the air in a circle around the Overseer.

"Now!" Terric yelled.

The crack of bullets unloading in rapid succession ricocheted off the buildings.

Nola stood on the side runner of the van, shotgun tight against her shoulder. She didn't stop firing until she was out of bullets.

Magic is fast.

Bullets are faster.

It didn't give us much time. Just a moment or two. The Overseer was caught off guard and without magic. She fell to the ground.

Zay and I didn't need to talk, didn't need to plan. We both broke the Shield spell and drew Impact with quick, clean strokes and heaved it at her with everything we had. Our spells joined, tangling into something more powerful than just Impact. It burned a path through the air and slammed into the Overseer.

A shadow spread out over her body, protecting her from the spell. The Impact spell hissed like lava hitting the sea.

The Overseer was bleeding from at least two bullet holes in her chest, but she was still breathing. And in a moment, Leander and Isabelle made sure she was standing again too.

Lightning wicked down out of the sky. Her people at the gates channeling more magic.

Not a lot of choices left. We either opened the wells to shut her people down and risked giving her a well to pull magic out of, or we somehow stopped her here and now.

With a flick of her wrist, the lightning reached out and wrapped around her fingers.

Lightning whipped up over the top of us. Because we weren't the target.

In the death of one second to the next, I knew who she was aiming at.

Nola.

She had shot the Overseer and was reloading. They were making sure she didn't fire on them again.

Nola screamed as lightning wrapped her in a crackling cocoon. Magic shook her like a limp doll, throwing the shotgun out of her hand and tossing her to the ground.

"No!" Cody rushed to her side.

"Nola!" I yelled.

Zay and I ran to her.

Just as I reached the van, just as Shame and Terric were hauling ass toward us, Zay spun.

And pulled on every drop of magic in the air.

Unleashing hell itself.

His spell hit.

The road broke in half, a sinkhole spreading out from just the other side of Shame's boots and crumbling away like a hill of sand as it stretched out toward the Overseer. She slipped down into that fissure, and disappeared from sight in the dust and debris.

"Fucking balls, Z," Shame yelled, running for the van. "Warning next time."

I tripped, fell. Zay's hand caught my arm just as I got one hand out to catch myself. That much magic was too much. Too damn much. My ears were ringing and my vision narrowed down to a single spot.

"Nola," I said. "Help Nola."

"We got her." Zay pulled me up to my feet. I wasn't steady, but the strength flowing through Zayvion to me meant I wasn't going to pass out either.

Cody and Terric were lifting Nola and carrying her into the van.

"She's breathing," Terric said. "Burned. We need to get her to a hospital."

"Where's Stone?" I asked.

"Flew away," Cody said.

"We need to get out of here," I said.

Zay let go of me for a second and I felt like I'd just lost a couple of pints of blood. Then his arms were around me again and I put some effort into getting to the van.

The world shook.

Shame wiped blood away from his eyes and glanced over at the huge hole Zay had punched in the middle of the street. "Aw, piss."

"What?" Terric said.

"Run," Shame said. "It's time to run."

Terric and Cody hurried to get Nola in the van and Zay practically lifted me up and shoved me in after her.

"Drive, Flynn!" Zay yelled.

Shame had the van in reverse before the side door shut. I was tossed against the window, and braced there while Zay wrestled the door shut.

The van spun, rocked, then straightened. Shame floored it.

"Fuck, fuck, fuck." Shame's gaze flicked to the rear-view mirror.

I turned, looked back over Terric and Cody, who were trying to keep Nola safely lying across the seat. She wasn't just unconscious, she was burned. Very burned. Third degree. If we didn't get her to a hospital, I didn't know how long she had left.

"Terric?" I said.

He used Life magic. Used it a lot. Couldn't he find enough magic in the city to help her?

His hands glowed a soft white-green and he was whispering healing spells. I didn't know where he was getting the magic, but thought whatever he was doing might be helping her. I didn't know if it would be enough. He wasn't a doctor. And there wasn't much magic available.

He kept glancing out the ripped-apart back doors of the van too.

The Overseer was rising—no, not rising, flying—up out of the sinkhole. A column of darkness surrounded her, carrying her into the air. Wild lashes of magic filled the sky and arced down as if she were a storm rod built to channel magic.

She was chanting. I could hear it inside my head, Leander and Isabelle's voices snapping and grinding through a spell that I knew would be our deaths.

All the warmth bled from the air. The van's windows cracked with a layer of ice as the sky went black.

"Z?" Shame said.

Zay grabbed my hand, and I laced my fingers between his. "Hold on," he said.

I had no idea what he was going to do.

Zayvion traced a spell and said one word.

He tore open the wells. And the world.

I didn't know how he did it. Didn't know that anyone could open the wells like that. But I saw a final flare of the glyphs that were worked into Zay's skin flash, and burn away. Guardian of the gate. Maybe that was how he did it.

I bit my lip to keep from screaming. Tasted blood. He had cast magic, a spell I could not fathom, and tripped all the spells we'd locked down the wells with, breaking them so he could access their magic.

Leander and Isabelle's spell closed down like a hand crushing the van.

Shame hit the gas. The world slipped away.

And suddenly everything was silent.

We were falling. I covered my head, wondering where the cliff had come from.

I hit my shoulder, the side of my face. Tasted more blood. I thought, for a moment, that we were upside down, tried to look out the window.

There was no street, there was no world. We were speeding, over a hundred miles an hour through a gate. A gate Zay had opened.

He yelled one word to close it again. I felt that spell rush outward. He hadn't just closed one gate. He had closed all the other gates in the city in a massive implosion.

Tires hit reality, gravity slammed into my chest. I thought I saw trees, buildings, grass. I thought I heard Shame swearing. Then an explosion of metal crushing and groaning filled my ears. And everything went black.

Chapter Twenty

A llison, you must wake up.

I ignored Dad. I didn't want to wake up. Waking up was a bad idea. As a matter of fact, I wanted to dig my way much, much deeper into sleep.

You must wake. This time he gave me a shove.

I snapped open my eyes and inhaled a hard, sharp breath that gave me just enough time to take inventory of how much of me was hurting. Easy answer—all of me.

Use magic and it uses you back. And we had been using a lot of magic.

I heard the ticking of a turn signal and tasted gasoline in the air. Everything flickered with orange light.

Fire.

Holy shit!

I pushed up, yelped as my left wrist shot with pain. Broken. We were still in the van. What was left of it.

Quick glance: Shame slumped against the steering wheel, Zay unconscious and tossed to one side. Behind me, Terric curled over Nola, shattered glass covering the back of his coat and everywhere else like tiny, perfect ice cubes reflecting the flames. Cody was thrown back behind the seat, just his legs in clear view along the side of the seats.

Stone, gone.

I didn't think we'd been out long, but had very little way to tell. We could have minutes or seconds before the gasoline exploded and killed us all.

"Hey!" I yelled. "Wake up! Come on. Shame, Terric, Cody, wake up!" I shook Zayvion's side and he groaned. He pushed up on one arm, his head hanging. Blood dripped from his nose, his mouth. The ripple of his pain over mine made everything go dark for a minute.

Ouch.

"Out, out!" I said. I grabbed at Terric's coat, tugged on him. He came to; Shame came to at the same time. They inhaled, held their breath and exhaled.

Shame: "Jesus."

Terric: "Christ."

Somehow we were all moving. The side door was bashed in so badly it wouldn't move no matter how much Zay yanked on it.

Since my window was broken, I pushed myself up and out of it, holding my wrist to my chest. I mostly managed a controlled fall to my feet, then stumbled to the back of the van to open the remaining door.

Shame got out of the passenger's side door. The driver's side was smashed in. He'd hit a tree. The tree was still standing.

I pulled the crooked-hinged back door open, and Cody coughed and blinked up at me. "Nola?" He sounded lost, frightened, young.

"She's still with us. Can you walk?" I helped him out and Shame clambered in. Between he and Terric, they got Nola moved as gently as possible over the seat and out away from the van. Zayvion limped around from the passenger's side door.

He looked like hell. I couldn't believe he was even conscious.

I held my good hand out for him and helped as much as I could. It took me a bit before I realized we were walking on grass.

Where the hell were we?

I glanced around.

"St. Johns?" I exhaled. "Why? We need a hospital. Nola needs a hospital."

"I was trying not to land us in a wall," he panted. "Or a river."

"We hit a tree," I said.

"Shame hit the tree," he said.

Stone, Dad said. *Where is the Animate?*

I don't know. I hoped he was smart enough to get somewhere safe and far away from the Overseer. I was hoping he'd found someplace to hide.

If Leander and Isabelle find him, they will use him against us.

They're already using magic and everything else in the city, including gravity, against us, I said. *Stone won't make that much of a difference. And he won't get caught.*

I helped Zay sit and went back to help Terric, Cody, and Shame with Nola. She was semiconscious, and shivering.

"Call," Shame said. "Allie, call an ambulance." He and Terric pulled off their coats and covered Nola with them.

I reached for my cell. Pulled it out of my pocket. The battery was drained. "Terric, your phone."

He fished it out of his pocket. "Nothing," he said, trying to thumb it on.

Shame glanced at his phone. "Dead."

Cody sat with Nola's head in his lap, gently brushing his fingertips over her forehead. He was on the verge of tears.

None of us looked strong enough to go call for an ambulance. All of us looked like we needed an ambulance. "I'm going to go get help. Stay here with her."

Mama, Dad said. *She can help.*

Her place is too far away.

"They want you," Shame said. "Leander and Isabelle want your father in you. You can't go off alone."

"She needs a doctor." I was already walking.

Shame grabbed my arm. "Allie, no. If Zay were conscious he'd kick my ass if I let you go."

It took me a second. Finally his words sank in. "Zay's unconscious?"

I stopped. Turned. Zay was lying on the ground, bleeding. The glyphs that always burned with black fire against his skin were ashy gray with no light, no magic.

Everything seemed to go silent. I didn't know what to do. Did I run for an ambulance to save Nola? Did I go to Zayvion and hope that being there, holding him, lending him my strength would ease his pain, hold him away from death?

Allison, Dad said. *I can help. Call Stone. I can make this all better.*

It was like he flipped on a light switch in my head.

I remembered when I was little—maybe in kindergarten—I'd snuck out of the house to ride my bike. I'd fallen down a hill. My arms and legs were bloody, but I'd pushed my bike all the way home. And when I got there, I snuck into the bathroom and tried to fix all the bleeding myself, but I couldn't get the bandages to stick right.

Dad must have heard me. He came out of his office and found me there, standing in the bathtub so I didn't get blood on the floor, with an empty box of Band-Aids in my hand and a pile of wrappers at my feet.

"Allison," he'd said. "I can help. I can make this all better. You should have come to me." He gently washed my arms and legs, wrapped soft cotton bandages around the cuts, then put me in a warm, dry bathrobe and gathered me up. He held me on the couch until I fell asleep, and made me my favorite lunch—tomato soup and a tuna sandwich—when I woke up.

I wanted that warm, safe feeling again. I wanted that father again.

I'd spent most of my life not trusting him. Maybe it was time to admit I could have been wrong. That I should let go my distrust. That I could believe he really wanted to help me. That maybe he really still loved me.

"Cody, can you get an ambulance?"

Cody was rocking softly now, shaking his head. No help there.

"Shame, get an ambulance."

I started walking back toward Zay and Nola.

I'm trusting you, Dad, I said quietly. *Please . . . please help make this all better.*

I knelt next to Nola. She was quieter, I thought unconscious. I could see the faint white-green light of the spell Terric had put on her. Something that eased the pain and gave her strength.

"She'll be okay," I said to Cody. "Just don't let go of her."

He nodded and nodded. "Doctor. We need a doctor. Are doctors coming?"

"Shame's getting the doctors."

Then I took the few steps over to Zay. Terric sat next to him, his hand on Zay's chest.

"He's breathing," Terric said, his voice rough. "That gate. Too much."

Too much for all of us. Terric looked like he was barely conscious himself. He was blinking hard, and swaying a bit even though he was sitting.

"I need to call Stone," I said. "So you might want to let go of Zay. This might hurt."

Terric peered up at me, and shook his head once. "Summon?"

"Yes."

"I got him."

It was great that he was willing to help Zay while I used magic. But I wasn't even sure I was going to make it to the end of the spell.

Who was going to get me?

I will, Dad said.

His presence filled me, and I felt stronger, as if he was standing beside me with his hand on my shoulder, encouraging, supporting.

You can do this, Allison. I know you can.

I cleared my mind, thinking through the lines and angles of the Summon spell before I even tried to cast it. Once I had it clearly in my head, I traced the glyph.

Then I called on magic.

There is no magic in St. Johns. Or maybe there was. I didn't care where the magic was coming from just as long as it came.

And it did, pulling across from the wells we'd worked so hard to close off, to purify.

It felt sticky, hot. I didn't want to touch it. Didn't want it to touch me. I knew it was going to hurt. Ever since Dad did that thing in my head so I could use magic again, I knew using it meant magic harmed me. Permanently.

But I held it, kept my concentration by focusing on my breathing, in, out. Ignore the pain. Ignore the world around me. There was nothing more important than the magic responding to my summons, the magic filling the glyph, and the glyph, finally, finally becoming a spell—a bloodred butterfly—that shot up into the air, winging off to search for Stone.

I let go of magic, shaking it free of my unbroken right hand.

The pains were stacking up. I felt sick, woozy. Just on the edge of passing out.

But Stone would come. I knew he would. And then Dad would help us . . . somehow. Terric slid his arm around my waist, and lowered me down next to Zay.

"Hold him," he said. "It will help."

I was sitting, so I put my hand on Zay's chest. He was breathing too hard, his eyes closed and far too much blood still slicking his face and chest. At my touch, his breathing settled some, and he opened his eyes.

Gold and filled with pain.

Where was Shame and that ambulance?

"Allie?" Terric said.

"What?" I guess I had closed my eyes for a second. For the first time, it occurred to me that I might have a concussion.

He pointed.

At the sky.

It was still red, still storming, now with magic gushing like geysers out of the wells Zayvion had blown open. And straight above us was a soft glow of pink. I'd seen the color before, that magic before.

It took me a minute; then I remembered. That was the color of the crystal Dad had found in St. Johns. The crystal Terric had somehow embedded into Shame's chest to save him.

It was the color of light I'd seen around Cody's hands when he'd first seen Davy injured by the Veiled. A soft pink light, a soft magic.

"What is it?" I asked, though I didn't think Terric would have the answer.

The well, Dad said. *The magic of St. Johns. You were searching for it, reaching for it. It is now answering you, Allison.* He said that with something like amazement, or respect. *The magic answered your need for it.*

How is that going to help us?

He didn't answer.

He didn't have time to. That soft pink light suddenly blew apart like someone had just shot a cloud of darkness into its center.

And out of that darkness emerged the Overseer.

She arrowed down, straight toward St. Johns, toward the park, toward us, magic carrying her on wings of fire.

I struggled up onto my feet. Somehow, so did Zayvion. He snarled in pain as he straightened and pulled his sword.

"Stay here, Cody," I said. "And help Shame get Nola to the hospital, okay?"

Cody shook his head. "Don't go," he pleaded. "Please don't do this, Daniel."

Daniel? What did he think my dad was going to do? "I won't let him do anything bad," I said.

"It's too late." He pointed.

The darkness in the center of the sky was still there. Obsidian black, flecked with arcing lightning shots of rainbows. It looked like the Rift—that band of dark magic that flowed like a river between life and death.

"Is that the Rift?" I asked.

"Dark magic," Zay said.

"You can see it?"

"Yes."

"They're using dark magic?" I didn't know how bad that would be, but I knew it wouldn't be good.

"Both," Zay said. "They're using dark and light magic."

Well, hell. Not only could very few people use dark and light magic—Zayvion being one of those people—anyone who did could use it only for a short period of time before it killed them.

Ever since magic had been broken to try to keep the living Leander and Isabelle from pretty much doing what the dead Leander and Isabelle were doing right now—taking over the world, killing anyone who got in their way, and bending magic to do whatever they willed it to do—it had been deadly to use any but the smallest amount of dark magic.

"Did you cast something?" Zay asked me.

"Summon. For Stone. He . . . Dad told me if Stone were here Dad could help us, could make it better."

"I wouldn't say no to some backup," he said. "Did you call anyone else? Let them know we have the Overseer's full attention?"

"The phones are all dead," I said. "Drained. We just got out of the burning car a couple minutes ago."

"Where's Shame?" he asked.

"He's gone."

A wash of shock and sorrow nearly took me to my knees. I grabbed Zay's hand.

"No, no," I said hurriedly. "Not that. Not dead. He's

alive. He's getting an ambulance. Gone to get an ambulance. For Nola."

Zay closed his eyes for a second and swallowed hard. "I thought . . ."

"I know. I didn't mean it that way. I'm sorry."

"We need a plan," Terric said as Leander and Isabelle rocketed toward the ground. They weren't going to land very far away. Maybe a block. Maybe two. "Who protects Nola and Cody? Who takes on the Overseer?"

"They're coming," Cody said quietly. "For Daniel. Just like he wanted. Just like he's planned all along."

"Allie?" Zay asked.

"I don't know. That's not what he told me. Dad seems afraid of Leander and Isabelle. I don't think he's on their side. Do you know something more, Cody?"

"He made deals. In death. With my father, Mikhale. I think he made deals about Leander and Isabelle. Deals so he could live. So he could be here, right now, when this happened."

Is that true? I asked him.

Of course I've made deals. No business comes to fruition by one hand alone. Yes, I wanted to be here if this came about. But I am not on Leander and Isabelle's side. I do not want to rule magic the way they do.

You want to rule magic?

I want it in the right hands. I have told you that for many months.

I knew he was telling me the truth. I could feel it in his thoughts. But I was also just as sure it wasn't all of the truth.

"I don't think he's on their side," I said. "I don't think this was his plan."

My plan would never be so haphazard, he said, a little offended.

"Whether it's his plan or not, we need to make some decisions," Terric said. "They're coming."

I glanced across the park to the street just beyond the grassy knoll. The street was a steep hill, rising over the railroad track, and lined by two- and three-story buildings, some that had been converted into warehouses, some that were just plain falling down.

Margaret Stafford, the Overseer, the body for Leander and Isabelle, walked down the center of that street. There was an awful lot of blood soaked through her shirt. Nola was a hell of a shot. I didn't think that body was going to be alive for much longer.

Darkness—an impenetrable black that sizzled with dark magic—followed behind her. The darkness swallowed up the buildings, the street, and everything she passed.

"That's dark magic, right?" I said.

"That's our death," Terric said.

"Not yet, it isn't," I said. "Cody, help me get Nola somewhere safe."

He shook his head. "There is no safe place."

Okay, convincing him would take too long, and trying to get Nola . . . where? Into one of the buildings that was being swallowed whole wasn't a good plan either.

"We take the battle away from here, away from Nola," I said.

"Allie," Zay said. "I can't cast Gate again. Not if you want me, and probably yourself, conscious."

"Not Gate. Just not here. We get far enough away from Nola so that she's not in the blast zone."

I strode across the grass. Toward Leander and Isabelle. Toward that storm of darkness devouring my city. Toward my death.

If I had to die, I was sure as hell not doing it alone. Leander and Isabelle were going with me.

You make any deals that might help us right now? I asked Dad.

Not . . . not that I can think of. If Stone were here . . . perhaps.

And just when I'd hoped he might be helpful.

I pulled my sword, felt Zay walking beside me, his sword clenched in his hand at his side. Terric was on my other side. He had a gun in one hand, an ax in the other.

I wished Shame were here.

Hells, I wished an army was here. Because if Leander and Isabelle were determined to kill us, I didn't see how we could stop them. Maybe the rest of the world could fight them, kill the body. But Leander and Isabelle would just find a new body, probably the next person in position of power. And since it was easy magic to Close someone, to take their memories away, no one would even know that they should be stopped.

But the three of us? We were not enough. I could hardly cast magic. Zay was burned out and bleeding, my pain his pain. Terric was exhausted. Without Shame, I wasn't even sure he could control magic or if he would, on accident, kill us all with the first spell he cast.

Not exactly the heroes to count on at the end of the world.

Cody didn't follow us. I had hoped he wouldn't. I wanted him to stay with Nola.

No one should die alone.

I swallowed down my fear for Nola and my fear that Shame may have been killed by that city-eating blackness, the Rift that followed the Overseer. Swallowed my fear that there was no ambulance coming for Nola, no help coming for any of us because there were no ambulances, or city for that matter, beyond the grass at my feet, and the park where my friend was dying behind me.

I reached out for Zay as we walked. Just as he reached out for me. Since I had the sword in my hand, and my left wrist was broken, he hooked my fingers with his own. We reached the edge of the park and stepped out across the railroad track, then onto the street beyond.

No one should die alone.

And no one should face the end of the world alone.

Margaret Stafford was there on the street. It made my angry little heart happy to see she was not unscathed. Our fight had left her burned and bleeding. Not enough to stop her. Not enough to even slow her down. Yet.

But by God, it was good to see her hurt.

No matter that Leander and Isabelle were the first Soul Complements, undead and more powerful than any person walking this earth, that body they were using was still mortal. Fallible. Killable.

Time to make her fall. Time to make Leander and Isabelle pay. Make this end.

A motion to my left made me glance that way.

Shamus Flynn strode down the street, smoking the ash off a cigarette, and throwing the butt to the side as he exhaled.

I could practically feel Terric's smile.

"Decided to join us?" Terric asked, handing Shame a spare ax from his belt.

Shame met his gaze with a wry grin. "Wouldn't miss this for the fucking world, mate." He took the ax, then fell into step next to Terric as we headed up the street. "Called for medical, Allie. Not sure when they'll get here. The whole damn city's under fire from the armies at the gates."

"Are we winning?" I asked.

"Hayden's still alive. And Mum. Don't know about your Hounds. The armies aren't going to be standing much longer. Gates are closed. Well done that, Zay."

"Victor? Violet? Kevin? Stotts?"

"Violet and Kevin are fine. Mum hasn't heard from Stotts. Figures he has his hands full coordinating the firepower. Guns against magic. It's a mess out there."

"Victor?" I asked again.

"Took a bullet to the chest," he said a little quieter. "They don't think he's going to make it."

Zay inhaled hard, and I could feel his anger and sorrow.

I swallowed against the need to cry. "Is . . . is someone with him?"

"Doctor Fischer and Mum. He won't go alone."

"Hell," Terric breathed.

"I could Close them," Zay said. "Kill them."

"The armies?" I asked.

"Yes."

"You'll be standing after that?"

"No. But the city might."

I didn't want him to.

But this wasn't about me. This was about magic. And the people of Portland surviving this attack.

"If you think—" I started.

"No," Shame said to Zay. "Allie can't take much more. I know. I caught her last time. No fucking chance I can do it again."

"I could—" Zay started.

"Zayvion," Shame said gently, bending a bit so he could look around Terric and make eye contact with

Zay. "Doing it won't change what happened to Victor. That's done now. Out of our hands. Out of yours."

Zay inhaled, exhaled as if trying to push down sorrow, or rage. Victor was more than a teacher to him. He had been a father.

"You know what he'd want you to do, Z," Shame said. "Go on now, mate."

"Cut off the head of the serpent that killed him," Zay said, squaring his shoulders.

"Fuck the price we pay," Terric said.

"That's it, boys," Shame said. "Let's do the old man proud."

We stopped, spread out along the street at the bottom of the hill where the Overseer was standing.

"That our plan?" Shame asked.

"Do we need more?" Terric said.

"Kill them," I agreed, letting go of Zay's fingers and adjusting the hold on my sword. "And don't get killed."

"Simple," Shame said. "Straightforward. A bit suicidal. I like it."

"You would," Terric murmured.

"You love me for it," Shame said.

"You do make life and death interesting."

Zay twisted and pulled something out of the satchel at his side. A disk. I had completely forgotten about them.

"How many do we have left?"

"I blew two opening the wells and closing the gates."

So one. We had only one disk left.

"Trust me?" he asked.

I nodded.

"Then don't let go." He held the disk and I had to sheath my sword to take his hand, the disk between our palms.

Zay started chanting.

The Overseer laughed. "Too late, Guardian. All the Complements will be dead soon after I kill the four of you. The world is ours. Magic, dark and light, are ours. None can stand against us."

Leander and Isabelle lifted their hand. And that wall of black roared down the hill, tearing apart the world and aiming straight at us.

Chapter Twenty-one

Shame and Terric cast a spell—maybe Block, maybe something I didn't know. Whatever it was, it erupted out of the ground like liquid fire. Pure power.

Shame shifted to stand slightly behind Terric, his hand gripping Terric's shoulder, whispering to him, chanting with or coaching Terric as he drew the lines of a spell over and over again, a different angle, a different line to direct the fire, to channel the power.

Their power.

Soul Complements.

Beautiful.

Around Shame's feet, the concrete cracked as he drank the energy out of it. Behind him, the grass on the other side of the tracks shriveled up to brown, then dust. I heard a tree snap, and fall.

Shame held his free hand down, pulling life and energy out of the world, to feed into the spell Terric manipulated. Magic shifted from black to blinding white as it leaped to Shame's hands, changed, and was passed into Terric's hands.

Shame bit down on a grin and whispered curses.

Terric forced that magic to do what they wanted it to do, breaking rules, writing new ones. He sent the magic he and Shame alone could form straight overhead in an arcing, fiery wall.

The wave of blackness and wave of fire met in an explosive scream. Ashes fell through the air with the stink of broken spells. They held back the dark magic.

Just. But it was all they could do. Two men, holding up the collapsing world.

They could not stop Leander and Isabelle from casting other spells.

I glanced over my shoulder. Could see Cody bent over Nola, hugging her against him and sobbing. She was limp, lifeless.

Dead.

No. Oh, God, no.

I wanted to run to her. I wanted to fall to my knees, wanted to scream. Wanted to do anything to make this stop.

This couldn't be my reality. I didn't know how to live in a world without Nola. I didn't know how to live in a world without Victor.

Who else would I lose?

Shame? Terric?

Zayvion?

Was Zay slipping away, closer and closer to death as he chanted? Would that be the price he paid for this magic? Would he die and leave me alone?

I looked away from Cody, away from his pain. From my dead friend, held in his arms.

No matter how much magic hurt to use it, no matter how much my body hurt, there was no pain as excruciating as losing Nola.

I would do anything, pay any price to end the people who had done this to her.

I fed that pain into my anger, my fury.

"I want them dead," I said to Zay. "More than dead."

He was still chanting, the most complicated spell I'd ever heard him use. Sweat and blood traced lines down the side of his face and fell in thick drops from his lips and nose.

Zay looked up at me. Golden eyes. No brown. No black. No white. Just a pure, hating gold, loving gold. Powerful.

Oh.

I could not look away. I didn't want to. I knew where I belonged. I belonged with him.

Belonged to him.

And he to me.

"Yes," he said, casting the spell from the disk that licked out and wrapped around me.

I let go.

Let go of the disk. Let go of the world. Let go of everything. And held on to him. Held on to Zayvion, just like I'd promised.

My body fell away with a dreamlike softness. Zay's hand was there to catch me. I laughed at the sudden freedom, the rightness of this moment, this choice. He kissed me as we moved together, a waltz, step-to-step, soul-to-soul. A dance promising joy, pleasure, and endless power.

Soul Complements.

Two minds. Two souls.

But only one body. Just like Leander and Isabelle.

Containing one fury, one purpose.

To break magic to our will, and kill Leander and Isabelle.

We turned—well, Zay turned. I was in his mind, somehow in his body too. It felt right, natural. It felt like all the cold and hollow places inside me were finally filled. Filled with the heat of him. With his love.

With his anger. Our anger.

I was aware of my body, still standing there next to us. I looked like I'd been run over by a truck. My jacket was torn, my hands bleeding, and a monster of a bruise seeped down from my forehead to the edge of my chin. It was a little like seeing a life-sized cardboard photo of myself, until I realized I—my body—was still moving.

Dad. He shook his head, my head. Held up my hands and looked at my fingers and palms. Then he looked up at me, at Zay, and gave us a sad smile.

It was very, very odd to see that. To see myself from the outside. To see myself being moved by him. Inhabited by him. Worn by him.

Hello, nightmare.

There was no time to worry about it. About my body. About what my dad might do now that he was alone inside of me.

Free to use me any way he wanted.

He had told me he could help. Keeping my body breathing, thinking, alive while I was joined with Zayvion could be help. But I didn't think that was what he had meant.

The Overseer drew magic into a line in the air in front of her. It cracked like a whip. Not at me and Zay. Not at Shame and Terric, but directly at Dad.

In me.

Dad lifted my hand and spoke a Block spell I didn't know. The spell skittered off the Block like black water. But I, Dad, stumbled back, fell, groaning when my broken left wrist tried to brace for the impact.

"Stone," Dad said. "Allie, call him."

I had already called for Stone. Doing it twice wouldn't make much of a difference. Also, there were a couple of crazy people trying to kill us. I didn't think Stone would tip the scales in our favor.

Zay? I thought.

Your Summon was strong enough, he thought. *If he can, he'll come. Now it is our time to make magic our own.*

We pulled on magic. I wanted to cry out with joy. Magic leaped sweet and willing to our hands. I knew we were still injured, in pain. But using magic was easy, soothing, sensual. It made the pain of our body a distant echo, leaving the sweet promise of pleasure, any pleasure we could imagine, behind.

Zayvion laughed.

This was the way magic should feel.

We didn't need a spell. Didn't need to carve a path to guide magic. It would become anything we wanted it to be.

Magic was like a second sight, a sixth sense that let us feel the entire city as if it were our skin. We were aware of every road, building, river, tree. We were aware of every person.

In an instant, I knew my Hounds were fighting, some hurt, but no one dead, all of them buzzing on the adrenaline of taking down Isabelle and Leander's armies. With a brush of thought, I could feel Maeve, Hayden, Kevin, and Violet. Their wash of concern and grim satisfaction of a fight coming to an end. The tide was turning. In our favor.

Leander and Isabelle may have brought an army to our town, but the town was still ours. No one could take it from us.

Farther off, if we reached just a bit more, I could feel the flickering emotions of Davy, Sunny, and Collins.

Alive. Safe. They had four people with them. Soul Complements.

And I realized, if we wanted to, Zayvion and I could find anyone anywhere in the world.

It was a heady feeling. Especially for someone who had spent years Hounding and tracking people and spells. It was an ability I did not want to let go of.

But even more, we wanted to bend magic until it became a weapon in our hands.

To kill Leander and Isabelle.

Now, we thought.

Magic pulsed over us, promising anything. Everything. We breathed it in, drank it in.

Magic hummed with an electricity I could feel in our bones. I liked it.

Proxy? I asked Zay.

No. We wipe them out of existence.

God, I love you.

I braced for the pain.

There was no pain as magic took on the shape of our desire.

The only way to kill Leander and Isabelle was to break them apart.

Terric yelled. Shame yelled, then started swearing with a vengeance. We could feel Terric's pain, and Shame's anger, before we looked their way.

Terric was on one knee. Blood poured from a wound in his side. The wall of fire, the Shield had fallen. Shame carved a spell through the air, then twisted back and threw it at the Overseer.

Terric lifted a gun, took two hard breaths, and aimed at the Overseer.

He unloaded the clip. The Overseer jerked back, hit

once, twice. Kill shots. That body was not alive. But Leander and Isabelle were still filling it, using it like a puppet. They couldn't maintain that for long. Could they?

The Overseer tipped her head to one side. Flicked her fingers.

Brushed away the rest of the bullets. And brushed away Shame's spell.

"Brush this away, bitch," Zay said.

We threw magic, raw, wild, arcing across the sky, licking flames along the ground, an inferno of magic, a tornado, spiraling down around her. Magic following our want. Our need.

It tore through Leander and Isabelle. Consumed them. Dug in fingers to tear them free of that body, to tear them apart.

They uttered a word. Our magic shattered, fell around their feet like a curtain of heavy rain.

It hadn't stopped them. But it had hurt them. The body stumbled forward, onto one knee. For a moment, I saw the shadows of Leander and Isabelle, two angry ghostlike forms that hovered over the bleeding and burned body. Then they sank into her again.

And pushed the body up onto her feet. She started walking our way, limping, a gory, inhuman mockery of life. Dark magic followed her, lashing and burning behind her like a storm. It bent the buildings, warping them into the strange shapes of the buildings I had seen in death.

They were mutating St. Johns. They were changing the world with magic.

Dad had said a hundred times that he wanted magic in the right hands. I just had never really thought about what magic might do in the wrong hands.

It could destroy the world. It could remake the world into something broken and alien.

It could kill us all.

This was why the ancient Authority had broken magic. To keep it out of Leander and Isabelle's hands. They knew what they would do with magic. Knew what they had done, and what they wanted.

Pure, utter destruction.

Shame and Terric yelled a word. All the light of day snuffed out. We were suddenly plunged into the blackness of night.

Then they blasted a spell at the Overseer. It howled and tore at her.

Zay and I threw magic, calling it from the sky, the earth, the air. To kill the undead Soul Complements, to break them, rip them apart, end them.

But nothing was enough. Not all the magic we could call on. Not all the magic we threw at them. We were too evenly matched. We needed something else, something more that Leander and Isabelle did not have.

I knew Dad, in me, couldn't call on magic. I'd . . . well, my body, would pass out.

Still, he was talking to himself, maybe a mantra to calm his mind and thoughts, maybe a spell.

The Overseer stood in the middle of the street, several hundred yards in front of us, magic responding to them just as quickly as to us, dark magic licking across their fingers, as they chanted, two voices filling the air with a new spell.

Fine. Just because we couldn't kill them didn't mean we couldn't stop them.

Enough! we commanded. *Hold.*

Magic answered, forming a cage around the Overseer. The cage stopped her from moving, which was good. But we wanted magic to do more. Instead of try-ing to pull them out of the body, we locked them in that dead flesh, trapping Leander and Isabelle so they could not escape.

They snarled, fighting the magic that we directed at them as we rebuilt our spells faster than Leander and Isabelle could tear them apart.

Terric pushed up onto his feet, and Shame held on to the back of his jacket to help him stay standing. Each of them used one hand to pour magic into a barrier to slow the dark magic that was still consuming the city, building by building.

Every time Zay blinked, the world went a little too dark for a little too long. He had lost blood. Too much blood, and I was pretty sure he'd cracked ribs that had just recently healed and maybe done more damage. A lot more damage.

I gave him all the strength I could, so we could stand strong, steady.

But it was all we could do to keep that cage intact, to force magic to hold them as they twisted, pushed, pulled, and blasted at the bars around them.

Our grip on magic was slipping. Our grip on con-sciousness was slipping.

We couldn't hold out for much longer. Shame and Terric couldn't hold out for much longer.

A shadow knifed down out of the sky, something big, coming at us fast. We glanced up.

Stone angled down and landed at the feet of my body, answering the Summon spell I had cast.

Dad lifted my hand toward him, but Stone's ears flat-tened against his big head and he growled.

He didn't like Dad running the show either.

"Stone," Dad said. With my mouth, with my voice.

Stone backed away from him, snarling.

"It is fine," he said. "Everything is fine. Allison is safe with Zayvion." He held out my hand—the unbroken one—again. "Come to me," he coaxed. "We can help her. Together, we can help her."

The Overseer yelled and raged. Leander and Isabelle's voices filled my mind, and the world went dark for a heartbeat. For two.

"Die!" they screamed.

They pulled on our magic. So fast, it slipped my control, slipped Zayvion's control. They drank down everything we were throwing at them. Drank down everything Shame and Terric hit them with.

Time seemed to slow. I felt the wrenching pain of magic being ripped, physically, out of Zay by Leander and Isabelle. I heard Shame and Terric yell.

And I watched as Dad cast a spell with a single finger, standing still in the maelstrom of power, drawing a simple glyph with his signature. He kissed my right palm and blew across it, sending the spell to softly float toward Stone.

Leander and Isabelle turned magic into a bolt of raw black power and hatred. Light and dark magic snapped, arcing out in a block radius.

They threw that spell. Straight for Dad. For me. My body.

Magic blasted into my chest.

I watched my body buckle, stiffen, and fall.

Lifeless as a rag doll.

There was a hole in my chest where flesh should be, skin should be, bone should be.

I lay there, staring, blank, as blood oozed out of that hole.

My Dad, a ghost, stepped up and out of me. He looked down at my body, maybe with regret. Maybe just with relief to be free of me.

Dead.

I was dead.

Chapter Twenty-two

*N*o, I thought. The pain was slow to reach me, but it found me. The world spun as that pain pulled on me. I didn't know how to hold on to living. Didn't know how not to die.

Don't leave, Zayvion cried out, wrapping his need, his love around me, holding me strong to his soul, as if trying to tie me tight against the wind.

I held on to him, too afraid to let go.

Dad, a ghost, turned. Looked at me inside Zayvion. Shook his head. Regret. But not sorrow. More like disappointment.

And then the spell that he'd blown on a kiss to Stone landed right in the center of the gargoyle's forehead.

"Thank you, Allison," Dad said. "For your sacrifice."

The spell sent out soft ribbons of light and darkness to wrap around Stone. Where the spell touched the glyphs carved into Stone, the ribbon sank in and caught up that glyph like a bead on a string. All the glyphs across Stone's body flickered to life, joined, and created a net.

The net surrounded Dad, lifted him, carried him, his ghost, his soul, and sank him into Stone.

Stone had carried Zayvion's soul out of death.

That had been my dad's idea.

Stone had carried both light and dark magic inside him to purify the wells.

That had been my dad's idea.

Stone had been carved by Cody, a savant, and spells of Passage and Transference had been carved into him. Spells that could carry someone's soul safely to another place, another state of living.

That had been my dad's idea too.

Cody had begged Daniel not to do something. I was pretty sure it was this. Here. Now.

Cody had begged Daniel not to possess Stone.

Stone lifted up on his back legs, his wings spread wide, arms out to each side, head tipped up to the sky.

And then the magic Dad had cast in him, the glyphs carved into him, strummed like an orchestra of instruments all playing their part of one chord, building a song, harmonizing light and dark magic into a glorious chorus.

Magic surrounded Stone. And changed him.

At the distant edge of Zay's awareness, I knew Shame and Terric had thrown up a Shield to protect us from Leander and Isabelle's attacks.

A blast rocked the air.

Shame and Terric fell, bloody, unconscious, the Shield they had cast broken.

"Die!" Leander and Isabelle's word carried our end.

Zay yelled.

My hold on him slipped.

I was pulled, dragged away from Zay and toward my dead body.

Then the world didn't just slow. It stopped.

Zay didn't move. I didn't move. Leander and Isabelle didn't move. Not even the wind or the river beyond the park moved. The only thing that moved was Stone.

Stone glowed with dark and light magic that pulsed through the glyphs carved into him. Those glyphs moved, as if forming the language of a spell I had never read before. As each glyph found a new place on his body, the spell formed and reshaped him, changed him. His body shifted like blocks being restacked.

Until it was not Stone, not a gargoyle at all standing there. Until it was my father standing there. My father, made of stone and magic and death.

He was taller than I remembered, the stone body offering him no color other than the shadows of magic that slipped over his face, his shoulders, his hands.

Jingo Jingo had asked Dad where the simulacrum was. Dad had said there wasn't one.

He lied. Stone was the simulacrum. A vessel my father had commissioned Cody to carve for his soul years ago. A plan he had in place for his death. For this.

This is what Cody made Stone for. It was why Stone had so many glyphs on him. Why Stone could hold dark and light magic, why Stone was an Animate, alive.

He was made to become a body for my father's undead soul.

Dad had always told me he wanted two things: for magic to be in the right hands, and immortality.

By the right hands, he meant his own.

And by immortality, he meant this. A body made of rock and powered by magic would never die. Especially since it wasn't alive to begin with.

Dad took a step toward Leander and Isabelle, who were frozen still. The earth shook.

"You," Dad said in a deep voice amplified by magic, "are done now. Magic is not yours. Has never been yours to rule. So the Authority decreed in ancient times. So they paid the price with their lives to break magic so that it would hold you apart and banish you to death. Your refusal of death, your refusal to bow to the sentence given to you for killing so many, will now be your end.

"If death will not stop your hunger to rule, then you will pay the price of bringing magic back together again, just as the ancient Authority members paid the price to break it apart."

Dad lifted his hands, one to the sky, one to the ground. And called on magic.

Light and dark magic answered his call. For a moment, he stood there, holding the two halves of magic in his hands, light in one, dark in the other.

Then he joined his hands together.

A bolt of magic sliced through the air like a blade, taking off her head.

The Overseer fell, lifeless.

But Leander and Isabelle stood in her place. They weren't completely solid, just enough to still look human. I could see the color of Leander's eyes—hazel—and Isabelle's hair—honey gold. I could see their anger, their fury twisting their features into hatred.

Whatever Dad had cast on the world, this huge stillness, held them frozen. They couldn't even cry out as he slung a bolt of light magic at them again, this time a hook that dragged them toward him.

"Such foolish, foolish souls," Dad said. "Did you really think you could cross me and win? Did you really think I would allow you to kill the woman I loved and let you walk free? I am not a man who gives mercy willingly. Not before you tried to destroy me. And certainly not after. There is no price I am not willing to pay to see you destroyed, body and soul."

He spoke a word and a Proxy spell spun in the air

then burned a brand into both Leander and Isabelle. They opened their mouths to scream, but I could hear no sound.

"Pay for your sins against me. Pay for your sins against mankind."

Dad clapped his hands together again and Leander and Isabelle writhed in agony. Dark and light magic joined in Dad's hands. Not clashing, not burning, not exploding.

No one could hold dark magic for long. Guardians of the gate trained long years to be able to use dark and light magic together for just the briefest spells.

But Dad pulled on another magic. The soft pink magic of St. Johns, pure, untouched. It poured up out of the earth, and wrapped around the magic he held in his hands, just like the pure magic from the disks had wrapped around the dark and light magic held in Stone.

With the healing magic of St. Johns, dark and light magic meshed together, magnet to steel.

A bell tone, louder than thunder, deep as the roots of reality, rang out. Leander and Isabelle screamed. Dad's voice rolled heavy, sharp across my mind, burning with power.

The world seemed to turn inside out as dark and light magic joined.

Dad had told me it would take a Focal, a person who could withstand the punishment, and pay the massive price, to join light and dark magic again.

Looked like a dead man in a stone body made just for this reason was a perfect Focal.

And the spirits of two dead Soul Complements were just what he needed to pay the price.

I'm sure that was in his plans too.

Time began again.

We fell, Zay and I.

I don't remember hitting the ground. One moment I was falling with Zayvion, the next, Zayvion was pushing up onto his knees. I stood beside him, my dead body on the ground behind me.

"Allie," Zay panted.

"I'm here," I said, but he couldn't hear me.

Oh, this wasn't going to end well. Not at all the way either of us had hoped for.

I turned and looked at Dad. He was . . . amazing, I suppose. Filled with magic, both light and dark, a Focal for magic to rejoin again. He used magic as easily as breathing while Leander and Isabelle's souls writhed in pain, paying the price for that magic.

He cast a spell over St. Johns and the buildings became just buildings again. The sky was blue, the world looking a lot more like it should.

I could sense him closing the wells again and opening the cisterns. I could feel him making sure the attackers in the city had no access to magic, so that the fight was now over. I was a little surprised by all that. I'd never thought putting all magic, both dark and light, in my father's hands would mean his first thoughts would be toward helping others.

"Hello, Angel," Dad said beside me.

Not the dad who was casting magic in his immortal simulacrum body.

My dad's ghost. Younger Dad, whom I'd only seen in death, was standing right there beside me.

"Hey," I said, realizing he was here to take me into death with him. "What happens now?"

"Now, you hold this, while I go talk to my living self." He held something out for me.

A pink rose, glowing softly. I knew that rose. It was

the small magic I had always held inside me. The small magic I'd given to Mikhale so that Zayvion's soul could escape death. So that Zay could live.

"I won't take it if it means Zay will die."

"That's not what it means." He glanced at Zayvion, who was frozen in place again. Concern darkened Dad's face.

"Your agreement with Mikhale has been fulfilled. This magic never belonged in death, or to Sedra anyway."

I didn't know if I should take it. I had never trusted Dad much, old or young. And the one time I did—this time—well, look at him. He'd gone megalomaniac, taken over all of magic, and killed me and my gargoyle in the process.

Not a great track record for the whole trust thing.

"Here, now," he said. "I really do need to talk to myself."

I took the rose. It was soft and warm, and gave off just the faintest perfume.

Dead Dad walked over to living Dad.

"Daniel," he said.

Living Dad looked down at him and arched his eyebrows. "Ah, you are here. As it should be. Join with me." He held his hand out.

Dead Dad shook his head. "If I join with you, we will hold all magic."

"Yes?"

"It is believed that whoever becomes the Focal of magic, to bring it fully together, darkness and light, will change magic in some way. Leander and Isabelle wanted power and destruction. Even when they were alive, that is what they sought. If they were allowed to join magic and rule over it, it would be a very dark world they created."

"Yes."

"We want that too."

"Not destruction," Living Dad said. "And ultimately, not a dark world. We would create, build. Of course it would be different. Efficient. Magic would be parceled out, controlled. The world would become a fine-tuned network of magic. A great machine."

"We would destroy. You know it is true." He smiled ruefully. "We are an ambitious man. A vengeful man. We do not compromise well."

"Don't lecture me on our qualities."

"Daniel," Dead Dad said. "We have already made our choice. Years ago. To sacrifice our life for those we love."

"I have sacrificed nothing."

"We have sacrificed our soul. It is the reason we dwell in life and death, parted." He pointed to his own chest. "It is why there are two of us."

"That was only temporary. Until I could join dark and light magic again," Living Dad said. "And join my living and dead selves."

"Our time is done."

"No."

"Then you will remain, however long the Animate can sustain you, among the living with half a soul. I will not join you. Not in life."

"Why would you deny life? Our life? Our immortality?" He actually seemed puzzled.

"Immortality is not enough reward for our daughter's life."

Living Dad looked over at where I stood, all ghosty

and insubstantial, the pink rose in my hand, next to my unbreathing body.

Something changed in his cool marble face.

"I . . ." He hesitated, unable to look away from me. It was the first time in my life I had seen my father doubt.

"There is no one else who can hold magic together," Living Dad said. "If I let go now, Leander and Isabelle will rise again. Magic will return to being broken, dark and light. And they will pick it up. They will rule.

"I will not allow that. No one else can survive becoming the Focal long enough to hold magic together, to mend it. I cannot hold it for long, joined without you. Without my whole soul healed."

"I'll do it," Cody said, stepping up on the other side of my prone body.

"Cody," I said, though I didn't think he'd hear me. "Don't. Don't die for my father's twisted plan."

Cody took another step forward, two. Until he was standing next to Dead Dad. "I never thought about light magic and dark magic joining until I met you, Daniel Beckstrom," he said in a quiet voice. "But you . . . inspired me. To think about what dark magic could do. What light magic could do if they were together again. Just one magic in the world. They way it used to be. The way it always had been before Leander and Isabelle.

"I think magic might be kinder, or maybe it would heal better, or just . . . I don't know. Be less trouble. Or maybe magic will always be like water: gentle on the one hand, destructive on the other.

"Whatever it becomes once it is joined, I think I can hold it long enough for it to do so."

"It will kill you," Living Dad said.

"We don't know that," Cody said. "We can't know that yet."

"I will not hand over all the power in the world to a broken-minded boy," Living Dad said.

"I'm the child of Soul Complements," Cody said, "My mother, Sedra, and my father, Mikhale, were very powerful before Isabelle possessed my mother and killed my father. You know that. You made deals with my father in death so that he could save my mother's soul."

Dead Dad nodded. "That is true. And Cody is a savant, an artist whose ability with magic is even more rare than Soul Complements. There is no other in the world like him. If any living being could hold light and dark magic together, I believe it would be this broken-minded boy."

It was getting harder and harder to stand here. I mean, Dad had done something to halt the world, and Zay had moved for a moment, but wasn't anymore.

I was still moving though. And it felt like the ocean tide was drawing the sand out from under my feet, pulling me with it.

I didn't know how Cody was moving when no one else was. Not Zay, who was caught, pushing up off his knees and reaching for me. Not Shame, who was unconscious, blood pouring down his face. Not Terric who was bent over, his hands gripping the collar of Shame's coat as he tried to drag him back away from where Leander and Isabelle screamed.

Not Eleanor, who pressed both hands over Shame's heart, as if trying to hold his soul to his flesh.

Not Nola, dead. Not me, dead.

And even with everything stopped, with my very life stopped, I had to move, had to go, had to leave this place forever.

Something soft and light was calling me. And I didn't think I could ignore it this time.

"Can I give this to someone else?" I asked.

Surprisingly, the Dads looked at me. So did Cody.

I held up the rose. "I won't need it in death. And you said it doesn't belong there. It's special to me. Just a small magic, but it always made me feel loved. I think someone else should have it."

I decided I didn't have to wait for their permission. My dad had made me bargain it away for Zayvion's soul once, so I knew it could be given away.

This time I was going to give it to someone I loved.

I walked over to Zayvion. Touched his face, caught in fear, anger, sorrow. Too much blood still on him. Too many cuts and bruises from our fight.

It seemed like since the moment I could remember meeting him, we'd been fighting something, pushing for things to be right again.

Protecting the world, protecting magic for a price.

And now this. The price.

Having to die and leave the world in my father's hands was never the outcome I wanted. But it was pretty clear I didn't get a say anymore.

I knelt in front of Zayvion so that we were crouched, eye to eye.

He looked so worried. Afraid that he'd lost me. That I was dead.

I traced my fingers over the arc of his cheek, setting the memory of the shape of him in my mind even though I could no longer feel him.

"This is my small magic," I said softly. "I've had it ever since I was little. It's the only thing that made me feel special. Until I met you."

He didn't move, didn't say anything. The blood on his face didn't drip; the pain in his eyes didn't ease.

I didn't even know if he heard me.

Still, I placed the rose against his chest. The rose was ghostly. Like me. The rose was magic. But I wasn't.

The rose pressed into Zayvion as if it belonged there, that small magic his now.

Maybe he would know he had it.

Maybe he would know I gave it to him.

Maybe it would help him remember me in the years he had left to live. Because I knew him. Knew he wouldn't stop fighting just because I had fallen.

"I'll be waiting for you, Zayvion Jones," I said, smiling even though I felt like I was made of tears. "Keep everyone safe for me. And don't forget me. Don't forget us."

I leaned forward and kissed him.

I could not feel the warmth of his skin, could not taste his lips, could not smell the familiar pine scent of him.

"I love you," I said, I thought, with every ounce of my soul.

"Allie," Dead Dad said.

"I know," I said. There was no more time left for good-byes. I had to leave now. "I'm coming."

I stood and turned.

It was not Dead Dad standing behind me. It was Living Dad.

And just behind him, with a look of kindness on his face, was Dead Dad.

"That small magic is yours, Allison," Living Dad said to me in his cool, marble voice. He held up his hand and a rose—no, not just a rose; my rose—glistened softly in his fingers.

"You can't have that," I said. For the first time since I'd died, I was angry. Really angry. "I gave it to Zayvion and you have no right to take it from him."

"He isn't the one who needs it," Living Dad said.

Dead Dad smiled. "Allison, we've made a choice. For you."

"You know what?" I said. "I am tired of you making choices for me. This is my life—no, this is my death. And I'm the one who's going to make the choices. Do you understand me?"

Anger was good. Anger made me feel stronger, pushed my sorrow to the side. Anger even made it feel like my feet were firmly beneath me instead of being swept away by that soft calling light.

"Give me back my goddamn rose."

Dad's cool, impenetrable face twitched. The corners of his mouth quirked up in a faint smile. "You have always had your mother's temper."

I held out my hand and raised my eyebrows. "My rose."

But he didn't give me the rose. Instead, he turned and walked over to my prone body. He stood there a moment, shaking his head. "I never meant it to be this way."

Cody stood on the other side of my body. "I know," he said.

Dead Dad walked over to Living Dad and put his hand on his shoulder.

Living Dad nodded to Cody.

I had no idea what they were doing. They must have come to some kind of agreement while I was saying good-bye to Zayvion.

Cody traced a spell in the air. Living Dad traced the same spell at the same time, mirrored movements to the other.

Magic answered that spell like a song waiting to be sung. It leaped up into Dad's fingers, rolled over his carved stone body, then jumped from him in a joyous chorus that somehow gave voice to my father's dreams, his desires, his brilliant and wild vision of the world.

The magic poured into Cody, who stood, quietly smiling, his eyes searching the sky as if he saw the dance of angels or the order of the universe there. Cody lifted his hands. Magic, light and dark, rolled up his arms, just as it had rolled up mine, carving dark whorls of multicolored ribbons from the tip of his fingertips on one arm, up to the side of his jaw, and light whorls of multicolored ribbons from the tip of his fingertips on his left arm.

Dad shimmered, the glyphs on his body flaring bright, then fading and fading until they were ashen gray.

Leander and Isabelle faded too, taken apart by the price of magic, dissolved, spent, used up, until they were gone, their soul nothing but dust that scattered in the breeze.

And then Dad stepped out of Stone. Stone very quickly folded back into the shape of a gargoyle, my gargoyle. He shook his big head and sneezed.

He was alive! That was good. So good.

"Allison Angel," Dad said.

I looked over at him. There was just one Dad standing there. And for the first time in my life, I saw my father. All of him. His whole soul and mind.

The stern furrow was still there in his brow, and the lines at his eyes that seemed made from sorrow rather than joy. But there was a spark to his eyes, a glint that made me wonder what secrets he still held, what joys he had experienced. He had a kindness, a humanness to him I had never seen.

But now that I did, I understood why someone would be drawn to him. Why someone might love him.

I suddenly wished I had known him. Wished this could have been the man who raised me.

"Dad?" I said.

"I gave you this flower a long time ago," he said. He was still holding the pink rose. "I want you to promise me you won't let go of it so easily again."

I nodded. Held out my hand.

"I have done . . . regretful things. So many . . ." His voice was filled with sorrow. "I cannot change the choices I have made. But this last choice is for you. For your life. For your world. For your love. Do not waste them, never let go, never stop fighting, daughter. Time is taken from us all too quickly. Even those of us with the best of plans. And my plans were always the best.

"I love you, Allison. My beautiful daughter. I am proud of you." He smiled and there were tears in his eyes.

And then he threw the rose. Not toward me, but toward my body.

I turned, stretching out to try to catch it.

Cody said a word. Dad said a word, and suddenly the world was fading away, washed in watercolor hues. I was caught in that, like a leaf carried by a soft wind. Watched as the world turned sideways, watched as I was rested gently into my body. Watched as Dad knelt beside me, his hand over my heart, as the pink light of the rose, my small magic, was placed once again in my body.

I wanted to ask him what he was doing, why I was lying here, but all he said was, "Good-bye, Allison Angel."

I tried to open my mouth. Couldn't find a way to do so.

Dad stood, glanced once at the world around him, then, with a satisfied nod, faded away.

The world started up again like someone had just slammed on a switch.

I inhaled, air in my lungs hot as fire as I screamed through the pain that wrapped around every inch of me.

And then Zayvion was there, his voice whispering ragged, soft words to me, the most comforting sound in the world. I wanted to tell him I loved him. I wanted to kiss him one last time with my lips, hold him with the arms of my very recently unbreathing body.

A body that was still burned and broken from magic.

My eyes were working though. And I opened them to see that beautiful, bloody man of mine. His eyes were brown, empty of all magic, filled with pain and sorrow. I wanted to tell him I was okay. It was okay. That at least Dad had stopped Leander and Isabelle.

And that he had given up Stone, given up immortality, given up holding all magic in his hands.

Which meant we won.

We had really, finally won.

Go, us.

"I love you," Zay said, over and over again. "Don't leave me, Allie. God, please don't leave me." He was crying.

I couldn't say anything. Couldn't move.

Cody came into the range of my vision, standing so I saw him over Zayvion's shoulder.

He wore magic, beautiful soft hues in every color of the rainbow, around him like a cloak. He looked ageless, both a young boy and a wise man, his blue eyes filled with joy and peace.

"It's all right, Allie," he said. "Everything's going to be okay now."

And then he began singing. A very soft lullaby. It wasn't a song I had ever heard before, but I knew it carried magic. And I knew what that magic, light and dark joined together with the pure untouched magic of St. Johns, would do. He used his fingertips to paint very specific spells in the air.

Healing.

Not just for me.

To heal the world. Dark and light magic were woven together again as they were always meant to be and cast for the first time by a child of Soul Complements, a savant. Cody was a rarity in this world. A brilliant artist with magic.

I wanted to stay awake, to see the world Cody was about to bring into life, but that song took away my pain, my worries, and rocked me gently to sleep.

Chapter Twenty-three

I woke up in a bed, the smell of roses all around me. I opened my eyes.

It was my bed, my room. And I was not alone. Zayvion lay on his side next to me, his hand resting on my stomach, his breathing easy and deep. He was asleep.

Soft amber light filtered through my window, and I thought it might be evening turning toward night. I had no idea what day it was. I thought about waking Zayvion and asking him a lot of questions, but instead, I just slid my fingers between his, and held tight as I fell back to sleep.

When I next woke, it was to a clatter of cups.

Zay was bringing in a tray with two coffee cups, the coffeepot, two bowls and plates. Smelled like toast and maybe oatmeal. The dishes clattered again as he set the whole thing down on the top of my dresser, his back turned toward me.

He had his shirt off. I expected him to be bruised, burned, and stitched up. But other than moving a little stiffly, he looked all in one piece.

Healed.

Alive.

Gorgeous.

"Morning," I said softly.

He half turned, a soft smile putting light in his beautiful brown eyes. "Morning. I thought you'd wake up if I brought you coffee."

"How long since . . ." My mind flashed with everything that had happened, the pain, the magic, the death. And then it all sort of went white, pushed to one side so the memories weren't so overwhelming. All that pain and trauma were right there, but behind a velvet rope line, waiting their turn for me to deal with them one at a time. When I wanted to. When I was strong enough.

"Since St. Johns?" Zay said. "Three days. Which you've mostly slept through. Maeve's been here, and Violet. Dr. Fischer said you'd probably wake up sometime today. I thought I'd celebrate with breakfast."

He got everything situated on the tray and brought it over to the bed.

"Think you can sit?" he asked.

"For coffee and breakfast in bed? Oh, baby." I pushed up gingerly, vaguely remembering a broken wrist and other wounds.

Like a hole in my chest.

Holy shit. I'd been dead.

I pulled at my T-shirt, lifting it up so I could see my chest. My usual scars were there, bullet wounds that I'd gotten used to. But right over my solar plexus was a shiny line about as wide as my thumb was thick. From that scar other lines, maybe eight or so, reached up between my breasts to arc just below my collarbone.

Almost like someone had tried to trace the lines of a bouquet of flowers there.

"Good morning to you too," Zayvion said, nodding toward my breasts.

I looked up at his smile, realized I'd just flashed him, and tugged my shirt back down. "So, I have a new scar."

He nodded. "You were hit by magic. Leander and Isabelle . . . hurt you. Do you remember that?"

I did, though that was still over there, with the other awful memories on the other side of the rope. And I wasn't sure I could deal with those before breakfast.

"I remember."

Zay got the tray settled, and then sat on the bed with me, grunting as he tucked up his legs crisscross.

"I remember you were hurt too. Badly," I said.

He retrieved a bowl of oatmeal and handed it to me, then took the other for himself. "I was. Eat first." He nodded to my bowl.

I stuck a spoonful of oatmeal in my mouth, then forgot about trying to ask him things and ate.

"Cody took magic," Zay said after we'd both made a good dent in our food. "Dark and light."

I reached for a cup of coffee, caught my breath on the pain in my ribs. I wasn't in agony—far from it. But I still wasn't fully recovered.

Zay smoothly retrieved the coffee cup for me with a look that said I should slow down and take it easy. Then he took the other cup for himself, and snagged up a piece of toast for both of us.

"Marmalade," I said. "You really went all out, didn't you?"

"Nothing but the best for my love." Zay finished his toast. Then shook his head. "Cody stood as the Focal for dark and light magic. All these years, and Cody was the one who was strong enough to join light and dark magic. No wonder Leander and Isabelle wanted him Closed, broken, and dead."

"Is he okay?" Dad had said there wasn't any living person who could hold both light and dark magic long enough for it to rejoin.

"He's fine. Except, no, let's finish breakfast. I'll tell you later. Also, there's a meeting today."

"Except what?" I asked.

"He can't use magic now."

"What? Why not? Did you take the ability away from him? Did you let the Authority take the ability away from him again?"

"No. Allie." He sort of sighed and brushed his hand back over his head. When he looked at me again, he was very serious. "Things have changed. Let's eat. Take a shower. Then we'll go to the meeting in a few hours. I'll tell you everything I know, which isn't really all that much."

Oh. From the sound of his voice, we hadn't won. We hadn't claimed victory without also claiming very high losses.

And while the memories of it all remained distant, my emotions—anger, sorrow, loss, fear, hope—cut that velvet rope and came swirling into my mind.

It was too much. I swallowed hard, trying to push it all away.

"Shower?" I stood, put my hand on the wall to keep myself steady.

Too many days running, fighting, throwing magic around like it didn't cost anything, like it wouldn't all catch up with me some day and make me hurt, hit me all at once. I was standing, but not for long.

Zay stood and put his arm around my waist.

I'd seen him exhausted before. He wasn't there yet, but he wasn't all that far from it. And he'd been sleeping for three days too.

I put my arm around him, and we leaned on each other, making our way down the hall to the bathroom.

Zayvion started the water while I got out of the shirt and jammie pants I must have been wearing for a while.

I shivered even though the room was warm and quickly getting steamy.

Zay had shucked out of his pants and pulled the shower curtain aside.

I got in the shower, and so did he.

The water was warm and gentle. Then his arms were around me and mine were around him, and I was crying, even though I didn't know why, but I couldn't stop, couldn't hold him close enough as I trembled.

I wanted the water to wash the fear and death and loss away. I wanted to feel safe and whole again.

I had died. I'd been so close to losing him, to never feeling him in my arms again.

And now that I was alive, now that the reality of that was right here, breathing, his heartbeat and mine beating with the same rhythm, I could not stop thinking of how close I'd come to losing him.

He didn't say anything. Neither did I. We both knew what we had. What we'd almost lost. How incredibly lucky we were.

There were no happy endings for Soul Complements.

Maybe there was now.

It took a while before I stopped crying. Took a while for my shaking to ease. And then I was so tired that washing my hair seemed like an insurmountable chore.

We managed, Zay washing my hair for me, me washing his back for him. After I toweled dry, I shuffled back to bed and crawled under the covers.

Zay shut off the water, turned off the lights, and moved the breakfast tray off the bed. Just before I fell asleep I heard him call someone on his phone and tell them we weren't going to make it today, but that we'd try to be there tomorrow.

Then I rolled over, tucking my head on his wide chest, my ear pressed so I could hear his heartbeat, my leg over his as his arm wrapped around me.

I didn't want to leave this bed, didn't want to face the real world right now. Maybe not for a long time.

Thankfully, sleep pulled me, all too willingly, down into soft darkness.

A cold nose pushed my hand open, then something that felt like a quarter pressed on the center of my palm.

I ignored it.

I heard the soft clink of a coin set on coin, still in the center of my palm.

Pause, then another coin went clink.

I was starting to feel the weight.

Clink. Coin number four in my hand.

I opened my eyes.

Stone sat next to the bed, his wings very carefully pressed against his back and his ears up. In his fingers he had a quarter, which he delicately stacked on top of the other four quarters on my palm.

"Stone?" I mumbled.

Hearing his name, he cooed and blinked his big round eyes. I could tell he was happy to see me. I was happy to see him too.

I did, however, wonder where he was getting those quarters.

Stone trotted off down the hall, then returned in a flash, another quarter in his hand. He sat, and placed it carefully in my hand on top of the others.

Someone must be out in the living room.

I curled my fingers around the coins and Stone gurgled approvingly, then tromped out of the room again.

Zay was sleeping soundly on his back, his arm over his eyes. No coins in his hand.

I got up carefully, made it to the door, and pulled on my robe. I walked out toward the living room.

Someone was lounging on my couch. That someone was Shame.

God, it was good to see him alive.

Stone sat in front of him and waited for another quarter.

"Did you just pay my gargoyle to wake me up?"

Shame looked over at me.

Pale, his face was all angles, too thin, but strangely vibrant, his eyes a very dark green. He raised one eyebrow and smiled. "Maybe."

"You cut your hair." I sat on the other side of the couch. His hair was combed back in the slick style of the nineteen forties or fifties. Looked good on him.

"Got singed. Was time for a change anyway. Like?"

"I do. I can see your eyes better."

Stone shifted so he was sitting in front of me, waiting for me to put my hand out. I gave him all my quarters. "You can go stack these if you want, Stoney." I rubbed his head.

Instead of running off to go make a mess, he settled down right where he was and rested his head on the couch between Shame and me.

I petted his head and he crooned softly. I thought about asking how everyone was, but I knew if I did, I'd have to deal with it. Deal with everything we'd been through. Face some pretty terrible things.

I didn't want to face any of it right now.

"Came by to take you to the meeting," he said. "Mum said you and Zay need to be there today."

"Is she the head of the Authority now?"

Shame shrugged. "Things are unsettled. And you?" he said. "I've never seen you so quiet."

I tucked my feet up and looked over at him. He was quiet too, studying me as if he were holding his breath for my answer. Over his left shoulder, I could see Eleanor's ghost in front of one of my bookshelves, scanning the books there.

"What happened?" I asked.

"When, exactly?"

"Just the end of it. The end of the fight with Leander and Isabelle."

He turned his face so that the cool yellow light of morning coming through the window washed his skin in yellow, leaving his eyes and the curve under his cheekbone in lavender shadow.

"We had them held off, but that was about it. The way they used magic"—he shook his head—"didn't think we'd survive it, honestly. Your da did something. Something with Stone, right?"

"He possessed him, and then tried to join light and dark magic."

Shame whistled, low. "Always knew he had balls. Also that he was a bit mental."

"Did he kill Leander and Isabelle?"

He shook his head. "I blacked out. When I came to, Cody was standing on one side of you, and your da was a ghost, standing on the other. Didn't see Leander and Isabelle anywhere. About that time, Zay reached your side. You were so still, Allie. Covered in blood. I thought you were dead."

"I think I was," I said quietly.

He didn't say anything for a while. Then, "Found your way back on your own this time, didn't you?"

"I guess I did."

"I brought you this." Shame twisted and pulled a box out from beside him. It was about the size of a shoe box, but made of wood. Across the top in my father's clean handwriting were the words: ALLISON ANGEL'S BOX OF DREAMS.

It was the box my dad had given me when I was a little girl. The box he had put a lock on and hidden away in his safe at his house. I had forgotten it until Shame, Zay, and I found it a few months ago. I didn't even remember what was in it.

"Found it in the trunk of my car," he said. "Thought you'd want it."

I nodded. "I do. I think I do."

He handed me the box and I held it a moment, wondering what I might have put in here, and why Dad would have thought it important enough to lock away.

"Morning," Zay said, walking into the living room. "Shamus."

"Jones. Done sleeping your life away while the rest of us take care of this damn mess?"

"No. When did you get a key to the apartment?"

"Never. Don't need a key. Got myself an inside man, don't I, Stone?"

Stone burbled.

"Coffee?" Zay said. He leaned down and kissed me softly on the temple.

"Yes," I said. "No, wait, Shame said Maeve wants to see us."

"Is that why you came by?" Zayvion asked.

"Mostly. Really are some things we all need to make decisions on. I'll drive."

"Let me get dressed," I said, taking myself and the box down the hall. "Where's the meeting?"

"Kevin's place."

Well, at least there would be coffee. I put the box down on my dresser and got into jeans and a couple of layers of shirts, topping it off with one of Zayvion's sweaters.

They were talking in the living room. Low voices, but I could still catch snatches of the conversation. They were glad to see each other alive. And the meeting had something to do with the Authority, with how it would be run.

Shame didn't seem to have many details on that, only that Maeve had asked that as many members of the Authority as possible please be in attendance, though the vast majority wouldn't be there due to the cleanup and reconstruction efforts.

Shame asked Zay how I was really getting on. Zay said he thought I was still in shock.

I paused while brushing my hair and glanced in the mirror. Green eyes too pale, even my skin too pale, as if I had faded out, worn thin. Had I changed so much in so short a time that I didn't even recognize my own eyes?

Maybe Zay was right.

I quickly looked away, and put the brush down next to the box. Too many questions hovered just on the edge of my thoughts. Too many fears I didn't want to face yet, held back by a tenuous thread of denial.

"What about her da?" Shame asked. "Do you know what he did?"

"Are we ready?" I asked from halfway down the hall. I didn't want to think about these things. Didn't want to let them become a reality to me yet.

Didn't want to know how much of myself I had lost.

How many friends I had lost. I hadn't even asked about Nola yet. The last I had seen her she was burned, bloody, dead. . . .

"Are you sure I shouldn't call the doctor?" Shame asked.

"Allie." Zay stood in front of me, putting both of his hands on my arms. Warm. Strong. Real. "Are you still with me?"

"Of course," I said, though I think I had missed some time. Had I just been standing here trying not to think about . . . anything?

Zay searched my eyes, so I tried to smile. Didn't manage that, but I nodded. "I'm here. I'm ready. Let's go."

I slid out of his grip and found my coat. As I shrugged it on, the notebook in my pocket slapped against my thigh. I reached in my pocket, pulled out the notebook where I always wrote down everything that happened to me. My life. My way of remembering who I was.

An awful lot had happened lately. Things I should record before they slipped away, were taken away.

I drew my fingers across the cover of the notebook. And set it down on the table, leaving it behind.

Zayvion and Shame followed me out into the hall, without a word. Stone slipped out too, trotting along beside me. His wing slid up across my back, the prehensile tip of it holding the collar of my coat.

Just like when we'd walked through death together.

Zay, on the other side of me, took my hand, and squeezed it once, before holding on.

I knew I was home. Knew I was alive. Well, I mean, I could see that, could logically think that. But I felt like a ghost drifting through my own life.

Maybe I didn't belong here. I'd died. Twice. Maybe I shouldn't be alive now. My dad had tried cheating death. Look at the mess he had made.

Dad? I thought.

Nothing. Not even the faintest feeling of him.

I was alone.

Very alone.

I was surprised how much it bothered me.

Shame's car was parked behind the building. We walked to it, and Shame unlocked the driver's side and got in.

Zay opened the front door for me. I shook my head and got into the back.

After a pause, Zay got in the back next to me.

Stone hopped in the front seat like he'd just won a ride in an ice cream truck, and Eleanor hovered in the space in front of Stone.

Shame started the engine. Other than Stone's mumbling, none of us had said a thing.

"All right," Shame said after easing out into traffic. "That's about all the quiet I can take. Allie, are you all right, love? Are you hurting? Do you need a doctor?"

I glanced up at Shame's reflection in the rearview mirror.

"I don't need a doctor," I said. "I'm just . . . I don't want to wake up yet. Don't want to face everything, you know?"

"Aye." Shame sighed. "I do. We'll get you some coffee, or whiskey. Whichever you think will do you the most good. Because there's an awful lot of messy living left for you to do."

"Is . . . is Nola . . . ?" My throat tightened and I couldn't even get the words out.

"She's going to be okay," Shame said.

I felt like the sky had broken open and let the sun pour across the world again. I'd been afraid to ask. Terrified to have lost my best friend, knowing her death would have been my fault.

"Oh," I said, not finding words to express my joy, my relief. "Oh."

Zayvion put his arm around me and pulled me against his chest.

I was tempted to close my eyes, to try to ignore everything about the world except Zayvion's heartbeat. But the longer we drove, the more I realized the scenery going by didn't seem quite right.

I sat up, looked out the window. And I mean really looked out at the world around me for the first time.

Suddenly the cleanup and reconstruction comment Shame had made became clear. Buildings were burned, some missing stories, or with holes in the walls, roofs torn off. It looked like the city had gone through an earthquake during a hurricane and forest fire.

"Did we do this?"

"Redecorate Portland in apocalypse chic?" Shame asked. "Pretty much. That's why wars between magic users are a no-no."

"Do people know? Has it been covered up?" I didn't even know how someone would go about covering up something of this magnitude. "They must have seen the magic. They must have seen the gates, the battles, things, people falling down."

"They did," Shame said. "And they think they saw an earthquake that damaged the networks and cisterns and natural gas lines. A lot of explosions, a lot of mess, and plenty of ways to explain it all. Even the gates."

"The entire police force was dispatched, wasn't it?" I asked. "And the National Guard?"

"Standard procedure for any disaster," Zayvion said. "Nothing to be suspicious about."

No one on the street looked panicked or particularly worried. They were all going about their business, side-stepping the broken sidewalks, walking around police tape. Workers were out with heavy equipment and dump trucks, moving rubble, or pulling up broken pavement in preparation to lay new.

It might have been a disaster, but it was not enough to tear this city down.

Soon we were out of the city, and after another twenty minutes of driving, we were off into the hills at Kevin's estate.

Shame parked the car and turned off the engine. "Ready for this?"

I took a deep breath and nodded. I might not want to face everything, might not want to have to look at what the world had become, but that didn't mean I could ignore it forever.

There were still people I cared for here. People I needed to know were okay.

Messy living to do. Wasn't that what Shame said?

I was surprised to see Shame still sitting in the car, his hands clenched on the wheel like he didn't want to get out. Finally, he said, "Fuck it," opened the door, and strode off to the front porch.

"Is he okay?"

"I think Terric will be here," Zayvion said. "I'm not sure if they've been around each other much."

I realized I hadn't really paid a lot of attention to Shame. Hadn't even asked him if his mother was okay. If Terric was okay.

Time to pull up my bootstraps and get back in step with the living.

"Have you heard from anyone? About anyone?" I asked as I opened the door and got out of the car. It was warm, and I was way overdressed. A nice day. We were headed well into summer weather now. When had that happened?

"Other than Shame, and Maeve? Not really." He shut the door and Stone got out too, jogging off up the steps ahead of us.

"I've been sleeping almost as much as you have," he said.

Shame was already inside. And while there were a lot of cars parked in Kevin's lot, and probably more around the back, there weren't any people milling about. Everyone who was here was already inside.

"How important is this meeting?" I asked.

"We're about to find out." Zay pushed the door open and we walked in together. There were a few unfamiliar faces in the lobby, but it was clear from the low murmur in the distance that most of the people were in the main ballroom.

I had a sudden, crushing need to check on Nola, to see how badly she was hurt. That whole "living" thing came back with a vengeance.

How could I have slept and ignored everything when my best friend might have been dying?

It wasn't only Nola I wanted to see. Were Terric and Violet and my little brother okay? Had Victor lived? Was Hayden still all right? Were any of my Hounds still alive?

Davy. Oh, God. I'd sent him into danger with Sunny and Collins. Had he made it home?

A million thoughts and worries and fears and questions flooded through my mind, making my heart pound.

It didn't take long to reach the ballroom. The door was open.

The room was filled with people, all of whom had glasses of wine or beer or champagne in their hands. This looked more like a celebration than a meeting.

So many people crowded the room—at least as many as when I'd first had to stand up on the stage and decide how we were going to fight Leander and Isabelle. A fight that had not gone according to plan. At all. But a fight I think we had won.

Still, I didn't want to walk in there. So many people in such a crowded place made my heart leap up and clog my throat. I was already having a hard time breathing and I wasn't even over the threshold yet.

Zayvion took my hand and we stepped into the room.

I don't know who saw us first, maybe someone Zayvion brushed past while trying to find a clear space on the other side of the room.

That person moved aside for us, and then another, and another, each person turning to look at us, to murmur and point, so that the person next to them turned, and looked at us, murmuring, pointing, as they moved to one side.

It was a little strange. A little uncomfortable to be noticed like that.

In a remarkably short stretch of time, the entire room full of people opened up in front of us, the crowd pulling away so that there was a huge space around Zayvion and me, a space that opened a pathway all the way up to the stage.

Zay and I stopped. We stood, hand in hand, looking at the crowd.

Someone clapped. And then another pair of hands, and another. The entire room filled with thunderous applause, everyone looking at us, smiling, cheering.

Cheering for us.

For our fight.

For our victory.

I smiled, a little embarrassed at all the attention. But more than that, grateful.

"Speech!" someone yelled. I shook my head, looked at Zay. He was smiling. Turned toward me as the crowd picked up the "speech, speech, speech" chant.

"This is all you, love," he said. "You're the one who got us through this."

"This is not just me," I said, squeezing his hand. "I never would have made it without you."

"Louder!" someone else shouted.

Zayvion took a moment to clear his mind, then very carefully cast an Amplify spell. It hovered in the air like the strokes of a painting, glowing from a deep turquoise at the first of the glyph to a soft gold at the final line.

A few people caught their breath. That's when I realized everyone could see the spell, that magic was no longer so fast it was invisible to the naked eye.

Different indeed.

The Amplify hovered like a Celtic charm in front of Zayvion and me. As soon as he finished the cast, it faded from sight, even though I knew it was working.

Expectant eyes waited, expectant faces with expectant smiles.

"We," I started, the spell carrying my voice across the big hall. I suddenly didn't know what to say. My dad had been good at these kinds of speeches. When he wanted to, he knew how to show his gratitude and tell the people working with him how much he appreciated their efforts.

What would my father have said?

"Thank you," I said. "I want to say thank you so much. We could not have survived this without all of you, all of the people of Portland joining together to meet this threat as a unified force. We are strong, stronger with each other than alone. And we've proven that by fighting for not just our city, but . . . but our world.

"We risked so much, lost so much, and used magic for a price. Fought for what we knew was right. But we have gained so much in return. It wasn't just a handful of people who secured this victory. It wasn't just the Authority, or the Hounds, or Zay and me. It was all of Portland's people: magic users, nonmagic users, the living, and even the dead, who stood side by side against overwhelming numbers.

"Those who fought beside me, Zayvion, Shamus Flynn, Terric Conely, Nola Robbins, Cody Miller, and . . . and my father, Daniel Beckstrom, never once faltered. I know that is true of everyone here as well.

"We have made a stand for what we know magic should be. What magic *should have been* all these hundreds of years before it was broken: dark and light together, whole. And even though magic has changed, I don't think this is an ending of what magic can be. I think it's the beginning of what it can become. And I am so grateful to be here among such strong, brave, caring people. Thank you."

Zay swept his hand through the air once, ending the spell.

Everyone was silent for a moment. Then the applause started again. Long and loud.

I scanned the crowd, saw Maeve up on the stage across the room. Hayden stood beside her looking a lot stronger than the last time I'd seen him. It was good to see them both. I couldn't see Nola, but Terric and Shame leaned against one wall of the room—where Zay and I had been originally headed, and were both applauding.

The Hounds were over there too, Jack and Bea and

Sid. Jack raised a glass toward me and Sid and Bea did the same. A toast. To us.

I suddenly wished I had a glass of champagne in my hands too.

I smiled one last time for the crowd, then tugged on Zayvion's hand, walking toward Shame and Terric and the Hounds.

The applause quieted and people went back to talking and laughing.

We secured a spot next to Shame and Terric. There was a little more breathing room here. Probably because Shame was sort of radiating that dark-and-death thing he'd picked up, and people avoided it like a cold wind.

He leaned on the wall and was smoking, even though I was pretty sure Kevin had said he didn't want anyone smoking in his house.

Terric had on a white T-shirt and black jeans. A fist-sized stone hung from a leather cord around his neck and a string of beads belted his waist. He brushed his white bangs away from his eyes and I noted the collection of bracelets on his wrist all studded with beads.

Not beads—Void stones. Just like the Void stones Shame was wearing beneath his black hoodie.

Terric was a good-looking guy under any circumstance, but without those Void stones to dampen the magic he carried around, he was mesmerizing. Even with the Void stones on, it was easy to want to smile when he talked, to want to watch him and not look away.

He smiled as we came near. "Very nice speech," he said. "And so good to see the two of you."

"And you," Zay said. "Are we late? Looks like people have been here a while."

"Just in time, I think." Terric nodded toward the stage where Maeve was approaching the microphone.

Already walking out onto the stage were a dozen men and women, a few whom I knew—like my father's accountant, Ethan Katz, and Dr. Fischer—most of whom I didn't. They all seemed to be here in some kind of official capacity, dressed in business suits and looking stoic.

"Good afternoon," Maeve said. "Thank you, Allie, for that wonderful speech, and thank you all for coming." She paused, giving the crowd time to quiet down. No one was sitting. The huge room was standing room only.

A woman threaded through the crowd with a serving platter of wine, beer, and champagne glasses. She stopped next to us. I took the champagne, Zay and Terric took a beer. Shame just waved her off.

"When there's whiskey, then I'll be drinking."

Maeve was talking again.

"I know we've had several meetings since the event, and I want to thank all of you who have attended each session. Some of this information will be old news to you, but to those who haven't been able to join us before, I want to touch briefly on a few points.

"Magic has changed. Quite a bit, really. Dark and light magic are once again joined as one. You'll notice spells, no matter which discipline you use, may react differently, are seen more easily, and many are much more subdued than what they were. Please be prepared and careful when casting.

"We should have the majority of roads reopened in the next two weeks, and reconstruction is going well.

"It is not my place as acting Voice of the Authority to assume the direction of the organization, but I can say that we have been in close contact with the new Overseer in Rome, and he is giving us his full support in reestablishing our city, and in our choice of those who will stand as Portland's Voices.

"And that is why I have called you all here today. We will be reassigning the Voices of Life, Death, Blood, Faith, and Flux magic."

An excited murmur rolled through the room, and the atmosphere took a tick up.

"This will be rich," Shame said, exhaling smoke. "Want to lose some money on it, Jones?"

Zay leaned both shoulders against the wall. "Who do you think is up?"

"Blood? Mum, of course. Think they'll put Victor on Faith—"

"Victor?" I said. "Is he well enough for that?"

"See for yourself." Shame sucked on his cigarette and tipped his chin toward the other side of the room where Victor sat in a chair. He had on a bulky sweater and jeans, not at all his usual business wear, but he didn't seem uncomfortable. He most certainly looked like he was healing. And the bandage over his eyes was gone, though he was wearing dark glasses.

"God," I exhaled. "I thought . . . the last thing I remember is you telling us he'd been shot and wasn't going to make it."

Shame held the smoke in his lungs. "Didn't you tell her anything?" he asked Zay.

"We haven't had time. Victor's going to be okay," he said to me.

The knot in my chest loosened a little. "Good," I said. "Good."

"Voice of Life magic will go to Carl, I'd wager," Shame said, "and Death to La."

"La doesn't use Death magic," Terric said.

"No, but she could pick it up." Shame grinned. "As a matter of fact, I'd be happy to teach her."

"That your bet?" Zay asked.

Shame nodded.

"I say you're wrong."

"'Course. Wouldn't be a bet if you didn't. So who? Go on."

"Blood, Sunny. She's been studying under your mom long enough I think she'd take it if Maeve doesn't want it. Faith . . . I think it's Kevin's time to give up the body-guard business and step up to a little more Authority business. Flux, which you forgot about, Violet. Life might be best in Dr. Fischer's hands. And Death? I think that's going to you, Shamus Flynn."

Shame snorted. "Like they'd give me responsibility." He stuck his cigarette in his mouth so he could talk around it. "Unreliable, remember? You're on." He shook Zay's hand. "Easy money."

"How much are you losing on this, Flynn?" Terric asked.

"Winning," Shame said. "Fifty?" he looked at Zay.

"Cents?"

"Ha-ha. Dollars."

"Done," Zay said.

"So Sunny is back? Is everyone else okay?" I asked. "Baby Daniel? Cody?"

Zay leaned down closer to my ear. "They're fine. A little worse for the wear, but when Cody joined magic, he healed everyone with magic."

"How?"

Zay shrugged. "Even he doesn't know. From what he can explain, it has to do with his vision of what magic really is. Cody, apparently, has always seen magic as a beautiful thing. Both light and dark. When he was hold-ing magic together, helping it join again, it responded to that, to his expectations and vision of it. It healed the

people he cared for, like Nola. Then it kept right on healing. Starting with you."

I touched my chest where the scar lay beneath my
shirts.

He nodded.

"And then all the people wounded in the fight, and
then all the people poisoned by magic, and then ending
with you again."

Wow. I searched the crowd for Cody. Found him. He
stood on the opposite wall from us, looking right at me,
as if waiting for me to notice him.

His eyes were clear, his body language comfortable,
and . . . adult in a way I'd rarely seen him. This, I thought,
was the Cody Miller who would have been, if his mind
and soul hadn't been broken. And here he was, all grown
up and put together again.

The real hero of the day.

I raised one hand in a small wave, and he lifted his
hand in a wave. Whorls of magic painted his fingers and
palm, all the way up his arm—both arms—to disappear
beneath the short sleeves of his T-shirt.

Marks of magic. Just like mine.

"You said he can't use magic anymore?" I asked Zay.

"Cody?" Zay glanced over at him. "No. He thinks it's
the price that had to be paid to join magic. Maybe his
ability will come back in time. We don't know. He says
he doesn't mind. He's painting again. I saw a picture of a
piece he's working on. It's . . . there aren't words. There's
something more than magic in his art, something . . .
amazing. I think he's going to be a very rich man."

"Allie!" Nola pressed her way through the crowd and
gave me a big hug before I could even get a good look at
her.

Detective Stotts was right behind her, and nodded to Zay. "Zayvion."

"Paul," Zay greeted him.

"Are you okay?" Nola and I both said at the same time.

She laughed a little, and gave me one more squeeze, then stepped back just a bit, still holding my hand.

"Are you?" I asked again.

"I'm good," she said. "Tired, still a little confused about everything, but catching on pretty quickly for a country bumpkin."

She looked good, and except for a thin inch-long line at the edge of her jaw, seemed to have made it through everything without any lasting injury.

"What about you?" she asked.

"I'm dealing. Not quite . . . up to speed yet."

"Oh, Allie," she said. "You saved the world. You can take a little more time to recover if you need it." And the kindness in her eyes almost made me want to cry.

"What, that?" I said, trying to push my sorrow away. "Just another day on the job."

She shook her head, seeing right through my ruse.

"It is my pleasure," Maeve said, loud enough that both Nola and I turned to see the stage again, "to announce the new Voices of the Authority."

Apparently, I'd missed some of her speech. I still wasn't quite tracking everything. The world was moving too fast, and I had been holding still for so long, I had to work a bit to keep up with it.

"The Voice of Flux magic will remain Violet Beckstrom," Maeve said. "The Voice of Faith magic will temporarily remain in Victor Forsythe's hands until he chooses a successor. The Voice of Blood magic will be given to Clyde Turner."

"Who?" I asked.

"Old friend of me mum's," Shame said. "Last I'd heard he was working with the Ward, Sam Arch. Guess he's back in town now."

"Hell of a Blood magic user," Terric said.

"And lastly," Maeve said, "the Voice of Life magic will be given to Terric Conely."

Terric straightened and looked a little shocked. "Shit."

"The Voice of Death magic will be given to my son, Shamus Flynn."

Applause broke out.

"She did not," Shame spit out.

Zay just laughed.

God, I hadn't heard him laugh in such a long time. "Oh, but she did," Zay said.

"But I'm unreliable. I can't have that kind of say in things. I can't have that kind of power. And Terric? He's, he's"—Shame waved one hand in the air as if trying to grab words out of it—"he's impossible to work with."

"Like working with you is some kind of dream?" Terric drank down the last of his beer and handed Zay his empty glass. With a final look at Shame, he started across the room toward the stage.

"Go." Zayvion pushed Shame to get him moving too.

Terric had been appointed the Voice of Faith magic by Bartholomew Wray, a position Terric did not want to take from Victor and a position he had never been comfortable with. Terric definitely leaned toward Life magic. I wondered if he'd had any say over which position he was appointed to this time.

Probably not. Knowing Maeve, and the dozen people

with her on stage, they'd done what they had thought was right for Portland for now, with very little or no input from the people directly taking the positions.

"How long will they be Voices?" I asked.

"Usually for many years. But I don't know," Zayvion said. "Maeve told me Sam Arch is on his way. If he doesn't agree with their stations, they'll be reappointed, or maybe there will be some kind of rule put in place so that Voices can only be in office for a limited term."

"Sam Arch is the Ward—the regional director of the Authority, right?"

"Yes, now, shhh. I do not want to miss this."

Zay stuck his fingers in his mouth and let off a sharp whistle. Then he yelled, "Speech, speech, speech!"

Each person took their turn at the mic, saying thank you.

I was surprised to see Violet there, as I hadn't spotted her in the crowd, but she looked calm and reasonable as ever, telling everyone that she hoped to pioneer the next advances in magical and tech innovation.

It was strange to see her, to listen to her speak and not feel my dad's reaction, not feel his love and sorrow for losing her.

She caught my eye across the crowd and gave me a smile.

Or maybe she was giving Dad a smile. Only he was no longer here to see it.

I smiled back and nodded. We needed to talk.

Clyde Turner was probably in his late thirties, early forties. He wore a baseball hat backward and had on flannel and jeans. Very Northwest. He looked more like a guy who worked in a microbrewery or a shipping company than an expert in Blood magic. He took off his hat and brushed a hand over his mop of black hair before stepping up to the mic.

"It's a pleasure, an honor, and a gift. I'll do my best to uphold a position so well represented by Mrs. Flynn."

Seemed like a nice enough guy.

Victor had not made his way to the stage, but remained seated in the chair. Terric walked up to the mic.

"This is a great honor. I will do everything in my ability to respond to the needs of the Life magic users in this community. Thank you."

He stepped away from the mic and Shame walked up.

Shame shook his head, looking out over the crowd. "Really, people? Have you gone completely insane? I mean, sure, yeah, I can see the others standing as Voices of the Authority, but me?"

The room filled with chuckles.

Shame pressed his hand against his heart, his pale fingers sticking up out of his black fingerless gloves. "I'll do what I can for Death magic users, all you dark, depraved souls out there. I'll try to do you right, or wrong, if that's the way you like it. Thanks for this then."

He stepped away from the mic.

Maeve took the stand again. "Good. That's our announcement. A meal will be served in the dining room, please enjoy the food. Oh, one last thing: Sam Arch will be in town soon, to verify these appointments and to hear any concerns you have. He will also help to select a Head of the Authority. We'll be sure to let you know more information as things progress."

Everyone applauded and then people filed forward to talk to those coming off the stage. Plenty of people wandered out of the room, heading down to the dining room setup for food.

"Hey, boss," a familiar voice said.

Davy was walking my way, Sunny beside him, her arm looped through his. They both looked well. Really well.

"When did you make it home?" I asked.

"Yesterday." He nodded to Zay. "Heard you two were still recovering from the confrontation."

"We're on the mend," Zay said. "How did things go with Collins?"

Jack and Sid and Bea wandered over. Looked like it was time for me to catch up with the Hounds.

"He did what he said he'd do," Davy said. "Kept the Soul Complements out of Leander and Isabelle's sights and safe from anyone following the Overseer's orders. But as soon as we got word that Portland was out of lockdown, and the situation was stable, Collins disappeared. It was . . . annoying."

Nothing worse for a Hound than having someone slip the trail.

"Think our boy Davy here is losing his edge." Jack strolled up with his arm around Bea. "Or maybe there's someone distracting his attention."

Davy grinned. "Like you're one to talk."

Bea giggled. From the rosy flush of her cheeks she'd had more than one glass of champagne.

"You did fine, Davy," she said. "Collins is a very . . . well, he's an odd sort of man. Maybe it's better he isn't around."

Sid reached over and patted Davy on the shoulder. "It's good to see you back, Silvers. And looking so well. Thought we'd lost you there for sure."

"Still not a hundred percent," he said. "But I'm better. Much better than I was."

"Zayvion told me everyone in Portland was healed when Cody joined magic," I said. "Did that reach you?"

"I think so," he said. "Magic's worldwide. They think the healing has been spreading out from Portland to the rest of the world. And no more ghosting out for me, if that's what you're asking. I haven't really tested to see what I can do with magic. Didn't want to blow myself up far away from home."

"Please," Sunny said, rolling her eyes. "Most of the 'different' about magic is that spells are less powerful rather than more powerful. Chicken."

Davy nodded. "Smart chicken, thank you."

"Allie," Sid said, "have you checked in with the others?"

"No. Are there other Hounds here?"

"A few. Want me to call a meeting?"

"How about tonight. Is the den still standing?"

"Like a rock. I'll let you know when I have the meeting nailed down. But first, I'm going to get in on that free food."

Sid and Jack and Bea headed off, stopping occasionally to talk to members of the Authority in the crowd.

Davy watched them go and grinned. "So much for the Hounds staying out of the Authority's business."

"Not such a bad thing," I said.

"Not such a bad thing at all," he agreed. "See you at the meeting, boss. Oh, and Allie?"

"Yes?"

"Thank you. For everything. For making sure I was alive for all this." He waved his hand at the room.

"You were the one who made sure you were alive," I said. "You never stopped fighting for it."

"Still." He let go of Sunny, then stepped over to me and gave me a hug.

I was so surprised I forgot to hug him back for the first second or two. Hounds avoid contact as much as possible. With pretty much everyone. The only safe way to stay untrackable, and therefore alive, was to have as little contact as possible with people.

I didn't think that was true anymore. The only way to stay alive was to rely on each other, to trust your friends, and your pack.

"You are welcome, Davy," I said. And I hugged him back.

Chapter Twenty-four

It had taken a month for things to feel normal again. Well, maybe not normal, but new, solid, real. Cody healing everyone in Portland with magic had some unintended side effects. One, the healing had spread out around the world, which was a good thing as far as I was concerned. Two, all the people who had been Closed by the Authority and had their memories taken away had regained those memories.

That had been every kind of not fun.

I was the exception and hadn't gotten any of my memories back. I didn't know why but most of my life was still filled with big, black blankness.

Which was pretty much normal, so I tried not to let it bother me.

Zay and I had spent most of the next month at the coast doing nothing more than eating seafood, walking the beach, and spending lazy, luxurious days in bed together.

Summer had slipped by too quickly.

Still, I'd had a chance to catch up with everyone. Nola had decided to sell the farm and move into the city with Detective Stotts. I was just waiting for Paul to ask her to marry him any day now. Maeve and Hayden had given the keys of the inn to Shame, while they headed off to spend a year together at Hayden's home in Alaska. For a "proper courtship," Maeve had said. Victor was still the Voice of Faith magic, and I wasn't sure he was ever going to choose his successor.

Cody couldn't use magic, but his paintings were nothing short of amazing, and he already had a backlog of buyers lining up for his next piece. He was also working on a statue to honor my dad. "Something permanent," he had said, "so the city will remember Daniel Beckstrom as a great man who changed magic, and really, gave his life to save the world."

Eli Collins was missing, completely disappeared off the map. Maybe that was for the best.

As for the Hounds, I'd called a meeting and told them I was stepping down. I didn't want to be the leader anymore, not for the Hounds, not for anyone in Portland. I was done making the big life-or-death decisions for a while.

I thought for sure Jack or Bea, or Sid or Jamar would step up and take over the den, and deal with the Hounds working not only with the police, but also with the Authority. But it was Davy and Sunny who said they'd take on the responsibility.

Pike would be so proud of that kid.

And I'd talked to Violet. Told her dad was gone, really and truly gone. I'd told her, in detail, everything he'd done, and everything he'd said during the fight, and anything else I could remember from the time he'd been possessing me. He had loved her. I told her I knew that was true because I had felt his love for her. That had made her smile a little.

Then Kevin had come in the room, interrupting us. Her smiled had brightened.

From the way she had looked at him, and he had

looked at her, it was clear they'd finally talked about their feelings. Their relationship. He had admitted he loved her. And it looked like she loved him too.

It was good to see her moving on. Kevin was going to be a great dad for little Daniel.

"Allie?" Nola said from the front seat of Paul's car. "Are you sure you don't want us to come with you?"

I pulled free of my memories and looked out the window. Paul had stopped by the park, and the arch of the St. Johns bridge speared the clear blue sky.

"No, I'm good. Zay's going to pick me up for lunch later."

"Are you sure?" Paul asked. He and I had sat down over a couple pots of coffee and I'd given him a full rundown of everything I knew about the Authority and magic and things that he'd been tracking in the city for years.

Oddly, he seemed pretty happy with the way things had turned out, and was currently coordinating his efforts toward the safety and crackdown on illegal spells with Sam Arch, the Authority's Ward of the region.

It wasn't just the Hounds who were working closely with the Authority. It was the police now too. Being a little less of a secret organization was benefiting everyone.

"I'm sure," I said. "Thank you both for the ride. Have a lovely time on the river."

"We will," Nola said. "See you Saturday for the movie."

I opened the car door and walked out into the sunny day. Autumn may be around the corner, but it hadn't browned the backs of leaves or put a chill in the air yet.

There were probably twenty or so people in the park. I made my way along the concrete path, and finally found a bench a little out of the way, covered in an equal spattering of shade and sunlight.

I had brought something with me. Something that I hadn't been brave enough to open before now.

My box.

ALLISON ANGEL'S BOX OF DREAMS.

Hayden had helped me spring the lock. The box had been sitting unopened in my apartment for months now, on my dresser where I'd left it.

I didn't know why it worried me, but I had a huge case of the butterflies thinking about what might be in it.

I took a deep breath, let it out, then opened the lid.

The lid hinged back smoothly, as if it had last been used yesterday, instead of almost twenty years ago. I exhaled, like I'd been holding my breath for years. Suddenly, the trees didn't seem so close and crowded, and the park took on an even more spacious and sunny feeling.

Inside the box were papers. Letters, photos, little origami cranes. I smiled, remembering some of these things — the origami in particular — but most of it was unfamiliar. I picked up the photo on the top.

A woman and child were smiling in the picture, both holding dandelion fluffs in their hands. The child — a girl — was probably only one year old, wearing a pink dress and striped tights. That must be me. The woman had dark hair, soft eyes, and a smile that set a cascade of memories rushing through my mind.

My mother.

She was so pretty, so young. Maybe about my age. We were in a park I think, even though I would have been too little to remember that day. I smiled. We both looked really happy.

I realized I didn't have any photos of my mother. Why hadn't I thought about that before?

Beneath the photo was an envelope. It was my dad's monogrammed stationery, and written in his handwriting across the front: "Allison, open first."

I turned the envelope, opened it, and pulled out the letter.

My dearest Allison,

I do not know when you will read this letter. At the time of writing, you have just turned twenty-one, are in college, hating me, and dating my assistant, Eli Collins.

Twenty-one. Already. Yet I find myself pacing the nights with regret.

I have had an entire lifetime to tell you the truth, and could not bring myself to do it. Better that you hate me for the things you know I have done, rather than for the secrets I have held from you.

Let me begin thusly: I have made enemies, very powerful enemies who are part of an organization called the Authority. They are strong magic users who are seeking to destroy Portland and magic. It may sound strange, but they are not afraid of stepping through death to see that their goals are achieved.

They see me as a threat to their plans of dominance. Rightly so. For it is my intention to remove them from power and see that magic falls into the right hands.

That, though, isn't the secret I've been avoiding all these years.

When you were five years old we took you for a drive, your mother and I. The brakes on the car failed. That is what the police report said. But I remember, just before blacking out, seeing another car pass us. Seeing magic users in that car casting dark spells. An Authority member named Bartholomew Wray was among them.

We hit the side of a warehouse in St. Johns at fifty miles an hour. I woke to the pain, the blood. Your mother, beside me, was silent. She wasn't moving. Wasn't breathing. She never did again.

They killed her. Trying to kill me, they had killed her.

I believe Sedra was behind it, though I have no proof. Or perhaps it was not Sedra, but something darker that holds her.

You were barely breathing, broken bones, and so very bloody. I carried you out of the wreckage. I am ashamed to say I panicked and ran down the streets looking for help. Looking for someone who could save you.

There is a woman in St. Johns. Her name is Rossitto. She and I have a deal, a secret between us I have never betrayed. St. Johns holds its own magic. That is the secret. The magic is different from all the magic in the city, perhaps in the world, because it is not broken into light and dark. It is pure. Other than a few crystals, I have not yet been able to study it thoroughly. I had planned to lay the network lines into St. Johns. But that day, my plans changed.

She found me, on my knees, with you nearly dead in my arms. She took us to her home and made a deal. I would never lay lines for magic to be accessed in St. Johns. I would keep the Authority away from her and the secret magic she guarded. In return, she would heal you.

Magic for a price. It is always the way of things. I gave her my promise.

The price of pulling your soul from the brink of death was my soul. Most of it, in any case. A trade-off I was more than willing to do then. One that I hope you will appreciate one day.

A part of me died so that you could live.

To hold you to life, she gave you a small piece of the magic from St. Johns.

And you breathed, and cried, and lived.

I have raised you on my own for all of these years. Up until you were thirteen, I created memories of your mother for you because I could not bear to tell you she had died. That I had let her die, and only barely saved you.

I am sorry, Allison, for that deceit the most. The false memories of your mother and your life with her. I don't know if she would have wanted it that way. I do know she loved you very much. I hope one day I will be able to tell you these things.

I hope one day to apologize for the changes I have made in your memories, and the memories I have taken away from you. Magic should not make you lose your memories, but I regret that in my hope to give you a happier, if false, childhood it has changed the price you pay when you use magic. Perhaps one day I will find a way to heal magic and make it whole again so that you will no longer lose your memories.

Perhaps one day I will be able to tell you all

these things. You deserve that. You deserve to hear this from me, and not from a letter hidden away with your childhood memories. Your real memories.

I hope you will find forgiveness for the things I have done and the choices I have, regrettably, made.

Lovingly,
Dad

After all these years, he finally explained . . . everything. Why did it make me so sad?

"Sitting on a park bench alone, Allie girl?" Mama Rossitto said.

I looked up away from the letter. I hadn't heard her approach, too lost in the reality of this letter. These truths.

"Is this true?" I asked, holding the letter out to her. "Is any of this true?"

She studied my face for a moment. I realized I had been crying, and wiped at my cheeks.

Then she took the letter. After reading the first bit, she sighed and sat on the bench next to me.

"The accident," she said after she read the entire thing, "is true. He was so afraid to lose you, his sweet baby daughter. And so broken with your poor mama's death." She shook her head. "He was a good man once. Before her death. Before his soul snapped in half so you could live."

"Why me?" I asked, both miserable with the knowledge, and on some levels, not surprised. I think, somewhere in the back of my mind, buried deep in my memories, I had known my mother was dead. I had seen it in my father's eyes, heard it in his voice for a long, long time. "Why didn't you try to save my mother instead? Give her the magic."

"St. Johns chooses its own. All the people here are called by its magic. They may not know it, but still, they come. They are nurtured by it, and in return nurture it. The guardian of the magic here is chosen by the magic. Touched, changed, healed by it."

"Are you its guardian?"

"Yes. But not forever, Allie girl." She gave me a knowing smile. "Not forever."

She shoved the letter back at me with a grunt. "Is this all in that box of yours? One sad letter?"

I looked down at the box of memories on my lap. "No, there's a lot more." I started digging. "Pictures of my mother." I handed her the first one. "Finger paintings, origami, a drawing of something that looks like a turkey." I shook my head.

My dad had packed these things away. Little bits of my life he had tried to keep safe for me. Little bits of my life that were mine again.

"I think these little cassette tapes are video, right? There's dozens of them." I read the label of one: ALLISON YEARS ONE THROUGH THREE. It was in a softer, more fluid handwriting. My mother's.

She had recorded memories, stories of me? Of my life?

Only the first few of the tapes were in her handwriting. Then there were others, in my father's handwriting. ALLISON YEARS SIX AND SEVEN. ALLISON YEAR EIGHT. ALLISON YEAR NINE. He had taken over where Mom had left off.

It was all so much—more than I'd ever thought he'd cared about me, more of my life than I'd ever expected to get back. And I'd barely scratched the top of the pile of stuff. I could see a few thumb drives, which might be full of photos, or who knew what else? It would take me a lot of time to go through everything.

And it made me really happy to have it all.

"Good. You're smiling now. Too nice a day for all those tears." Mama pushed up onto her feet. "You come by again soon. I feed you dinner." She patted me gruffly on the shoulder, then stumped off toward the street.

I sat and looked through a few more things: a key that said it fit a safety deposit box, my birth certificate.

"Allie?"

I glanced up. Eli Collins stood in the shadows near the trees.

"Eli?" How long had he been standing there?

"I just wanted to tell you it was a pleasure working for your father. I know he's dead now. Truly at rest."

"We dated?" I blurted out, holding up the letter.

He nodded, the light not quite reaching his glasses. "We did. For two years, actually, while you were in college."

"Why?"

He smiled a little ruefully. "Because we liked each other?"

"Are you sure? Are you sure you didn't use magic to make me like you?"

He laughed. I think it was the first time I'd ever heard him laugh. It was a joyful outburst, and I found myself smiling too.

"No," he said. "I have never used magic to make a girl like me. We had . . . something. And we were both happy for a while. But I came here to tell you something about . . . about our past."

I braced myself. For the life of me, I didn't know what he could say that would shock me now.

"Your father once told me that he was very sorry for the choices he had made. For the things he had done to you. Especially for his years of influence on your mind causing heavy use of magic to take your memories away. He also told me that if magic could be healed, dark and light joined, it might make it so that you didn't lose your memories any longer."

"I read the letter," I said.

"Good. There's one more thing he told me. He said he knew you were strong enough."

"What, to survive what he did to me?"

"No. To question him. He counted on that. And he counted on you being strong enough to trust him one day."

I was quiet for a moment or two. "I guess he was right about that," I finally said.

"Yes. Well. He was brilliant," Collins said. "And, Allie, please don't look for me. You won't be able to find me."

"Look for you? You're standing right there."

He smiled again. "No," he said. "I'm not." Then the image of him, the Illusion of him that had seemed so real I was sure I could smell his cologne, winked out of existence.

Sweet hells. Magic.

Without thinking, I cast a small Sight spell. Magic flickered into the spell I drew, and I caught my breath. I saw the dusty remnant of the spell Collins had cast, draped across the dry grass at the base of the tree. He was nowhere to be seen.

But that wasn't what had surprised me. Magic felt easy again. It didn't hurt, not one bit, to cast it now. Whatever healing Cody had done included my ability to cast magic too.

Oh, that was good. So very good.

Then I felt a familiar, and very real, presence.

Zayvion was walking across the park toward me, his thumbs tucked in his belt loops, relaxed in the sunlight, smiling.

I folded the papers back up and tucked them in the box. I stood up and walked toward Zayvion, my soul, my love.

There would be time enough for the past later. Time enough to explore what I could do with magic later. Right now, I just wanted today, with a promise of an awful lot of tomorrows with him.

Epilogue

It was the morning of my twenty-sixth birthday, and all I wanted was a decent cup of coffee, a hot breakfast, and some time away from the gargoyle who had been given a dozen squeaky toys by Shame and was chewing on them. All of them. At once.

It sounded like an entire flock of rubber ducks were screaming out their death quacks.

I'd asked Zay if he wanted to go out today to do something to celebrate, and had received vague promises in return. Something about him needing to help Shame and Terric with important Authority-related stuff.

He'd gotten up before dawn, given me a kiss, which I'd been too sleepy to return properly, and left.

Not that I expected him to remember it was my birthday. Things had been busy the last few months.

Reappointing the Voices of the Authority was just the beginning of restructuring the Authority. There was a lot of information that needed to be exchanged about how magic had changed worldwide. It meant establishing contacts throughout the various systems and agencies so the Authority could now operate as a semihidden organization.

But Sam Arch and the Overseer had finally chosen who should be the head of Portland's Authority.

They'd given that position to Shame and Terric. Said that they thought the head of the Authority might best be handled by two people, Soul Complements, with a lot of experience dealing with a town that sat on five wells of magic.

Terric was shocked, but as is his way, took the appointment with gravity and grace.

To say Shame was reluctant to take the position was a massive understatement.

To say he threw a bloody fit was more like it. He'd argued against it for three weeks, brought up his lengthy past history of irresponsibility and slackerdom as proof of his incompetence.

Zay had finally taken him out for a drink and a long talk.

The next day, Shame had agreed to the position.

I hadn't yet gotten Zay to tell me what he'd said to Shame.

But there were plenty of things I'd probably never understand. Like why I had dated Eli Collins in college.

Use magic, it uses you back. That was still true, though the magic was much gentler now and the price to pay was also more moderate. No one knew if that was a temporary state of things or not.

I guess we'd just have to keep living to find out.

I shoved the pillow off my head and got out of bed. "Stone! For the love of God. Stop torturing those ducks."

There was a pause in the noise from the living room. Then one long, sad squeal that ended with a pop.

Oh, sweet hells. He was killing them.

Fine. Let him have his rubber minions. I wanted a shower, clothes, then a big cup of coffee at Get Mugged. Because it was my birthday and I planned on doing anything I wanted to do today.

By the time I got out of the shower, dressed, and had put on my shoes, Stone had stacked his toys across the windowsill in the living room. Even the slightly saggy duck with the missing head.

At least he wasn't eating them anymore.

"See you later, Stoney," I said. "Be a good boy, okay?"

He whuffled at me and trotted over so I could pet his head.

"You are such a goofus," I said, rubbing behind his ears. "Don't get seen, okay?"

Sure, people had gotten memories back, and the Authority was a little more out in the open than before. But Stone was still the only gargoyle in the city. The fewer people who knew about him, the better.

It didn't take me long to make my way to Get Mugged. Even though it was September, the sky was mostly clear, patched together by clouds that sent the sun dipping into and out of shadows. No rain yet. That was nice.

I just kind of wished Zay was here. That maybe he would have had time to spend with me on my birthday.

Maybe Grant would take a couple of minutes and sit at my table. We hadn't had a chance to gossip for weeks.

Just before I opened the door to the coffee shop, I realized something was not right.

It was too quiet, though I saw Grant, and only Grant, standing behind the counter. He smiled and waved me in.

I put my hand on the blood blade I still carried at my side and cautiously opened the door.

The snap of a canceled spell filled the room with the sweet scent of lilac.

"Happy Birthday!"

The entire place was filled with people. No, not just people. My friends. All the Hounds, all the members of

the Authority, Maeve and Victor, Nola, Stotts, Violet and
my little brother, and Terric and Shame.

It was back-to-belly crowded, but I stepped right in.
And for the first time, I realized I didn't feel the slightest
twinge of claustrophobia.

All the world seemed a lot more open to me now.

Zay stood at the door and shook the last wisps of the
Illusion spell off his fingers.

Victor started singing the happy birthday song, and
everyone joined in.

I couldn't stop smiling. This—all this, all of them—
was worth every price I'd ever paid.

Zay stepped up and wrapped his arms around me.
"Happy birthday, love," he said. "Can I buy you a cup of
coffee?"

"Yes," I said. "You can. Today and every day." I
reached up and kissed him. And oh, sweet loves, how he
kissed me back.

ALSO AVAILABLE
FROM
Devon Monk

MAGIC WITHOUT MERCY

Allison Beckstrom's talent for tracking spells has put
her up against some of the darkest elements in the
world of magic. But now, magic itself has been
poisoned, and Allie's undead father may have left
the only cure in the hands of a madman.

**"Monk's writing is addictive, and the
only cure is more, more, more!"
—*New York Times* bestselling author
Rachel Vincent**

Available wherever books are sold or at
penguin.com

facebook.com/acerocbooks

R0128

Penguin Group (USA) Online

What will you be reading tomorrow?

Tom Clancy, Patricia Cornwell, W.E.B. Griffin,
Nora Roberts, William Gibson, Catherine Coulter,
Stephen King, Dean Koontz, Ken Follett, Nick Hornby,
Khaled Hosseini, Kathryn Stockett, Clive Cussler,
John Sandford, Terry McMillan, Sue Monk Kidd,
Amy Tan, J. R. Ward, Laurell K. Hamilton,
Charlaine Harris, Christine Feehan...

You'll find them all at
penguin.com
facebook.com/PenguinGroupUSA
twitter.com/PenguinUSA

*Read excerpts and newsletters, find tour schedules
and reading group guides, and enter contests.*

Subscribe to Penguin Group (USA) newsletters
and get an exclusive inside look
at exciting new titles and the authors you love
long before everyone else does.

PENGUIN GROUP (USA)
us.penguingroup.com

S0151